EASTSIDE HEDGE WITCH

T.J. DESCHAMPS

Edited by
EMILY PAPER

EASTSIDE HEDGE WITCH

T.J. DESCHAMPS

Edited by
EMILY PAPER

❀ Created with Vellum

1

No one expects to run into a hellhound on their pre-dawn run in the Seattle suburbs, not even me, and I've had a long history with the stinky mutts and their master. I stop dead in my tracks, my heart thudding faster than the beat in my earbuds. After pressing the bud in my right ear, the music ceases. Ambient noise filters in.

Luck is on my side, sort of, as I am downwind of the monster, not the other way around. The reek of sulfur was what had given away the hellhound circling my neighbor's begonias long before I spot the glowing red headlights where eyeballs should be. Besides the glowing red eyes, there's no mistaking the hellhound for a lost pooch or a coyote on the prowl. The arch of its back reaches about as high as my chest, and I'm about 5'6", not tall but not short either. It's three times as wide as my hips, and I'm, as my daughter's generation puts it, "thicc." Under a sleek coat of slate-gray fur, sinewy muscles ripple. Even without looking inside its muzzle, I know viscous slobber covers several rows of razor-sharp teeth. But what really gives away the doggo is not a helpful Lassie are the shadows, darker than dark, swirling about the killer canine.

Those shadows will suck you into a whole new world. Somewhere you don't want to take a magic carpet ride, Aladdin, not one little bit.

Too busy sniffing at my neighbor's hedges, likely distracted by a bunny, the hellhound doesn't even realize I'm there. I don't mind if the demonic beast eats Peter Rabbit, the circle of life and all that, but I sure as hell mind if the hound tries to devour me, or worse catch me up in those swirling darker-than-dark shadows forming around him.

My stomach knots with unease and I bite my bottom lip to keep from crying. I'd grown complacent over the years since I left Hell. I want to stomp my foot and cry out that this isn't fair. I'd gotten away from His Creepiness and all his bullshit evil machinations a long time ago. I have a nice, albeit bland, life in the suburbs. I'm on the freaking Parent Teacher Student Association!

I give up my pity party. I am a middle-aged mom, not sixteen. I've known for a long time that life was never going to be fair, as life never is when someone has way more power than you have.

I'd grown complacent, but like all middle-aged mothers, I still came prepared. I'd thought I was safe from Hell, but the world is filled with a lot more things that go bump in the night than hellhounds. I ease off my backpack.

My kid likely thinks I carry around weights, tasteless nutrition bars, and a water bottle like a normal person. The water bottle is the only true part. What I do have in my bag stops all kinds of monsters from devouring me while I get my heart rate up to "cardio" on my smartwatch. I push aside ash and rowan wood stakes, a silver dagger in its sheathe, a jar of cream to distract fae—not that the high fae courts are even allowed on Earth after the angels kicked them out, but the tiny low fae love the stuff and keeps them on your side.

Among these contents, I retrieve a container of Morton salt, tear off the sticker, and flick the spout with my thumb. My stomach dips when the friction causes the metal of the spout to squeak against the cardboard of the container.

My gaze still on the hellhound, who is still tearing up my neighbor's garden, I exhale in relief.

With great care, I pour the salt in a circle, whispering the words

I'd learn by rote. I'd learned them in another tongue but say the spell in English—a focus. The words don't matter. The intention does. The power comes from within me, as it does all witches. I contain a metaphorical light inside that can blaze with the brilliance of a thousand suns, or so my mother said.

Mom was more poetic than I could ever be. She read Ralph Ellison, Alice Walker, and other greats of the twentieth century. I read comics and listened to Biggie and Wu-Tang Clan. She belongs to a coven. I am a lone witch, living a continent away from the women who raised me. Generational disconnect happens to the supernatural, too. Especially when your mother gave you to a fallen angel as a tithe when you were only a teenager.

When I'm done with the setup, I return the salt to my backpack and steel myself for what's to come next.

I whistle. The first comes out dry and soundless. I moisten my teeth and try again. A shrill sound, loud enough to wake the dead, let alone the neighborhood, departs from my lips.

The hound pauses the search for the rabbit, lifting its head. Alert. The beast's nostrils flare as it sniffs the air. Red glowing eyes lock onto me.

Yeah. That's right. I'm much better prey.

A low growl emits from the beast's throat. Claws the length of my fingers click on the sidewalk as the hound stalks forward toward me.

Inside, I'm quaking with fear. I have not done this spell in a long time. If something happens to me, my daughter will have no one. I push that out of my head and plant my hands on my hips.

"Go tell your master to take the hint and leave me alone." I point as I speak, not intending a literal destination but a general begone direction.

The idiot looks where I pointed.

I roll my eyes. Hellhounds are not like Earth dogs. They have no instinct to protect, but they have the same instinct to hunt and follow signals. When the evil pooch realizes his master isn't there, the predatory red gaze narrows on me, but it doesn't move.

Doubt and confusion sets in. I'm not sure why he's not pouncing and dragging me back with him to Hell nor ripping me to shreds. Am I not its target?

I curse under my breath.

I clear my throat. "Also, tell him stalking is a little gross and so creepy that he's still got a thing for a me. I made it pretty clear I didn't want to be with him anymore." I throw up a hand and shake my head. "Wait. Why am I telling you? You're too stupid to deliver a message."

I spin on my heel like I'm going to walk away. Part of me wants to run. Wants to lure this beast away from my home, my kid.

The movement triggers instincts. In my peripheral, the monster snarls and lunges.

My heart leaps into my throat. The creature is doing exactly what I want it to do, however, a massive hellhound is launching in my direction. That and swirling magic that promises to rip me from everything I love to carry me to my least favorite ex scares the bejesus out of me.

After a moment of frozen terror, my brain revs into gear. I find my voice, murmuring the final words of the spell. A silly little rhyme stammered more than said—*but stammered with intention*!

The ground shakes beneath my feet, rumbling like a thunder cloud. Within the salt circle I've created, a swirling vortex appears. Fire erupts from the center, but I don't feel the heat. It's all contained by the salt I bought in a three-pack from Costco. The beast snarls and whines but cannot escape the flames toasting its flesh.

Oopsy. I've opened a portal to a less hospitable part of Hell. Guess this hellhound won't be delivering my message.

I murmur another spell, voice still shaking. The swirling vortex sucks the hellfire and burning beast down like a flaming turd down a flushed toilet.

As I've said, I'm no poet.

The portal between worlds vanishes, leaving behind my salt art.

Sweat cooling on my body and adrenaline waning, all I want to do is go home and shower, but I need to clean up the salt first. If I left it,

Seattle's infamous constant drizzle would wash the salt into the neighbor's yard and kill all the plants.

Television and movies with demon slayers never mention that salt will kill plants if absorbed into the ground. The ostensible heroes walk away from their salt circles, leaving a destructive mess, not caring whose yard they've destroyed, but I do.

As I sweep up the salt circle with a pocket-sized dustpan and broom, dumping the contents into a Ziploc bag, a sadness envelops me. I'd found safety and community on the Eastside—albeit while pretending I was something I was not. I don't want to move again, but I have to.

The thing is, you don't just leave my ex and get to live happily ever after, not after he's shared his ambitions. Not after he's named you his Harbinger of the Apocalypse. I'd only deluded myself that I could.

His Creepiness had once said that he'd tear the heart out of anyone whom I loved more than him, so they'd know how he felt. I used to think of the declaration as terribly romantic, instead of simply terrible. I certainly loved my daughter more than I ever loved him. Would he kill her or try to use her for the purpose he wanted to use me? New fears arise.

With the salt all swept and bagged up, I head to my house with a heavy heart. The life I've built here on the Eastside is over, and I have to break that, and so much more, to my daughter.

2

Two stories, four bedrooms, three thousand square feet of new construction, and yards so small you could spit in any of your neighbors' windows from your house, if you felt so inclined. Since real estate was tight, I used every bit of outdoor space to grow herbs and flowers and all kinds of plants.

The tingle of magic brushes against my skin as I step onto my property. The aroma of flowers and various green and growing things washes the stink of sulfur and burnt hellhound from my nostrils. The frogs in the nearby watershed preserve, who had stopped making noise with the appearance of the hellhound, return to their croaky night song. A myriad of tiny lights dance in the air, illuminating my path. One could almost mistake them for fireflies, if Washington state had fireflies.

Instead of the buzz of insects, minute voices flit through the air, speaking in a language unbeknownst to me. Pixies, sprites, nymphs, spirits, or whatever name you fancy for the tiny supernatural creatures who live in my garden, have always had an affinity for me, showing up wherever I roam. As far as I knew, I was the only witch whom low fae followed, but I don't mind. They'd proven good friends on more than one occasion.

The whole superhero story about a refugee from a dying planet explains the presence of most supernatural beings on Earth, but on a much grander scale than a singular Kansan. Many live here because they have no other choice, their world long destroyed by the wars between the governments of the Angelic Anocracy and the Kingdom of Hell, not to mention the Fae Wars. The angels seemed to like to fight everyone for supremacy over humans.

Eons after these great battles, mundane humans are just beginning to understand that we live in a multiverse. It'd blow their human minds if they'd learned that the multiverse has as many populated worlds as there are snowflakes in a blizzard...with just as much trouble as a storm.

The pixies congregate around me, their teeny voices a din in my ears. I don't understand what they're saying, but I know what the wee folk are upset about. I hold my hands out in front of me in a halting gesture.

"I know. I know. Hellhounds like to gobble your kind up, but I kept you safe. The threat is gone." *Burnt to a crisp*, I don't add.

The light sprites coalesce into an arrow pointing behind me. At that moment, the hairs on the back of my neck rise in warning.

A low growl rumbles, too close.

Cursing under my breath for not reinforcing the wards around our property, I turn in slow motion fully expecting to see another hellhound. Apex predators don't like sudden movements, tending to trigger their instinct to pounce. I'm torn between sighing in relief and screaming in frustration when I see a sleek black panther emerging from my herb garden.

The relief is short-lived as the panther crouches down low, yellow eyes narrowing on me. Jada, my daughter in cat form, growls.

Confused why she'd be angry with me, I hold up a finger and use my mother tone, "Don't you dare growl at me young lady."

She does worse.

Without thinking, I say the word for a deflection spell and pour my light into it. The panther bounces off the forcefield I've generated.

The cat shimmers and then scrambles to its feet. Two legs, at first feline, stretch and morph into a human shape, brown skin replacing black fur. The midsection goes through the same sort of transition. Moss green curls sprout from the morphing skull, spiraling down to cover the teenage girl's bare brown chest.

"Ouch! That hurt!"

"You were going to pounce on me!"

She looks down at her hands, likely still tingling from the deflection spell, and then at me, slow realization fills her features. "Mami... you know magic." It's not a question. Betrayal limns her tone and a world of hurt resides in her eyes.

Inwardly, I flinch, outwardly I maintain a semblance of calm. All I want to do right now is grab her, a few necessities, and flee, but I can't. She's seventeen and will need a better explanation than when she was small and Raf and I would say, "We're going bye-byes."

She may be part goddess, half witch, and wholly able to shift into deadly animals, but I am still in charge. I clear my throat and give her my best impression of the scariest person I've ever met—my mother.

"Inside. Now." I point to the door.

For a moment, I think she's not going to listen. That she's going to pull a "I'm going to be eighteen in nine months" on me, but she doesn't.

Jada picks up her clothes from the porch, petulantly glaring in my direction as she does so. Oh, she's going to go full teen angst on me about this. All the big feels and pouts.

I deserve it.

A keen ache develops in my chest and part of me wonders if she'll ever trust me once she learns the truth.

Inside our home is much like the exterior, covered in plants. On my left there's a winding staircase, on my right a door that leads to a dining room. Jada stomps down a hall shooting from the foyer between the two. I follow, collecting my thoughts about what I'm going to say.

I circumvent my daughter's dressing session next to the kitchen's breakfast bar, and start up the coffee maker I set up before my run so that all I have to do is press a button.

Like her father Raf, Jada doesn't care for coffee. Hands shaking from left-over adrenaline, I put some water to boil in the electric kettle and scoop out some loose-leaf tea from a container. I used to drink tea and spent an inordinate amount of time in shops selecting different blends, but I'd adopted the habit of drinking coffee after moving to the Pacific Northwest and finding out two thirds of the year offers very little sunlight.

The clothes she's donned are the same as I saw her wearing when I checked in before bed: black pajama pants with skulls pierced by daggers and an oversized black t-shirt with the words "Black Girl Magic" in silver glitter. Jada slides onto one of the stools at the breakfast nook and pulls her mass of dyed green ringlets back with a Scunci. Her face is so like Raf's, with round, apple cheekbones and dimples when she smiles, and large, intelligent eyes.

"How can you practice magic?" Her eyes thin into accusing slits. "What are you?"

"I'm a witch. A hedge witch, to be exact. My natural ability lies with nature." I gesture to the plants, which isn't hard. The house bursts with green.

"We're such freaks." She groans and rolls her eyes. "At least you're *kinda* legal. I thought you were going to say a fae princess. That would be so cool."

"Hardly." I laugh, ignoring the niggling itch at the back of my head. I don't actually know what my father is/was. However, my mother feared fae.

Jada regards her hand. "Why haven't you told me before?"

I plate some scones and scoop a dollop of strawberry jam on each. "Your father and I thought it best. I—I have a past...I got involved with some unscrupulous dealings I'd rather not talk about."

I hated being vague while confessing, but I also didn't want to scare her.

"Everything is better with tea and snacks," she remarks in a mocking tone, but doesn't refuse the plate I set before her. She eyes the food.

I leave her to it and start making her tea.

"Are you wanted by the Angelic Anocracy or something?"

I almost drop the tongs that I'm using to parse the loose-leaf into a metal tea infuser. "How do you know about the Angelic Anocracy?"

She scoffs and says like I'm an idiot, "They run the supe community."

"Soup community?"

"Supernatural community." She laughs and then asks around a bite of scone, "Mami, are you an unregistered supe?"

"Not exactly." I'd once been registered, but I'd faked my death years ago to get away from His Creepiness. "Did your father register you with the local archangel?"

"He kinda had to. But, why hide that you are a witch if you're not in trouble?"

I can't answer right away. I can't speak. Stunned by the betrayal. Rafael never told me he'd done that after we'd *agreed* we would live as latents, almost magic-less as mundane humans.

After I'd pissed my pants the first time there was a little bunny instead of my baby in the crib, Rafael was supposed to teach Jada how to manage her powers. He was *not* supposed to introduce her into the community.

"How much do you know about witches?"

Jada shrugs. "Nothing. I've never met one."

I see a kernel of truth I can give her, sparing her of being complicit. "That's because all witches belong to covens. You live your whole life on a coven's property, doing the coven's bidding and not involving yourself with the outside world."

"Sounds like a cult."

I frown. It certainly does. "I was from a very powerful coven, very well known in the supe world. The only way to leave was to fake my death."

Jada's face shifts from irritation to worry, eyes widening. "What happens if they find out you're still alive?"

"Trial. Possible execution." The coven is the least of my worries, but the consequences made for a far less scary story than the King of Hell was looking for me.

"Shit."

"I think I've been discovered. We might have to pack our things and leave as soon as tonight."

My daughter shakes her head. I'm not sure she's aware of the movement because she asks, "Leave? Where we would we go?"

The kettle whistles. We both jump.

I take it off the stand and pour our tea for my daughter with shaking hands. I don't know. "Somewhere we can pretend that we're mundane humans. Japan, maybe?"

I grate some cinnamon over her mug, handing Jada her tea. I pour my coffee. I need this mundane morning ritual to balance how off-kilter I feel.

"No. I'm not leaving." Jada's firm declaration pulls me out of my spiraling thoughts. She clears her throat. "The archangel will protect you from your coven. Just explain your situation."

"I—I don't know."

Rafael and I had specifically picked the Pacific Northwest because of the lack of covens in this area, and we'd heard rumors the archangel was lenient and didn't make any indigenous cryptids or latents register. I was safe as long as I didn't practice magic—or so I'd thought.

"So, no running?" Her face is hopeful, breaking my heart.

I want to tell her that we have no choice, but I blow on my coffee. I don't want to shock my daughter further. She's only just learned I'm a witch and feels betrayed. There is so much she does not know, that I have—we have when Raf was alive—hidden from her for her own safety.

Jada's eyebrows scrunch together in a disapproving scowl that is very much like Raf when he was annoyed. "Mama! Don't do that thing where you zone out and don't answer as an answer."

"I need a day to think." A day won't hurt. I could take several. If His Creepiness knew exactly where I was, he'd send a vampire to snatch me up at the very least, not a non-verbal dog.

Hope lights in my chest. A small and weak flame, but there. Maybe the hellhound was here on other business...but that would mean there is something or someone in the neighborhood that my ex or a demon wants. Upheaving both my and Jada's life would be foolish if it were only a hellhound on an errand for a demon. If another comes around, I could just do a spell to elude it. No banishing necessary.

Jada chugs her tea as if it weren't scalding hot—one of her abilities is to withstand heat. She stands, stuffing a chunk of strawberry scone in her mouth.

"Where are you going?"

She rolls her eyes. "School. I have a math test first period. I can't be late."

I want to tell her to stay home, but Jada can take care of herself. Not only will she be eighteen in a few months, she is a descendant of the Orisha. Raf trained her well in his magic—her magic. She's a witch, too. A familiar pull in my gut visits, the longing to teach her all I was taught, to share that part of me. Having the power of a god at her fingertips, would she even want to bother to learn witchcraft?

As if reading my thoughts, Jada pauses and turns to me. "Can you teach me how you got rid of that monster? Banishing that thing was the coolest magic I've ever seen."

"I would love to," I respond, grinning. *I have to,* I don't add. If one hellhound disappears, more will come in its place. Something occurs to me. "Before you go, what were you doing outside at 5 a.m. and in the form of a panther?" As if the word panther calls him, our cat PC rubs his warm, furry body against my leg. Then he goes to Jada, the fur boy's favorite next to yours truly.

Jada scoops the elderly cat up in her arms. "I woke up scared for no reason. My chest was all tight." She wrinkles her nose and rubs her hand over her sternum as if still experiencing the sensation. "Then I had like sleep paralysis and this trippy vision of you being devoured by—I don't know, like shadows or something. I couldn't sleep after that. So, I went to your room, but you weren't there, soooo..."

Rafael, too, had experienced glimpses of the future in the form of visions. Sometimes they'd come to fruition, sometimes not. Obviously, the gift had passed to Jada. Despite the disturbing prophetic vision's near accuracy of what would have happened if the hellhound had taken me by surprise, it warms my heart that my teenager went out to protect me.

Jada has become so independent, which is good, but I miss the little girl who used to crawl into bed with Raf and I, wedging her little body between us. I miss Raf's complaining that it was his time with mama.

"So?"

"I know you go night jogging. The dream felt so real. I went looking for you." She sets PC down and then shrugs. "I thought being a panther would add a little stealth and deter anyone if you were being robbed or attacked. The pixies *acted* like they wanted to help but kept me going in circles around the house pointing arrows this way and that until I *saw*." She puffs her cheeks and makes a noise simulating an explosion and waves her hand dramatically. Then she lowers her head. "All my power and I *hid*, mami." Her eyes are luminous. She then admits, "I was so scared. Papi told me there were monsters in this world, but I didn't think I'd ever see one. That thing could've eaten you."

I breech the distance between us and hug my daughter. At the same time, I make a mental note to put out the big bowl of fresh cream for the light sprites in thanks. She may be almost eighteen, but she's still a kid and didn't need to face down a hellhound. She hugs me back.

I draw back, pushing stray curls out of her face. "I will teach you all you need to know. Hellhounds are frightening, but you're stronger. There's no reason to fear them." I kiss her forehead, hoping it to be true.

Not one to be coddled, Jada disentangles herself. "Okay. Got to hurry up. Roxy will be here soon."

I force a smile. I'm not fond of her best friend Roxanne, but from experience I know not to let Jada know—teenagers always love best the ones that their parents hate most.

"Love you."

"Yep, me too," she throws over her shoulder.

3

The upper level has five doors leading to four rooms and a bathroom, but only four doors are visible. I wait outside Jada's bathroom until I hear the spray of the shower before I go to the end of the hall to the secret room. The wall is spelled to hide that there is a door there. Even if you can see past my illusion, I have warded the door so that you have to say 'open' in a tongue only coven-raised witches know to enter, or you'll suffer a shock akin to being tased. Another ward would make you forget why you were flat on your back.

The precautions were not necessary when Jada was small, but as she grew older and had friends around, I couldn't risk someone accidentally entering.

I whisper the word, the barest of sounds. A door appears. I turn the handle. The tingle of magic grows stronger, my skin ablaze with the sensation as I pass through my wards.

The room possesses a singular chair, a small table, and bookcases filled with thirty-three leather-bound grimoires—well, not leather exactly. Only the witches who bound the grimoires knew what creatures of the old world they'd skinned to make them.

I descended from a long line of Archivists, witches dedicated to preserving our heritage and magic through grimoires. These thirty-three grimoires, separately, contain an Easter egg spell. Alone, the spell means nothing, but combined, could collapse a universe within the multiverse—even Heaven could not withstand this spell. These grimoires were what His Creepiness would still be after, not me.

The grimoires were supposed to have been destroyed along with me when I faked my death to get away from His Creepiness.

I have to tell Jada about this library, but not now. Later, when she comes home from school, when we start our lessons.

I go to a shelf and pull the grimoire I need. I glean from a section on casting wards that would fry anyone with ill will towards me. I jot down on a little notebook the symbols I need and commit the words of the spell to memory before returning the book.

Instead of exiting from the door I entered, I use another door that leads to the back of my closet. I part my dresses and leave the walk-in closet to enter a bathroom adjacent to the master bedroom, and start the shower.

I need to think and clear my mind before casting the wards, and I have time.

In fiction, demons, hellhounds, and other Hellish creatures can just blip from one world to the next. In reality, it took a lot of magical energy to banish that hellhound, and I come from a very powerful line of witches. My coven is not romantic about choosing a breeding partner—their words, not mine.

Witches do not marry and believe warlocks are good for one thing, breeding more witches. Witches live in coven communes. The communes only taught witchcraft to girl children. It is sexist as hell and transphobic. Like many people who grow up in homophobic and transphobic religions, I hadn't realized how problematic covens were until I left.

While I wait for my shower to heat, I remove my clothes, retrieving my cell phone from my hoodie pocket before tossing the laundry into the hamper. I check my messages and notice an alert on my calendar. I let out an exasperated sigh. I have a PTSA meeting at eight this morning. I am the board's secretary, and this is my snack week, hence why I'd baked strawberry scones.

I should feign sickness more often. As it is, I never have. If I didn't show, my best friend Lucinda, who happened to be the PTSA president, would show up to the house concerned. I couldn't let down someone who'd been there for me when I was at my worst.

My phone says it's still only 6:30 a.m. If I hustle, I could set the wards around my property after Jada leaves for school and still make it to the meeting on time. I scrub up and dress for the meeting: sweater, leggings, and sensible shoes.

I spell my hair dry because I don't have time to blow-dry. I'm not into much makeup, but I like flavored lip balm and apply some.

When I exit my room, I collide with a perfumed black and blue something...or someone. It takes a moment for us to untangle and for me to get bearings straight. Somewhere in the confusion, I swear I heard...

"Did you just growl at me?"

"Ugh! No." Roxy curls her deep purple lips and rolls her vivid blue eyes, made brighter by her heavy layer of black eyeliner circling her lids. Jada's friend is about my height, model-gorgeous like her mother Kirsten, except Roxy wears heavy goth-emo-scene-emo-depending on her mood of the week-makeup. Roxy's blonde hair is teased into a style reminiscent of 80s punks and dyed electric blue, a few shades darker than her eyes. Her clothes are a mashup of Victorian-era funeral wear and Harajuku chic.

"Maybe you should stick to Jada's end of the upstairs." Instinctively my gaze shifts to the hidden door.

I realize my mistake when I turn my attention back to Roxy.

She sniffs the air, a smirk curves a corner of her black lipstick-painted mouth, like a hound relishing the scent of prey. "My, my Ms. Diaz. Here, I thought you were a boring normie."

"I don't understand what you mean, dear."

Her eyes flick up and down the length of me. "I think you do. Don't worry. I won't tell. I got secrets, too." Her eyes flash gold.

I struggle to speak. Roxy is some sort of shifter. She's been in my house a thousand times over the years, and I never knew. At the same time, she's never suspected me of being something more than Jada's mother. Then again, I'd never practiced magic strong enough to rip a hole through the fabric of reality and toast a hellhound over a hellfire spit. That kind of magic leaves a trail. Every supe can detect it differently, but shifters use their noses.

Just then my daughter bounces out of her room, black leggings, tutu, and ripped up black t-shirt. Black cat ears peak from her green curls and she has darkened her nose and drawn whiskers—the irony is not lost on me.

PC dashes past me into my room, back arched and hissing at Roxy before disappearing under my bed. No wonder the cat never liked her. She's likely a canine sometimes.

My face grows cold. Shifter packs are the Angelic Anocracy's Earthbound Guardians, serving archangels. She's too young to be a Guardian, but her parents, at least one of them, might be one. How did they hide what they were from me so long, so well?

Of course, they would do everything they could to not let me know. They thought I was a mundane or at the very least a latent. Supernaturals were in the closet and liked to stay that way.

Roxy turns to Jada. "You didn't tell me your ma was a supe."

Jada's smile dims, gaze darting between the two of us. "Barely. Latent stuff, I guess. She's not a danger to anyone." Her voice is high and pleading, so unlike her usual snarky banter with her friend. She gestures to me with a shaky hand. "Obviously."

A scrutinizing eye sweeps over me, again. Roxy duckbills her lips and shakes her head in mock pity. "Yeah. Not a threat not at all." Her gaze flicks to the illusion covering the hidden door. "I suppose."

"What exactly *are* you?" I ask. It's impolite, but I don't care. I need to know if she's one of the bigger animals. The bigger the predator, the higher the pack status for her parents. The higher the status, the closer to the archangel.

She grins. "A little bit of wing and fang."

"Hilarious," Jada says, pulling on Roxy's arm. "We need to go."

Her friend wriggles free and gets close to me, too close, inhaling deeply. "I'll tell you what. If you tell me what you are, then I'll tell you what I am. Because I don't believe for one minute your little latent story anymore."

A car horn beeps outside—either Roxy's mother or father, depending on whose week it is. My heart drops at the sound. Either one could take me in for practicing magic without being registered, if they get a whiff of the area where I banished the hellhound.

I force a smile. "How about the three of us sit down for a little chat after school and discuss this?"

"Sharing secrets. Tight." Roxy flashes a wolfish grin, retreating. She starts down the stairs, throwing over her shoulder, "Jada, come on. It's dad's week. I don't want a tardy and get grounded. Again."

My daughter hesitates, gaze darting between me and Roxy. Concern wrinkles her brow.

"Go to school, Jada." I force myself to sound calm when I'm anything but. "We'll talk later."

"Don't worry, mami. I'll make her swear not to tell her dad."

So Gabriel, not Kirsten, is the guardian. I've known him for years tangentially through Raf and Roxy, but never realized he was a shifter. Gabriel had been one of Raf's few acquaintances outside work—some paintball league or something I hadn't been interested in, or so Raf had told me.

Why was my late husband consorting with shifters? Raf could not hide his demi-godliness. He didn't practice magic, he was magic.

My gut ties in knots as I follow the girls downstairs and out the door. I don't know why I'm following them, some faint hope I can *do* something about my world unraveling.

They hop into Gabriel's SUV parked along the foot of my driveway. I can't see him past Roxy's big hair. Gabriel beeps as they pull out.

I wave at the departing vehicle, knees threatening to buckle.

My daughter is in a vehicle with two shifters, driving off—and there's nothing, nothing I can do about it, lest raise suspicion. I'm an unregistered, non-coven affiliated witch. If Roxy spills to her father, Gabriel could arrest me for not registering and bring me to the archangel. The archangel would only have to do a little digging to find out...

Not practicing magic had protected me from Gabriel sniffing out what I was, and my husband's lies by omission had kept me from knowing what Gabriel was--and had put me in danger of discovery for *years*. The betrayal on Raf's part on top of all the risk is too overwhelming. Bile rises in my throat.

I hold the vomit in until the sleek black SUV turns a corner, out of sight. My stomach empties the coffee, but I keep retching into my bushes until I have nothing left. I collapse on the porch in a heap. The jig is up. Heaven and Hell would soon be pounding down my door.

The light sprites come out of hiding and comfort me, like tiny ladies in waiting soothing their queen. They clean up the mess and bring me water to sip from flowers while I gather my senses.

This is totally normal. Right?

Forget fortifying the house with better wards. I need to get out of here. Raf had played a dangerous game with my life. He had an out. He'd played by the rules. If I messed up, he could have claimed he hadn't known I was a witch.

If I hadn't practiced magic this morning, Roxy would have never known. The door had never ever been something she'd even been interested in. She must have sniffed around after smelling the residual magic from earlier outside.

All these thoughts race through my mind.

Why, why would Raf interact so closely with the Guard after we'd *agreed*?

I cry into my palms. Useless really. I will never know why he betrayed me. The dead cannot answer.

I take deep cleansing breaths. I knew my husband. I had to connect how exactly he'd kept up the charade of a non-magical wife so I could feed into the story when Gabriel inevitably interrogated me—I didn't trust Roxy to keep the secret.

Raf likely decided on his own to set up an acquaintance with a low member of the pack and register Jada to both protect our daughter and me. Hiding in plain sight. Yes. Raf was protecting me. I was a terrible liar. I bet he thought I could lie better if I didn't know I was lying at all.

With a shaky hand I pull out my cell phone and text my daughter that I will pick her up after school. I don't need Gabriel literally sniffing around after I cast protective wards. My phone dings right away, a notification of her reply.

JADA: K.
Roxy isn't coming.
Her dad says she's grounded for not doing her homework
Be cool. She hasn't said anything...she won't.

I RELEASE A QUIVERING sigh of relief. I brush myself off and return inside. Time to practice some magic.

THE CONVENIENT PART of being a hedge witch is that all I need is my own internal magic and a few basics found around the house...filled with plants. I hum to relax myself as I gather a small bowl, a knife, a basting brush, a mortar and pestle, and some herbs drying in the corner of the kitchen.

I cut my arm, hissing. It stings like heck as it drips into the bowl. Witches may be alien stock, but I bleed red just like any human. Most supernaturals do. I have yet to see blue or black blood like in the movies. Using blood magic shows my desperation. Blood isn't often used in spells, because the story of our ancestors and the power passed generation to generation is in our blood, making blood magic the most powerful—at least that's how my mother explained it.

After as much blood as I'll need collects, which is less than what I lose monthly, I use my light to heal my own wound. The mending of flesh itches terribly. I sing to myself, so I don't scratch at it.

Next, I grind the herbs and add them to the bowl. On their own, herbs and blood are just a gruesome soup, but used in a spell they become magic. The herbs and blood are not enough to do anything. Just like chemicals in a solution sometimes need a catalyst for a reaction, my light, words, and the act of drawing the symbols of the wards are the catalyst to make the ingredients of the spell work.

I go out into the yard and paint small symbols with the mixture at the very edge of my property, whispering the words of the spell and throwing my light and intention into the act. Like most witchcraft, it's a tedious, unglamorous process and takes forever to do the entire perimeter.

I go inside, clean up, and get scones loaded in the Subaru in the garage. Lucinda texts that she'll bring coffee from her café. I smile. One less worry. Enough witchiness, I have a PTSA meeting to attend.

4

I get in my Subaru, pausing to glare at Rafael's little red convertible parked next to mine. I should sell the thing. Owning a convertible in Seattle suburbs, where it rained, or at least drizzled, almost two-hundred days out of the year was ridiculous—and it is just sitting there. I decide I'm going to sell it as soon as I can...but what I really want to do is torch the thing and laugh maniacally over the flames. Raf had loved that car. It wouldn't change that my husband had kept secrets from me, but *oh Mother*, the petty act of destroying something he'd cherished would feel good.

I press the clicker to open the garage and put the car in reverse, slamming on the brakes when I see white fur in my rearview belonging to the most massive wolf I've ever seen.

Crap.

My heart somehow jumps into my throat and pounds in my ears at the same time. Eyes locked with the wolf, I remain frozen, unsure of how to proceed.

What I wouldn't give for a raw steak to toss into the yard and peel out of the driveway as soon as the wolf runs after it. I bite my lip, trying not to laugh at the image of the giant wolf unable to help its instincts, reporting back to his alpha, *"But it was a porterhouse, sir."*

Okay. I'm losing it.

I draw in a deep breath and gather my composure. I am a mom on her way to a PTSA meeting. *Blood magic? Oh my, I have no idea how that happened.*

I throw the gear into park, unbuckle my seatbelt and get out of the car. I force a smile. I'm sure I appear a Stepford Wife kind of creepy, but he or she is a frickin' wolf.

"Hi, could you please move out of the way? I have a PTSA meeting, and I'm running late."

Oh, my god.

Kill me now.

I just made a polite request of a freaking *wolf*. I won't have to worry about appearing before the Angelic Anocracy or His Creepiness finding me and my grimoires. This Guardian is going to transform back into a human and promptly have me committed.

A bunch of gruesome wet, popping sounds, and a whole lot of gross morphing occurs, before a man stands in front of me. He's at least 6'1" or 6'2", muscled like an athlete, and light brown head to toe. I can't stop noticing there's no tan lines. I'm seeing a whole lot more of Gabriel than I ever have before. I force my eyes to his face.

Not that it does me any good. Gabriel isn't just perfectly proportioned, he has won the lottery in the features department: high, prominent cheekbones, a jaw that could cut glass, a cleft chin, and eyes that tilt slightly upward at the outermost corners. His mouth is so damned full and shapely it could belong to a woman.

I lick my lips. His gaze tracks the motion. My cheeks flare and I warm other places. How have I known him for so long and never noticed how smoking hot Gabriel was?

Oh, because it had never been appropriate before to gape at my late husband's friend!

I shake my head. What is wrong with me? It's not appropriate now. My world is falling apart and all I can think about is how I'd like to rock his. I shake my head a second time and force my eyes to stay *mostly* on his face.

He runs a hand through tousled dark brown hair.

Yes, please keep my eyes from dipping down. Again.

His wolf eyes turn to a human shade of green close to mine, but there's a bit of otherworldliness about them. Again, I ask myself why hadn't I *noticed* Gabriel before? This time for entirely different reasons. Humans could be beautiful, but not flawless.

We continue to stare at each other as if *seeing* each other for the first time. This is a man Raf met with for beers often, but I had little contact with. After Raf died, I'd only seen Gabriel waving from his vehicle as he picked up and or dropped off Roxy. If I think about it, my husband always managed to keep us separate.

Same went for his wife—ex-wife. She wasn't the PTSA type. By the way their daughter acted, the divorce was messy and complicated. I didn't know shifters divorced. They were so about mate-bonding for life, weren't they?

"Did you banish a hellhound, Miriam?" He points to exactly where the incident occurred.

An icy tendril of fear slithers up my spine. I swallow hard. "Yes."

He takes a step forward, planting his hands on his hips.

I'm not going to lie. I look exactly where I shouldn't. This is not an average dude. He's physical perfection. Too perfect. Fear that he might be more than a shifter snaps my gaze back to his face. There's something familiar about him now that I'm *really* looking at him for the first time, but I can't place what.

"Raf give you some sort of protection that does that?"

I could lie. He's giving me an out. It could also be a test to see if I lie. Also, I really, really hate lying. Outright lies put me in a kind of pain that feels like full-body labor. I've always had the reaction, even when I was a small child. My mother called it "a case of a good conscience in overdrive." The back of my head always itched when she said that.

I blow out my breath. "I'm a non-practicing witch. I remembered the spell in self-defense."

"I get that…but trans-dimensional transference and blood wards are not things a non-practicing witch should know," he says with an air of authority that goes way beyond a low ranking Guardian.

Okay. Time for half-truths. "I was coven raised. I fell in love with Rafael and—marrying is frowned upon. I would have registered, but there's bad blood between me and them for leaving and I didn't want to be found." I hold up my hands. "I swear, I haven't practiced until I saw that hellhound on my run this morning. Please don't turn me in."

I'm trembling now. Tears are running down my cheeks.

He's going to bring me to the archangel. He has to. That's what Guardians do.

Gabriel breaches the distance between us and puts a hand on my shoulder. "Hey. It's okay." He lifts my chin with a finger so I have to look into his eyes. There's no judgment, only concern. His voice is gentle. "I'm sure seeing that monster was terrifying, but you're okay now."

Yeah. I'm just a non-practicing witch, scared out of her wits because she faced a monster. Totally learned from other witches that magic, not the devil himself.

He smiles. Blessed Mother, he's handsome when he smiles. I find myself smiling back.

"You have a PTSA meeting now?"

I have what? As if waking from an enchantment, I realize I'm standing in my driveway with a naked man where *all* my neighbors can see.

I back up, brushing off my clothes as if I could brush off my newfound attraction to him. "Um. Yes. And...Do you need some clothes or are you going to shift back into a wolf?"

Gabriel glances down as if realizing his nudity for the first time. He curses under his breath. "My clothes are in my SUV. I parked a few blocks down because I wanted to shift without being seen." He taps his nose. "I can scent better in my other form, but I don't want to shift back now."

I nod my head along as if I know what he's talking about. Half of what he says doesn't make sense to me. Not wanting the Angelic Anocracy in their business, witches tend to stay away from their watchdogs on Earth.

I point to the garage. "There's a box of Rafael's old clothes I've been meaning to donate. You two are close enough in size."

Were close enough in size. Raf no longer has a body.

Gabriel's gaze swivels to the garage. "It's been two years, hasn't it?"

"Three," I correct. Before today, I wouldn't even suggest someone wear Raf's old things, but at the moment I'm too angry at my husband to care.

He scratches the back of his head. "I'd meant to check in on you… afterward. I— You understand why I stayed away, right?"

His question summons a memory I'd rather forget. Raf had just ascended. I left the hospital room, falling into Gabriel's arms in a hallway. I'd been so stricken with grief. No protector. No father for Jada. Alone, and I'd never been alone before. Gabriel had been solid, warm, lifting me like I was nothing.

My phone dings. The vibration against my leg startles me out of the half-recalled memory. I pull my cell waving it in front of me like a shield, protecting me from this conversation, from the memory.

I don't want to think of Gabriel coming into Raf's room. Raf asking for me and Jada to give them a moment alone. I don't want to know what they discussed. I don't want to think of Gabriel holding me, or when he had to practically carry me to his car so the cancer ward nurses could take my husband away. The memory of that drive home and anything that happened afterward is vague. The month after Raf's death, when I couldn't get out of bed and let my friends take care of Jada, are not times I want to remember.

"I have to go."

Gabriel gently clasps my arm, halting me. His dark eyebrows draw together. "We're friends, but I'm obligated to get a full report from you. A hellhound making an appearance, whether you took care of it or not, is not something I can ignore."

My heart leaps to my throat, rendering me speechless. None of that friendship counted. All hounds had a master.

"Can I swing by later—after school?"

I nod, slipping away from him and into my car. As I start the engine, I look out the front windshield. Frozen in place, I stare at

Gabriel's back. It's a testament to how flustered I am and how gorgeous Gabriel is that I had not noticed what appears to be an intricate tattoo of wings covering his back. I know better. I've seen that "tattoo."

"Nephil," I whisper, voice quaking with the word. The nephilim are half angels, half human. Usually mistakes, curiosities, or sometimes taken under the proverbial wing of their angelic parents. Sometimes they ended with His Creepiness in Hell, spies against their own parent.

At least I don't have to worry about him telling the archangel about me, I thought, heart sinking. Gabriel *is* the Archangel.

5

The Parent Teacher Student Association meeting is held in a community room at the local library. Despite the organization's name, only parents attend and today is a board meeting, not a general assembly, which we hold at the school gymnasium.

I pull into the lot. After I park, I take a deep cleansing breath with my hands gripping the steering wheel. I blow out my breath through my mouth. I need to get my crap together. Lucinda would notice I look rattled and would worry, with good reason.

I conjured my alibi of half-truths. I had a scary experience. A wolf in my driveway. I'm definitely *not* thinking about withdrawing as much cash as possible from the nearest ATM, pulling my kid out of school, and seeking some old connections to get me out of town in a hurry.

I'm not thinking about how Jada is always talking about anime, Japanese fashion and happened to be in her third year of Japanese in school. I'm not thinking about how the kitsune and the Shinigami weren't too fond of the Angelic Anocracy and couldn't care less about His Creepiness.

My phone dings—again. Notifications have been going off at a steady rate while I sit and scheme. Lucinda is normally easy going, but budget meetings are always the most stressful. Everyone has an idea how the money should be spent, usually conflicting ideas.

Past my white-knuckled grip, a stay-at-home mom is unloading her brood. I was like her, taking Jada to the toddler story hour before she started preschool. It bored the heck out of me, but Jada liked it. This library and story hour is where I met Lucinda.

She's been there for me. I can be there for her. *Okay, get through this budget meeting and then plan our escape, Miriam.*

I text Lucinda to let her know I'm here.

Me: Unloading snacks. BRT!

Lucinda: Hurry, or I'll serve roast Chad.

I snort and get out of the car, going first to the trunk. I've packed the strawberry scones that I baked last night for today's meeting. I take the container into the building, nodding to the librarians behind the desk. They all know me from years of interaction.

The backs of my eyes sting and my throat tightens. I wouldn't have that anywhere else. It would take years to build the life I have now, and it wouldn't be the same. The funds wouldn't just keep coming. I wouldn't be a comfortable widow. Jada and I would be on the run.

My phone dings, reminding me I need to move. My destination is in the back of the library, and I head straight there at a brisk pace. On my left, I recognize a few of the elderly sitting at the public computers. A few telecommuters work at tables over in the silent section. The parents with small children head back to the colorful section with lots of bean bag chairs—where I used to take Jada for story time.

Before he became too important at the mega software company, Raf would sometimes take a morning off and come with us. He'd liked taking her to the Spanish story time on Saturday mornings. It was their own little thing. An achy sadness washes over me. This is home. I don't want to abandon it.

Because I'm late, I enter the meeting room tentatively, closing the door behind with a soft click.

Inside, Lucinda is facing off with our vice president, Chad. Chad has salt and pepper hair, and a chin that's quit on him. He seems to leak out of the waistband of his khakis. Lucinda is short and compact, possessing a triathlete's body. My bestie loves to compete in events with the word 'fun' in the title that don't sound fun at all. Her curly black hair is pulled back from her heart-shaped, ageless face. She's classically beautiful with large, dark eyes and a pert mouth, now drawn in a sneer-smile. Even in leggings and a sweatshirt, she looks nine times better than I do dressed up.

Chad uses his height and size to loom over Lucinda as they argue. That kind of posturing is why I've never found him attractive—the moms that volunteer at the school call him a silver fox with a dad bod. Rafael used to say Chad "strutted like a cock in a hen house" when we'd observe him at the school functions. I just didn't see it.

Then again, I'd never been interested in any man except Rafael… and His Creepiness. An image pops into my head unbidden of Gabriel's well-muscled body, glistening from the ever-present northwest rain misting his skin, which is an unfair comparison.

If you want to talk about unrealistic beauty standards, compare a normal human of any age to nephilim, fallen angels, and demigods.

The thing is, I don't find Chad unattractive because he's a typical middle-aged man. I don't like Chad because he's new to the PTSA world, already is the VP without putting in the years of work the rest of us have put in, and is trying to call the shots.

Chad throws up his hands. "So, what you're saying is that you want the football players to share mouth guards and jockstraps so the drama kids can have cool props?"

Lucinda's hands clench, but her smile is all honey. Years ago, after imbibing several glasses of wine, I asked her why she never once lost her temper. She confided, "Men love to rile me, especially white men. They want me to play into that fiery Latina stereotype. They hate when I meet their barbs with a smile. Every time I answer their anger with calm, sugar-coated wit, they don't know what to do."

"Oh my, Chad. Did you eat breakfast? It isn't like you to make ridiculous accusations. You must be hangry." She turns her thousand-watt smile in my direction. "Look. Miriam's brought goodies. I suggest you try one, so we can discuss the budget in a calm, logical manner."

I have to hold back a giggle at the sight of Chad's red-faced, impotent fury. He cannot fire Lucinda. All Chad has is his anger and bluster, and it is absolutely hilarious.

Chad swivels his anger in my direction. "You could have just picked up donuts and made it on time. Some of us have jobs to go to."

I clench my fists, fingers tingling and mouth itching to curse him. There's *nothing* worse than dealing with a mundane, mediocre, middle-aged man and that's coming from someone who knows the devil personally. There's a curtained window between the library and the meeting room. I see my reflection in it: a woman smiling in a way that says she's about to hex the asshole in front of her so that more than his rage is impotent.

"There was a wolf in my neighborhood. I had to speak to the authorities about the beast's removal."

Both sentences are separately true. They didn't need to know that the wolf and officer were the same person.

Lucinda's eyes widen, but she says nothing, which means I'm going to get interrogated later.

Chad has the nerve to poach one of the scones before I've finished setting them out for everyone. "It was probably a coyote, more scared of you than you were of it."

"The officer thought different. He did a thorough job of making sure the neighborhood was safe."

He rolls his eyes and waltzes over to the only other man on the board. "How much do you wanna bet the cop was extra thorough because he hoped to score the hot widow?"

Micah has the good sense to pretend he didn't hear the snide, misogynistic remark. He bypasses Chad, approaching me. "Those scones smell delicious. Need any help, Miriam?"

"Thanks. I got it." I give him a real smile, but feel a bit of concern once I take him in.

Micah is attractive with strawberry blonde hair and a smattering of freckles that make him look younger than his forty-one years. His husband Shawn, a local lawyer, is equally good looking with a whole Idris Elba vibe. But, today, dark circles ring Micah's pale blue eyes—a tell-tale sign of a parent with children still not sleeping through the night, but he returns my smile.

I stand aside so Micah and the others can refill their coffees from the portable dispenser and grab a scone. I've made enough for an army, not a PTSA board. While I wait, I go to the double stroller parked in the corner of the room to get my baby fix. The twins are fast asleep. I sigh, remembering when Jada was that teeny with no small amount of nostalgia.

Disposable cup in one hand and one of my strawberry scones wrapped in a napkin in the other, Micah sidles next to me. "I didn't see an officer in the neighborhood this morning, but I did wake just before dawn. I had this overwhelming sense of—I don't know, not doom—a disturbance in the force, maybe?"

"Oh, wow. Didn't know you were a Jedi." I laugh to hide my shock that he could sense something. Humans had intuition, some natural clairvoyants and telepaths, but ignored most of their small magics. Usually, they had a little extra in their blood if they were in tune with it.

"Sounds, silly right?" He chuckles and a blush spreads across his freckled cheeks. There's a reason Jada calls Micah a cinnamon roll. He's endearingly sweet. He lowers his voice. "The thing is...my gut is usually right about these things. I had to check on all of the kids before the feeling went away. I'm actually kind of relieved it was only a wild animal. Did you see the wolf on your ridiculously early run?"

I blink. I had no idea he knew I took a pre-dawn run. The knowledge only throws me for a moment before I gather my wits. I squeeze his arm.

"I didn't see a wolf on my run. I just don't want Chad knowing my business," I answer half-truthfully, in a low voice, not wanting Micah nervous about his middle child playing outside.

"A home invasion?" Micah's hand flies to his chest. He lowers his voice to a conspiratorial tone. "Did someone destroy those gorgeous gardens trying to break in?"

"No. An ex of mine might have caught wind that Raf is—" I choke. I couldn't say dead. I couldn't outright lie; it would be too painful. Literally. Demigods don't die, they ascend. Raf decided to give up on his material body, but his consciousness is very much alive—somewhere. "—gone. I think my ex found out and had…someone track me down."

Concern fills Micah's sweet face. "Is that why you don't ever have family visit and it's so hard to get to know anything about you? You moved out here to get away from a stalker, didn't you?"

I realize that in order to relieve his concern, I've said too much. The walls I've built up over the years snap into place. "The authorities are aware of the situation. Your kids are safe."

Micah gives me a rueful smile and places a hand on my shoulder. "Sorry, Miriam. That was intrusive. It came from a place of wanting to help."

I squeeze his hand. "I know, friend."

Lucinda calls the meeting back to order, saving me from the urge to spill everything to Micah's understanding face. I go to my seat at Lucinda's right and Micah returns to his space as treasurer to Chad's left.

Chad's eyes are on me as he munches on his second unappreciated scone. Ignoring him, I get out my laptop and pull up a Word doc to take the meeting minutes. The inane feud over the funds begins again. After a twenty-minute debate with a reminder that Chad's wife runs the damned sports club booster that finances the equipment, we vote. It's Chad and a football mom vs the rest of the board, so the decision is made to give the drama club the funds.

The next item, funding the school's learning center, to purchase more noise-canceling headphones and other sensory items for kids with special needs, is a non-issue—even Chad is onboard voting yes.

"Now that we've taken care of how we will spend money, let's talk about raising some," Lucinda begins.

"We have all the fundraising committees in place," Chad argues. "Pass the hat and the silent auction works. Let's not reinvent the wheel here because someone's bored. *Most* of us work." Chad's eyes are on me when he says "most," but poor Micah squirms uncomfortably in his seat—my friend has to justify being a stay-at-home dad all the time too.

Lucinda clears her throat. "No one is looking to reinvent the wheel, Chad. While our own private high school PTSA is as well-funded as well as many of our public feeder middle and elementary schools, there are schools on the fringes of the Seattle tech-money bubble that are struggling to fund basic programs we take for granted."

"We should advise them to follow our lead," Chad replies.

I sigh. "You can't bleed a rock. Those parents are putting in just as much effort as our PTSA does, but the funds just aren't there. We are privileged to have more than enough. Let's give a little from our bowl to make the whole community better."

Chad doesn't respond, only raises an eyebrow at me when I mention the word 'privileged.' He opens his mouth, but Lucinda speaks first. "I was asked by the district board to nominate a chair for the committee that will host a district-wide fundraiser, an event, open to not only parents, but the entire community. We want everyone involved."

"You'll need someone who knows people with deep pockets," Chad says, nodding. "I'll have to think about it, but I might be up to the task."

By the way Lucinda's mouth twitches, I doubt she had Chad in mind. Her gaze lands on Micah and she quirks an eyebrow.

Clearing his throat, Micah sits ups straighter. "I'd like to nominate my husband, Shawn. He knows all the local judges, politicians, and media. Through his volunteer work, he also knows which schools need the money the most."

Lucinda jumps in. "I second the nomination. Can I get a third?"

"Hold up, before anyone speaks. I play golf with Shawn. He's a busy dude. Guys like me and Shawn will say yes just because we're stand-up fellows. God knows Tina abuses my charitable nature. You know, if it weren't for Tina's henpecking, I wouldn't have even —" Chad cuts himself off and readjusts in his chair. "What I'm saying is, check in first before you offer Shawn up to the charity gods."

Micah swivels toward Chad. "I wouldn't dream of volunteering my spouse if I hadn't already discussed it with Shawn." He wrinkles his nose. "Also, I would never *henpeck* him to take on more than he can handle. Perhaps don't project your marital problems onto mine?"

I bite my lip to keep from chortling.

"Okay. Cat's out of the bag," Lucinda adds, quickly before Chad can open his mouth and piss Micah off further. "I've spoken to Shawn. He has lots of good ideas."

"I third the nomination," I say.

Lucinda calls, "All in favor?"

Everyone, even Chad, gives a grudging 'aye.'

"Okay, meeting adjourned."

Micah tears a sheet of paper from a legal pad and passes it across the table. "Took these for you before you arrived."

I thank him and stay seated to type up the notes, while the rest of the board mills out of the room. I want to have all the minutes in one place before I leave so that all I have to do is copy and paste them into an email tonight.

It doesn't escape my notice that Chad claps Micah on the shoulder as the latter is pushing the stroller out the door. It doesn't sit well with me that Chad is likely going to worm his way onto Shawn's committee for cred with his wife and the community, but it's not my business.

"You alright?" Lucinda asks as she packs up the snacks for me.

"Yeah. He's just a little much."

She chuckles, gaze slanting to the door. "I mean, what happened this morning, really?"

"Not much more to tell." I close my laptop and slide it in my bag.

She throws over her shoulder. "Need to talk about any feels around it?"

"Nope."

Lucinda quirks an eyebrow but leaves it. We've been friends long enough for her to know not to push. She's about to leave the meeting room but pauses. "You're never late. When you're ready to talk about it, call me."

I nod and force a smile when all I really want to do is hug my friend tight and tell her everything. She'd post herself at my house if I told her what I, in a moment of weakness, told Micah. I can't have her there if any more danger heads my way. If I leave, I will not have friends like Lucinda and Micah or the wonderful community where I've made a life, but I will also be protecting them from my past.

6

———————

My first stop after the meeting at the library is the credit union where Raf and I have banked for the past fifteen years. Like most Eastside businesses, the credit union is situated in a storefront of a newish-construction plaza. I access the ATM outside, breathing in the petrichor and scent of fallen leaves. Autumn is in full swing. The machine won't let me take out the amount I punch in, which is a ballpark of what Jada and I will need to start a new life. The screen keeps screaming at me, *"insufficient funds."*

When I check the amount in my savings and checking accounts, something seems off. The total sum is significantly smaller than what I estimated should be there. It's definitely not enough to buy tickets at the airport, let alone start a new life. I frown, disliking that I'm going to have to go inside and deal with a person, not knowing whether they're a spy for His Creepiness or the archangel.

Inside, a teller, a spiky-haired, jovial-looking man in his twenties, smiles at my approach. "Hello. How can I help you?"

"I'd like to withdraw all of my money, but it seems all of my money isn't there."

An inscrutable expression passes over his features before a white-toothed grin returns. "What's your account number?"

I rummage in my bag for my purse and get out my checkbook. I don't do a lot of banking. Almost everything was set up on automatic payments—thank goodness. Shawn had set everything up for me. I slide the checkbook onto the counter. "Would it be on this?"

"Yep. And some ID?"

I hand over my driver's license. Spike does some typing then makes a face. He then walks around the counter and beckons me with a nod of his head toward the back. "Follow me."

I follow him to a woman in a pantsuit with her very own office that has a plaque that reads 'Branch Manager.' Huh, not one of the customer service reps at desks. *Look at me, so very wealthy and important the branch manager has to approve the withdrawal.*

She gestures to the chairs facing her desk. "Have a seat Ms.—" Her gaze shoots to Spike.

"Diaz," he provides before I can, as he sets my ID and checkbook in front of pantsuit. "She has some questions about her account. She believes the funds available are wrong."

I take a seat in the modern-looking office with very little personal effects.

Pantsuit looks at my ID and my checkbook then taps at her keyboard. Her smooth forehead wrinkles as she stares at the screen. "No. This is the correct amount. The dividends from the trust fund stocks deposited at the first of the month and all the withdrawals are ongoing. I see no anomalies."

"What's a dividend?" I'd heard of trust funds from television but thought that was something only wealthy kids of billionaires had. I wasn't sure how it worked. Raf had taken care of the banking, then Shawn set everything up so I wouldn't have to worry about it, and there were people at the commune responsible for the coven's finances. Finances had never been a thing I had to take care of.

Pantsuit blinks. Then she adjusts her clothes, seeming uncomfortable with what she's about to say. "It's true that you have more money than what is in the savings and checking, but you can't withdraw that money. It's tied up in investments."

"Why?" I rear my head. "It's my money."

Pantsuit takes a deep breath and then explained that the manager of my trust fund—i.e., Shawn—took all the money Raf had saved plus the life insurance settlement and bought little pieces of companies, making me the part owner of them. "In return for your partial ownership, you receive a portion of those companies' monetary value, but you no longer have access to the cash amount. Do you understand?"

I do. Also, I'm pretty certain she'd explained something a lot more complicated in terms I could understand, yet in a way that didn't make me feel like a complete idiot. I appreciate that so I temper my tone. "Yes. Perfectly clear. How would I go about selling my partial ownership and how long would it take?"

Pantsuit gives me a pitying look. "*You* can't. You'll have to see the manager of your trust fund."

"Oh."

My stomach feels queasy. That would be Shawn. There would be questions around why I want the money and what I am going to do with it. Questions I can't answer.

Pantsuit folds her perfectly manicured hands on her desk. "May I ask a personal question?"

I shrug. "You may. Whether I answer or not, will remain my prerogative."

"Are you of sound mind and body, and if so, can you have that verified by a health professional?"

Confused, I shake my head. "Yes, of course I'm sane. Why would you ask a question like that?"

Pantsuit gives me a rueful smile. "Inability to take care of oneself due to mental illness or dementia is why people hand over full power of attorney over their assets...or someone takes advantage of them. I could get fired for telling you this, but I feel a moral obligation to warn you that if you attempt to withdraw all the money available from your accounts, there's a note to notify Attorney Shawn Johnson

—he has legal guardianship over you. The question is, why does he have control over your life?"

That is a horse of a different color. If I hadn't known Gabriel was a nephil, could Shawn be something else? No. The Johnsons are charitable. Shawn is simply looking out for me.

I rise and thank Pantsuit.

"Let me walk you out. Just let me print up these notes really quick." Her fingers tap away at her keyboard and she clicks with her mouse a few times and then stands.

Pantsuit pauses next to a printer outside her office. She lifts her eyebrows, nudges her head toward the papers on the tray, and then turns her back to me.

I glance at the papers, notice my name on a printout and snatch up the documents, shoving them into my bag. My gaze sweeps the storefront. It all feels like a television show with corporate espionage. Except no one gives a crap that I'm taking papers off the printer. Not a single head in the office turns my way.

Pantsuit walks me the rest of the way to the door. She smiles. "Hope it all works out."

I mumble something before rushing out the door to my car. The papers contain the names of lawyers, groups for abused women, resources for disproving dementia or mental illness...so much more. From my car, I research more about inheritance, trust funds, power of attorney, and learn just exactly how much control Shawn Johnson has over my life.

7

The gray concrete and glass office building of Milner, Baker, Johnson and Associates, is situated in a lovely office park with plenty of trees to obscure my Subaru from the view of anyone gazing down from Shawn's fifth floor office. I've sat in my car for forty-five minutes, hoping to come up with some sort of plan that doesn't rouse his suspicion.

Shawn's gray Tesla pulls into the parking lot, cruising right past me. One hand is on the steering wheel, the other gesturing as if he's on a conference call. When I see Shawn get out of his car, movie-star suave in his expensive suit, able to live his life however he wants, I practically jump out of my seat to pounce on him.

"You!" I shout, pointing at him. "I trusted you, and you swindled me." *Way to go, Miriam. Very unsuspicious.* But, I'm furious. I'm tired of people, male people, doing things behind my back 'for my own good.'

Shawn blows out his breath and runs his hand over his short-cropped curls. Something behind me catches his eye that causes him to freeze. His gaze returns to mine and I don't sense danger, so I don't check it out. He gives me an Idris Elba look-alike smile and says in a conversational tone, "Miriam, I need you to calm down."

I throw up my hands and shout, "When in the history of *forever* has telling a person to *calm down* ever worked?"

"Miriam, let's go inside and talk this out." Shawn uses the same voice I've heard him use when his kid is about to lose her shit because she needs a nap, and it does nothing to ease how angry I am with him.

I jab a finger in his direction, using all my self-control not to put a spell on him to make him talk. Coercion is what he did to me and I'm not stooping that low. "Not until I know why you're monitoring my doings." I narrow my eyes, suspicion colors the question, "Whose side are you on?"

"I'm on your side." He slowly puts his hands up as if to show he's unarmed. Through gritted teeth he points out, "I understand you're troubled by what you learned today, but there's a nice police officer over there very interested in this conversation. I'd like for his interest to go away." He pleads with his eyes. "For both our sakes."

My anger deflates, replaced by worry. I'm angry, but I don't want Shawn hurt. I force a laugh. *Yes. It's all a joke.* "Got you!"

Shawn eyes me warily, then catches on, forcing a deep rumbling laugh. "Good one."

I allow him to lead the way into his office building, and walk through the door he opens for me. Inside is your typical Pacific Northwest foyer for a multi-story office building: *stupid* fake plants, a couple of *stupid* metal and pleather chairs, *stupid* stairs to my left and a *stupid* elevator directly ahead. A *stupid* directory on the wall lists of the names of the independent offices within.

I may not have calmed down as much as I've pretended.

Shawn closes his eyes and lets out a shaky breath. He then presses the button for the elevator and turns to me. Even in the suit, it's clear he works out and he's tall. His eyes are mournful. "I knew this day would come."

I open up my mouth to give him an earful, but Shawn holds up a finger nodding to the elevator door. The elevator chimes before the doors slide open, disgorging people dressed in business suits. Shawn and I take a polite step back out of the way so the newcomers can exit

—I don't know how banks or finances work, but I know some etiquette of the mundane world.

Thankfully, the elevator is completely emptied so Shawn and I have it alone. He lets me go in first and hits the button for the fifth floor. "Let's put a pin in this conversation until we're in my office."

I agree with a dip of my chin. Once I open my mouth, the words aren't going to stop.

The elevator opens to a hall that smells of cleansers and old carpet. We exit and turn a corner to go down a long hall. Shawn opens one of the double glass doors. Inside, the office is modern and sleek in shades of gray and blue. The chairs and table in the waiting area are expensive looking. The plant in the corner is real—I can sense it, like I can all things green and growing.

A receptionist looks up from her monitor and greets Shawn. Her gaze shifts to me then him, eyebrows lifting in silent question to her boss—I'm not on the schedule, an admin's nightmare.

"Hold all my calls. Reschedule my one o'clock. If they press, tell them it's a family emergency."

"Yes, Mr. Johnson."

We go past the reception area and glass offices filled with books, lawyers, and meeting rooms, all the way to Shawn's office in the rear. The file system, books and desk have a modern sleekness and meticulousness that I find antiseptic, but suits Shawn. From his close-cropped hair, neatly trimmed beard, manicured hands, and tailored suit, Shawn Johnson presents a flawless image.

"Please, take a seat."

I settle in one of two chairs before his desk. Shawn sits opposite of me.

I can't ask if he's an agent of His Creepiness. That plan flew out the window when I realized how that will sound to someone who thinks I'm mentally unwell in the first place. Instead, I stare at my hands.

Shawn adjusts his tie, which was already perfect, and clears his throat. "Okay. I'll begin. Someone who manages your account left a message saying you were poking around your assets, that you were trying to liquify them. I was in the middle of a trial, so I let the call go to voicemail." He leans forward and his eyes have a look I haven't seen in a while. It was the look he gave me when Raf died. "The message concerned me, so I returned her call before I listened to the whole thing. I just finished speaking with her in the car and was about to call you when I returned to the office. She didn't say it directly, but I could tell the credit union manager was under the impression I was taking advantage of you. I don't care what she thinks, what I want to know is do you really believe that I would do that?"

I shrink into my seat. He knows everything and makes it sound like I'm doing something irrational. "You never told me anything about power of attorney."

He gives me a rueful smile and sighs through his nose. "Raf asked me not to. He said that you wouldn't understand anything financial and might get swindled. Why do you want your money, Miriam?"

My chest aches with the stab of betrayal of Raf doing things behind my back all over again. "I'd like to have control of my finances. I'm in a place now that I can do it." I hate the way my voice quivers as I speak, and I feel like a child asking for permission. "I'd like you to make that happen."

"I would agree, but you claimed someone was stalking you to Micah and within an hour sought to liquidate all of your assets. This isn't typical behavior. It reminds me of when..." His voice drops off, but we both know I had a mental breakdown after Raf ascended.

"I spoke with the authorities about a prowler in our neighborhood. I have the officer's number right here." I wave my phone, hoping he won't ask me for Gabriel's information. Gabriel is not an authority to mundanes. I'd look even more mentally unstable if I give him the number of a man who owns a construction business.

"No. No." Shawn waves his hand in front of him. "No need. I believe you. Do you think the prowler is related to the coven devoted to the devil that you told Rafael you allegedly escaped?"

I realize he's testing how sane I am. "Coven? I grew up on a commune on a Pennsylvanian farm. They were pagans, not a cult." I laugh softly and shake my head. "No. I thought it was a possessive ex. He gave me a lot of trouble before Raf, and I got nervous."

Shawn steeples his fingers in front of him, remaining silent for a seeming eternity before he finally replies, "Pagan. Huh? Some of your odd habits and quirks make more sense now."

"I've never mentioned my practice or the commune because people are judgmental." There's bite in my tone.

"Fair." He smiles. "You're doing much better than when Raf passed. I'll look into giving you power over your assets, but it will take time. There's a lot to file and the courts are slow."

Somehow, I manage to thank Shawn and murmur an excuse to leave. He walks me to the door of his office. "It'll be alright, Miriam."

I nod as I exit his office, unsure it will. I have yet to meet with Gabriel. I have no recourse. I can't run until I have my funds. How long will that take and how long can I keep up the innocent, non-practicing witch façade if His Creepiness sends more of his minions after me and my grimoire library?

I manage to get inside my car before I cry. How could Raf do this to me? I try to look through an objective lens instead of the one wrought with the pain of betrayal. Knowing Raf, he thought ahead and wanted me and Jada taken care of, but he left me without means to run. Why had my husband pinned me here with inaccessible money?

Again, I have no answer.

8

I have thirty minutes to kill before I need to pick Jada up at school and have Gabriel coming, so I go to the only grocery store in town where I haven't embarrassed myself. When Jada was small, white people would approach me while I grocery-shopped, compliment how beautiful she was, and then would ask what Jada was mixed with. At first, I assumed they were supes, asking because they could sense her power. Terrified they would find out my secret, I would pick her up and run out of the store. Soon, I was running out of places to shop. Supes seemed to be everywhere. When I told Raf he needed to buy groceries and why, he laughed.

"Mi amor, they're not supernaturals, they're racists."

While I wasn't glad people racially profiled my child, I was glad that I found the store I was going to now. I know which carts have a wonky wheel and where everything is located. The baker knows Jada's favorite cookies—madeleines and macarons—and used to have one of each set aside for her every Tuesday morning. Not one, but two cookies made the weekly trip easier—a kid with a cookie in each hand didn't reach for things on the shelf or complain she wanted to leave.

The clerk in charge of the dry goods in bulk has learned from those who came before them to have certain things ordered for me, ready to go as soon as I run out. Because the layout only changes every few years, I know where everything is, so it takes only minutes to find everything I need to entertain a possible archangel.

A young clerk comes around and bags the groceries with my totes and sets them in the cart.

As I put my bags in the trunk, I chew my lip, wondering just how many people in the neighborhood have met the ostensible officer. If Gabriel gets to Micah and Shawn, the wolf story won't match up with my story about the stalker. I shut the trunk and round the car, cursing to myself. *Could this day get worse?*

My phone rings.

The caller ID says Papillon Academy, Jada's school. She attends a STEAM school that is part of the public system but for kids who need a little extra. I sigh and pick it up with a halfhearted, "Hello?"

"Miriam?" The voice sounds incredibly young for high school faculty. I don't go for honorifics, but it also feels strange for staff to call me by my first name. I would get suspicious of this call if I didn't remember meeting a teacher briefly at parent night a few weeks ago. Kimmy, as she'd asked us all to call her, looked like one of Jada's peers, not old enough to not only have finished college let alone teach advanced Math. Her name didn't help with that representation.

"This is Miriam Diaz speaking."

"This is Kimmy—Ms. Brodie—your daughter's AP Calculus teacher. Got a sec?"

No, Kimmy. I do not have a sec.

Forty minutes until I told Gabriel I'd be home. I also had cream and other perishables in the trunk. It is a cool Pacific Northwest afternoon, but it isn't fridge cold in this car.

"As long as you don't mind me putting you on speaker in my car."

After a moment's hesitation, Kimmy Brodie replies, "If you're alone, I'd be comfortable with that."

"I'm alone," I assure her, starting the engine and patching the call into the stereo so that I can talk hands-free.

Her exhale is loud over the system. "I'm calling because I want to help Jada succeed. She is a very popular girl. The students seem to have a sort of respect for her that almost borders worship. She's also very intelligent."

I back out, ready to hear Jada is up for an award and a list of checkboxes she'll have to hit to earn it. My daughter has received citizenship and academic awards since she was in kindergarten and it's part of the reason she got into Papillon Academy. She and Raf bonded over Math and Science homework. I pull my car onto the street and head towards home.

"If she applied as much to her work as she does for her arguments against why I am a failure as a teacher and why her peers should boycott my class, then she'd have an A in this class."

Traffic is light, but I concentrate on what I'm doing as I listen. My daughter has never in her life disrespected a teacher, let alone started this level of trouble, and I'm not sure what to do or how to feel about Jada being described as problematic.

"What would you like me to do about this, Kimmy?"

"Tell her to stop riling the students. To give me the same respect she gives any other teacher. I've talked to my peers. It seems I'm the only one who has fallen prey to her bullying."

Ah, that's the problem.

"Ms. Brodie, this is what I hear. You allowed a child to take over your classroom. I will speak to Jada, but she won't be the only child who will usurp your authority if you don't know how to deflect the situation yourself."

"You don't understand. Jada is very charismatic. It's hard to present the material in a way that is engaging while they are in her thrall. I've never seen a student whose every word is so utterly obeyed."

Now *that* is worrisome. My daughter is part god and she could potentially assert her will over others.

The teacher continues, "I may not have a lot of experience, but I do have a Master's in Teaching and Mathematics. You know how hard it is with this age group. You either get their attention right away or you lose it completely. Jada hasn't given me a chance. She formed an opinion on day one, saying, 'Who let the Freshman teach?' She doesn't have to agree with how I present the material. All I'm asking is that she keeps silent about it long enough for the other students to form an opinion."

Suddenly, I'm a young woman again, attending my first PTSA meeting. The older parents see my younger-than-them appearance and scoff at all of my ideas. I could choose to tell Kimmy to put on her big girl pants and leave it to her to get control of her classroom against a teenaged-demigoddess, or I could choose to be the kind of woman who helps lift another woman up. Blessed Mother knew it would have been nice if a woman had explained to me the way my finances work before today.

"I tell you what. I'll tell Jada to back off and give you a break, but I can't make her or any of the other students respect you. That's on you."

"Thank you, Miriam. I appreciate your help."

I hang up and head for the school. Jada and I need to have a talk about more than witchcraft.

9

I pull up to Papillon High School a few minutes before the final bell, weighing what I will say to Jada. The parent car queue is as long as ever, but it'll give me more time to think. Students disgorge from the front and side entrances of the two-story glass and concrete modern-looking building. Some mill about, others head directly to the bus lot or their parents' vehicles. I inch forward as the line-up begins to move.

Instead of coming straight for my car, I spy my daughter flanked by a group of teens goofing off by the bike racks. I slap the horn. There are signs posted with steering wheels with a big red X covering them, and I get the stink-eye from a parent volunteer directing traffic. Jada parts ways with her group of friends and slides into the passenger seat.

"Not supposed to do that," travels in behind my kid from the parent volunteer.

Jada and I roll our eyes at the same time. As soon as she slams the door and buckles up, I veer out of the curb queue and into the steady flow of traffic in the main parking lot. When we're clear of the school and chaos of afternoon pickup, I glance at Jada.

"Your father had the power to convince anyone to do anything he wanted. He didn't. Want to know why?"

In my periphery, Jada crosses her arms across her chest and the other hand plays with the lesbian pride flag pendant on a chain. Her gaze focuses out her window, not on me.

"I'll take your silence as a no."

She scoffs. "I didn't say that."

I'm focused on traffic now, but I can hear the eye-roll when she adds, "Whatever, you're going to tell me whether I *want* to hear it or not."

I don't say anything. Not because I feel like punishing her, but Jada never talked to me in that tone before Raf passed. I'm not sure if it's teenaged angst, her father's passing, or Roxy's influence.

Maybe all three.

After a bit, Jada blows out her breath and faces me. "Sorry. Please, tell me what papi said."

"He said there was more power in moving people by earning their respect than to force them against their will."

She sits up. "Like literal power? Will I level-up if I gain followers that way? I mean. I do want to be a goddess someday—not now, but someday."

"I don't know." I shrug, feeling bittersweet ache over the fact that she doesn't want to ascend *now* but will someday. "What I do know is that magic is a give and take. If he controlled people, that would take from him because he was using magic."

"Papi said that gods and demigods gain power from belief, but it has to be willing worship," she agrees.

"So, math class..."

"No, mami. I'm not influencing anyone. The teacher—"

I cut her off before she says something unkind. "Is inexperienced and trying to find her way."

Jada groans. "Mami, she's the worst teacher ever!"

"Somehow, I doubt that." I give her a dubious look and then sigh. "Look, I'm not saying she doesn't lack skills in managing a classroom, but this is an educated woman we're talking about here.

She's new to the job. Give her a chance by at least being respectful."

She chews on that for a bit. "I'll tell people to be quiet if they talk to me while she's teaching. If she still bombs, that's on her."

"That's all I ask."

We pull into the garage with an hour to spare before Gabriel should arrive. Jada helps me unload and put away the groceries, munching on an apple after we're done.

"Leave that on a plate for a sec," I say, getting one out for her from the cupboard. "I have something I want to show you."

Jada does as I ask, following me upstairs.

She gasps as I seemingly pass through a wall. I extend a hand through the spells. "It's just an illusion." I tell her the word she needs to say to pass through without harm.

Jada repeats me and takes my hand, following me into the library. After spinning in a circle with her jaw dropped, she says, "This. Is. So. Cool."

"These grimoires are only a small portion of a much larger library kept by the coven I left. The Archivist covens library is one of a kind and the only written knowledge of our former world."

"Why did you take these books? Did you write them?"

I give her a rueful shake of my head and take a deep breath. I am going to tell her a secret I haven't uttered in twenty years. Only Raf knew. "Within each of these grimoires is a spell that is a step of larger spell."

"What's the spell for?"

"To destroy a world."

Her mouth closes and thins into a straight line. "These grimoires are why you hide you're a witch?"

My chest tightens. Truth time. "Yes. I don't want them in the wrong hands."

"This world destroying spell is what that monster was after?"

"I believe so." My daughter could always make connections faster than some adults. I couldn't fathom a mind of a demigoddess.

Jada crosses her arms across her chest. "Mr. Crowfoot is the archangel of the Pacific Northwest. We need to tell him what you have so he can protect us."

At least that question is confirmed. The information would have been more useful this morning.

"Does he know you know that he's the archangel?"

She shrugs a shoulder. "Yeah. It's not a secret among supes. He's also the alpha of a shifter pack."

"Alpha isn't a real thing," I answer, dumbly.

She rolls her eyes, then grows serious. "Not among animals, but with shifters it's real. Like if he orders Roxy to do something she can't disobey. Her mom couldn't stand it. Can you imagine being married to someone whose word could—oh."

Raf could have used his godly influence, but— "Your father would never have done that to me. Does Gabriel use his influence on Roxy or Kirsten?" That would explain Roxy not wanting to tell her dad about me—the power of knowing a secret.

Jada shakes her head. "Nah. With her he's real careful about commands versus asking. Apparently if he says, 'can you take out the garbage?' she can say no. But, if he says, 'Take out the garbage.' and she doesn't, Roxy will get sick and barf."

"I'm beginning to understand why Roxy likes to push boundaries," I sigh.

"She says it hurts so much to disobey him that shifters will black out, and when they revive the urge to obey starts again. The only way it will stop is if the alpha rescinds the command, the shifter is abjured, or the shifter caves and obeys."

I wrinkle my nose. "Should I ask how Roxy knows this?"

"All shifters know, but she's seen it. As soon as he abjured Kirsten," Jada snaps her fingers. "Roxy's mom didn't have to listen to a word he said."

Interesting.

"Does he have an influence on you?"

Jada wrinkles her nose. "No. I'm a demigod, not a shifter. Turning into an animal is all they got. They're one-trick ponies."

I laugh at the expression. "Sometimes actual ponies."

She giggles. "Exactly." Her gaze slides across the grimoires and then back to me. She lifts her eyebrows, a grin dimpling her cheeks. "Wanna teach me how to banish the hellhound?"

I pull a leather-bound book, the only book that is not a grimoire, and hand it to Jada. Like the grimoires, the Kairska primer is spelled to resist the elements, tearing, fire, bombs, magic, etc., so I'm not concerned she'll damage it.

Her eyebrows knit together as she flips through the pages. "What is this?"

"A children's primer on how to read and write in Kairska, a language that is from the world all witches are from."

Her gaze snaps to me. "We're aliens?"

"So are angels, fae, demons—basically all supes. Only humans, shifters, and cryptids are indigenous to Earth...as far as I know."

The corner of Jada's mouth quirks. "Makes sense. We're all seeds from the ancients spread across the galaxy and the gods are just alien, symbiotic creatures inside humans, right?"

I roll my eyes. "You've watched too much Stargate with your father."

She snorts. "I remember you being there with us."

I had. Shows that touched on the truth always fascinated me. "Supes having fun with mundanes," Raf had called it. I took the stance that the human mind is capable of imagining the possible and impossible.

"The truth is, the multiverse is a lot more complex and weirder than what's on television. I cannot tell you how you and your father's godly powers work, but witchcraft is science and all science takes is study." I gesture to the Kairska primer. "You must learn Kairska first, and then the theories behind witchcraft before you can delve into spell casting and banishment."

She gazes down at the primer, flipping through the pages again. "I feel cheated. I mean, I know you're trying to protect yourself from your former coven, but..." Her voice trails off.

"You could have known this for a long time," I finish for her, knowing the burn of betrayal that likely seared her chest. Raf had kept things from me, maybe for my own protection. Maybe because he'd lost respect for me after I stopped being a powerful witch. Men often lost respect for their wives when they became a stay-at-home mom. It is hard, unglamorous work undervalued. He may have betrayed me by rejoining the supe community, but he'd kept my secret. I guess I could find some comfort in his loyalty.

"The thing is, even only having knowledge of the whereabouts of these grimoires is dangerous. You saw why."

She nods gravely.

I check my watch. "Speaking of Mr. Crowfoot. He is coming by at 4 p.m. How about we go over basic pronunciation, and maybe experiment a little with some basics while I set up snacks. Language and lab combined makes for quicker study."

Jada's face brightens. "Okay."

Later, the charcuterie board and fresh squeezed lemonade are ready to present upon Gabriel's arrival, and I switch from preparation to giving my full attention to teaching Jada. PC snakes through my legs as I lean against the breakfast bar, going over pronunciation and magical purpose of the symbols.

The written language of Kairska resembles Cyrillic. I show her how to push a bit of her light into the words she's learning. We manifest small magics. I'm fine with this because the traces of our spell work will burn away before Gabriel, and his keen nose, arrives. Jada's enthusiasm is contagious and it's fun to share the knowledge I'd kept to myself for so many years.

"I think we can study herbs and their uses as a supplement to this tedium."

She looks up from the Kairska primer. "It's not tedium. I'm enjoying myself."

We both turn to something tapping on the glass back door. The light sprites softly glow in the dark. It's autumn, so the sun sets early, but it's full dark outside. I check my phone for text messages. My mouth gapes as I see the time—a quarter 'til eight. Gabriel is hours late. I would have chucked it up to him being a busy archangel, but the sprites are acting bizarrely.

They smack themselves against the class frantically as if trying to bust in. Remembering that I owe them for distracting Jada from danger this morning, I gather their bowl and some heavy whipping cream from the fridge.

Jada accompanies me as I slide the door open. The sprites flood my kitchen.

"Hey, you weren't invited. That's just rude!"

The hairs on the back of my neck raise as something crashes into my blood wards. I slide the door shut and lock it—which is totally logical because glass and a little metal bar are definitely stronger than powerful blood magic.

"Mami, look!" Jada's voice comes from much farther away than it should.

I swing around to find she's no longer next to me. I dash, along with all the pixies, down the hall. Jada's at the front door gaping out the window.

A group has gathered on the asphalt of the cul de sac, concentrating in one area and piling on top of each other like a mosh pit. I can't distinguish from this far how many bodies there are...maybe ten, maybe more.

A few stragglers meander toward my property—their limbs make awkward, choppy movements as if marionettes. My wards zap them more effectively than an electric fence. The intruders flop on the ground as if they're being tasered.

An arm falls off a lady in a tank top as she pushes to her feet. A man in a track suit shakes his head, as if dazed, then stares straight at my house. His mouth widens until it is a gaping maw, bearing innumerable elongated fangs where teeth should be. He resembles a human-ish version of an anglerfish.

"Vamps," I hiss, running back inside for the interior door to the garage.

Jada follows. "I've never seen a vampire. They're...kinda gross."

"That's because they're rotting corpses with fancy dental."

"If we get bit will we become one?"

"No. Their venom will kill you—well at least make you very sick."

I honestly didn't know what a vampire could do to a demigod. Raf wasn't afraid of them. I go for my backpack of tricks and Raf's crossbow and quivers—I've never actually used it.

"So they're just monsters that exist?"

"They bargained for immortality with a demon." I notch an arrow in the crossbow and check the sites.

She wrinkles her nose. "Who would want to be *that* forever? It's like the Walking Dead but with fangs—and not the sexy kind."

"They assumed what immortality would be like. Sparkly and good looking. They should have read the fine print of the contract. They get to live forever, but under the demon's control and they don't get to stay young."

"That's awful!"

"Deals with demons never turn out good for anyone, except the demon," I throw over my shoulder before firing an arrow into a poster on the garage wall. It hits its mark close enough.

Jada's eyes grow wide as saucers. "Mami, what are you doing?"

"There's someone under that pile."

And I have a good idea who it might be.

Vamps alone will feed only to slow decomposition, attacking a victim at a time, usually people who wouldn't be missed. If they attack in a group so blatantly, they have orders from a demon, maybe His Creepiness himself.

Jada goes for her combat boots.

"No. Stay here and protect the pixies. Vamps love their blood." Vamps would pop the light sprites like candy. No wonder they were terrified.

Jada nods, straightening. She looks so much like her father did when he'd made up his mind to be a protector. The pixies have been her playmates her whole life. I can be comforted in the knowledge that Jada will stay inside to protect her friends.

"So brave." I cup my baby girl's cheek and then head out the door.

10

Vamps are notoriously silent killers, even in groups—their brains might be rotting, but they're smart enough to survive. As I march off my porch, I scan my surroundings —focusing on the windows of the houses facing the cul de sac melee. No one is in the windows gaping at the attack. One of my neighbor's dogs usually barks, but everyone has learned to ignore him.

Ah, the anonymity of the suburbs.

When I spot Gabriel's SUV parked down the street, my stomach drops. He's for sure under that pile.

I need to create a distraction. I just hope his angelic blood is keeping him alive.

I aim the crossbow at a vamp's head. There are two ways to take vamps out: put a hole in the brain or the heart; or stab the vamp *anywhere* with rowan or ash—something about those two types of wood cancels the demon contract and their body goes lifeless.

I pull the trigger, shooting the nearest vamp in the head. Or, at least I shot *a* vamp in the head. She happened to be nowhere near the one I meant to kill. The vamp crumbles to dust. The other vamps are so busy in their feeding frenzy they don't realize their buddy's demise.

Despite killing one, my confidence wavers. I'm not as good a shot as I once was. You really *do* lose it if you don't use it. Still, I grab another arrow from the quiver. I assure myself I don't have to be perfect. With all of the vamps gathered in a gruesome puppy pile, I'm bound to hit something. Like shooting fish in a barrel, or something like that.

After hitting another vamp in the arm and her resulting hissing and screaming, a few of the undead break away from their feeding frenzy to face the new threat. More join them. The vamps don't charge, they stumble as if drunk. I wonder if it's a reaction to Gabriel's blood.

"Do you feel inebriated?"

I get a lot of confused stares.

A gasp escapes my lips when I see the bloody, shredded remains of what had been Gabriel. My heart sinks. I'm too late. There's no way he survived that.

When he turns his wrecked head to face me, dangling eyeball and all, I almost piss my pants.

"Run." His voice is a hoarse whisper.

I blink at his command.

He shouldn't have *any* voice. There isn't anything left of his vocal chords.

Angels are really hard to kill. I didn't know the same went for nephilim.

"No. I'm not running," I reply.

Well, I plan on running, as soon as I have control of my money, but not right now. Right now, I have to face these fools, who chose to be bloodsuckers, fooled into thinking they were going to be glittery and young forever. Gross. I want to kill the vamps on the sheer principle. These abominations were a spit in the eye to the dignity and beauty of life and aging.

"Who is sick of their contract?" I reach over my shoulder and pull another arrow and load the crossbow. "I have your loophole, right here."

A few of the vamps fall for my ploy, charging my wards hard

enough to not just get warning zapped a bit, but deep fried. Their bodies crumble to piles of charred ashes. Neat. It's always validating to see theoretical magic work. Also, now I know a third way vamps can die that His Creepiness hadn't told me. See? There was a benefit to growing older. Learning!

A vamp in a sundress approaches, staying on the edge of the ashes of the fallen. Her skin is a mottled bluish gray and she's missing an arm. She's deteriorated enough to have lived more than a few years since being turned, yet she's not a grade-A killer—the more blood vamps drink, the less they deteriorate. She may have been Serial Killer Lite up until now, but her face has the flush of a fresh nephil blood.

Furious, I notch another arrow, aiming it at her head. I hate killing women, but this one ate my friend.

"If you come with us, we will let the nephil live." At least that's what I think the monster says. It's super hard to understand someone talking through a mouthful of fangs. The lisp is awful.

"You're all drunk off of angelic blood. The young ones among you will not be able to control themselves." I'm guessing by their behavior.

What's left of a man in a frayed and tattered track suit, hisses. *Aw. Sorry. Did I offend you with the truth*?

"Give us your treasure," the vamp in the sundress says, ignoring Tracksuit.

"Treasure?"

"Witch or her stolen treasure were our orders."

Interesting. His Creepiness didn't trust the vamps to tell them what the "stolen treasure" was. I could give them anything, and they'd go away, but I can't make it easy.

"Well, this witch is staying right here and there's nothing you can do about it."

Tracksuit must be under the distinct impression I'm bluffing because despite the litter of ashes he charges right into the wards.

My pulse races and pressure builds from within my own body as he stretches the boundary. Others take notice; he's not frying. I'm well and truly screwed if they all make it through. The tension is almost unbearable as he pushes the magic supported by my blood and witch light. Sudden relief washes over me as Tracksuit's body bursts like a confetti popper, bits of vamp and ashes flying everywhere.

The vamp in the sundress rolls her eyes. Vamps didn't live long unless they're smart or gluttonous, so she's smart. "A trade? Treasure for that." She gestures at Gabriel.

I pretend to scrutinize him, wrinkling my nose. Hopefully this reprieve gives the nephil time to heal. That he's not healing is concerning. Angels have incredible regenerative powers. I've seen it in their wayward siblings.

"I don't think so." I shake my head. "It's broken."

"We could kill your neighbors one by one until you give it to us," Sundress says. The vamp doesn't even look at Gabriel. No. All eyes are focused on me, where I want them.

"You wouldn't be able—"

I don't have enough arrows to kill them all. I need to piss them off. I need to piss them off so badly, I get them in a frenzied state of murder death kill where they forget all logic and charge...like Tracksuit.

I slide my backpack off my shoulder and rifle through it, triggering another brainless vamp to charge and get fried.

Sundress narrows her eyes.

Inhaling deeply, I walk to the very edge of Tracksuit's ashes, raising a silver dagger for all to see. Pressing the blade to the delicate inner skin of my arm, I slice. Tears blur my sight. The cut stings like heck.

The vamps snarl and hiss. Even Sundress's gaze narrows on the blood.

I raise my bloody arm.

Like cats, who can't help but pounce on a moving target, their logic stops working and their cursed instincts kick into overdrive, propelling the vamps forward to their final death.

I pick up the crossbow and loading it with an arrow, I cautiously step over the boundary, scanning my surroundings for lurkers.

My stomach lurches at the sight of Gabriel's mangled body. I kneel next to him. "Why aren't you healing?"

Somehow with very little face, he manages to look indignant. His arm flops as if he's trying to use it. His good eye locks on me. "Phone."

The voice is inhuman and what feels like an attempt at compulsion taps at my natural defenses.

I shake my head. *No way.* I'm not having some angel brigade showing up, or shifters sniffing around. Gabriel is my friend, but the grimoires cannot get into the wrong hands. Again. "No time for that," I say in a soothing voice, placing a comforting patch of non-shredded head. "I can heal you long before help could arrive. Okay?"

Gabriel doesn't answer. His good eye just stares up at me until it flutters closes.

Crap. I want his consent, but I can't get it from an unconscious patient.

When I was very small, my mother told me every witch has two gifts, the gift to manipulate the natural world through the science of what is called witchcraft. The second gift is a gift that all witches keep to themselves, sharing with no one but immediate family. Mine was the ability to see the color of magic and heal any wound no matter how grave.

Upon learning how my sight-gift worked, I realized what my mother said about two gifts was bunk pretty fast, and that whatever this gift was, it was unique to me—and whatever my dear ol' dad is.

I dip into my light, the secondary light I got from whomever my father is, seeing the colors of magic. A beautiful shimmering gold aura surrounds him with sparks of sapphire—his angelic and shifter lights. I see null patches growing steadily within the aura. The null patches indicate life threatening wounds.

Partial relief washes over me. Gabriel is still alive.

Only three people knew about my healing gift: my mother, Rafael, and His Creepiness. If I save Gabriel, he'll know my secret. I could let him die. I could use this terrifying event to rush Jada out of town, money or no. Even though I sometimes forgot it and began believing the lie, I'm a witch, after all. I could conjure money and IDs and disappear—the only person who knew I could practice magic, dead.

My gaze darts to the house.

Jada watches from the front window, expectantly.

Right now, whatever I decide will change her life forever. She's registered. Protected. It's not her fault she possesses unknown witch blood.

As I debate, the null spots in Gabriel's aura grow. I have to act now.

I don't have it in me to leave him. I lean over his shredded body, dipping into the pool of light within me.

"Please, don't make me regret this kindness."

I lay my hands on Gabriel like I'm one of those TV preachers, ignoring the icky feel of his damaged flesh. I push my light into him, not the yellow witch light, but the other one. With my other sight, I see green light pour from me into Gabriel.

My light doesn't heal right, serving as patches instead of healing. At least the wounds stop leaking. However, the null spots in his aura don't repair themselves as null spots usually do with other magical people I've healed. They don't grow further, simply remain. I push more and the green light not only fills the nulls in the gold and sapphire light, it starts drawing them close.

Gabriel's massive wounds stop bleeding, the flesh binding as the nulls repair. I can feel I'm draining my inner well to the place where I should stop, where I know the pain will begin. I pause the flow.

Instead of continuing the work, the null patches stop repairing. His body hasn't repaired enough to function. He's in danger of dying despite my efforts.

I take one look back at my daughter. I say, "I love you." Then I dive back into the healing work.

As I scrape the bottom of the well, the corners of my vision darken. Pain I've experienced before makes me break out in a sweat and shake. But...

Gabriel is healing!

I've made a choice.

My life for his.

His only word to me when I left the house was "run," not "get help." He knew what the vamps would do if I did. He had made the same choice I'm making now. His eyes flutter open, green and intense.

"Protect Jada," I whisper just as the pain is too much to bear and my world slips into pitch black.

11

The first thing I'm aware of is the smell of bacon. The afterlife serving my favorite breakfast side is definitely a perk. I wonder briefly *which* afterlife I'm in since I never particularly subscribed to one belief. More importantly, I'll have to figure out what this bacon eating deity would want as a bribe to send me back.

I blink a few times before my vision comes into focus. The afterlife looks a lot like my four-poster bed and decorated like my bedroom suite. Wan light pours through the blinds. Dawn, judging by the accompanying aroma.

As my body revives, I'm aware of every ache head to toe, like I have the flu, or at least how others have described the flu. I've never been sick a day in my life.

"Mami?"

I turn my head slowly, with much effort to the sound of Jada's voice. A slow, tearful smile spreads on my daughter's lips. She's sitting on the edge of my bed. She body slams me—okay. It's a hug but it's a forceful one and painful.

It takes a conscious effort, but I lift my hand to pat her back. "I'm okay." My voice sounds rough as if from disuse.

She sits up and wipes her tears with the back of her hands. "I was so scared. I—I thought I'd lost you, too."

Her heartbreak hurts more than my physical pain. "No. I'm here to stay." I squeeze her hand. "Do I smell bacon?"

As if on cue, there's a knock on the door. Healthy and hale, Gabriel enters with a serving tray loaded with delicious foods. "Jada, I thought you'd—" whatever he was about to say, dies in his mouth. He gapes at me. "They said your healing sleep would take a month. How?"

My brow knits together and panic rises in my chest. "They?" There's definitely a whole lot of fear my tone.

"A demigoddess named Leilani," Jada answers, brushing some of my hair aside.

I sigh audibly. No angels.

"She was so cool! She said you had some sort of hex that's bound up your power—like you're really, really powerful, but someone put a lock on it and there's booby traps if you try to access your full potential. That's what happened, huh?"

I swallow. Another secret I didn't want out. I died once to keep my secret.

Gabriel hands the tray to Jada, glancing at me. "I have some official archangel business I have to go over with your mom. Why don't you take this and eat with Roxy downstairs?"

Jada's gaze swivels to me, the same protective expression Raf used to get in our early days filling her features. I want to tell her to stay because I'm too weak to fight for myself, to speak in half-truths. However, hiding behind my seventeen-year-old, who just so happened to be a powerful demigoddess, is cowardly.

"When you're done eating, bring me some water." There, I'm giving Gabriel a time limit and her a reason to come back.

"Of course, mami." Jada kisses my cheek.

To my surprise, Gabriel follows her out.

I would like to face the interrogation with the archangel and get it over with. I saved his life so Jada would have more protection, not so I could have the Angelic Anocracy breathing down my neck.

After a pitiful and painful attempt to sit, I give up and stare at the ceiling. The minutes tick by. My eyelids grow heavy.

Gabriel returns with another tray filled with food and drinks, rousing me again. He sets the tray on the nightstand next to the bed. I gaze at the tray longingly, but I'm still too weak and sore to *do* anything about it.

With a cellphone cradled between his head and his shoulder, Gabriel doesn't notice at first. He's too busy saying, "Uh huh" and "Right." His gaze flicks to my face. He puts a hand over his phone and tilts his head questioningly. "Can you sit up on your own?"

I don't like admitting weakness, but I can't take the pain of a lie, not in this state. "I can turn my head and move my arms." Barely. I wave in demonstration. Torment wracks through my body with the simple movement.

He gives me a sympathetic smile. "I see." Then, he says into the phone. "She can barely move." His jaw tightens in response to whatever the person says. To me, he asks, "Are you in any pain?"

"Loads."

His eyebrows furrow. His throat works as if he's swallowing hard. "Why didn't you say so?" He shakes his head. "That's the first thing I should have asked you, I'm sorry. Where does it hurt?"

"Everywhere."

His muscles, on display in a white t-shirt and fitted gray jogging pants, tense. "Miriam said yes...No. It's not localized, Leilani...I hear your concern about that but what *can* I do for her?" He worries his bottom lip as he listens to whoever is on the other end, presumably the demigoddess with healing powers.

I'm a healer and could suggest many herbs for physical symptoms, but this doesn't feel like a bodily type of hurt. It feels more like when I tell a lie, and that is something that can't be eased with herbs.

He approaches the bed and leans over me, cupping my chin. He smells like soap and fabric softener—and bacon. The simple, domestic aromas are unexpected. I would have pegged him as an expensive cologne kind of guy.

"Her eyes are clear, but her lips are dry—yes both Jada and I have put on lip balm...hold on, I'll ask. Is your vision okay?"

I have to process his casual mention of applying lip balm.

"Miriam?"

"I see fine."

He places the back of his hand to my forehead and cheeks. The gentle touch almost feels like a caress.

I close my eyes. It's been a long time since I'd been with someone. Commander Buzz Feelgood locked away in my closet met some needs, but I didn't realize how much I missed tenderness until I had someone leaning over my bed touching me gently.

I open my eyes when his hand draws away.

"She's not overly hot. I don't think she has a fever. Yes. I'm judging by feeling her forehead. I'm in her bedroom, not a clinic." His gaze is intent on my face, but he angles his mouth toward his phone. "Can I try the same course of action?"

Same course of action?

Gabriel listens to the person on the phone intently. "Alright. Yeah. Of course, I'll tell her the risks. The first time was an emergency. K. Thanks for your help. Bye." He ends the call and stuffs the phone into his pocket. His gaze turns to the food. "Oh, I forgot. Leilani says if you can talk, I can try feeding you. But first, we need to get you out of pain." Blowing out his breath, Gabriel scratches the back of his head. "Do you know about the analgesic effects of angel dust?"

I quirk an eyebrow. "I know the aphrodisiac effects of angel dust." I also know that if I lied, angel dust soothed that pain, but I wasn't going to share how I'd gained that knowledge.

He clears his throat. "Yes. There'll be that too."

I close my eyes. Only two things would make my agony go away: time or countering it with a magical substance. I don't know if I can bear being weak and in pain for a month.

"I promise. I won't let anything happen. You know I wouldn't take advantage of you, right?"

I nod, closing my eyes.

They fly open to the sound of rustling clothes, catching Gabriel shedding his shirt. I may be in agony and weak, but I'd have to be dead to not take in all that bronze muscle. More importantly, the few red areas on his throat and chest. Scarring from the vamps ravaging him? I sincerely hope the scars and the trauma of that experience will fade. He was protecting me by sacrificing himself.

Gabriel touches his chest on the healed tissue. "You saved my life and are suffering for it." The mattress dips with his weight as he sits on the bed. His hand encompasses mine. "Please, let me help you ease your pain."

I look away. "I can't."

He blows out his breath. "I wish I'd come around more, so you'd know that I'm not the type of person who would want the side effects. I—I thought it best if I left you alone, after what happened."

I do. In a moment of weakness and grief, I'd kissed Gabriel. I had no feelings for him. I hardly knew him. I'd simply felt so utterly alone, and he was there. The kiss was not unreciprocated—quite the opposite—but he'd come to his senses first and stopped us from going further.

We'd agreed to never mention it and I can tell he's extremely uncomfortable about bringing it up, especially now.

"It's not you. I've had firsthand experience"

"Miriam, I know you're not just hiding from your coven." His voice is gentle, not accusatory.

There's no need to ask who Gabriel means. He had been conscious when the vamps tried to bargain.

"I was a teenager when he started grooming me with his angel dust," I admit and then just let it all out. "At some point, I knew I'd never escape him alive. I faked my death and escaped. Raf found me half-dead in a Florida swamp while I was going through withdrawal." I sigh, even breathing hurts. "Raf took care of me. Helped me start over."

His hands envelop mine, comforting. "You wouldn't have been the first witch Lucifer groomed, promising her to be at his side if she only helped him get back at his brothers."

I cringe at the use of His Creepiness's name and the truth of it.

The spell and the light, albeit locked, to power it. Witches had both diluted blood and light these days.

I grow tired, the only thing keeping me awake is how much everything hurts. I don't want to talk about His Creepiness anymore. I sigh. "Once. I will accept what you offer once."

Gabriel pushes to his feet. Unlike when he shifted from wolf to human form, his feathery wings manifest like a parachute expanding all at once. White and shimmering gold magnificence; softer hues of pale pinks stretch, spanning at least six feet on either side.

He angles his stance so that the downy feathers are within reach.

"This isn't very scientific," I protest, but I already know what to do.

A seemingly involuntary shudder is Gabriel's only reaction as I stroke the downy feathers covering my fingers with the powdery substance coating his wings.

It's a herculean task to lift my hand to my mouth, where Gabriel's gaze fixes. My heart races and my cheeks flush as I suck the honeyed substance.

A moan of pleasure escapes my lips as the pain subsides, giving way to euphoria. Time stops and pure bliss settles in.

I smile, rainbows bursting around me. "This is *different.*"

"I'm a different person." Gabriel assists me into an upright position, rearranging pillows. His wings are woefully absent, once again nothing but a shimmering tattoo.

Lazily, I run a finger up his bicep and over his shoulder, watching his bare skin pebble into gooseflesh under my touch. "Maybe a little more?"

His gaze turns from where I'm touching him to meet mine. For a moment, I think he's going to spread those pretty wings for me. He wants to. It's in his dilated eyes and the way his nostrils flare.

"Are you still in pain?"

His voice is rumbly and sexy, tickling my ears.

I wrap my arms around his neck, he lets me lead him closer. A voice deep inside screams for me to stop behaving like this because I'll be mortified later. I ignore it, brushing the sensitive part of his ear with my lips on purpose as I whisper, "Don't you want to make me feel good?"

Gabriel's muscles tense. A low growl rumbles in his chest. Something about him shifts. Shaking his head, he gently removes my hands. His face is all hard lines. "You need to eat."

I groan. "So serious."

A muscle feathers in his cheek. "Always with someone inebriated."

I wag a finger. "If I were twenty years younger and skinny, you'd be tempted. I was so hot."

"No. I wouldn't," he assures with a 'no thanks' wave of his hand. "I'm not attracted to women over twenty years younger than me."

I snort. "Or me."

He grimaces. Breathing out his nostrils with impatience. "Most of the time, my attention is extremely focused on whatever task I have at hand. Peripheral people escape my notice...I notice you. I've *always* noticed you."

I grin. "You had a crush on me?"

"We were both married when we met," he hedges, pressing a glass of boring water to my lips. "Sip."

I place a hand over his that's holding the cup. We maintain eye contact as I drink.

He sets the tray on my lap and ends up feeding me because I'm too stoned to understand how silverware works, apparently. I don't have the stomach for much, but I try several times to lick his fingers. He's patient and even laughs a few times, but there is no seducing Gabriel.

My eyelids are too heavy to keep open. I'm vaguely aware of him taking away the tray and tucking me in.

"Get some rest, Miriam. I'll send Jada up" are the last words I hear before I drift off into lucid dreams of a sexy nephil.

<h1 style="text-align:center">12</h1>

The second time I awake, Jada's sitting in an armchair, asleep, textbooks and notebook sprawled around her. I'm in no pain and I don't feel symptomatic of angel dust withdrawal. In other words, I'm not convulsing, vomiting, and wishing I was dead, nor do I crave Gabriel like he is necessary to breathe. A lesson on just how messed up my relationship with His Creepiness really had been. Not that I needed one.

I take my time sitting up. No vertigo. No weakness. No pain. Good. My mouth feels cottony and my body odor reeks enough to make my eyes water. Enough time in bed.

Quietly, I tiptoe past Jada into the master bath and through to the hidden door to the library. Nothing is missing, but Jada's been in there. She left a notebook and pen on the stand next to the reading chair. Studying, I suppose.

Next, I take a shower. The steamy water feels so good, I stand under the spray until I muster up the energy to scrub myself and shave—I've rested long enough that an army of red stubble has made camp on my legs and underarms.

After I've brushed my teeth and dressed in my closet, there's a gentle knock on my door.

"Everything okay in there?" Gabriel calls from the other side.

My face and chest burn with embarrassment as I recall my role of the Clumsy Seductress. I clear my throat. "Yeah, I'm fine. Excellent, actually."

A pregnant pause follows, then, "Good. I will wait for you downstairs."

I don't reply. I'm too embarrassed. I don't clearly recall all of the conversation, I'd been in too much pain, mostly flashes of the really, really embarrassing bits.

When I hear the door to the bedroom open and close, I reenter my room. Jada is no longer sleeping on the chair. Her schoolwork disappeared along with my daughter.

Stalling on purpose, I check her room. The floor is a disaster of discarded clothes and accessories. She, and I assume Roxy by the electric blue hair, are fast asleep on her bed. I close the door with a soft click and head downstairs.

Gabriel is in my kitchen, loading the dishwasher. He's in a tank top and joggers, all black and fitted.

In the sitting room adjacent to the kitchen, Raf's flatscreen is playing the local news, the volume low. Upon seeing me, Gabriel uses the remote to mute the TV. He nods to the screen. "I can't stand silence. My pack lives in my house."

"Pack," I repeat, still getting used to the fact someone I'd thought was a mundane was half-angel and shifter. "Raf said you had a lot of extended family living with you." I don't keep the bitterness from my tone.

"It's why Kirsten and I would only have dinner with you two at restaurants."

That's what Raf had said too. How many lies and half-truths had my husband told me? My daughter had stayed at their house, growing up around shifters, and I had no idea.

"Is Kirsten a shifter too?"

He nods, gaze falling to the floor. "She's not pack though." He ran his hand through his hair, clearly uncomfortable talking about it. "Not anymore."

"Why?"

He frowns. "The same reason we got a divorce."

Kirsten was on her third husband since they'd split seven years ago. Raf had told me Kirsten cheated on Gabriel with many people. It had taken Gabriel years to see it was happening. According to Raf, he simply hadn't believed she'd lie to him.

"Sucks to be lied to," I say, folding my arms across my chest. I'd thought that was the best part of my marriage. No secrets. No lies. All loyalty. It hurt. I think it hurt more that I couldn't even have it out with Raf.

"Look, Raf lied to both of us. He said you were mostly a mundane human, maybe with some latent magic you weren't aware of, not a highly trained witch with a past. I trusted him, too. I've been thinking about it a lot...I don't think he meant to be devious. I think given who you ran from, he would have done anything to protect you and Jada."

Except stay in his mortal coil, I think bitterly. "I could have cured his cancer, and he knew it. He refused." I climb onto one of the stools at the breakfast bar.

"I don't think it was that simple as treating the cancer." Gabriel countered, pushing the buttons on the dishwasher and throwing a towel over his shoulder. "Rafael sustained his human form as long as he could. I think an abundance of magic, building in a shell not made for that amount of power, is what caused the cancer. It had to be torture, knowing he had to go but also wanting to be there for his family."

That took some of the sting away. But, part of me questioned if Raf would have not grown in power if he had not kept ties to supernaturals. "I'm not a demigod. I'll never know."

"True empathy isn't the ability to relate to someone's experience but taking in their perspective."

I chew on that for a second.

He heads for the fridge, tossing over his shoulder, "Hungry?"

I rise from the chair. "I can—"

Gabriel waves his hand dismissively. "There are leftovers from dinner." He dives into the fridge. "Hope you don't mind, but I've been cooking for them."

I blink. I imagined an alpha or an archangel having others waiting on him. Raf didn't know how to cook because his family had servants who did everything. I took over that duty when we settled down as mundanes, or at least one of us pretended to.

I push the thought aside and smile. "I not only don't mind but would like to thank you."

"I didn't always know how to cook. I grew up in Heaven, where everything is done differently," he says as he digs through my refrigerator, as if mentioning growing up among angels is an everyday thing. "When my mother brought me to Earth to be with her people and learn their ways, I learned how to cook, among other mundane tasks. Mom wanted me to be able to understand how humans and the supes who live here function. I had to learn to be good at it too." He smiles, memories clear in his eyes as he takes a pile of containers from the fridge to the counter. "Shifters have high metabolisms and are always eating."

I've known Gabriel tangentially through my husband and daughter for years, so it doesn't feel strange to have him in my kitchen, but it seems I don't know him at all. Learning of my past, I suppose he must feel the same.

He plates the leftovers, relating a story about his early attempts at cooking. I laugh at his story. My gaze falls on the play his muscles make in that well-fitting tank, the golden wings. Suddenly my mouth goes dry. Heat builds deep in my core and I *want*.

Gabriel punches the settings on the microwave, thankfully unaware of my attraction.

I shake my head. The attraction isn't real; a side effect of the angel dust, no doubt. He may be okay with my past but getting involved with him is a *very* bad idea. Our daughters are close.

He's the archangel.

That's a cold bucket of water dumped right on my heated lady bits.

While the microwave runs, Gabriel grips the counter of the island opposite of me, leaning my way. His cheeks dimple with his smile. "I think I have a solution to your problem."

I lick my lips, already forgetting what I just remembered. "You do?"

His gaze momentarily drops to my mouth before flicking to my eyes. "About our common enemy."

"Oh?"

"I think he's counting on you running or trying to maintain the life you've been living. Separate from those who can help you and desperate to keep your secrets."

"What else can I do?"

"Come out of the supernatural closet. Go out in public with me, meet my pack, and my council. He wants to send emissaries to bring you back? It's time to show him you are not the scared young woman who left. You're grown, you're powerful, and you have *friend*s." His eyes flash with excitement. "Maybe he'll stop sending his minions to bother you."

I stammer for a reply.

The microwave beeps. Gabriel retrieves the plate and sets it before me. He also gets me a glass of ice water before I even think about needing a drink. It's then I notice the dark circles under his eyes.

"Where have you been sleeping?"

"Haven't done much of that. Dozed off in the armchair in your room a couple times." He grins sheepishly. "Hope you don't mind. Jada wouldn't rest otherwise."

Guilt twists my gut. My daughter had lost one parent. I hadn't thought about the emotional repercussions, only her protection. "No. I understand."

Gabriel busies himself putting away the containers of leftovers and wiping down the counters.

I work on my food: steak, a rice dish, and a sautéed vegetable mix. It's delicious. I wish I could enjoy it. I'm too busy weighing whether I should take Gabriel up on his offer and take a stand, or continue with my getaway plan.

Jada deserves more than a half-existence where she has to run and hide what she is. If worse comes to worst, I'll destroy the grimoires before I let His Creepiness have them, but with new alliances I may not have to. I take a deep breath.

"I'm dead on official records. I would have to re-register..."

Gabriel holds up his hands. "Raf registered you as a latent years ago. As far as higher ups are concerned, that's what you are. We can keep between us what you really are."

By higher ups, he means the Angelic Anocracy. Technically, he's their Earthly rep and he has people to report back to. I point up. "What about the official report?"

"No need." He rests his hands on his hips. "I like to keep matters like this up to my discretion. I now know why the vampires and hellhound were here. Lucifer wants back what he believes is his. He's not making a move on my territory."

It's true. His Creepiness isn't making a move on the territory. He wants to destroy the whole damned world. I debate whether I should tell him about the grimoires.

"The Pacific Northwest Supernatural Council is meeting in a few days. I'd like you to come and meet all of them. I can introduce you to my beta there and then the rest of the pack whenever you're ready."

"Okay." I shrug. Best I make some friends while I wait for control of my finances.

Gabriel pulls out a cellphone from a pocket in his joggers and starts tapping.

I resume eating with the hope that I haven't made a mistake.

13

Sitting cross-legged on the floor of the library wearing leggings with rainbow skulls and a black t-shirt that says, "Ask me about Anime," Jada sighs and stretches. Then she goes back to practicing drawing the Kairska alphabet in her notebook.

I mark my place in the grimoire, close it, and rub my eyes.

Jada lifts her amber gaze and raises her eyebrows questioningly.

I shake my head. "Nothing."

"How many grimoires does that make?"

"Technically, I'm not finished with this one, but," I sigh heavily. "This is the last one on hexes, curses, and bindings."

"The coven you came from would know."

"Likely." Funny that. I had a sneaking suspicion someone didn't want His Creepiness to use me to power the spell. Definitely not my mother.

"How did you get so many books from their library without getting caught? Did you sneak and stash them away one at a time?"

"I took all of them at once."

Jada's eyes widen and she leans forward. "How?"

"I can create a pocket of reality, a dimension for storing. My mother called it a cache."

"Whoa!" Jada's face is filled with the kind of wonder I haven't seen from her since her father ascended. "Can I learn how to make one?"

"This is something you will not need a grimoire to learn," I say. "Either you are born with the ability to make a cache or not."

"Like the way some people can sing, and others can't carry a tune if they tried?" Her amber eyes light up. Even when she was very small Jada had a curious mind, absorbing knowledge like a sponge.

"Exactly, but rarer. I was the only one in my coven who could do it." That included my mother. She could make plants grow like I could, but healing and making caches are bonuses only I had. "I wasn't taught how to make caches, I just *could*. There are witches who can move earth or brew storms. Nobody taught them either, it's an ability that comes around puberty." Thank goodness. Both abilities were not one a toddler should possess.

Jada chuckled. "Witches sound like X-men."

"X-men sound like witches," I counter.

"So, a witch's natural ability is like the ability to shift forms," Jada says, understanding registering on her features. "Either it's part of your metaphysical makeup or it's not."

"That's always been my theory." I smile. "It's considered wild or natural magic."

"So are you going to make one?" There's pleading in her eyes.

"Okay. Just be warned. A cache requires tearing a hole in the fabric of reality and making a pocket universe in the interstitial space between universes."

"Whoa. Do you think I have this ability and don't know it?"

"Perhaps. I'll tell you how I do it as I make one, and you try to see?"

She nods.

Before my run-in with the hellhound, I couldn't even entertain the idea, the risk of someone detecting I possessed unregistered magic too great. I feel almost giddy to practice this type of magic.

"First I dip into my other sight. If you don't have it, then you will not be capable of making a cache." I can see Jada's aura. She's a brilliant spectrum of light showing her mixture of supernatural lineages. It's so beautiful, I could cry.

"Other sight?" she asks, drawing my attention back to the matter at hand.

"That's what I call using my light, my magic as a lens for the world." I don't have better words to explain it.

"I have latent energies within me. Papi said to leave them alone because he didn't know how to control them."

"I can see them." I smile, remembering that the force I call 'light' Raf called 'energy'. Magical terms vary between different supernatural groups because they all came from different worlds and cultures. Magic doesn't work like DNA, the split isn't even. Magenta, the color I associate with Raf's light and gods magic, dominates Jada's aura, but green and white threads of light, my magic, are woven throughout.

"You have three lights—three sources of magical energy. Two from me, one from your father." I pause to let it sink in and take a deep breath. "I use my green light to see the color of magic. You could use your green or magenta, I think."

Jada scrunches her eyebrows in concentration, looking so much like Raf when he was deep in thought. She blinks rapidly. "Whoa... One of your energies, er lights, has—" She screws up her face. "Something like a knot of vipers coiling around the light. No wonder Ana didn't want to mess with the hex no matter how much Roxy's dad begged her to lift it."

An icy frisson skitters across my shoulders hearing the binding on my light described as such. It didn't bode well for ever releasing my full potential. Why bind it? I wonder who my father is and *what* he is, not for the first time. What could he be that he cursed me to not be like him?

Jada echoes my thoughts. "What energy does the green represent?"

"My mother hedged the subject." That's putting it politely. My mother forbade me to even think of the sower—a witch euphemism, an equivalent to sperm donor. My mother feared my father, which make me fear him.

Given His Creepiness could not break the binding on my magic without killing me meant whoever my father was or *whatever* he was, was as powerful as a fallen seraph. Perhaps more powerful.

Jada scoffs. "Guess keeping secrets is a family trait."

"Let's concentrate on what we're learning now, not the past," I redirect. "Unless you're no longer interested in learning how to make a cache?" I lift my eyebrows.

Jada frowns but nods.

"Okay. Focus your green light or your energy in your dominant hand." As I speak, I do as I instruct, pausing for Jada to do it as well. "Then you're going to use that hand as a blade to cut a very small hole, reach in. This is the interstitial space called 'the null' that is between universes."

Jada's eyes widen.

"Now imagine a—a balloon. It has a definite barrier, but it's elastic, stretched as far as you want or need to. Pour your light into that thought and make it exist."

My daughter's expression is all I need to know she was successful. "Got it!"

"Now put something material inside and then close it by sealing the entrance to the cache the same way you made it."

She puts a pen inside her cache and then seals it shut.

"You'll be able to access the item from anywhere by just thinking about your cache as you open the seam."

"Huh? How does that work?"

I shrug. "I don't know. I learned by trial and error."

She rears her head, incredulous. "You messed with the fabric of reality by *trial and error*?"

"I didn't know that's what I was doing. I was playing with magic."

"I thought you said that this ability didn't come until puberty," she countered.

"Why don't you try to retrieve your pen?"

She glares at me for a moment, but curiosity wins out. Jada opens another hole in the fabric of this universe and reaches inside, pulling out a pen. Her eyes bulge. "Whoa. I have this same light, mami. How did you know how to do it? Something like this didn't even occur to me to *try.*"

I try to remember, but my childhood recollections are spotty at best. Suddenly, a blurry image of a person looking down at me—an antlered humanoid—comes to mind. I can't quite make out the distinct features of the creature-person, but the being shines with the green light within me, but theirs isn't threaded with anything else and more brilliant. Who is this person?

A single word echoes in the memory, *"Papa."*

I cry out as searing agony shoots from my center when I try to focus on the face and *remember* what my father looked like. I let go of the image, centering myself in my surroundings, and find immediate relief.

My father clearly doesn't want me to remember him.

Funny, neither did my mother.

Jada is at my side, on the armrest of the overstuffed chair. "Mami, are you alright?"

I give her a reassuring smile and pat her hand. "I'll be alright."

Though I'm not exactly sure this is true.

14

Shawn, Micah, Lucinda, and I sit with Chad in the library conference room. It's supposed to be a preliminary meeting for the fundraiser committee. I'm not on the committee, but I'm there to take notes because Lucinda begged me.

Her exact words were, "Please don't make me the only waffle at the sausage fest."

I laughed at her euphemism and told her that I'd be there. I had a lot going on but couldn't leave my best friend hanging.

"I plan on holding the event in Seattle proper rather than the Eastside," Shawn says. "I really wanted to go with a Cirque theme." He spread his hands. "Picture it: performers on a stage and among the guests, selling raffle tickets and tricks for donations."

"Sounds pricey," Chad grumbles. "Where are we going to get the funds for the upfront costs?"

"I'll call in a few favors," Shawn says with a dismissive flick of his wrist.

I nearly squeal with delight at Chad's pinched lips. Shawn is out busy-important-manning Chad. Instead of gloating, I exchange amused grins with Lucinda.

"At the end of the evening, we'll have a silent auction. All the local businesses can donate services or goods: salons, spas, pastry shops—for my own firm, I'll have one of the junior members do a free will consultation."

Chad opens his mouth, raising his hand to interrupt with another objection, I'm sure.

Shawn either doesn't see or doesn't care, continuing with, "I figure we'll have more than enough businesses who will volunteer. We'll push it as a promotion to get more patrons with disposable cash at their fingertips."

"I'll donate a latte a day for a year," Lucinda says. "People who get something for free always end up spending on other items."

Shawn gestures in her direction. "Perfect."

I look at my notes, wishing I had something to donate or contribute, but I'm not a business owner. Lucinda nudges my foot under the table and then nods toward the pile of cookies I've brought to the meeting.

Picking up her meaning, I perk. "I can make up gift baskets of homemade baked goods. We can auction those off, too."

"That's what I'm talking about." Shawn smiles.

"I'm crap at baking, but I can totally help with assembling the baskets," Micah offers.

Chad clears his throat. "Why don't we get a professional bakery to do that? I mean Miriam is a good baker, but who would want amateur goods?"

I bristle at the way he not only dismisses my contribution but also talks as if I'm not there. "You, apparently."

"You've eaten three of Miriam's snickerdoodles since this meeting started," Lucinda adds.

Ignoring us, Chad turns to Shawn. "I'm sure there's OSHA laws or something we'll be violating."

What does this guy have against me?

All eyes turn to Shawn, as if he's a great king, not the committee chair. He ponders the matter for a second. "Chad has a point. Miriam doesn't have a food handler's license or a commercial kitchen."

"Oh," I deflate. I know nothing of laws around food service.

Lucinda clears her throat. "If Miriam bakes in my café's kitchen, then everything will be up to standard."

"Then that settles it," Shawn says with a smile. "That makes three businesses altogether."

"If we hold this at the high school gym, my wife and I could provide the decorations as our contribution and get students to do the performances and tricks," Chad offers. "We could save calling in the favors for monetary donations."

I gape at him.

"That's not the same as professional performers," Lucinda jabs.

"She's right. We want this to be an event people want to attend. No one with deep pockets wants to attend a fundraiser where hormonal teens play basketball," Shawn says, checking his watch. "That's all the time I have for today. I'll email everyone the next meeting time." He rises without further ceremony, kissing Micah on the cheek on the way out.

"I need to get back to work too," Chad announces for no reason. Lucinda, Micah, and I also rise to leave, since the meeting is apparently over.

After Chad leaves, Micah laughs. "I think he thought we were going to make him stay and help clean up for once."

"I would never do that," I reply, grinning as I lid the container of snickerdoodles. "He has a job, you know, not all the time in the world like us slobs."

All three of us chuckle.

On our way out, I stop Lucinda just outside the library. "Hey, do you think you can give Jada a lift home tonight after closing?"

Jada and Roxy work part-time at Lucinda's Café as baristas.

"Sure." Her eyebrows furrow and her eyes fill with concern. "You alright?"

I'd missed a lunch date with Lucinda, when I was recovering. Jada even called off work because I was "sick."

"I have a date, I think." I didn't know what else to call it.

Lucinda read her head. "A date? With whom? When did you start dating? Oh, nena, we have to talk. You can't spring this on me and not give me details."

My cheeks grow hot. A real blush? What was wrong with me, calling our dinner out a date? "Gabriel Crowfoot. He asked me out to dinner. I don't know if I'd call it a date or a friendly meal."

Lucinda's mouth pressed in a flat line. "I know you only know him as a dad, but— Do you have time for a quick coffee?"

We go across the street to a small coffee house similar to Lucinda's, order, and seat ourselves among the cozy chairs and small coffee tables.

Lucinda wastes no time voicing the reason for her concern. "Gabriel dates a lot of women. Sometimes guys. Never more than one time. So if anything happens, good for you, but don't put your heart into it."

I chuckle at the thought of Gabriel using me for a one-night stand, or anyone for that matter. He did kiss me back, but he stopped things. "You think he wants to bone and dump me?"

She laughs. "Yes. I don't know what he's thinking dating his daughter's best friend's mom, but you are hot and definitely single.

"There's a reason why Gabriel hasn't dated anyone seriously over the last seven years."

"Why?"

"Even though she's remarried *twice*, Kirsten will drop everything and do anything to make sure any new relationship doesn't work."

"Oh." I sober. "Poor Gabriel."

She clears her throat. "It wouldn't be a problem if he didn't let it. They have this...bond, a codependency or something. Whatever." She waves her hand. "He's a nice guy. The best. But not someone to think of settling with. Besides, Kirsten turns into a whole different person than the one we know, if she thinks someone is moving in on her baby daddy."

All I needed was a shifter getting territorial about their ex to add to my list of problems. Given I'm not quite sure if Jada and Roxy are simply best friends or dating also complicates things. "I'm not actually dating Gabriel. He's extending friendship. It's a friend date. Thanks for the heads up."

She eyes me. "Make sure he understands you simply want to be friends. Something might have changed with him that I don't know about. He might be ready to move on."

I nod. Something had changed. The person he "always noticed" saved his life. Still, I want no drama between the three of us. Roxy and Jada are best friends. Even if I don't always approve of Roxy's behavior, Jada needs a friend.

A barista calls us to pick up our mutual orders. We grab the coffees and return to our chairs.

Lucinda lifts her mocha but doesn't drink. Instead she sighs. "You two would have made a nice couple if his relationship with his ex-wife wasn't so messy."

Other than the tea she spills about Gabriel's ex, we have a lovely chat, catching up on what we've been up to. I, of course, have to omit a *lot*, but enjoy listening to her talk about her kids and husband.

After parting ways with Lucinda in the parking lot, I receive a text from Gabriel. He wants to pick me up at six. I text him that I'll meet him at the restaurant. Date-dates get picked up. He doesn't reply. I pocket my cell and keep going.

My cell phone rings as I settle into my car. I wave to Lucinda, who drives past, before pulling out my cell to check the caller ID. It's Gabriel. I shut the door before taking the call.

"Miriam?"

"Yes?"

"Everything okay?"

Well, my husband led a double life and brought my daughter into the supernatural world without my consent, my ex has found me and his minions tried to bite you to death in my cul-de-sac...also, my father might be a more powerful and an eviler monster than the aforementioned ex and he really, really doesn't want me knowing who he is, but other than that everything is perfect.

I take a deep breath.

"Yes. I'm fine. Just coming out of a trying PTSA meeting."

His exhale is loud enough the mic on his phone picks it up. "Oh. Okay. Sorry to bother you. It's—I thought you didn't want me to pick you up because you were worried about how it would look to the kids."

"I told Jada that we would be having dinner. Was I not supposed to?"

He's silent for a moment. "No. It's fine. What does she know about...your past relationship?"

"Nothing."

He blows out his breath again. "I don't ever like giving anyone advice about parenting; however, she'll learn about your past from other sources if you don't tell her."

"Did you tell anyone?" I adjust my mirror and set the cellphone in a holder on the dashboard like everything is normal and my heart isn't hammering in my chest.

"Only those who needed to know. No one who would speak about it to anyone else. However, I have enemies who will use whatever they can against me and people I care about. After you show in public as my date, they'll watch you."

How very cryptic, Mr. Crowfoot. Of course, an archangel had enemies. The Angelic Anocracy wasn't exactly the do-gooder org religion would have you believe. Just ask the fae.

"Alright. Thanks for the warning. I'll see you at the restaurant at 6:30 p.m. sharp."

"I'm looking forward to it." From the smile I hear in his tone, I believe he really means it. At least that'll be one of us.

15

Bangkok is a standalone building, modeled to look like something cut out of a travel magazine and pasted into a supermarket parking lot. I hover outside the restaurant. I've been loitering outside for an incalculable amount of time. Immobile. My eyes sting and a hollow ache expands in my chest. I knew where I was going when I drove here. Bangkok was Raf's favorite restaurant. I had not expected to become rooted to the asphalt, staring at the bench.

"Miriam?"

Gabriel holds the restaurant door ajar, coming out.

I'm not the only person in the busy lot but he must have noticed me, my inertia, from inside. He waves. People move out of his way as his powerful legs eat the distance between us.

"Miriam?" My name takes another tone as his face softens. He softens.

"I can't—" I hiccup "—eat there." Tears slide down my cheek. They're not the first. Stupid eyes.

He slings one of his long, muscle-y arms around my shoulders. The gesture is gentle and comforting as it's meant to be. Softly but firmly, he declares, "Then we won't."

He leads me to his black SUV and opens the passenger door for me. I get in, allowing him to close the door. Gabriel slides into the driver's seat, buckles, and pulls out. No fuss. No questions why I can't eat there.

Neither of us speak. I don't even ask him where we're going. I don't care. As long as I'm not spending my first evening out on a maybe date at somewhere that reminds me of my husband.

We stop at a traffic light. Gabriel glances my way. I've had my cry and I'm now drying my eyes.

"I forgot who originally raved about that place," he says, apology in his tone as well as his eyes. "Sorry."

"I feel silly." I sniffle. "It's been three years."

"Grief strikes at odd times." Gabriel takes my hand in his and keeps holding it after the light changes.

I don't mind.

He gets on I-405, heading south. Traffic isn't bad at this time of day, for once.

"He's not dead," I say, eyes on the majestic Mt. Rainier ahead. The mountain is awe-inspiring in the true sense of the word. Also, cold and distant, despite seeming near.

"I know," Gabriel takes his eyes off the road long enough to glance at me. "Grieving a relationship ending is hard too."

I've played the widow role so long, I forget that Raf left me—by choice or not, it feels like abandonment.

We get off on an exit for Kirkland, a small town that's grown up to suburb status replete with trendy stores, gyms, and pretty parks. He pulls into an area that has a marina, a grassy park with a pavilion, and a man-made sand and gravel beach shoring Lake Washington. It's a rare clear day in early fall, and the sun hasn't set ridiculously early like it does in winter, so everyone is out enjoying the weather. Families with strollers and tots trailing behind, couples holding hands, teens on skateboards and bikes all mill about. Gabriel turns down a narrow street lined with shops, restaurants, and more pedestrian traffic, parking in a pay-per-hour lot.

I cannot say I'm not nervous. I grew up on a commune in rural

Pennsylvania and lived in a quieter suburb than Kirkland for a good reason—fewer people and fewer eyes and mouths to report back to His Creepiness.

As if reading my thoughts, Gabriel squeezes my hand. "We want him to know, but if you're uncomfortable..." His voice trails off, as if allowing me to decide how to finish the sentence.

I want to go home, do this date again another night when I don't feel so raw, but I have a sneaking suspicion that if I don't get out of the vehicle now, any other attempt would turn out the same. I shake my head. "No. I just—"

I flip down the sun visor and open the mirror, frowning at the mess. Without me needing to ask, Gabriel releases my hand. I use a wipe from my purse to fix my ruined attempt at makeup, as in remove it.

"I'm ready now."

We exit the vehicle and meet around the front. Gabriel places a hand on the small of my back, guiding me through the pedestrian traffic as he fiddles with his phone to pay for parking. I don't mind the weight of his hand or the warmth. I don't mind Gabriel touching me casually.

It makes no sense, given that I was lamenting my lost life with Raf, or perhaps it makes perfect sense to want touch, connection when feeling sad and vulnerable.

"Mexican?" He points to a place called La Cantina with sidewalk seating and a roll up storefront akin to a garage door. People dine at fire lit tables outside as well as inside, soaking up the nice evening.

I shrug. "I'm not picky."

A hostess behind a stand greets us. She's in her twenties, I think. Her gaze passes quickly over me and slowly over Gabriel. A smile appears. "Bienvenidos."

"Gracias. Una mesa para dos, por favor." Gabriel's Spanish has a different accent than hers or Raf's Dominican, but his pronunciation is as flawless as theirs. Given he'd said he was raised in Heaven then came here, I'm surprised. I assumed he got this territory because he was indigenous to the Pacific Northwest on his mother's side.

"Bueno," the hostess replies, her smile turned up a few notches, her lashes fluttering in Gabriel's direction as she gathers menus. She asks him a question in Spanish.

Gabriel replies.

She raises her eyebrows and makes another comment.

They converse in Spanish as we follow the shapely waitress. Even though I don't understand, I don't mind. Raf and Jada liked to speak in Spanish sometimes. It made them both happy. I never learned, but I guess by Gabriel's gestures, he's telling her where he'd like us to sit and other mundane small talk.

With his attention diverted, I take a moment to actually take in my "date" for the first time since the parking lot fiasco. He's in a pale blue dress shirt that flatters his wide shoulders and trim waist. The shirts rolled up at the sleeves to reveal brown, muscular forearms. I fall behind a little to take in the rest. Fitted gray slacks with a black belt that matches expensive shoes. His clothes are decidedly tailored. A man his size would have a hard time getting such a nice cut to fit so well. Gabriel's dark curls have been recently cut and are artfully styled, not the mussed tangle when he sat at my bedside.

Heat fills my middle and blooms in my cheeks when I think of how soft those curls felt, how hard the planes of his body under my fingertips...How long had he tolerated me running my hands all over him?

The waitress lays the menus down on a table for two that has a great view of the outside foot traffic, but inside enough that we can avoid the wind that's picked up outside. She steps aside.

Gabriel draws a chair for me.

The hostess whispers, "lucky lady," as she slips past.

"I didn't know you were bilingual," I say over my shoulder, taking the offered chair.

"I'm a polyglot, actually," he replies and then leans down. His hands grip my chair and his warm breath tickles my ear as he whispers, "A gift from my father."

The growing heat inside me battles with the frisson of fear from his admission. His father is The Herald, Gabriel, *the* archangel that heads the Angelic Anocracy.

To make matters worse, the person rounding the table and sitting across from me is His Creepiness's nephew—technically. All the original angels, either the heads of the Angelic Anocracy or the fallen generals under His Creepiness, supposedly spawned from the same Creator, so they all considered each other siblings.

How? *How* did I not put that together?

I know the answer. Ever since he showed up in my driveway naked, I haven't been thinking with my head when it came to Gabriel.

"You alright?"

"I'm on a date with my ex-lover's nephew. No. I'm not alright," I admit.

A server appears. An average-sized man with dark hair threaded with silver, bearing a tray with a pitcher of ice water, two glasses, tortilla chips and salsa. His gaze fixes on me, but he says, "Hola amigos! Me llamo, Juan. I'll be your server this evening. Can I get you an appetizer or—"

"We're going to need a minute, Juan," Gabriel interrupts, tone impatient.

Funny. All of the sudden he's forgotten he speaks Spanish.

"Bueno, señor." The server pours the waters.

I give Juan a sympathetic smile. "Thanks."

"De nada, señorita." He winks and rushes off.

Gabriel leans forward. "I've never met, let alone spoken to the person you're referring to." His green eyes do a sweep of the room before landing on me again, intense. "I'm not comfortable with you calling him my uncle."

"Sorry."

"Don't be." The hard angles of his face soften as does his tone. "I don't know if we bear any resemblance, but I—hope you will not associate me with him for multiple reasons. Most of all, the harm he's done to you."

"You don't, not in the slightest."

He says nothing, so we both look at our menus.

I don't want to admit this to him, but this is my first date, as in ever.

"I'm aware angels are perfect in their form and beauty, even fallen ones," he says with a sigh, gaze decidedly fixed on the menu he's gripping. "I bet he is incomparably attractive."

I don't comment. There are no other beings I'd ever come across as gorgeous as angels/demons—not witches, not gods, not demigods, not halflings with fae blood enhancing their looks, not even nephilim, but I see I've injured his pride. Gabriel is likely accustomed to the response of the hostess to his looks. I might have also reminded him of a time when he wasn't the most attractive person around.

I focus on my menu. "I think I'll have the enchiladas verde." I glance up to find Gabriel scrutinizing me. It's disarming. My throat grows tight. I grab my water and take a drink. "What about you?"

"Carne asada, tamales, and some queso," he replies. "You didn't answer my question."

"What was that?"

He shakes his head. "Doesn't matter."

Juan returns and takes our order.

Gabriel and I sit in silence. I don't think it's companionable. I think I've hurt him somehow.

"Did I say something to offend you?"

"No." He shakes his head. "I haven't been on a date in seven years. I don't have the time. Actually, I've never dated. It was sort of assumed by the pack that Kirsten and I were suited for each other. I wanted to fit in...I did what I thought the alpha at the time wanted. So did she."

I'd gone into the woods to summon a demon as a coming of age ritual, and got their king in my circle.

"I've never dated either," I admit.

His eyebrow shoot up. "Really? I heard witches don't have monogamous relationships."

I waffle my hand. "There are some. It's more of a partnering that's preferred, no ceremony. If one wants to leave, they can."

"Yet, you married Raf."

Juan returns with our food, setting down the sizzling plates with a warning they are hot. Once he leaves, I answer, "Rafael saved my life and gave me Jada. I loved him for it, but I married him to fit in mundane suburbia."

"Were you two monogamous?"

I nearly choke on the bite of chicken from the enchilada. "What?"

He hands me my water. "Let me explain why I'm prying. Do you have lovers who can be harmed or used to manipulate you?"

I get my choking under control, lean forward, and say in a conspiratorial tone, "Since we're being blunt here, I don't think Commander Buzz Feelgood is capable of manipulating me. I barely remember to change his battery."

Gabriel releases a belly laugh so infectious I almost laugh despite being miffed. He holds up his hands. "Point made. None of my business."

The rest of the meal goes well, as in, we talk about our food, the kids, and Gabriel stops trying to compare himself to my ex and doesn't ask me about my sex life again. When Juan comes with the check, we both whip out our credit cards.

Gabriel fires off in something in rapid Spanish with a smile. Juan's gaze shifts to me and then shakes his head as he walks away with both cards.

"What did you say to him?"

"I said to itemize the bill. My meal was more than yours a fifty-fifty split wouldn't be fair."

"An even split would have been better. You paid for parking."

"I wanted to pick you up and take you somewhere nice and to pay for everything like an old-fashioned first date." Gabriel grins, pillowing his head with his hands. "Call it growth."

"This is a date, date?"

"Our first of many, I hope." He smiles.

We're both smiling, actually.

"Alpha?" A feminine voice calls. A leggy brunette with the sleek silhouette decked out in leather makes her way from the street, hopping over the rail with the liquid grace that only someone who turns furry and stalks prey possesses. She's drop-dead gorgeous in a bad-ass biker chick sort of way.

Her gaze swings to me.

I can't help but smile. What can I say? I really dig bad-ass biker chicks with an attitude.

I don't realize the newcomer is a threat until Gabriel swears under his breath and is on his feet, physically putting himself between me and her.

16

I stand, too. A shielding spell forms in my mind as I take a place at Gabriel's side.

The biker chick's gaze sweeps over me the same way Roxy's had a few weeks ago. She wears the same sneer. Eyes on Gabriel, she juts a chin in my direction. "What are you doing with a mundane?"

"Last I checked, I don't answer to you," Gabriel says in a tone I've never heard him use before. I don't know if I like it.

I've met other beings who postured until someone is not considered a threat. Also, I'm growing aware of the number of patrons no longer eating and the wait staff skirting us. Gabriel is massive and this shifter equals him in height. Tension crackles between them. Their expressions are hard, like they're ready to throw down any second.

"Hello. I'm Miriam. And you're?" I smile to diffuse the situation, ignoring her wrinkled-nose slight of my extended hand.

She cocks her head, her lips curling into a disgusted sneer. "Gabriel might not kick latent groupies out of his bed, but I'm not touching you."

She's really trying to get a rise out of me. I turn up the volume of my smile and pour honey into my voice. "From mundane to latent? At least I'm moving up in your world, princess." I mock curtsy.

She narrows her eyes. "How do you know my name?"

I bite back a laugh. Okay. I snort a little. I can't help it. This bad ass shifter is named Princess, and I'm not big enough not to laugh about it.

"No. I'd planned on introducing you when she meets the pack." Gabriel is grinning, but there's still tension in his body. "This is Miriam."

Something registered in her features. "Raf's latent who isn't a latent, after all." She sniffs the air a lot like a poodle and then eyes me. "You don't smell like you handled that many vamps."

A spell that would make her burst into flames comes to mind. *Oops. I don't know what happened, Gabriel. Perhaps she just spontaneously combusted?*

My smile is so wide my cheeks hurt. "Thanks, I showered."

She grows closer, threat in her glare. "No one snags two council members. I think you're a temptation, testing Gabriel's loyalty to pack and his position."

"That would make me a temptress. A Temptation is a retired Motown singer."

She snarls, snapping her teeth in my face.

I raise my hands. I'm going to blast the shifter to next week. "I don't want to fight, and trust me, neither do you."

"It's time for you to leave, Princess," Gabriel says. The tingle of magic pushed into his words brushes my skin and tickles my ear.

Princess's eyes widen with shock. Suddenly she makes herself smaller, hunching her shoulders and lowering her head like a chastised child.

"Yes, alpha." She scurries away.

Gabriel pulls out a money clip filled with a stack of hundreds, handing it to Juan. "What this doesn't cover for everyone's bill, charge from my card."

As soon as we leave the restaurant Gabriel takes my hand, leading me toward the park I'd seen from the car. It's dark now and the number of passersby has thinned out. "We need to talk."

"Oh, that statement is never good. Does that mean no second date?" I ask with a grin.

"Ha, ha, very funny," Gabriel replies, but he's smiling.

He leads me to a bench in the park overlooking the water. We sit.

The night sky is clear and the lights from the boats and buildings reflect on the water. It's dark but early evening, so there are still a few families clearing out from the hill that slopes down to the beach.

He licks his lips. "She tracked me there."

"She seems very concerned with your sex life, too. Is she a jealous ex-lover?"

"Princess and me?" His chuckle melts some of the tension. He shakes his head. "No. It's more complicated than that."

A small child toddles up to us, her large eyes widening as they take in Gabriel's size. Her mother rushes over, scoops her up, and takes her back to where I assume the father is pushing an empty stroller.

"There's another reason I don't date. Whomever I choose as a mate will be part of the pack. There's a lot of bitterness and anger about Kirsten's infidelity. By pack law, I had to abjure her. By Angelic Code, I should have executed her."

His questions earlier make more sense. He was testing out my potential. But— "Infidelity is a reason to murder someone?"

"No." Gabriel leans toward me, lowering his voice so that only I can hear him confide, "I would have forgiven her for cheating if it was a one-time thing, maybe even an ongoing affair, if she apologized and we sought counseling, but Kirsten consorted with an incubus."

"Oh...I'm so sorry."

I truly am. Incubi and succubae aren't demons that haunt your dreams to fulfill sex fantasies. They are His Creepiness's honeypot spy network. Kirsten not only cheated on Gabriel, she betrayed him. Princess's protectiveness makes sense. I am someone new to her and that would be troublesome to me too.

"My ex-wife has her faults, but she swears she never told the incubus anything, and I believe her."

My mouth opens to disagree and closes. Incubi and succubae can draw whatever they wish from the minds of their victims, even influence them to the point of doing things they wouldn't normally do. That's why I don't disagree.

Even if she betrayed him, Kirsten shouldn't die for something she could not help. I also don't want to be the hand that forces Gabriel to commit such a heinous act as killing the mother of his child. I shudder.

He runs his hands up and down his thighs as if in physical pain. "There are some in the pack who think I have a weakness or a blind spot when it comes to those I love. Princess is one of them."

I lay a comforting hand on his shoulder. "I think it's admirable that you showed Kirsten mercy."

Gabriel's gaze lands somewhere on the water. "Seven years we've been divorced, nothing has happened, yet the pack still wants me to take revenge. they resent that I have forbidden anyone to lay a hand on her. Some of them think it's an abuse of my power as archangel but dare not say anything directly to me. I have to hear it all through Roxy."

My heart hurts for the poor kid. No wonder she is rebelling.

"To question an archangel is to question the Angelic Anocracy," I say.

He nods. "Roxy has had to face a lot of scrutiny and challenges because no one can challenge me or her mother. If I forbade it, the pack would find another way to ostracize her. She's grown strong enough I don't have to worry, but the kiddo had to go through hell to get to the point challenging her isn't worth the ass kicking."

"The poor kid."

He grins. "She's angel and shifter. The pack learned quickly that's a powerful combination."

His gaze lands on my hand, still resting on his shoulder. He covers mine with his larger hand. "Anyone I'm interested in, who isn't pack, will have to face the residual anger from the pack over Kirsten's betrayal. It's unfair to ask that of anyone, no matter how I feel about them."

His hand slips away and mine finds its way back to me. We sit staring at the water, each in our own thoughts. I have so many questions, but I don't know how I feel about all of this.

"The council meets tomorrow." He pushes to his feet, turning to offer me his hand.

I accept and rise. We're not exactly face to face because he's so much taller, but we're standing close, still holding hands. I feel a tug to move closer, but it's not him. The draw is internal.

Either I'm more attracted to Gabriel than I care to admit, or there's residual effects of his angel dust. That and the warning he shared, I should withdraw my hand and step away. Instead, I tilt my head to meet his gaze.

His chest heaves with his rapid breaths. I'm close enough and can see well enough in the dark that I notice his pupils dilating. His gaze drops to his mouth as I wet my lips.

"I think we should drive separately." His voice is husky and low, turning up the heat between us.

Until, I realize *what* he said. He's trying to keep this friendly, not a date date. We agreed three years ago, hooking up was a bad idea. I reach for my purse. "Should I get a ride service?"

He stays my hand. "No."

Now he's holding both our hands so close his breath fans my face as he chuckles. "I meant when we go to the council."

"So, I still have a ride back to my car?"

Gabriel's cheeks dimple when he smiles. "Oh, yes."

He leans down and almost kisses me. I wrestle my hands from his, place them firmly on his chest and dodge his mouth.

His eyebrows furrow after he recovers. "I thought there was something stirring between us. Did I assume wrong?"

"Not wrong, exactly. I'm all right with you having casual sex, you live how you want to live, but I'm not all right with me being a secret mistress to the archangel. It feels icky." *Icky?* Way to handle this like a teenager.

He points in the general direction of the restaurant. "Do you think Princess would challenge you if I wanted to just hook up?"

It does seem odd. "There are rumors that you're like that."

He looks at his feet as if ashamed. "I was for a bit. I was getting Kirsten out of my system and immaturely trying to prove something to myself."

"Why did you stop...before?"

"You were in pain. I could have been anyone. I wanted you to want *me*." He scratches his head. "I should take you back to your car."

"Yes. You should," I agree, though I believe he is thinking out loud.

He winces. We walk to the car further apart than we'd been all evening. I didn't realize how much we'd touched since the date began until the absence of it.

He says nothing during the ride, turning on the radio.

As I get out of the car, he says, "I'll text you the location of the council meeting the day of."

I nod and close the door. I didn't thank him for dinner because I paid my half. I didn't tell him I had a wonderful time because I didn't—well okay, maybe a little before Princess barged in. The awful first date served its purpose. If His Creepiness had spies, it would have looked like I had aligned myself with the archangel. I had friends. I could stay in my home.

Gabriel drives off before I start my car, likely figuring me safe once inside my vehicle. He is wrong.

17

I realize I'm not alone when I smell sulfur. I look in my rearview and swallow my scream. Drawing attention to the four-eyed demon staring back at me from my backseat will not help my case. The red glow of their eyes is the only thing I see. The rest is shrouded in darkness, but I know they have four arms, four legs, and four rows of teeth. How a demon fits in my backseat is a testament to the vehicle's roominess.

"Happy to see me?" Their voice sounds like four people speaking in unison. I recognize all four.

"Shit, Velja. You scared me." My voice comes out shaky and my hands tremble on the steering wheel.

"The archangel is not exiting the lot. He's likely waiting for you," Velja says, looking over their shoulder. "Start the car and leave through the east entrance."

I do as they say. Having a demon friend would take a lot of explaining. *If* Gabriel would allow me to explain and not just murder her. I can't let him do that. Velja is the reason I managed to escape His Creepiness.

Velja clucks their teeth. "What d'you think you're doing? I save you from one asshole, who'd use you for your power, and you line yourself up with another?"

"What else was I supposed to do? Your king knows I'm not dead," I reply. The road is clear, so I exit the parking lot. "Can you see if he's following us?"

"No one is following us. What do you mean he knows you're not dead?" There's real fear in their voice.

"Why are you here?"

They bear their fangs. "Because there are rumors flying my king is suddenly interested in this place."

I rear my head. "Rumors? Aren't you part of his inner circle?"

They laugh without humor—all four voices echoing. "He didn't say so, but I think he blamed me for your suicide. He posted me far from Gehenna. I'm supposedly spying on some rural governor, but everyone knows it's because I reminded him of you."

During my years spent in Hell as His Creepiness's consort, Velja was my guard and companion. It bothered Velja to watch me grow more and more addicted to their king, lose myself in it, and slowly become nothing but his puppet. In a moment of lucidity, I'd asked them to kill me because I had no will to do it myself. Instead, they helped me fake my death and then escape Hell without anyone's notice.

"I'm sorry helping me cost you so much."

Velja grunts and shifts in their seat. Apologies make demons uncomfortable—I'd forgotten so much of their ways. They lean forward, carrying the stink of their world with them. "Why do you believe my king is looking for you?"

I break down the events of the past few weeks, saving the bit where I accepted Gabriel's angel dust to ease pain.

"Where are the grimoires? I thought you destroyed them."

I grimace inwardly. Velja may have helped me in the past, but they might not like being in some hick region of Hell. Rural places are the same throughout the galaxy, beautiful, but boring if you're used to the pace of city life, especially if you're part of the social elite of a city. I can no longer trust Velja. They might want to pretend that I tricked them too, but *aha!* they found me and all of a sudden find themself in the inner circle again.

"I hid them throughout the multiverse twenty-years ago." I grip the steering wheel as my nerves set ablaze throughout my body. The lie hurts so much I almost lose consciousness.

Velja blows out a breath of relief that whistles through the rows of their dagger-sharp teeth. "You'd said you'd destroyed them."

I had said that I did, hadn't I? Pain isn't the only reason not to lie. Keeping track of untruths is harder than telling the truth and remembering. But, although the demon helped me, I never have completely trusted Velja.

"I tried," I admit, and it's the truth. "The grimoires are indestructible. Nothing short of a god could destroy them."

In my early days with Raf, he'd tried to destroy the grimoires. Not only could he not do it, he sustained pretty serious injuries from the protective spells placed on them. Blood magic was powerful, sacrificial magic even more so. Witches gave their own lives to preserve what they'd written in their grimoires.

"Does anyone else know where they are hidden?"

"A god named Rafael—or at least that was his name before he ascended."

Velja makes a disgusted sound. "You stayed with that demigod? I thought you'd use him to heal you and move on."

I not only stayed; I had a daughter with that demigod. I don't share this.

"Tell me, Tati, where do you find these powerful supernaturals and get them to be your protectors?"

I cringe at the use of the old nickname. "A forest in Pennsylvania, a swamp in Florida, and the Eastside suburbs of Seattle."

They laugh. "Always so literal. Would you be able to track down where you placed the grimoires?"

"I don't remember where they are." Suffering through the agony of telling another lie, I stiffly flip the turn signal and get on the highway. There's no way in, pardon my expression, *Hell* I'm going straight home with a demon in my car.

"It sounds to me that he doesn't know you're alive but knows the grimoires are still around, which until he possesses them, he can't go after me for that *lie*." There's much relief in their voice.

"Why do you think he doesn't know I'm alive?"

"Unlike his other witches, his little toys, he did love you. His grief was great. Your funeral was an event like none I'd ever seen." The demon's voices grow quiet. "My king would not leave it up to hell-hounds and vampires to retrieve you. If he thought for a second you were still alive, he'd breach treaty with the Angelic Anocracy and come for you himself, or at the very least, he'd send a full-blood like me."

A knot in my chest loosens. Velja is here to cover their tracks for their part in my disappearance, not out to get me or the grimoires.

"So, he doesn't know?"

I see the rows of teeth flash in my rearview. "No one makes my master go through the sort of suffering and get away with it. He cannot know you still live. He might believe the grimoires still exist and that a witch has them, but you need to leave this place before he discovers you're that witch, and we both face the consequences. I must go before I'm missed."

Shadows swirl in my rearview. Velja is gone.

The relief I felt is short lived. If His Creepiness had spies on Gabriel, they'd report back soon that the archangel was seen with a redhead in the same area my ex sent the hellhound and vamps, who all haven't returned.

Shit. No witch would know how to banish a hellhound or kill a vamp but me. I have lit a giant neon sign that read, "Tati is alive."

After Velja disappears, I pull off the highway and follow directions on my GPS to a carwash. It's not that demons naturally have a foul odor. Hell stinks, literally. You get used to it when you're there, but I haven't been in Hell for over two decades and the smell, and all I associate with it, nauseates me.

There are no quarters in my purse or in any of the compartments of the car. Thankfully the machine takes credit cards.

With the nozzle set to high, I open the door to the backseat, hosing the interior with the pressurized soapy water.

An attendant for the automatic wash in coveralls passes by. What I'm doing must not sit right, because he comes back to the stall. "That hose is meant for the outside, ma'am."

Oh, my white knight. Good thing he rode in to save me or I wouldn't know how to function.

I force a laugh as if he's telling the funniest joke ever, not minding business that isn't his. "No one said being a parent would be so gross." It isn't exactly a lie, so I feel no pain. *Don't come closer to inspect. Don't come closer to inspect. Don't—*

He chuckles and shakes his head. "They sure don't."

I let out a sigh of relief when he moves on.

Questions come up as I work. Mainly, how did Velja know where to find me? Did they have some sort of tracking spell? If so, that meant they had to have some of my hair or blood. His Creepiness likely had plenty of that lying around. If such a spell existed, he would have a way to find me. Maybe Velja was lying. Maybe they want me to run so that I don't have Gabriel's protection.

I'm glad I stopped to do this task and the time it gives me to think. If I'd gone straight home, I might have ran, compelled Jada to come by telling her everything. I might have summoned Velja to help me run to another world. All rash decisions.

I use the vacuum hose next to suck up the excess water. The smell of sulfur is not nearly as strong, but not gone entirely, especially where Velja sat. I buy the option of perfumed sprays.

I get a blanket from the trunk I keep there for emergency purposes and lay it out on the driver's seat.

As I drive out of the carwash stall, I decide I'm going to stay. It can't be coincidence Velja appeared the same night I went out in public with Gabriel.

18

Jada follows me into the kitchen, rubbing the sleep out of her eyes. It's early on a Saturday morning, before dawn, and she worked the night before at Lucinda's Café, but the time of day and that we have fasted for six hours is important for the spell I plan to cast. I direct her to which items she'll need as I gather my own.

I'm tired myself. I haven't slept a wink all night, scouring the grimoires for the spell.

"What exactly is this?"

I put everything we've collected on a tray, setting them in their proper place. "We're going to make you untraceable."

She rears her head. "What?"

"You possess fifty percent of my DNA. Anyone who can track me, can track you." This had occurred to me on my way home from the carwash, hence why I spent all night looking for counter spells to a *possible* tracking spell.

"Why would anyone want to track me?"

I jab my pointer finger in the general direction of the grimoire library.

"Oh." My daughter, fortunately, has the good sense to not comment further.

I pull a pair of scissors out of a drawer and cut a piece of my hair and then Jada's, binding them with twine.

Jada follows me out to our back garden, where I set up the materials. I make a circle of salt. Within the circle, I place a ramekin with herbs and one with oil. I place candles around the circle, marking the four cardinal directions and the half-winds.

"Stand here," I instruct Jada, pointing to a spot within the circle. "Take off your slippers first, you need to be grounded."

I light each of the candles and then pull the grimoire from a cache.

Jada gasps. "That's so cool! I mean, I know how to do it, but it's fun to watch. It looked like you're pulling the book from thin air."

As I open the grimoire, I smile, happy my daughter knows this part of me—of us. "Okay, repeat after me and as you repeat, feed your light into each word with the intention of protecting yourself from a tracking spell. Intention matters more than the words, so don't be afraid of saying it wrong." I had no time to translate the spell and memorize it.

Jada nods.

"Etso luci—" I enunciate each word of the spell and she repeats after me with perfect pronunciation, if not accent.

The candle marking the north snuffs out.

We chant the words together again, snuffing out the candle marking the south. We repeat the process until all the candles are out.

"That's it?" She asks, eyebrows furrowed and scratching the back of her head.

"That's it." I bend down and start collecting the items we laid out. "It's a protection, a counter spell that activates when someone tries to track me."

"What will happen on their end?"

"According to the grimoire, the spell will protect the blood of my blood, but it doesn't say what happens on their end other than they will be blind to your existence."

"Can I go back to bed now? I have to work this evening."

"Sure." I follow her inside. "Do you think you can get a ride home from Lucinda? I have a thing tonight."

Jada turns on her heel and crosses her arms across her chest. "You're not going out with Mr. Crowfoot again, are you?"

"He'll be present, but it's not a date. Why?"

She chews her lip as if weighing telling me bad news. "Roxy texted last night." She folded her hands. "She was so mad. She thinks you hurt her dad somehow and like broke his heart or something. She told me to tell you to stay away from him."

Breaching the distance between my daughter and myself, I brace my hands on either of her shoulders and wait for her to lift her chin so that she's looking me in the eye. "Let's get something straight. I am not responsible for a grown man's reaction to rejection. Roxy is allowed to feel empathy for how it affected her father, but she is not allowed to tell me, an adult, what I can or cannot do. If she has an issue with me direct her to me. Do you understand?"

"Yes, mami." Jada nods solemnly, her amber eyes glisten as if she's going to cry but holds back. "It's just...she's like my only supe friend, you know?"

"I know."

Which is one of *many* reasons why I couldn't be with Gabriel. I kiss her forehead. "Go get some rest."

19

Gabriel sends me a text directing me to meet him in the parking lot of the same shopping plaza where Lucinda's Café is located. I figure he gave me the familiar landmark since both of our daughters work there, but when I pull into the lot, he's waiting at the front of the café.

He's dressed in faded jeans and a gray, fitted long-sleeved tee, holding a cell phone to his ear, pacing. When his gaze locks on my approach, he stops in his tracks, ending the call and shoving the cell in his back pocket.

"We're the first to arrive," he says by way of greeting, opening the door to the café.

My heart thuds in my chest as he flips the sign from open to close. He gestures for me to enter. Confusion brings on a wave of vertigo. I take a deep breath, entering the empty café. A collection of oversized chairs and tables and the aroma of roasted coffee beans greets me. My brain is trying to register what is happening, but everything feels distant, surreal.

"Sorry it's just us for a bit," Gabriel says behind me, his tone cautious. "Lucinda is dropping the girls at your house. They wanted to stay, but we agreed, council business isn't kid business."

I whirl around. My brain not making a connection it should, I ask, "Lucinda knows about the council?"

Something akin to pity forms on his features. His throat works. "Lucinda is on the council. She represents sirens."

During my time with His Creepiness, I had met Persephone and Hades. I had seen her winged army of women warriors. My mind has a hard time reconciling the image of those women with my triathlete friend. I plop in an overstuffed chair.

"Oh."

Gabriel sinks in a similar chair next to mine. His hand reaches for mine, but he seems to remember himself and braces both of his massive hands on my knee. "If it's any consolation, she thought you didn't know you were a latent. Rafael did a good job of protecting your secret."

"I'm beginning to wonder if I actually know any mundanes," I murmur.

"Supes are quiet about what they are even among our kind, you know that."

I do. It doesn't lessen the sting of perceived betrayal.

"My territory is a haven for those who don't quite fit in. Cryptids running from deforestation and urban sprawl. Sirens who fell in love with naval officers and no longer want to live in the Underworld. Fae halflings. Latents." He blows out his breath. "I know it's Angelic Decree, but I don't agree with the supernatural registry. As long as a supe doesn't behave as a threat, I don't see the need to catalogue people and their powers."

I angle my head to get a better look at Gabriel. His confession and belief is nothing like what I'd been taught of archangels, or angels in general. I'd thought them sticklers for all laws. Fascists. I realize my perception is biased.

"Aren't some powers inherently a threat to the Angelic Anocracy?" Like mine and the knowledge contained in the grimoires.

"That's not my concern. None of the Angelic Code is, really. The safety of the people in my territory is all I care about."

I believe him. "Because your pack takes precedence with you and to the angels, shifters are servants, not kin."

A dark eyebrow quirks. Then he nods. "Yes. If I were full angel or perhaps even half mundane, I'd feel differently, but I'm biased because I don't like that hierarchy applying to my people. I want to be a leader because I'm good at it and I deserve to be in charge, not because someone ordained me archangel. I don't think one person should run a whole territory. One person can't possibly know the needs of a diverse set of people."

"How is alpha decided?"

He doesn't answer right away, simply narrows his gaze. Finally, he relents. "The position can either be inherited or someone challenges the alpha."

"You inherited the position?" That sounded like nepotism.

He shakes his head, a haunted look in his eyes. "The alpha happened to be my mother's Earthly husband. He didn't like she'd had a kid with an angel. Thought it made him look weak." He blows out his breath and clenches his shaking hands. "My stepfather challenged me. I didn't want to fight him, but he would have killed me to prove a jealous point. I had only meant to incapacitate him, but... what I meant didn't matter, what I wanted didn't matter, the alpha magic passed to me all the same." There is not a shred of alpha pride in his retelling. No angelic arrogance. Simply Gabriel, sad and ashamed by the whole affair.

"You didn't want the position of alpha?"

He glances over his shoulder and then shakes his head. "No. It should have gone to one of my step-siblings, Princess."

A lot more makes sense, now. Princess wasn't only protecting her alpha from a spy. She doesn't want her big brother hurt again. I wonder why he hadn't mentioned they were step-siblings before.

"It's a conflict of interest to be archangel and alpha," he says with a shrug. "I *should* have a degree of separation. In this meeting, I will act as archangel and Princess will act as representative of shifters."

The bells attached to the doors jingle as Lucinda walks through. She and I lock gazes.

"You have a lot of explaining to do," she says, squaring her shoulders. "After all these years, how could you have not trusted me but trust *him*?" She gestures in Gabriel's direction.

"Because I didn't know you were a siren," I reply with equal amount of hurt. "All these years you knew about Raf and Jada and didn't say a word."

She stiffens and juts out her jaw. "I was protecting a latent. Raf told me you didn't know what you were."

"Then Raf lied to you."

Lucinda mutters to herself in Spanish, cursing Rafael. I wonder if she's only half siren since she doesn't have a siren form. Her husband likes to tell the story of how they met off the coast of Puerto Rico: a sailor knocked unconscious gone overboard, saved by a local triathlete.

"He lied to us all," Gabriel interjects. "Let's put a pin in this argument until later." I hear a note of command I'd only heard when he sent Princess off running.

Both Lucinda and I exchange the same sort of glance we share in PTSA meetings when Chad butts in, then we turn our glares on Gabriel.

He raises his hands as if surrendering. A grin ticks up one corner of his mouth. "I'm just saying, let Miriam tell her story to the group so she doesn't have to retell it every time someone walks in."

The doorbells chime as a tall, broad-shouldered woman enters. She has dark brown curling ringlets that hang to her waist. She's as thickly built as she is tall, and her beauty shines the way Raf's did, giving away she's a demigoddess without doing a thing. Her dark-eyed gaze lands on me, lighting up. Her round face flashes a dazzling white smile. "You look so much better, Miriam!"

I struggle for words because I'm having trouble placing her. Had I met her in Florida while I was still going through withdrawal from His Creepiness? I hope not. That was a dark time for me, and I may have not been very nice.

"She does. Doesn't she?" Gabriel smiles as he turns to me. "Miriam, this is Leilani, the demigoddess I told you about."

The one who knows my secret. Pulse thrumming in my ears, I force a smile. "Nice to meet you."

I'm not sure if I should thank her. My body healed itself with the aid of Gabriel's angel dust keeping me unconscious.

She squeezes my shoulder as she passes. Her touch has that familiar zing of gods magic and I relax a bit. She smells of plumeria and loam, earthy and verdant.

On Leilani's heels enters a shorter than average man, dressed like he came directly from a construction site, steel-toed boots and all.

"Sorry we're late, traffic was a beast." His voice has a slight Irish lilt.

"Cian, this is Miriam," Leilani says. "Miriam, this is my fiancé Cian. He's a leprechaun, in case you can't tell."

I blink. Leprechauns are a form of fae, and all full-blooded fae have been banished from Earth by the Angelic Anocracy when the Romans brought Christianity to the Celtic world. Druids and fae were both banned, supposed allies of the devil. My mother had said fae of all sorts were nastier than His Creepiness could ever be. The fae aren't evil, per se, they simply don't think like everyone else. For example, eating someone for their power is acceptable behavior.

My mother taught me never to trust any fae—she even tried to kill the light sprites that follow me. Thank goodness she was unsuccessful. They've been my truest companions.

"Pleasure to meet you." Cian smiles, his freckled cheeks dimpling.

I stare at his outstretched hand before remembering my manners and clasp it. I can't help a niggling sense of fear despite his warm handshake. The coven backed my mother's distrust, teaching that the fae drank witch blood and feasted on our livers to gain our witch light. The light sprites did nothing but tend my gardens and serve as an alarm system. Cian might be just as kind.

As Cian takes his seat, Gabriel leans over and whispers, "He might be able to help you with your problem."

"Who are we waiting for?" Leilani asks everyone in general.

"Princess and Aurora," Lucinda replies.

As if on cue, a willowy blonde, taller than both Gabriel and

Leilani, enters the café. She has to duck her head to get in. Her colorful broom skirt sways as she walks. Her tie-dyed t-shirt says "Aurora" in glitter.

I clamp my mouth shut so I don't gape openly at her height. The woman must be close to seven feet tall, if not over.

Following her, Princess seems diminutive. She sneers when she sees me but says nothing.

Everyone takes a seat, or pulls up a chair in a circle, all eyes on me.

Gabriel leans back in his chair, hands on the armrests like a bored king conducting court. "Before we start our official council business, I'd like to introduce everyone formally to Miriam Diaz. She is here to tell her story, and I am here to nominate her to take a position on the council to represent—well, we'll let her tell you what she is."

20

____

I'm not the only one who gapes at Gabriel.

Princess growls. "Who, exactly, is she going to represent? Latents who got lucky?"

Leilani jumps to my defense. "Miriam isn't latent."

"You know the rules. It is not your turn," Lucinda adds. "Let her speak."

"I move that we all enter official capacity," Princess says, eyeing me with even more suspicion than before. "She's falsely registered and that needs to be addressed."

Gabriel clears his throat. "Fine. As long as you remember the No Violence in the Council mandate."

Princess stands. "Sure."

Gabriel approaches her. "For the purposes of this council, you are alpha of the Seattle pack, representing all shifter-packs of the Pacific Northwest who serve the office of archangel. No others."

Magic tingles my skin. Who doesn't serve the archangel that he feels the need to mention them?

Princess's gaze is upon me as she resumes her seat. I don't like the predatory gleam in her eyes, but she doesn't unnerve me. I've faced much scarier supes than this shifter.

Gabriel sits and turns to me. "Every person here represents a group. I represent angels on earth. Princess, the shifters. Leilani took over Raf's place as the representative of the demigod community."

Leilani nods.

"Cian represents the solitary fae unaligned with the Seelie or Unseelie Courts or any of the other lower fae courts, who are all officially banned from Earth. Aurora represents the cryptid community."

The willowy blond wiggles her fingers at me and smiles. "Hi! I'm a Bigfoot, in case you're wondering."

Admittedly, I was. I suppose it's my turn to fess up since Gabriel announced what they all were. I clasp my hands so everyone doesn't see them tremble as I explain, "I am a witch. Coven raised under a different name."

"Why don't you use your real name?" Princess asks, eyes narrowed.

"I was seduced by the king of Hell when I was young. I became an addict of his angel dust, a shell of the witch that I was. I eventually faked my own death to escape him."

The shifter's face loses all anger, but her arms are still crossed.

"Rafael Diaz, who I assume you all knew, saved me. We fell in love. Any lies he told you were to protect me from my past, from my abuser." What Raf did by setting himself up as a trusted member of the supe community sinks in now. By telling Gabriel to watch over me, Raf had set me up to eventually come out on my own. He'd planned this moment.

A tear escapes my eye. I forgive Raf in this moment, but I still prefer he'd told me his plan.

Leilani leans forward. "The hellhound and the vamps must mean that he knows you're alive. Lucifer doesn't like to let his playthings— sorry—his lovers go. Not with the bound power you possess."

"I'm not sure if he knows it's me or another powerful witch." I take a leap of faith and tell them the truth. "I also stole and hid about thirty grimoires from my coven's library. There's a spell contained within the grimoires he'd use against this world. He knows a witch has them but not necessarily that I'm still alive."

"That's the witch's treasure," Gabriel says, comprehension limning his features as if he'd been puzzling it out.

"I'm sorry you were a victim of an abusive supe, but we're talking about the devil here. You're a liability to this territory and all who live in it," Princess says. "I'm sorry, but I vote banishment."

All eyes turn to Gabriel. He's glaring at Princess. "Miriam is not the first witch I've harbored from him and likely not the last. We must remain a territory that accepts witches without a coven. Solitary witches are like solitary fae, unaffiliated. Making Miriam part of the council will draw witches away from Lucifer's hold and back to autonomy. I say we take a stand against him and not cower in fear. That's why I nominate Miriam to take a place here on the council."

An icy frisson swims through me. *I* don't want to take a stand against His Creepiness.

"You can't nominate me. I'm not registered," I protest before someone seconds the nomination.

"You are. Rafael registered you as latent," Gabriel disagrees. With a shrug, he adds, "I see no need to change that."

"Are you asking me to join the side of the Angelic Anocracy and go after Hell?"

"Why would that bother you?" Princess hisses.

"Because I'm afraid of *him,*" I admit, my body trembling. "And if you all aren't, you're either ignorant or fools."

Gabriel lays a hand over my trembling one.

I meet his gaze.

There's so much hope and empathy in Gabriel's face as he says, "I'm not asking you to ally with the Angelic Anocracy or to war against Hell, I'm asking you as the head of this council to help protect and guide the witches of the Pacific Northwest by representing them here and seeking them out. To help others like you."

"Then I won't be hidden anymore. He'll know I faked my death." Doesn't Gabriel understand what kind of danger that would put me in?

"You won't need to hide." He gestures to the room. "Ally with us and have all of these groups behind you."

Gabriel doesn't notice Princess's scowl. He's too busy building his own little faction here on Earth. He is uniting multiple earthbound groups in a way no other archangel can. Normally, supes squabble or avoid each other. Joining them would be safer than being a lone witch anywhere.

"There's no reason why *they* should rule us all," he says, as if reading my thoughts. "Either side, angels or demons. The shifters are sick of being enforcers. The rest of the supes don't want to live in fear of ridiculous laws. This council is something different. Something new." The excited gleam in his eyes reminds me of someone else I once knew.

"You will unlock your power and bring great change. With you by my side, I will oust my treacherous brethren and retake my rightful throne. It will be better for everyone, not only angels and demons."

I shake the voice out of my head. "Your council is working within the framework of the Angelic Anocracy, which is something old, Archangel."

Gabriel stiffens at the use of his title but quickly recovers. "Exactly. Change from within."

"We need you, Miriam," Aurora says. "There's a witch up in the Steven's Pass area. She doesn't bother mundanes, but some cryptids have gone missing. Maybe you could talk to her to see what she knows?"

"Why haven't the shifters investigated?" I direct the question to Gabriel, but he nods to Princess.

Princess props her feet on a coffee table and crosses her arms. Again. "We have. She attacked shifters investigating the disappearances." She lifts her eyebrows. "Without any provocation, I might add."

Somehow, I doubt that.

"I think she may be in a similar state as you were in when you left your coven and Hell behind, hiding and lashing out only because she doesn't know who to trust," Gabriel says, face grim.

"Poor thing." My hand flies to my chest. Homeless and heartless would make for a desperate witch. If Raf hadn't found me, I'd likely have become something other than what I am today. "A witch alone in nature is a good thing as long as she's grounded by others. Witches are a communal lot, in need of each other's company to keep our powers and minds in check. A witch isolated from her peers out in nature would become aggressive, if not feral, especially if she'd been through what I have."

There are Baba Yaga, and other witches in the woods, stories for a reason. Self-protection would look like malicious intent.

"There are witches in need of your help, friend," Lucinda says. "I know you, Miriam—you're not one to let a sister in need down."

If I could draw more witches to me, aid them, teach them, I could better protect the grimoires. A niggling voice says, *Or form that army he wanted, but for his nephew.* I push those thoughts down. Gabriel is trying to set this territory apart, not grow in power.

"I will represent witches as their voice, look after their interests, and I'll even help you talk to the one in the mountains, but I will not take on the role of their leader. If they left covens, they did so to get away from supernatural politics."

Aurora flashes a toothy smile that doesn't quite fit her glamour. "Cryptids are the same. I play grievance listener more than leader."

The council votes. To my surprise, even Princess votes me to be a member. After picking a day and time that we'll all be able to make it out to Steven's Pass, the council meeting adjourns. Princess and Aurora take their leave. Lucinda as well, telling Gabriel to lock up.

To me she says, "We're going to have coffee and a chat. Soon. Welcome to the council."

When Lucinda leaves, Gabriel locks the door behind her. He nods to Leilani.

She glances at her fiancé. "After talking to Cian, I believe your binding is of fae origin."

I laugh. I can't help it. "My mother fears fae. My entire childhood, I was warned against them wanting to drink my witch blood. So, I doubt that she found a halfling and thought 'I'd like to have a baby with them.'"

Cian shifts uncomfortably.

"I don't believe you want to drink my blood. All I'm saying is that my mother is very anti-fae. I grew up terrified of them—Sorry, Cian."

The Leprechaun exchanges a furtive look with the demigoddess. "Does it hurt when you lie?"

It's a yes or no question I can't get around. "Yes."

Cian smiles. "Me too. 'Tis a trait of the fae. Danu made us as such."

"Oh," is my eloquent response.

Leilani clears her throat. "If you're afraid of fae, why do you have pixies living in your garden?"

"They've always followed me since I was a kid."

"The wee ones follow the strong of the Tuatha dé Danann—the old gods. You have a binding on your faelight to disguise what you are, but I can see you're a halfling plainly as I can see my own face in the mirror. Any fae could. Other supes would just find you pretty."

There'd been no other fae around to point that out.

"Next you'll say I'm a fairy princess." I bark a laugh, sounding as manic as I feel.

When I think of fae, I don't think of human-looking men on the short side, like Cian, nor the little light sprites who tend my property. He might as well have said that I was half-thing-that-goes-bump-in-the-night.

My mother had described fae as nightmarish creatures, who only glamoured themselves to look beautiful to humans and witches to lure us to our deaths. Even His Creepiness was leery of them and disliked my light sprites.

Cian shrugs. "Don't really have monarchies the same way humans do, but a king or queen of a faerie realm is a god who created it."

"Well, I have no faerie," I reply. It's almost a compulsion to disagree, to avoid the topic of fae. I don't like that I feel this way. It feels like the influence of something like angel dust but more powerful. It's almost painful for me to ask Cian, "Can you look at the binding?"

"Sure, I can." Cian's eyes go unfocused for a moment then come close, staring at me as if he could peer into my very soul. He swears under his breath and shakes his head. "You don't have a binding spell or a curse. You have a geas."

Gabriel stiffens and Leilani frowns.

I'm the only one in the dark. "What's a gash—gesh?"

The Leprechaun sighs out his nostrils, then patiently explains, "A geas is an agreement between you and another fae. You've agreed to let someone damned powerful, likely a fae god, to put that geas on you. No halfling or low fae possesses that kind of magic."

"I don't ever remember meeting a fae. My mother wouldn't have ever allowed it."

"You don't remember *befriending* the pixies either, yet you have them tending you like servants." Cian's gaze moves to Gabriel. "It's my bet they're her attendants, placed to keep an eye on her where the fae who put the geas on her could not." He turns to me again. "You might very well be a fae princess and that, not your books, is why the devil wants you so."

21

Gabriel asks me to wait for him after Cian and Leilani leave. He makes sure the back is locked up as well as the front, turning out the lights. My husband trusted him enough to tell him to watch after me and Jada. Lucinda trusted him with her livelihood. I feel I should trust him too, but a niggling worry that he wants to break this geas for other reasons won't go away.

I stand in front of the building, waiting for him. It's a starless night, chill and damp with a constant drizzle. Like any local, I don't need an umbrella, used to the mist-like rain kissing my skin. The lot is dead at this time. An occasional car passes by, nothing like the early evening traffic when I got here. My phone reads that it's almost ten o'clock. Early for a Saturday night in a city, late for this neighborhood of families.

Gabriel approaches me. "Do you mind if I come over and say goodnight to my kid? I won't stay long."

The knot of tension twisting in my chest releases. I smile. "Of course not."

The relief in his face is palpable.

Gabriel follows me out of the parking lot, tailing in his SUV.

I smell the faint scent of sulfur as shadows form into a demon in the back seat. Velja smiles in my rearview mirror.

"Good news. My king doesn't know you still live. The vamps and hellhound were looking for a witch he believes stole your grimoires."

"The archangel is directly behind me," I say without looking back. My heart is pounding in my throat.

Velja sneers. "He won't see me."

He'll smell you. "What do you want me to do?"

"Leave this place before the king learns who you are. As it is, the witch who killed his hellhounds and the vamps has piqued his interest. The next step is to send one of us. You cannot kill one of us. You'll be caught and I'll die for it."

The demon is right. I couldn't kill a fallen angel or their demon spawn, not with my light bound...

"I can slip you through the cracks right now and deposit you on a world where no one would suspect who you are."

Ice cold fear crawls through me, draining my face of all color.

"You can't. My car will crash. The archangel will smell demon. He'll follow me into Hell, and we both can't afford that. Let me conjure a reason to disappear. A vacation or something, so he doesn't come looking until the trail is cold."

My plea is met with stony silence. Something shifts in Velja as if they have come to a decision.

"You have two Earth weeks to make this false vacation plan plausible. If you give me excuses the next time I appear, I will kill you. I did not risk my life and my position so that you would get us both caught."

Smoke and shadow swallow Velja before I can reply, not that I had an answer to that threat. I'm trembling so badly, I have to pull my car over onto the shoulder. I rest my head on the steering wheel.

A light rap on the window precedes Gabriel's tentative voice, "Miriam?"

He tries the door. The automatic locks keep him out.

I sit up and press the button for the window to roll down. His nose wrinkles, likely at the onslaught of sulfuric stench Velja brought with them.

"Miriam, what happened?"

I turn toward him slowly, unable to produce a lie, unable to hide the truth with the evidence stinking up my car.

"The demon who helped me escape Hell came with the good news that their master believes a witch has the grimoires he wants but doesn't know it's me."

"That's good."

I laugh without humor. "They also came to warn me. I have two weeks to get my affairs in order before they come to take me to a new hiding place. I'll have no choice but to go with them, or they'll kill me."

He grips the door, his face all protective fury. "I won't let them."

I shake my head slowly. "Velja ruined their career, risked their life to get me out of there. I owe them to run before he finds out I am alive."

Gabriel circles the car and jiggles the passenger door handle. I unlock it and he slides into the passenger seat. His face and tone gentles. "This Velja made a choice to help you, knowing the consequences. That doesn't give the demon the right to dictate the rest of your life. Besides, is it really fair to Jada for you to disappear or to have her uproot her life?"

My throat tightens and tears flow unbidden. Gabriel unbuckles my seatbelt and pulls me from the driver's seat into his arms like it's no more effort than lifting a rag doll. There is something about the tender way he holds me and doesn't try to fix it or make me stop crying that makes me break down more—we're talking snot bubble, body shaking sobs.

Gabriel manages to retrieve some tissues from the glovebox and hands them to me.

I dry my eyes, suddenly feeling infantile for sitting in his lap and crying. That feeling lasts only as long as it takes for me to realize there's nothing fatherly in the way he looks at me, and he's sporting a massive erection with emphasis on the word massive.

"Oh! I didn't mean to—" I scramble back to the driver's seat.

"It's not what you think," Gabriel says, face coloring.

"I didn't think—" I shake my head. Nope. No. I didn't want to consider why my meltdown got Gabriel hot and bothered.

He waves his hands in front of him. "You don't understand. It wasn't like that. I wanted to comfort you."

My eyebrows shoot to my hairline. "With your—" I nod to his pants.

"That didn't come out right either." He pinches his brow. "I don't think my cock is magically going pound your problems away."

I snort laugh at that and push away any images my mind conjures up of what the attempt might look like.

He meets my gaze. "I'm sorry if I've made you feel uncomfortable."

"Just surprised me." I grin. "I don't feel sad anymore."

He chuckles. "Glad to be of assistance. Can you drive now?"

I nod and blow out my breath as Gabriel gets out of the vehicle, watching him as he circles the front of the car.

22

oxy and Jada are on the driveway picking up what looks like an entire wardrobe. The pixies buzz around them, aiding their efforts. I park on the curb near the bottom of the driveway. Not a single neighbor is looking at the scene unfold. I'm beginning to believe I have lousy neighbors.

"What happened?"

Roxy opens her mouth then bursts into tears.

Jada mouths, "Her mom."

"This is all your fault," Roxy yells, finding her voice and directing her anger all at me. "If you would just leave my dad alone this wouldn't have happened."

Understanding registers. Although I've always known Kirsten to be the kind of parent who picks up and drops off without much chitchat, Lucinda told me Roxy's mother supposedly makes a big deal every time Gabriel dates someone new.

"I wish my interaction with your father was simple as dating, but—"

"Fan-fucking-tastic!" She cuts me off, throwing up her hands.

I turn to see what else has upset her. The headlights of Gabriel's SUV shine on the three of us, as he pulls up to the driveway.

Roxy folds her arms across her chest and lowers her eyebrows. In a voice that comes close to a growl, she asks, "Did you narc on my mom?"

"No. Your father was already coming to say goodnight to you."

She rolls her eyes and groans dramatically. "Uh, huh. And then, you two will have coffee after *the kids* go to bed, one thing leads to another, and then my dad is replacing my mom with you."

I take a deep breath. Arguing would be senseless. "Roxy, I'm sorry you're stuck in the middle of what should be between adults. It must feel awful, thinking you have to side with me or your mom."

Her shoulders slump, nodding slowly she acknowledges, "It does."

Gabriel bursts out of the vehicle and says completely the wrong thing, "What did you do to upset your mother now?"

Roxy laughs but there's no humor in it. I can see the defenses I'd lowered a bit slam back into place with the quirk of her eyebrow. "What did I do? Kirsten made this mess without me saying a damned word."

"Don't call your mother by her name. Pay her some respect."

Another swing and another miss.

"I'm supposed to respect this?" Roxy spreads her hands. "She kicked me out because *you* have a new girlfriend. How is that fair?"

Jada and I exchange glances. Her dark eyes glisten with tears. Raf and I used to take our differences to the garage or table them until she wasn't around. She's not used to this type of family discord.

I put an arm around Roxy. "Why don't we all go inside and have some tea and muffins. Then we can figure this out? The pixies will clean up the clothing."

I half expect her to push me away and laugh at my motherly suggestion, but the other half knows she needs someone to act like a mother while her mother acts like a petulant child and her father a screaming idiot. She nods and lets me lead her inside. Jada is on her other side. Gabriel seems to calm by the time we're indoors.

He touches my shoulder in the hall. "Can I speak privately with my daughter?"

I hesitate, the urge to intervene and protect this kid great, but I'm not her parent. I point to the dining room.

Jada and I make ourselves scarce. In the kitchen I busy myself putting water in the electric kettle and getting out calming blends of teas. While I scoop tea into individual metal infusers, Jada plates the blackberry muffins I baked this morning.

Gabriel and Roxy remain in the dining room speaking in low tones.

Jada stands next to me and whispers, "It was bad, mami. Mrs. Jenkins just stopped by to give Roxy her retainer. Roxy blows up on her, telling her she never gave a crap about the retainer before and accused her of wanting to cock block Mr. Crowfoot. Twenty minutes later, Mrs. Jenkins is throwing out all Roxy's stuff into our driveway. She said, 'Tell your dad to have fun with the mommy he's always wanted for you.'"

I pour the tea. "Why would she say that?"

Jada shrugs. "I don't get it either. It's not like you and Mr. Crow-foot ever hung out before now."

I'd meant Roxy, but my daughter has a point.

Gabriel's voice raises loud enough for us to hear. "You said *what*?"

Of course that's the moment the doorbell rings. I hand Jada the tray of tea and muffins to take into the dining room and go down the hall to answer the door, passing the open door to the dining room.

Gabriel looks up. "Expecting someone?"

I shake my head slowly. "Everyone, have some tea and muffins. I'll get it."

The doorbell rings again. I steel myself for an ugly conversation.

A man in sweats and a Harvard sweatshirt stands where I'd expected Kirsten to be. I recognize him as Roxy's stepfather, Dave. He gives me a watery grin. "Sorry to bother you so late, but I saw your lights are on. My wife here?"

"No."

He furrows his brow. Despite his Harvard alumni status, thinking seems really hard for Dave. He hikes a manicured thumb toward the driveway. "Come on. I see her ex's car." His brows draw together. "You can tell me if they took off together. Wouldn't be the first time."

Good to know. It irks me given the state of the driveway and his missing wife that he didn't ask if his stepdaughter was alright. "No. Gabriel is here with Roxy. None of us know where your wife is."

Comprehension lights his features. "Ah, I get it now. That's what's got her so worked up. Gabby and you are a thing. How long you two been dating?"

I don't think you're capable of 'getting' anything, Dave. "Sorry, that's none of your business."

Dave scratches his head. "If it's got my wife distressed because she thinks she's gonna lose her kid to the two of you, I think it kinda is." His gaze focuses behind me as he speaks.

 I glance over my shoulder. Gabriel stands behind me so close that I almost jump. A look of pure hatred burns in his eyes as he glares at the other man. "You and I both know I wouldn't take Roxy from Kirsten. We've had joint custody for seven years."

"Gabby, this deal permanent? Like are you two getting married or something? 'Cause I'm kinda done tracking Kirsten down every time she thinks she's got a chance of you two getting back together."

"Goodbye, Dave."

Gabriel pulls me by the waist and slams the door. He makes a little choking sound as if stifling a sob. I turn around and see tears. I wrap my arms around Gabriel's thickly muscled torso and lean my head on his shoulder. He cries silently, but I can feel his sobs as he grips me as if I'm a lifeline.

"Are the girls still drinking tea?" I ask, stupidly, after we stand like that for who knows how long.

"I sent them to bed," he answers in my hair. "She does this. Every time I think I might be happy with someone else, she does this. You're right to not want to start anything with me."

So, Lucinda was right.

I pull away enough to see his face. "This isn't your fault. Unless... you're leading her on?"

He rolls his eyes and shakes his head. "I try so hard to maintain this friendly relationship with her for Roxy's sake, but she mistakes it as me wanting to get back together. She never understood that I come with the pack, my position. I have responsibilities and an image to uphold. Whomever I'm with can't just be my lover and friend. They have to be a leader themself. Someone who looks out for the community, takes on responsibilities." His arms tighten around me, the way he holds me changes. The look in his eyes change. "Someone like you."

I lick my lips, mouth suddenly dry. I'm aware of every inch of his hard-muscled body pressed against mine. It's hard to pay attention to his words. It's hard to think of anything.

Gabriel is so damn pretty.

So. Damn. Close.

He leans down, and we're sharing breath. His hands trace my sides and my back. "Are you ready for this?"

I find myself nodding. *Oh, yes. I'm ready.* Then I shake my head, unclear of his meaning. "Ready for what?"

He laughs softly. His cheeks dimpling.

"For us." His scent grows stronger, forest and musk.

I furrow my brows, unsure if he means sex or dating, or I don't know what. I definitely want him, but I don't know what "us" means.

"I love that even though you want me, you don't give into impulse. You're thinking about my offer and what it means."

I had given in to every impulse when I tasted his angel dust. I'm about to say that I don't exactly know what he's offering, but he breaches the short distances between our mouths, brushing his lips against mine. Then he moves to my jaw and my neck, the heat of his mouth scorching through me straight to my core. His teeth graze over where my shoulder and neck meet.

He whispers against my skin. "Are you ready?"

This is a bad idea. A very, very bad idea. But, I want Gabriel and I don't want to fight it. I wrap my arms around his neck and a leg around his hip, grinding against his erection to show him how ready I am. "Let's go upstairs."

Suddenly all his mouth, heat, hands, and scent are too far. Gabriel shakes his head as if snapping out of a daze. "I—I think we're not on the same page. It's my fault. I'm not explaining myself well enough." He maneuvers around me to open the front door. "I'll be here to pick up Roxy in the morning."

23

I pack my backpack to go on my pre-dawn run, including rowan branches sharpened at both ends in the mix. There haven't been any more vamps in the area, but I don't see His Creepiness giving up now. He wants the grimoires and his witch battery to power the spell.

The air outside feels cool and damp on my face. I take a deep breath, inhaling the subtle shift to early autumn. The fae lights dance as they busily tend the fall blossoms. Enchanted, my gardens bloom year-round, but on a rotation.

I turn on my music in my earbuds and get a good three miles out, taking a longer run than usual before heading back. By the time I reach my little alley leading back to my house, the sun limns the horizon, glinting on the morning dew. In a few weeks, it won't be light until well past my run.

I'm feeling the euphoria of adrenaline and dopamine kicking in. Gabriel's car is already in my driveway, which spikes the sensation.

The neighbors sometimes have a relative or two visiting, so I don't notice the extra car parked on the cul de sac until Kirsten gets out and positions herself between me and the house. She's wearing fashionably ripped jeans and a leather jacket over a low-cut tank. Her thick blonde hair is artfully tousled, and her makeup done despite the early hour.

"Can we talk?"

Like I have a choice? I curse under my breath and tap the wireless earbuds to turn off the music. I keep my distance. I don't know what kind of shifter she is. Packs aren't actually animal packs, but shifter communities.

"Sure."

"I came here to warn you."

I raise my eyebrows. As far as I know, as persona non grata to the pack and no part of Gabriel's council, Kirsten doesn't know that I'm a witch or anything about my past. However, she had fallen victim to an incubus. "About?"

"Gabby." Leaning against her car, she crosses her booted legs and arms. "I like you, Miriam. I know how much you suffered when Rafael died, and I want you to be happy. You see, Gabriel and I come from a different world than you do. A different culture. It's a closed culture that you couldn't possibly understand." Her eyes well up with tears and her voice shakes. "Gabby will always choose our people over anyone he dates, especially an outsider. You might have heard different but that's the real reason why we didn't last. He *always* puts them first."

I balance on one foot, grabbing my shoe to stretch my quadriceps. "Okay. Anything else?"

She bites her bottom lip. "Are you going to keep seeing him?"

"Our daughters are best friends," I hedge. I won't explain that I'm on his council, not when it's clear her daughter and ex-husband haven't told her anything about me.

She gives me a pointed stare. "It's six a.m. and his car is in your driveway. His scent is on you."

I hadn't showered yet since he held me last night, but it had been last night since I saw him. Whatever furry she shifted to possesses a keen sense of smell.

I cock my head to the side, raising my eyebrows as if surprised. "You can smell all that from there?"

Kirsten shifts uncomfortably. "Never mind. Just watch your back, Miriam. You have a nice, cozy life. Bringing Gabby into it will change everything, and it won't be for the better."

"That's where we'll have to agree to disagree." My smile is cloyingly saccharine. "I appreciate your concern, but I'm a big girl. I can handle myself. Have a good day, Kirsten!" I resume walking toward my house.

A stupid mistake.

Never turn your back on a shifter.

With preternatural speed, a hand grips my wrist, spinning me around. "Stupid latent. I'm going to have to show you." Kirsten's eyes flash gold as she uses her inhuman strength to drag me toward her car. "We're going for a little ride and then I'll show exactly what we are and what you're getting into."

Fear freezes my voice. Freezes me. Is this how she got rid of women Gabriel slept with? Instinct tells me she's going to do more than take me to some location and shift. Without a pack, she's gone feral. I'm not going to survive this.

Then I remember I am not a *latent*.

The words to a spell which conjures flames come to mind. I say them. Kirsten yelps and lets go as my fingers light like wicks of a candle. Off balance, I fall to the ground, smacking my cheek on the pavement but manage to get to my feet, hands still flaming.

"Witch!" Kirsten gasps.

"I am." I grin in response, other hand lighting. "A powerful one."

Her gaze flicks to Gabriel's car, and then to my house. She's likely considering ratting me out and how good it will make her look in his eyes. Anger as hot as the flames at my fingertips burns in my chest. I *really* hate women who betray their sisters for a man's attention.

"He knows. That's why we've been seeing so much of each other. You'd have known too, if you were still part of the supernatural community."

The look of utter betrayal fills her face. I hadn't set out to hurt her, but she came after me.

"Go home, Kirsten," I say. "Your warning is appreciated, but you have nothing to tell me that I don't already know."

Instead of a look of defeat, Kirsten's mouth twists in a grin that doesn't reach her eyes. "No wonder he's harbored feelings for you for so long, waiting for you to get over Raf like a dog waiting for scraps. Angels can see so much more than everyone else. Gabby must have sensed your power and how you could benefit him. He's likely using you for it."

I shake my head against the kernel of doubt she causes in me. Raf trusted Gabriel, and I trust my erstwhile husband would protect me and his daughter more than a jealous ex's accusations.

"For someone who professes she wants to work things out and loves me, you don't mind weakening my position and slandering me to my allies." Gabriel's voice sounds like it did when he chastised Princess, but it's laced with an icy anger that he didn't have for his beta.

Kirsten laughs. "Your position? I don't give a fuck about your position. You chose pack and *position* over your *mate*."

"You gave me no choice." He steps forward, pointing away from the cul de sac. "Go home, Kirsten."

Bristling magic scrapes over my skin with the command.

Kirsten laughs but there's not mirth in it. "I'm *abjured*. That doesn't work on me anymore," she challenges, but slinks around her car away from him in retreat.

"You're permitted to stay in my territory because you're the mother of our daughter. You have twenty-four hours to reconcile with Roxy, or I'll banish you."

"No. You won't." Kirsten shakes her pretty head, laughing and ducking into her car.

I step out of the way as she starts the car and pulls out, not giving her the chance to make any more stupid moves. Gabriel follows as if tethered to me.

After Kirsten's Lexus pulls out of the cul de sac, Gabriel's green-eyed gaze turns to me. His brow furrows with concern as his hand goes to my cheek. "You alright?"

I'm not. I was accosted, a demon threatened my life the night before, and my ex wants my grimoires, but I don't wish to talk about any of it right now. Adrenaline still courses through my system and all I want to do is fight my way out of this feeling that my life is spiraling out of control. I clench my jaw, but nod.

Gabriel's assessing gaze sweeps over me again, landing on my fists. A wry grin curves his full lips and his eyes gleam with amusement. "You can turn those off now."

My hands are still aflame. I withdraw my light.

"She was trying to drag me to her car," I explain.

He nods. "I felt her anger. She wasn't in her right mind. I'll have someone to follow her for the next few days."

I quirk an eyebrow. "You're bonded? I thought she was abjured."

"Shifter mate bonds are different. I didn't sever them because I like keeping an eye on her. I hope you can see why."

I nod, rubbing my cheek.

He puts an arm lightly around my shoulder. "Want some breakfast?"

Nice change of subject. "Sure."

Inside the girls are eating eggs, bacon, toast, and hash browns, all whipped up by Gabriel during my run. I spy two lunch boxes already packed next to their backpacks. The girls give me a cheery hello. A woman could get used to this.

"Scrape your plates and grab your bags," Gabriel chides in a cheerful tone. He slips past me into the kitchen. His hand brushes my back, sending electric tingles down my spine.

The girls do what he asks with no whining, no bargaining to finish this or that.

Jada kisses my cheek on her way out.

"Thanks for letting me stay the night," Roxy says, glancing briefly at her dad. "Sorry about the drama."

Flabbergasted, I simply nod.

The girls leave out the front.

This glimpse of a life that seems out of a television show is too sharp of a juxtaposition from the discord outside and last night.

"What's happening?" I ask.

Gabriel rinses off the plates and places them in the dishwasher, closing it with his hip. His smile is almost shy. "I wanted to make breakfast for you and the girls to make up for..." He blows out his breath and rakes a hand through his hair. "That's not true. I wanted to show you giving me a chance wouldn't be only dealing with the drama of my pack and my ex. I wanted you to see being with me would have its perks." He turns the dishwasher on and makes to leave. "So much for that plan."

I take his hand as he passes, stopping him. "Thank you for making the girls breakfast and packing lunch. Everything else, wasn't your fault."

Gabriel gives me a rueful smile. "It is. I could have severed the mate bond when I severed her bond with the pack. I thought I was protecting her by keeping it, protecting others. All I was doing was leading her on. I'm going to sever it tonight. Ending things cleanly will make my intentions clear."

He leans over, covering my mouth with his. Despite the way things ended the last time he kissed me, the madness with Princess at the restaurant, and despite Kirsten's warning, I let my lips part to receive him.

The kiss is different than last night, surprisingly gentle, an introduction with a promise the story will build. He tastes like orange juice and something bolder, sweeter. His forest and musk scent fill my nostrils again.

Gabriel breaks away first. We're both breathless. His gaze reaches past me to the door. "I have to take the girls to school, but we need to talk."

"Okay."

"There's a plate for you in the dining room," he says over his shoulder with a smile.

I watch him leave, dazed, and then head into the dining room. At the head of the table there's a covered dish, a pitcher of orange juice that smells fresh squeezed, a carafe of coffee and cream and sugar in little containers, and a full place setting with a single red lily in a vase

I don't recognize—actually none of the dishes or set up are things from my house. A little card sits on top of the covered dish. I open the card. It reads:

You were the last thing I thought about when I went to sleep and the first thing on my mind when I woke. I offer you food made by hand.

-G

I lift the lid of the dish and there's a savory galette with a crust in the shape of a heart. The savory aroma of caramelized onions, cheese, sausage, and veggies makes my mouth water.

I've been seduced by the King of Hell, I'd gone from friends to lovers with a demigod, but I've never ever had anyone bake something in the shape of a heart just for me. A niggling voice whispers this is more than just breakfast, that the nip at my neck means more than foreplay, but I tell that voice to shut up. I'm hungry and until Gabriel uses his words like a grown angelic shifter, I've agreed to nothing.

24

"But Roxy gets to go," Jada whines. "I don't see why I can't go."

I shove the last of the sandwiches we're packing into the cooler and then twirl on my daughter, giving her my sternest expression. "Different houses. Different rules."

Jada throws up her hands. "We're not talking snacks or bedtimes, mami."

"Exactly." I lift my eyebrows and give her a pointed look. "We're canvassing for missing, possibly murdered cryptids with a potentially feral witch in the forest. Roxy has had a lifetime of training in tracking and hunting and has gone on patrols with the pack for years. You, young lady, barely make it to the first viewpoint on the Wallace Falls trail without getting bored and needing your phone."

She rolls her eyes. "This isn't a boring family hike. Papi taught me defensive magic. I could be of use."

"Your father taught you self-defense and how to get away, not how to contain a potential threat."

She thrusts her hands on her hips. "How am I going to learn?"

I squeeze her shoulder. "Study and practice. Spend the day learning how to read the script of the grimoires. Once you master that, you'll be able to learn any spell and go on these kinds of expeditions."

Her shoulders sag with defeat. "Fine."

My cellphone chimes, notifying I have a message. I open it up to see if it's Gabriel. To my surprise, it's Micah.

Micah: Shawn wants to discuss your gift baskets for the gala. Want to come over for dinner?

I'd totally forgotten about using Lucinda's kitchen and buying the supplies. Chad would have a field day with my lack of planning.

Me: Can't tonight. I have a date. How about brunch at my place tomorrow?

Micah: *gasp* A date? Who's the lucky man?

I should have known Micah would want the details. I hope he doesn't know Gabriel well.

Me: Gabriel Crowfoot.

Micah: Ooh. Tomi and Jada's friend Roxy's father. Never met him but heard he's hot. Yay, you!!!! Anyway, brunch works. Maybe your new beau can come?

Me: We'll see.

I have no intention of inviting Gabriel, but I don't know what might happen between now and then, so if he was there, there would be no surprises.

The doorbell rings. Leave it to Gabriel to come to the door when a text he is in the driveway would suffice. It's a good thing though, saves me the trouble of asking him to come in and ruin the surprise I have for the pack.

"Go tell Roxy her dad is here," I order Jada over my shoulder.

"Are you sure I should? I might hurt myself going upstairs untrained."

Ignoring the snark for what it is, bitterness over not being able to go, I jog down the stairs, strapping on the backpack laden with a change of clothes, healer supplies, and a few defenses against His Creepiness's minions.

Gabriel waits outside in a fitted muscle shirt and sweats. He's braced against the top of the door frame by one sculpted forearm. His gaze sweeps down the length of my body, lingering here and there—I'm in leggings and a form fitting jacket, my running gear. A wolfish grin dimples his cheeks and his voice lowers a couple octaves when he says, "Good morning. You look pretty."

"Back at you." I can't help but smile in return. I may have batted my eyelashes a bit.

Gabriel glances over his shoulder, as if hearing something. His gaze centers on my face, his expression sobers. "There are members of the pack in the car who are not too fond of witches. Others are curious about you and what kind magic you possess, and they have a *lot* of questions. They all have orders to be on their best behavior."

I could only guess that by 'members' he means Princess, but there could be others. I shrug. "I can handle myself."

"I know." He leans forward, his voice a low purr when he asks, "Did you enjoy your galette?"

Little butterflies dance in my stomach and heat rushes to places long left cold. "I did, thank you.—Oh, food! Thanks for reminding me." I swear I feel his gaze on my backside as I turn to go to the kitchen. I pause, and motion for Gabriel to follow.

He follows at a leisurely pace. Yep. Definitely checking me out. *Gabriel must fancy big butts.*

On the counter, I have a container of muffins I'd baked last night with the girls, and a cooler filled with twenty sandwiches and bottles of water.

"Breakfast and lunch."

Gabriel chuckles. "I have a big appetite, but not that big."

I roll my eyes. "Ha. Ha. I'm not going into the woods with hungry shifters."

He eases closer, one hand grips my waist. "Devouring you wasn't in the plans, but it's always good to feed a hungry wolf when you look so delicious, Red." He touches one of my curls with a positively hungry look in his eyes, his head lowering for a kiss.

I angle my head to accept it.

"Ew, dad. Your game is gross," Roxy huffs, startling us apart. She grabs the muffin container. "So, Jada isn't allowed to come for real?"

"For real."

Roxy shakes her head, but says nothing more, taking the muffin container with her.

Gabriel pulls me to him, brushing my lips with his—an exchange of flesh and breath—before letting go and grabbing the cooler.

I shake myself from the stupor his affection puts me in and follow.

Gabriel's SUV takes up my driveway. The doors are all open. Three muscle-bound guys dressed similarly to Gabriel all look in my direction. One of them sniffs the air. My favorite person in the whole world, Princess, gets out of the front passenger seat and takes a new seat in the back.

I want to protest that Gabriel's beta doesn't need to move for me, but I think I'd make him look bad if I did, or offend her gesture of respect. I only peripherally know of their culture and I want to make sure that I am making friends, not enemies, here. The more they like me the less likely they are to be cruel to witches.

I take the muffin container from Roxy so she can get in. I get in the front seat and crack open the container.

"Anyone hungry?" I ask, shaking a muffin.

"Shit, yeah, I love muffins. Name's Syd," the guy sitting behind the driver's seat says. He can't be more than nineteen or twenty. The youthful appearance might be in part due to a sprinkling of freckles on his pale, narrow nose and cheekbones. Syd's short-clipped brown hair reminds me of a grizzly bear's fur. He is also massive enough to be a small bear.

I pass him a muffin. "Nice to meet you Syd, I'm—"

"Miriam," a deep voice interrupts from behind Syd. The owner of the voice looks to be in his late twenties, perhaps early thirties. He has long hair in small dreads neatly pulled back into a ponytail. He's dressed all in black and his ebony skin gleams. The shifter is impossibly handsome when he flashes straight white teeth at me with admiration in his dark eyes. "We all heard about the Miriam who saved our alpha and your bad-assery killing all those vamps. My name's Lance by the way."

I pass Lance a muffin, smiling. "Nice to meet you, Lance."

"He left out you were a total MILF," a guy in the way back calls. His head is shaved around the sides and nape but the hair on top is half green and half blue in the hues of the Seahawks' colors, contrasting against his extremely pale skin. His eyebrows are blue and green too. He's either a fan or really likes those colors because his t-shirt is green and blue too.

"I'm not sure how to respond to that," I say, passing a muffing to Syd to pass back. "But have a muffin."

"Don't be gross, Nate." Roxy chides, taking the muffin from Syd and shoving it at Nate.

"What have I told you about speaking to women that way?" Gabriel asks from the rear.

Nate lowers his eyes to his muffin. "Sorry I called you a MILF, Miriam."

I roll my eyes, not commenting. I offer Princess a muffin. She accepts, making a humming sound of appreciation after taking a bite.

Roxy refuses a muffin, by folding her arms and looking out the window. I didn't tell Gabriel the reason she was late getting ready was that she had been part of Jada's petition to go on this canvassing expedition, but she's as miffed as my daughter.

All the doors close and Gabriel hops in the driver seat, starting the SUV. His gaze slants to the muffins in my lap.

"Want one?"

"Please." The way he says *please* and his expression seem to imply he wants more than the baked goods.

I peel the wrapper back, so he won't have to while driving, and hand it to him. As Gabriel backs out of the driveway, I hear a whisper in the back that I act more like a proper mate than Kirsten ever did.

Gabriel grins, likely glad of his pack's approval, but the statement makes me uneasy. I don't like women being compared to other women.

I glance over my shoulder to see Princess and Roxy both glaring at Nate. I add my look of disapproval into the mix, but he seems oblivious.

"You alright?" Gabriel asks, as he pulls up to the stop sign.

I have the distinct feeling we aren't leaving until he is certain I'm comfortable, so I nod, not quite able to speak without showing how upset I am that I made snacks for my first council mission like the PTSA mom that I am, and that's somehow deflecting my purpose to simply "mate." I should have showed up in leather with magically imbued swords or bow and arrow like a supernatural badass.

"You look upset." He glares at the pack with a distinct alpha-ness and then looks at me with a gentle expression. "Do we need to talk in private?"

"No. I'm fine." I shake my head and force a smile. "A lot on my mind. Let's go. We still need to meet the others."

Gabriel gives me a look that says he's not buying that I'm fine, but pulls out anyway.

I eat one of my muffins, listening to the banter in the back. Nate tries his best to flirt with Roxy, who tears him apart with acerbic wit. I wonder if she's "out" to the pack. I side-eye her father, who grins at his daughter's comments. Nate doesn't push too far, so there's no need for Gabriel to step in as alpha or dad, apparently.

We reach Lucinda's Café in no time. Lucinda, Leilani, Cian, and Aurora are already waiting with coffees in hand. Lucinda has a carafe and cups for the others, making me feel a lot better about my decision to bring food. We're just better at remembering the basics, I suppose.

Aurora is in clothes that make more sense for a music festival than for canvasing the heavily wooded and dense underbrush of the North Cascades. There's not a lot of clear forest floor for pretty, sparkly vamps to run around. Her large eyes take in all the shifters. They are all pretty, and pretty intimidating. When her gaze lands on me, she gives me a thin smile.

"We're going to Wallace Falls State Park. I know someone who cleans the Sultan Police Department and the Snohomish County Sheriff's Department. She called me last night, saying campers reported seeing a Sasquatch around Pebble Beach area of Wallace Lake a few days before my cousin Svetlana went missing."

"Why would she drop her glamour in a place so heavily visited by humans?" Gabriel asks, coming to my side, rather close too.

Roxy sidles to my other side, picking at a second muffin.

There's plenty more in the SUV, but we've gone straight into planning, so I don't want to offer any. There are eleven of us total, eating later, anyway. It's best to conserve food.

Aurora's shoulders heave with her sigh. "The only two times a Bigfoot drops their glamour are when they are sick or injured. Badly."

"That's not all," Cian says, tipping his trucker hat by way of greeting. "I live out in Gold Bar. There's been reports of a feral woman attacking anyone who goes off trail up at Wallace Falls and finds her in the woods. There're all kinds of theories. Some say she's a spirit. Some say she's a witch. Some are saying she's some sort of mental health case and the authorities are starting to think it's not just rumors. Townies, not just tourists saying it, too."

My stomach knots. This is not good.

We all turn to Gabriel, watching him weigh all this as he sips his coffee. We might be a council, but he's an archangel. It's their job to put supes out of commission who attack mundanes.

"How do you think we should approach her," Gabriel asks me.

"A witch without her coven is not a dangerous thing," I begin, raising my voice a little to be heard by everyone. "A witch alone in nature, however, is. Her powers grow, but her capacity to relate to people diminishes. If you come across her, please leave her where she is and come for me."

Princess, all bad ass with *another* one of my muffins in one hand, plants her other hand on her hip. "What can you do that we can't?"

"I can bind her so she's not a danger to herself or others," I say.

Lucinda grimaces. "What if she's more powerful than you?"

"It's not about power, but rather knowledge. Most witches have only passed on subtle magics and only a range of spells passed down from their mothers. I'm from a coven of what you'd call scholars. I know traps she won't be able to break."

"Are you sure," Princess asks, taking a bite of muffin.

I clear my throat. "Most witches no longer understand the science behind the craft as I do. It's like they have recipes, but I know the chemical composition of all the ingredients and how they'll react to different catalysts. I not only know the how, but the why of witchcraft."

"How come you and these scholars are the only ones who have the information," Lance asks, moving closer to the circle. There's no accusation in his tone. He seems genuinely curious.

"Witch hunts. Covens became secretive."

Lance shakes his head. "Damn. That's sad but makes sense."

"How about this?" Gabriel asks, drawing everyone's attention to him. "Miriam, you set up a binding trap and the rest of us lure the witch into it. Once we make sure she's not a threat to anyone, we can free her."

"I can do that."

"It's best to not get too close," Lucinda advises. "How about if you see her, you howl, growl, or whatever in your other form and then I use my song to draw her to Miriam's trap?"

A couple of the shifters shudder. A siren song is inescapable.

Gabriel tips his coffee at Lucinda. "Excellent idea. Minimal risk. Minimal casualties."

"What if you can't lure the witch with your song?" Princess asks.

"No one can resist siren song." Lucinda shrugs and gestures broadly. "It's a compulsion gift from Persephone herself."

"Then we'll flush her out the way we do prey on a hunt," Gabriel says.

Aurora wrinkles her nose. "Sasquatch are vegetarians."

"It's like forming a net, forcing the pr—witch in the direction we want to go. You can do it, babe," Princess explains, squeezing Aurora's hand.

I want to laugh out of the sheer audacity of Princess's double standard. Aurora wasn't a shifter, but Princess, the pack's beta and shifter rep in the council, was allowed to date her without anyone challenging her?

Gabriel clears his throat. "We'll go to Gold Bar and meet at the lower entrance to Wallace Falls park. My pack, Leilani, and Aurora will canvas the woods on the ground. Cian, Miriam, and Lucinda will stay behind to set the trap. We'll head back to Miriam's trap to reconvene at noon. That'll give us three hours to cover the majority of the off-trail territory along the river. If you run into the witch, do not engage. Stay out of sight and signal to Lucinda where she's needed."

We head to the vehicles. Gabriel catches my arm and whispers, "The double standard my beta holds about mating outside the pack frustrates me too."

I simply nod and get in the car. That was a confrontation that had to happen between Princess and myself. Alone.

25

Even at the early hour, I would expect someone to be in the parking lot at the entrance of the trail, but Gabriel's SUV and Lucinda's minivan are the only vehicles.

When we disembark, I realize why the lot is abandoned. My stomach turns, threatening to release my breakfast. A frisson of fear dances across my shoulders although there's nothing to be frightened of. Every instinct screams at me to leave this place, but I know better.

The defensive wards I have around my property are a blunter "stay out," but I recognize spell work at play. A repulsion spell is a good defense if you want to deter people from entering without drawing notice. They'll think it's their own body revolting and have the negative association keeping them from returning.

Lance and Nate vomit up their muffins and coffee. Roxy joins them, whining she wants to go home. Aurora hunches over like she wants to crawl into a hole and hide. Syd and Princess snarl and shake their heads. Lucinda, Leilani, and Cian, who have joined us, all look like they're barely holding down their breakfast.

"There's definitely a witch here," I tell the group, stating the obvious. It's a habit I picked up from being a mom and having to explain the world to a kid. "She has repulsion wards up. That's what you're feeling."

Even Gabriel looks a little green as he rounds the SUV. "Doesn't bode well for our purpose. She knows spellwork."

"I wanna go home!" Roxy whines again. "I don't want to die here."

"She's laid iron somewhere nearby. I gotta get out of here," Cian says with a shiver. "I gotta go before I'm too weak to move."

"There's no iron, and you're not going to die, Roxy. The spell is seeking your fears," I tell the group.

Gabriel presses his palm to his forehead. "Can you combat it?"

I take a while to understand the weave of the spell, then I unshoulder my backpack to retrieve a stick of vine charcoal out of my sack.

I draw a symbol on each of their foreheads that will counter her wards, starting with Gabriel and ending with Princess. I whisper words and push a bit of light into each ward.

"As long as you have these symbols un-smudged, they will help you combat the repulsion spell."

Once everyone has a ward and seems to have shaken off the lingering effects of the spell magic, I say, "The repulsion spell will make anyone who comes here turn around and run, which is why this lot is empty. I can set up the trap right here without mundanes bothering me."

"We need to shift. The underbrush is too thick for us to make good time in human form," Gabriel says, pointing to his ward.

Crap. I'll have to ward them all again. I convey this.

The pack all start stripping right then and there. Leilani, shier than the shifters, undresses behind a car. I wonder what animal form she'll take.

When Gabriel strips, my gaze and my thoughts are nowhere else. Even among the well-muscled shifters, he is damned near perfection. Our gazes meet. The corner of his mouth quirks.

His face grows longer and his skin sprouts fur. His bones snap, crackle, and pop until a wolf on all fours stands before me. After that gross display, all the heat building inside me peters out. The other shifters transform, and it's just as gross.

Roxy, Lance, and Nate are wolves. Like I suspected, Syd is a massive grizzly. Princess is a...oh, mother! Princess is a *honey badger* the size of a standard poodle. Leilani trots out as a giant black and tan lizard. I mark them all with the ward against the spell again. A chuckle rises in my throat at Princess in honey badger form, but I swallow it down, biting my lip as I redraw the symbol on her big furry forehead.

"Well, what d'you know? I'd figure Princess, a harpy," Cian says, as the supernatural animals and Aurora take off into the woods.

"Never seen her shift before?" I ask, rifling through my backpack for the items I'll need.

He shrugs and gazes off into the forest. "I'm not usually invited on these things. I'm not fast or a hunter. Luck is all I can bring."

"Must be the archangel wanted extra insurance for his lady friend." Lucinda winks at me.

I roll my eyes. His lady friend had plenty of skills which didn't need luck.

"Do you need any help?" she asks, grinning.

I shake my head. "I got it."

I spend a good twenty-minutes drawing the circle and symbols that will trap a witch with the vine charcoal, pouring my light into it. I hiss as I cut my arm. I let the blood drip onto the correct points.

"I never seen anything like what you're doing," Cian says.

Lucinda wrinkles her nose. "What kind of spell is that? Blood magic is rare."

Demonic spells always require blood. I don't tell her that. I don't answer at all, pretending to be too focused to hear. The spell is something His Creepiness had taught me, not witchcraft. I don't like making portals to Hell or traps that bind people with my blood, but I also don't know how to neutralize her magic any other way. If there was such a spell as neutralizing a witch's magic, witches weren't writing it down in grimoires for their enemies to learn.

The ground rumbles, followed by an inhuman screech. Yips and roars trail. Something bursts from the trees. A winged creature.

I gasp at the sight of Gabriel in his angelic form.

"Guess that's my cue. Turn around Cian," Lucinda says, undressing.

Cian looks away as she hands me her clothes. "Mind putting these in my car?"

I blink as wings sprout from her back. They're rainbow hued and iridescent. Her brown skin shimmers, turning gold, and feathers that match the wings replace her tan skin. Her fingers and toes sharpen into golden talons. Her eyes glow electric blue when she nods at me. Lucinda takes off in a graceful sprint, then launches into the air.

A white wolf and silver wolf shoot out of the brush at top speed, Roxy and Lance. The ground shakes, dispersing more animals from the forest.

I squint to see Lucinda join Gabriel in the air. There is some sort of exchange, but I don't wait to hear the siren's song; I slip on a necklace with the amulet that Velja had given me years ago. I don't know how the amulet's magic works the way I know spellcraft, but I do know the amulet makes the wearer immune to mind control magics, called persuasives, like angel dust and, hopefully, siren song.

Lizard Leilani stomps out of the forest with Aurora running inhumanly fast past her lumbering gate. Next comes Princess in honey badger form. Finally, grizzly Syd tramples and crashes his way out of the forest, his roar deafening.

Lastly, Gabriel flies in, landing on the ground next to me.

I know it's not the time to think this, but holy shit he's beautiful. Freaking angels. It's really unfair how gorgeous they are. He smiles at me checking him out and then draws the attention of the group.

"Did the witch get anyone?"

The shifters all shake their heads. When the ground shakes again, poor Roxy pisses.

"Rock witch," I sigh. "They're natural geomancers. She doesn't need spells for that."

"Yeah, I figured when she started erecting walls of earth. If I couldn't transform, I'd be stuck on one of her—guh—" He bends over, gagging.

I remember the repulsion spell and grab the charcoal. There's not a lot left, but enough to ward him. I try not to think about the fact that I'm touching him while he's naked.

"Thank you."

A sweet soprano fills the air, turning everyone's gaze to Lucinda in the sky. Magic beats against my skin, but does not permeate, thanks to the amulet. The ground stops shaking.

"I—I should go to her," Cian says in dazed voice, but he's cut off by lizard-Leilani. The leprechaun tries to circumvent his fiancé but thinks twice when she hisses at him.

I notice the song doesn't have an effect on shifters, but Aurora's eyes glaze over.

"Animal form keeps them in control," Gabriel grits through his teeth.

"Should you shift?"

He shakes his head, drawing closer. He buries his face in my neck, inhaling deeply. "I just need you." His voice is husky and I feel a poke on my hip.

Being a witch who's been to Hell, I've been around some weird shit, but this has got to be the strangest situation I've ever found myself in.

He trails his nose along my neck, loosening my hair with a deft hand. "I broke the bond with Kirsten. I'm free to mate with whom I wish."

"I—uh—your daughter is right there."

A low chuckle reverberates against my skin. "I'm not trying to fuck you Miriam. I'm trying to keep my sanity. The siren call is too much, even for me. That's why it's forbidden."

I snort. "Seems to me the Angelic Anocracy doesn't like beings they can't resist, or pound, into submission."

He presses his lips to my ear. "I can't resist you. Hmmm...I wonder if I can p—"

Just then, Lucinda flies closer. Siren song, loud as amplified music at a concert, drowns out the rest of Gabriel's filthy suggestion. Mostly. I hear enough to learn Gabriel is a little freaky.

I turn toward the rustling in the forest that follows Lucinda, expecting—I don't know what. The brush parts, and a woman of indeterminate age emerges, her dirty face awestruck by the siren. Her long, dark hair is tangled and matted. Her bedraggled skirt and sweater are covered in dirt, and perhaps moss? She stumbles forward, not seeing any of us. Her focus is on the siren.

"Everyone clear," I order, dragging Gabriel, who is still whispering filthy suggestions, with me.

When Lucinda draws the rock witch into the trap, the song suddenly stops. The messy haired woman blinks. "What the shit?"

The witch tries to launch herself back into the woods but gets zapped onto her butt. She shakes her head and looks around. "Well, I'll be damned. Didn't expect that. So, are you all working for the devil?" Her eyes narrow on me. Despite her disheveled appearance, there's a lucidity, a keen intelligence in her gaze. "Or, just you?"

26

I hand the witch, whose name I've learned is Rhiannon No-Last-Name, a third sandwich and another bottle of water. I wish I'd brought wet wipes. Her nails are overgrown and covered in the gods know what.

"We're heading out," Lucinda says, back in human form. "I'll check in on the kiddo."

I nod and wave to Leilani and Cian helping Roxy, now in human form, into the car. Gabriel escorts Aurora to the SUV. Rhiannon refused to speak in front of her, insisting she could have ties to demons.

The shifters are all human again, dressed and standing around eating by the SUV.

Gabriel returns to me, wings folded against his back, not trusting Rhiannon enough to shift into human form. He has, however, donned some pants after the witch told him he'd "poke someone's eye out with that thing."

"Since the cryptids could report my whereabouts to you-know-who, I couldn't very well let them go," Rhiannon says around a mouthful of sandwich, her brown eyes twinkling with amusement.

"What did you do with them?" I ask.

"Took them home."

"Where is that?"

She points to the woods. "Second star to the right and straight on to morning."

I furrow my brow, not understanding.

"You live in Neverland?" Gabriel asks, squatting down beside me. He'd been silent so far, letting me talk to the witch since I am one.

"I live beyond a neverdoor," the witch replies. "Get it? Never door. Neverland. It's all faerie."

I blink in disbelief, as goosebumps pillar my skin. Never doors are what my mother said the fae used to travel between their world and ours.

There is no emotion on Gabriel's pretty face or his tone when he asks, "Are you fae?"

Rhiannon grins, sandwich bits in her teeth. "One sixteenth brownie. That seems to be enough to get between this world and faeries."

Gabriel curses under his breath something about wishing he hadn't let Cian go home.

I clear my throat. "So, let me get this straight. Earlier, you said you were attacked by several cryptids, who were working for the devil to capture you. Then, instead of harming them or fleeing, you took the cryptids home, which is faerie?"

"Not Tir Na Nog or any of the royal turf, I'm not stupid. The faerie is a pocket realm, created by some fae princeling, who wants nothing to do with the rest of them."

"How did you end up in a faerie at all? Did one lure you?"

"When I ran from my coven, I met some pixies who showed me my first neverdoor. I got a sweet setup there. Want to see it?" Her face brightens with hope.

My insides churn. Instinctively, I want nothing to do with fae or faeries, but I want to find the cryptids and see what they know about His Creepiness. Also, this princeling might know who my father is. I force a smile. "I do. However, I'd like to ask you something first. Why did you run from your coven?"

"Feel that earthquake? That was me. I know a spell or two but you-know-who wanted to get up close and personal with me because my light is pretty strong...plus I'm one-sixteenth brownie. The devil really likes fae-witches. That's why he sent so many cryptids after me. He wants a fae-witch for some reason. I got my ass out of there before I could find out for what."

I can't help but shudder. I know for what.

Gabriel places a hand on my shoulder but doesn't comment. Instead, he says, "Can you take us to the cryptids?"

Rhiannon's gaze focuses on his hand. "An angel and a witch. Never thought I'd see the day." She sighs. "I suppose you can come too."

"May our friend come with us as well," I ask, knowing Aurora was anxious to see her cousin again. "She might find out how the cryptids came into the devil's employ."

The rock witch squints at the SUV and then angles her head at Gabriel. "You sure she's on your side?"

"I trust Aurora," Gabriel answers without hesitation.

Rhiannon stuffs her water bottle and the remnants of her sandwich down her shirt. "Okay. Let's go then."

Gabriel excuses himself to speak to the shifters. Princess balks at whatever he says but doesn't complain. Aurora gets out of the SUV and joins us. We follow Rhiannon through thick underbrush of the forest, skirting blackberry brambles.

She walks straight into a tree, disappearing entirely. Aurora goes next.

It's my turn. As I approach the tree, my heart thunders in my chest, threatening to break free. Sweat beads my brow, sliding down my cheeks. I can't seem to get enough air.

Gabriel rounds me so we're face to face. His hands are sweeping over my hair and arms. "What's wrong?"

"I need to go." My voice is a whisper.

He shakes his head. "It's the geas."

I fight the panic-driven racing thoughts and breathe. Gabriel is right. I can feel it in my core that I'm being pushed away from this place. As much as I fear what my father might be or why he doesn't want my light free, moving toward where the geas doesn't want me to go will be moving toward answers.

"Help me through," I plead.

His arms wrap around me. We walk together, me slumped against his side, arms trembling. There's a shift in the density of the air as if it grows thicker, like walking in a muggy summer afternoon. My stomach drops, and falling, falling, falling.

Except Gabriel is holding me tight, and we're walking.

How are we walking?

I can't see anything except swirls of color, then we're in a meadow. The grass is a pale blue and the sky is a verdant green. The air smells like honeydew melons. Sprites flitter around Rhiannon. They're not like my sprites. These are earth tones of brown and tan, they buzz about.

I turn to Gabriel. "I'm fine now."

After a brief scrutinizing gaze, he comes to the same conclusion, I suppose, and releases me.

"What the hell? My glamour," Aurora exclaims, her voice suddenly gruffer and she's no longer a tall and willowy human, but something akin to Chewbacca.

"This isn't Earth," Rhiannon lectures. "You have no bars and there's no wireless router to connect to for Wi-Fi."

Aurora wrinkles her furry nose. "Huh?"

"Your magic is earthbound," I clarify. "A force of nature there does not apply to the forces of fae-made universe."

"Oh," Aurora doesn't look pleased.

"Okay, Okay, I'll say it," Rhiannon says, swatting a sprite buzzing next to her ear away. She gives Gabriel a wary look. "You look like an angel who killed multitudes of the High Fae courts." She lowers her voice and talks out the side of her mouth, "I don't mean to disinvite you, but this may not be the best place for you to be, buddy. The princeling might not like it."

Gabriel glances at me. Embarrassment or perhaps guilt fills his eyes, I can't tell. He doesn't have the same look when his gaze returns to Rhiannon. "That war is long over. I have no quarrel with the fae." He glances at me again. "I'm here for her protection."

As if an afterthought, he says, nodding to Aurora, "And hers."

"Gee, thanks," Aurora says, folding her arms across her furry breasts. "Are we going to see the cryptids or what?"

"Yeah, yeah," Rhiannon answers, motioning us to come.

The sprites buzz around me, an aerial dance that seems like a greeting. One *bites* me, narrowly escaping my swat. The swarm flies away, buzzing excitedly.

Rhiannon's gaze follows them and then narrows her eyes at me, that keen intelligence I saw only briefly before returns, until she says, "Alright, let's go see if the dryad's ferry is around.

WE TRAVERSE the strange meadow filled with odd creatures of the likes I've never seen, some humanoid, some more animalistic, none I could name. I'm on edge because of my mother's warnings, but they don't seem to pose a threat. The fae creatures pause in their activities to stare at our little party. Some dash away in fear at the sight of Gabriel. Some venture closer as if to get a good look at us, but their gazes fixate on me until Gabriel notices them and glares, then they run like the others.

I want to tell him not to look so mean, they're only curious, but my mother's warnings that all fae are far from harmless prevent me from defending them.

We reach a river that is a deep shade of wine red. A tree with twisted branches making up their legs and arms stands by the river, giant staff in hand. The dryad's slits for eyes grow green, no pupils or sclera. Some demons have completely black eyes or red eyes, so I'm not bothered by this.

Dryads, from my limited knowledge of mythology, are not water fae, and are of Greek not Celtic origin, so it is strange to see one— then again since most supernaturals exist and I'm using human pop culture as a reference for what dryads are supposed to be, maybe it's not strange at all.

The tree-person speaks. Their voice is a papery rasp like dry leaves scraping together. I don't understand a word the creature says, but Gabriel stiffens.

"They want a drop of our blood as price to pass," Rhiannon translates.

"No." Gabriel, Aurora, and I say in unison.

The rock witch shrugs. "Guess you're not going."

Expression dubious, Aurora asks what I am thinking out loud, "How do you understand the sprites and the dryad?"

Rhiannon shrugs. "They speak the same language. Kinda. Root sounds the same, kinda like Spanish and French are derived from Latin."

"She's translating correctly," Gabriel confirms. Then he turns to the dryad, speaking in the strange fae tongue.

The dryad spreads their hands. Gabriel scowls in response. "They say it's the price they're made to charge by the fae who made this faerie." He adds, darkly, "They're collecting information, not tolls."

"Is this the only way," I ask Rhiannon.

She nods. "If we start walking downriver in either direction, we'll end up right back here. If we walk away from the river, we'll end back up here."

Gabriel curses under his breath, muttering about illogical faeries.

We could test if Rhiannon is telling the truth, but I don't like the idea of wandering around a faerie. We have no idea what her house looks like and would likely have to battle something vile and danger-ous. Besides, I'm still fighting a vague sense of unease from the geas.

"So how do we do this?" I ask.

Rhiannon holds out her hand. The dryad grows a thorn from a gnarled branch finger, pricking the rock witch. Blood wells and the dryad lets her onto a long wooden raft.

Aurora goes next. The dryad uses a separate thorn for the Sasquatch. She takes a place beside.

Gabriel stands in front of me. He says something in the dryad's tongue. The fae nods, replies, and then pricks the nephil's finger. Gabriel doesn't board until I go through the same process.

With all five of us loaded, the dryad pushes off the dock. The further down river we go, the stronger my unease builds. Perspiration makes my face damp.

Gabriel takes my hand in his. "Are you alright?"

"Same problem."

I notice his hand is wet. He's still bleeding. I don't even think. I push my light into his finger to heal it. A wave of nausea crashes over me like the sea soaking a rocky shore, pain follows. It's nothing like when I'd overextended myself saving Gabriel, but more like a warning. Like the geas is telling me "*Don't use that here.*"

I feel *noticed.* I don't know how to explain it, but using the green light drew attention of a terrible power. Part of me wants to confront that power and see if it is the fae that bound me. Another, more primal part wants to run.

Gabriel's head is in constant motion as we float down the river, eyes scanning the entire valley to the west and the rust-colored cliffs in the distance east. He glances over his shoulder occasionally to the dryad.

Something catches my gaze above, but it flies too high to make out what it is. The flying entity follows our path before soaring off.

"Be prepared," Gabriel whispers in my ear. "I think that was a scout."

I nod.

The meadow on either bank unexpectedly gives way to a dense forest. The abrupt change of scenery startles me. I blink to adjust to the sudden shift in light.

Aurora whispers, "What the shit? How—"

"Faeries make no sense until they do," Rhiannon says from the front of the craft.

I exchange an uneasy glance with Gabriel. The fae are not simply magical creatures, full fae are gods able to create pocket universes.

The dryad docks the raft on a bank. We disembark, taking in our surroundings—mainly, slender gray trees. There is no underbrush, only dirt and roots. Following Rhiannon through the forest, we come to a cottage that slouches to one side as if it's disappointed in life and gave up. She leads us around to the back where we find cages made of the trees themselves.

I gasp at the sight of the cryptids in these tree prisons. It looks like something out of nightmares fueled by my mother's tales of wicked fae.

The cryptids stir when they see our approach. Two are Sasquatch, there's a mothperson and something like a coyote, but humanoid.

"Aurora!" one of the Sasquatches shouts in a growly voice.

Another Sasquatch keens in an inhuman wail and sobbingly cries, "Cousin! You've come for me."

Aurora sprints past us to the first cage, clinging between the branch bars. The other cryptids perk, hope lighting their faces.

"You're a healer," Gabriel says, gesturing to the cryptids.

Getting his meaning, I inspect the cryptids. None show signs of malnutrition, dehydration, or abuse. I have a few power bars in my sack that I hand to each, but I don't offer them escape. According to Rhiannon, they all tried to kidnap her.

Rhiannon snorts. "Don't be too happy, this here's the archangel of the Pacific Northwest." She makes a grand gesture to Gabriel. "Go ahead. Tell him why you're here."

Aurora's cousin releases her and shrinks back. I hear a soft, "I'm sorry."

"Don't apologize. Just explain," Aurora replies, reaching for her cousin.

The cryptids all hang their heads. The coyote-looking one whines.

"We've all had time to talk about how we ended up here," the Sasquatch gestures a brown, hairy arm to the rest of the cages. "And we all have the same story. A crossroads demon told us to find a witch hiding in these woods."

"Did they say why?" I ask, hoping they could not hear my pounding heart.

"No."

Gabriel steps forward, face harder than I've ever seen it. "What were you supposed to do when you found the witch?"

"He gave each of us an apple. We simply had to share it with her."

"Oh, they were all crafty, acting like they just wanted to help the poor, lost witch in their wood with a little food." Rhiannon rolls her eyes. "I recognized the fruit for what it was and captured them before they went back to the devil with my whereabouts."

"How did you come upon this demon?" Gabriel asks Aurora's cousin.

A very good question. Demons don't simply make forays to angel-occupied worlds without a purpose.

"I want to marry a human. The thing is, if we have children—" A shuddering sob cuts the sentence short.

Aurora offers her hand to her cousin and finishes for her, "Any child from such a union will be born as we are, without glamour." She gestures to her furry body. "She's been living as a human. Her fiancé doesn't know."

I feel sorry for Aurora's cousin despite how angry I am she bargained with a demon to capture a witch.

The Sasquatch collects herself. "I went to a crossroads that intersects the ley line. The one near Stevens Pass, not the Snoqualmie one."

Gabriel nods. I have no idea where she's talking about, but I do know that a ley line is a magical point that can be used to access magic or travel between worlds. You have to know how to travel to different universes to use a ley line, and there's usually an inconvenient price...like being drained of most of your light for a few days.

"I must have waited there for at least three days. A demon showed up. They heard my case and told me that if I did this favor, they would make my child favor the human side."

"That's impossible," Gabriel replies. "They don't have that kind of power."

Despite Gabriel's gentle tone, the Sasquatch cringes and then shakes her head, not in disagreement but defeat. "I've had lots of time to think about how foolish I was." She nods her furry head toward the other cages. "We all have."

We interview the other captives. All have a similar story—an impossible wish, and a demon ready to give it to them if they do this simple harmless favor of finding the witch and giving her an apple.

The last one, a mothman, says in a high, insect-like voice, "I didn't even give her the damned apple. She—" He points a fuzzy finger accusingly in the rock witch's direction, "—trapped me here against my will."

Rhiannon cackles. "You had one on you when you followed me through the never door." She makes a sweeping gesture, indicating all the cryptids in cages. "You all came here by choice, thinking you'd convince me to take the fruit. For all you knew, the apple could have been poisoned. Attempted murderers don't have it good as you."

The cryptids hang their heads. They'd had time to consider that too, I bet.

"Where are the apples?" Gabriel and I ask at the same time.

"In here." Rhiannon motions for us to follow, guiding us to the cottage. Leaving the captured behind as they are, a few protest and one demands to be set free.

Gabriel makes a sharp turn, throwing angelic power into his voice when he speaks. "Be thankful the witch is kind enough to care for you after you deceived her. You are outside of my jurisdiction. You've consorted with my enemy against a person under my protection. It will not be better for you if I take you back."

Aurora gapes but does not protest.

I whisper to him, "Are we any better luring Rhiannon with a siren to speak to her?"

"We are the authorities," Gabriel replies without batting an eye. "We arrested a suspect in the cryptid disappearance case. I think that's a far cry different than our enemy's intention."

27

We leave Aurora behind with the other cryptids, following Rhiannon into her cottage. The interior looks like Thoreau lived here. One of everything. One table and chair, one chair for sitting, and a bed big enough for a single thin person. Rhiannon does not plan on guests, let alone ever living with anyone else.

She motions and the dirt floor trembles, churning in the corner of the hut until a solid shaft appears. Dirt falls away revealing a chest atop a mini-mesa. Rhiannon opens the chest with a wave and murmured incantation I recognize but am surprised she knows. Inside the chest, magic, *His Creepiness's magic*, pulses off red apples.

My gut twists yet I take a step forward toward his magic, compelled toward *him*. I shake my head and step back. "The devil himself imbued those with his light."

Gabriel, who seems to not notice my internal battle, takes an apple, examining the perfectly normal looking Red Delicious while I fight the urge to bat it out of his hand.

He turns to me, offering the apple. "I've never seen anything like this. What does it do?"

I wave my hands in front of me refusing his offer to take the apple for my own inspection. I don't want to touch the thing reeking of my ex. At the same time, a minute part of me wants to take the apple and sink my teeth into it. That scares me more than I care to admit. It's been so, so long. His Creepiness and his angel dust shouldn't be a temptation, but anyone who's known addiction knows the urge never goes away, only lessens over time by learning to cope without your vice.

I switch my focus on Gabriel's handsome face instead of the apple. "The apple's a mockery of the forbidden fruit from the book of Genesis. Instead of granting you knowledge, one bite transfers the victim directly to Gehenna, Hell. I used to have a whole chest filled with these apples." I smile bitterly. "His way of saying I was welcome in his presence at any time."

"The devil wants easy access to his baes." Rhiannon cackles, the sound eerily manic.

"Did he give you one?" I ask, curious how she knows this.

She shakes her head, her expression serious. "No. I've never met him personally. A witch in my coven much more powerful than I am, like a quarter fae, and a real looker received one from a demon. We all knew it was some icky courtship between you-know-who and her. She'd take a bite and disappear for an hour, a few days, a week. She'd come back, predicting the end of the world was nigh and she had the special privilege—" Rhiannon makes air quotes with her fingers, "— of being Harbinger of the Apocalypse."

A shudder passes through me accompanied by an odd sense of betrayal and hurt. Once, I'd thought he truly loved me, I'd thought I was some Chosen One hand-selected, but it turns out anyone with the fae/witch combination could power the spell.

"Everyone in the coven was envious, but to me she looked like someone suffering and didn't know it." Face haunted by something only she could see, Rhiannon crosses her arms over her chest, hugging herself. Her voice softens to a whisper. "Eventually, she never came back to us."

"Is that why you left your coven?" Gabriel asks.

Rhiannon fists the material of her dress in her hands, her gaze distant. "After she disappeared, the demon, who presented her with an apple, popped up in my quarters. The stinky thing wanted me to bite the apple right then and there like it was some great honor. I told it I needed to pee. I climbed out the bathroom window and ran. The pixies you saw earlier led me through a never door to here. The princeling who rules this faerie was put off by my presence, said he wouldn't stop any fae from eating me, but let me live here. He showed me the never door to Wallace Falls because I'm not enough brownie to survive on faerie food."

I nod in understanding, glancing at her shelves of canned foods and water bottles. This princeling seems nothing like the fae in my mother's stories.

"I need to take these apples as evidence of the attempted kidnapping," Gabriel demands, tossing the apple in his hand into the chest.

Rhiannon narrows her eyes. "Evidence for whom?"

"The families of the cryptids."

She grumbles for a few minutes and then says, "Okay. Fine."

Gabriel tucks the chest under his arm.

When we all exit the cottage, I say, "I need to speak to Gabriel in private for a moment."

Rhiannon makes herself scarce.

Aurora is sitting below her cousin's cage, conversing. She doesn't even glance our way. Neither does her sobbing cousin.

"Are we going to leave them here?" I gesture to the cryptids.

Gabriel tenses. "They're not safe on earth. You don't break a deal with a demon and expect to live."

I lift my chin. "You can if you have the protection of the archangel. They made a mistake. Spending forever away from their native land is not a just punishment for the crime."

By his expression, Gabriel does not agree. "Since you know Lucifer personally, what exactly would the king of demons do to Rhiannon?"

I lower my eyes.

"That's what I thought."

Furious, my gaze snaps to him. "This isn't about what *he'd* do. This is about what we'd do." I know I've already lost the fight but can't see these people here indefinitely. "Cryptids need the world they're from, or they'll die."

"Say we do take them back. Attempted kidnapping of a person in my jurisdiction, conspiring with a demon. What do you think the Angelic Code demands *I* do?"

"What?" I have no idea what his position requires of him to carry out because he seems to not follow any rules.

He closes his eyes and exhales. "Execution."

I blink. My reply spills out before I even consider how he might take it: "You didn't execute Kirsten when she consorted with a demon. Why can't you be merciful with these cryptids, too?"

That earns me a dark look. He's next to me, but I feel him distance himself as if he'd taken a step back. "That was different."

My gaze returns to the captured. "So, we leave them like animals in a cage?"

He doesn't answer for a long time. "No." He runs a hand through his curls. Drawing close, he says, "I don't like it either, okay. Leaving them here for now gives me time to think about how I can bring them back without killing them."

My mood brightens as I see a way to further my appeal. "You can't execute them because you need to find the demon giving out apples. The best way to do that is to bring the cryptids back. The demon will follow up and when they do, we can have a trap waiting."

Gabriel stews on this a bit. "Okay." He holds up a finger. "However, they'll be in my custody until this demon is caught, and we figure out his purpose."

"I'd like to take these cryptids into my custody. Could you release them?" Gabriel asks Rhiannon.

"They're in custody right here." Rhiannon jacks a thumb at the tree-branch cages. "I feed them and take them on walks once a day, but they aren't leaving this faerie. Princeling's orders. I think he wants to spar with Ol' Horny over kidnapping halflings."

I couldn't care less what a fae princeling wants to do with His Creepiness, and don't like the idea of using these cryptids as bait. I try a different approach. "I'm a mom. I know what goes into the care and keeping of another person. I also know you can't really trust food in faerie to feed cryptids, so you have to get it from Earth. Do you want to be their caretaker for the rest of your life? What if one of them gets sick, or hurt by a malicious fae while you're out? Do you want to be responsible for their injuries?"

The cryptids all hang on my every word. Their attention shifts to Rhiannon—their desperation, their hope, palpable.

Rhiannon mulls on what I've said for a bit. Not wanting to give up her prisoners, the rock witch grumbles about meddling and the princeling not liking it, but finally relents. The branches part, setting the cryptids free. Aurora and her cousin embrace. The rest of the cryptids stand about awkwardly. All eyes are on Gabriel.

He puts power into his voice when he says, "By the authority given to me by the Angelic Anocracy, you are all under arrest. Any attempt to run will be considered an act of admission to collusion with Hell and its King, which will result in your prosecution and immediate execution."

After the release of the cryptid prisoners, we all stand on the shore. The ferry and dryad have departed and there's no sign of when they'll be back.

"Where is the boat?" Gabriel barks at Rhiannon.

The witch shrugs. "The river runs the entirety of the faerie, the boat could be anywhere but if I had to guess, the dryad is done for the day."

"Can you summon the dryad," I ask, trying to keep my patience, but I'm as eager as Gabriel to return to our world. The feeling of being observed only strengthens the longer we remain. There are no answers here to my parentage, not from anyone who was willing to speak to me anyway.

"The dryad knows when we need them and comes if they wish. They won't come when they're on a break or done for the day. Fae are stubborn about getting their 'me time.'"

"So, we wait here on the shore until the dryad returns?" I ask Gabriel.

He clenches his jaw tight, judging by his expression, debating something. He launches into the air, flying downriver.

Rhiannon rolls her eyes and sighs loudly. "It doesn't work like that."

Within seconds Gabriel flies over the river, coming from the opposite direction he left. He shakes his head, landing. The soil billows around his feet. He glares at Rhiannon, a threat of violence in his every movement. He jabs a finger at her. "Did you trap us here?"

The rock witch sidles closer to me, shaking her head.

"Gabriel, Rhiannon was with us," I say in her defense.

"Why did the dryad need our blood?" he asks, his anger unabated.

"There's no way beyond the meadow but death or the ferry. It's a protection the princeling gave me. The dryad must collect a drop of blood," Rhiannon answers. "The princeling requires it."

I lick my lips. "*Who* is this princeling?"

She lowers her head and plays with her tattered skirt. "I dare not say. Come to my cottage, stay the night. By morning, I'm sure if this is his doing, he'll bore of it and let you go home."

I glance at Gabriel, who looks like he could murder someone. He eventually sighs and gestures in the direction of the cottage.

We all make our way back to the cottage. Rhiannon whispers to the trees and they make entwined branch awnings for the cryptids to camp under.

Gabriel draws close, whispering, "She's got an awful lot of control of her surroundings for only being one-sixteenth brownie."

I feel the same way.

Rhiannon returns to us. "You two can stay in my cottage. The rest of you can hunker down over there." To Aurora, she says. "Don't worry. Nothing nasty comes in this part. The princeling wouldn't allow it."

Aurora hugs her furry arms around herself as if fending off cold, but I can see in her eyes she's as afraid as the rest of us, excepting Rhiannon. "Is time here similar to back home?"

Rhiannon laughs, sobering only after she notices we don't join her. "Oh, you're serious?" Her mouth twists as if she's thinking of an explanation, but only comes up with, "In short, no."

Aurora frowns, I think. It's hard to see under all that fur. "Is there a way of knowing when morning will be? The light hasn't changed since we've arrived."

Rhiannon scowls as if in deep thought and then her face brightens. "When the dryad returns!"

With that we part ways with the cryptics and head into Rhiannon's cottage. She busies herself opening rations and cooking us beans and rice in a cauldron hanging over a wood fire. Since it's food from Earth, therefore safe, we join her in her meal.

I engage in conversation with Rhiannon, discovering that she's from a Baltimore coven. She tells me she's learned all her spell work through oral tradition. I find that impressive. Gabriel is silent the entire time, scowling.

"He excels at brooding for extended periods," Rhiannon remarks as if 'he' isn't there.

I giggle.

Gabriel grins, but his wariness doesn't leave his eyes.

Eventually Rhiannon tires. She gives us a blanket to sleep on before settling on her cot. She's snoring before we can even make a bed.

Gabriel lays the blanket out, props himself against the wall, and pats for me to sit next to him. I do so.

"You can rest your head on me. I'll watch over you," he whispers.

I arch an eyebrow. "You're not going to sleep?"

"I—I was in the Great War," he sighs. "I have too many enemies here to sleep."

I know the war he's referring to and it's not the one on Earth. It's much more ancient by Earth standards. "Exactly how old are you?"

He twists my ponytail around his finger. "I don't know. Angels take a long time to mature and time is different in Heaven. I served at the very end of the war...I did things for the Anocracy I believed in then that I don't now, but the fae will not see it that way. Sleep Miriam. I'll wake you if there's trouble."

I rest my head on his bare chest, closing my eyes and inhaling his scent. He strokes my back, my head. Although I'm afraid to sleep here with my unknown parentage, I'm somehow too exhausted to care. His lips pressing against my crown is the last thing I'm aware of before I drift off.

28

Something nudges my shoulder. I roll over. "Just give me five more minutes, Jada."

"Tati, aich larro," a deep, unfamiliar voice replies.

My eyes flutter open. I'm in the middle of a garden, on a bed of flowers softer than a down mattress. More flowers are woven into a blanket covering me. Most importantly, a black boot rests next to my pillow. I follow the black boot up a black leather-covered leg. Something that looks like writing and glows green covers the boot and the leather getup the bronze-skinned fae is wearing.

When I say that the fae is bronze, I don't mean he's brown. His skin has the appearance of burnished metal. His black hair, a curtain of silk, shimmers like a starless night. Black horns curve from each temple, reminding me slightly of His Creepiness. Preternaturally gold eyes stare back down at me, curious. He says something in a questioning tone. The melodic language is somehow familiar, though I can't understand a word of it. He smiles, bearing fangs. The fae is gorgeous, prettier than any angel or demon...and more terrifying.

My heart races, because I don't know if he's smiling or if he's showing off what he'll use to puncture my skin and drink my blood. I scoot away. My gaze dashes around, searching for ways to escape.

He holds up his hands like he means me no harm and says something in a soothing voice, ending it with "Tati."

The pet form of my name. My *real* name.

I shake my head and try to calm myself. "You know me? Do you speak English?"

"I do." Gold eyes with dark lashes sweep over the length of me, taking their sweet time. When their gaze meets my eyes, a wicked grin touches their lips. "I said, 'Very interesting way to return to me, Tati.'"

I blink. "Return to you?"

The grin falters. "Why else would you be *here*?" He indicates where I lay with a gesture.

"I don't know. I fell asleep in Rhiannon's cottage and woke here. Where is here and how do you know my name?"

Confusion limns his fine features. He squats down to get at my level. "You should know whose faerie you're in and who *I* am, too. Is it that I've changed so much? You have." His gaze sweeps over my body again. "You've grown taller and fatter, but I recognized you."

I scowl. "Not okay, buddy."

His eyebrows, thick, black slashes, furrow. Genuine curiosity fills his tone when he asks, "Why are you insulted?"

"Where I live people use 'fat' as an insult."

"What an odd notion to insult prosperity!" His indignation is real. So is the look in his eyes as he gives me a once over *again*. "Perhaps they're jealous of your ample bosoms and shapely—"

I held up a hand. "That's enough."

"I know that I look different than when we were young, but you truly don't recognize me?"

I spread my hands. "I'm sorry. I don't." A thought occurs. "If you know me, then perhaps you know who put the geas on my light?"

He nods, then glances over his shoulder. "I have an idea. What troubles me is that you do not. Have you no memory of your years before you left your people?"

I shake my head. I'm more confused than when this conversation began. I know I forgot most of my childhood, but I've always thought that was the lasting side-effects of angel dust overuse. My mother hates fae. Is this why?

He grimaces. "This is troubling."

Indeed.

"Who are you?"

"For now, you may call me Phyr, P-h-y-r in your alphabet. It means warrior. Though I've been called many other names in human tongues, Phouka my least favorite." He makes a sweeping motion gaze settling in the distance. "I am prince of all that you see. Not much, thanks to the angels." Bitterness curves his lips to a grimace, and then his face shifts back to mildly curious so quickly I might have imagined the bitterness. "You truly didn't mean to come here?"

I shake my head. "I came to a faerie to investigate why some cryptids went missing. I found them, but the dryad who ferries the river disappeared. I fell asleep in a cottage and ended up here—what the hell?" I look down. I'm not only *not* in my clothes, I'm in a diaphanous gown. My nipples are showing, and goddess knows what else would be apparent if I weren't covered in flowers.

He rolls his eyes, muttering something about meddling fae. "I apologize. Some well-meaning, but socially inept matchmakers brought you here, it seems. I should have known better. You're wearing my sibling's dress." His gaze sweeps over my head and shoulders. He rolls his eyes dramatically. "The flowers in your hair were a bit overkill in symbology, even for them."

He offers a gloved hand.

Before I take it, I say, "Wait. Do you know who put this geas on my light?"

"I do." He glances over my shoulder as if expecting someone to be watching. "Well, I can assume. Only your father could have and lived to tell about it."

"Do you know my father," I ask, hope and dread welling in my chest in an awful combination.

"I do," he replies, eyeing me as if I'm daft to ask that.

"I'd like to meet him. Could you take me to him?"

Phyr grows so still it's hard to tell if he's still breathing. When he finally speaks, his words are devoid of the teasing tone he's used thus far. "If you have no memory of him, and he's bound you from your full potential, you may be asking me to forfeit my life."

I wave my hands. "I wouldn't ask you to risk your life. Just tell me how to get to him. I won't say a word about your part in it."

The fae looks as if he's about to agree to my terms but then shakes his head. "I should not meddle in his affairs. I'll take you back to wherever you came from, then you go return to your home. It's safest for all."

I take his offered hand and we're standing face to face. I don't let go and pull him to me when he tries to draw away. "Please. I've made a powerful enemy. I need the light to defend myself and my daughter."

"You're a mother," Phyr whispers, no small amount of wonder in his tone. Hope lights his eyes. "Is the child here? I would like to see the young one before you leave again."

Technically, if my father is indeed fae, she's only a quarter fae. Given Rhiannon lives here as one-sixteenth brownie, fae seem to claim all their kind. "No. She's safe on Earth."

His disappointment is palpable. "It's been so long since I've seen a young fae. Halflings are impossible now. No fae dare risk Earth."

I feel sorry for him, I do, but my need presses me to ask, "Will you tell me how to find my father?"

He broods on the decision for a few moments before he replies, "I will deliver word that you seek him. Perhaps that will move him to seek you out. Who is the owner of the cottage who offered you lodging?"

"Rhiannon?"

"Ah, the refugee. She knows nothing of her brownie heritage, but she's fae. That's enough for me to permit her to stay," Phyr says, offering me his arm with a smile. "Shall we?"

As I take his arm, I get a glimpse of a shimmering castle in the distance. Even at a distance, I can see the marvelous structure is something out of fairytale. "Whoa. Do you live there?"

Something flickers his eyes, there and gone. He smiles ruefully. "Yes."

He slices through the air with a hand, reminding me of the way I make a cache, and then he takes a step forward, taking me along with him. My skin feels tight and vertigo dizzies me as we step through the interstitial space called the null into the backyard of Rhiannon's cottage.

The tension in the air is thick. Gabriel and Rhiannon argue, their shouting so loud their words are intelligible. Aurora stands in the middle, a physical barrier. The other cryptids group together away from the argument, cowering.

"What's going on?" I ask.

Heads whip in our direction just as I let go of Phyr's arm.

"Miriam!" Gabriel cries, his wings unfurling at the sight of me, and then his gaze narrows on Phyr. He charges the fae, an inhuman growl surging from his throat.

At the same time, I hear the whine of metal scraping against leather. Sword in hand, Phyr takes an offensive stance. The blade of the sword blazes with brilliant green light.

I hold up my hands, placing myself bodily between Gabriel and Phyr. "Stop! He's a friend."

Gabriel stops short, his eyes glowing with angelic light. Confusion paints his features. "He kidnapped you." His face pleads with mine to understand—what? That I should let him pass and kill Phyr? "You don't know him," he adds in a calm tone, hand raised slightly as if speaking to a skittish animal. "You didn't even know you were fae until recently. He's manipulating your mind to distort reality."

"Ignorant nephil," Phyr retorts, the sneer in his voice apparent. "So quick to violence. So quick to vilify my people. Mind tricks don't work on fae or halflings."

"It's true," Rhiannon provides. "Some of the fae here tried to mind hump me when I first came. Even my tiny bit of fae blood protects me."

"Trust me, if he tried to control me, he did a piss poor job of it," I say, glancing over my shoulder to see Phyr still has his sword drawn. "Can you put that thing away?"

"Not as long as he trespasses on *my* faerie, accusing me of misdeeds toward *my* people," Phyr snarls, because of course he does. Why be reasonable when you can be stubborn?

Gabriel lifts his chin, because of course he can't be the better of the two, either. "I'm here investigating a crime committed in my territory by your people." He gestures to Rhiannon.

Planting her fists on her hips, the rock witch cries, "Hey! That's not true. I'm only one-sixteenth brownie, not a highborn fae like these two. You know what? I'm the real victim in all of this. These cryptids tried to kidnap me. Then you and this witch worked with a siren to trap me, then forced me to give up my prisoners and the apples with your big muscle-y threats about being an archangel. This is my turf you're all on." She wags a dirty finger in Phyr's direction. "Even you, Prince Phyr. You said this bit of the faerie was mine for as long as I liked."

Phyr smiles. "My apologies. Would you like me to execute the angel for trespassing?"

I whirl on him and get so close our noses are almost touching. Anger and frustration at this ridiculous situation make me not care about getting on the bad side of a fae with a giant magical sword. "You will not hurt my friend."

Because Phyr is taller than me, he looks down his nose. His imperious glare softens. "I would let him tear through me just so you could see his true nature is to kill and oppress anything or anyone who freely have what his kind must take. I drew my sword for *your* sake, not mine."

"Bullshit," Gabriel shouts behind me, *not helping.*

"Fae can't lie," I say without turning around.

Phyr's gaze doesn't leave my face. He says in lilting English, "Tell him to swear to do you no harm, no matter what truths you may uncover about yourself, and I'll gladly sheath my sword to prove it is you I protect."

I turn to Gabriel, pleading with my eyes.

At that, the archangel deflates. "I swear I'll do Miriam no harm."

Phyr shakes his head. "Not good enough. Say, no matter what."

"Fuck." Gabriel throws up his arms. "Of course, no matter what!"

The fae princeling eyes the nephil for a moment, assessing. Finally, he sheaths his sword. Phyr smiles at me in a way that's much more familiar than he's been thus far. "I find it intriguing you call him friend but haven't given him your name."

I cut the fae a glare. "I changed my name years ago to protect myself. Please use Miriam."

Phyr wrinkles his nose and says in teasing tone, "Miriam doesn't suit you."

"It's not up to you to decide."

He smiles, blue eyes twinkling. "No. It is not."

"So, who is Miriam's father," Gabriel asks.

"None of your business," Phyr replies not taking his eyes off me. "If I'm going to deliver your message to your father, Miriam. You shouldn't tarry here. You have a daughter to return to." He reaches out his hand, slicing through reality.

Gabriel gapes. "You're a planeswalker."

"One of the last, thanks to you," Phyr says, with a sardonic grin. He gestures. "Go on, nephil, take your friends home. Miriam, you go last, there's something I want to tell you in private."

Gabriel motions for Aurora, they make a quiet exchange out of earshot. She and the cryptids go first. Aurora comes back. "It worked."

Gabriel picks up the chest of apples. His gaze passes between Phyr and I, something ugly fills his eyes. Jealousy. Why? I don't even know this fae.

"I'll be right there," I promise, not knowing if it were true but feeling it is.

"I will not hold her here against her will," Phyr adds.

Gabriel gives Phyr a final glare before going through.

"That's my cue to go inside," Rhiannon says, backing into her house.

"Would you like to stay with me?" I offer.

She shakes her head. "No, thanks. I don't like your boyfriend."

"Boyfriend," Phyr says, chuckling. He produces a silver hand mirror seemingly out of thin air. He offers it to me. "Here. I'll be in contact."

"I don't need a mirror."

He chuckles softly. "It's a magic mirror. We'll be able to communicate at any time. Hide its existence from humans." He rolls his eyes. "They cause all sorts of trouble with these things."

Before I can walk through the never door he's made, Phyr takes my hand and draws me close, whispering, "I saw into the nephil's mind. He has ambitions that are rather interesting and might prove useful as an ally to you. Use him for your needs, but don't trust him and for the Danu's sake, don't fall in love with him. He sees a future with you *serving* him as his mate, not as he equal."

"Good to know," I say and mean it.

Phyr slowly frees my hand, backing away with a grin. "If I don't contact you, your father has killed me, and you should watch for fae assassins."

On that cheery note, I leave.

29

The time that passed between when Gabriel crossed and the moment I came through must have been a while, because more vehicles and more shifters are present—at least, I assume they're shifters by the way they hang onto Gabriel's every word as he speaks to the group of people gathered around him. The cryptids, Princess, and Aurora are missing. Leilani, Cian, Roxy have returned, accompanied by Jada.

My stomach drops. Phyr kept me longer than a few minutes.

I clear my throat and wave. "Hey! Looking for me?"

Gabriel's head lifts, relief washing over his features. Jada pushes her way out of the group of shifters, running to me. Her arms wrap around me. She throws her weight into the kind of bear hug she gave when she was little. Caught off guard, I stumble back a step.

Tears stain her face and she's sobbing so hard she can't speak. "We—couldn't get." She buries her face in my shoulder slobbering on me.

"Only moments passed for me," I say to her and to Gabriel, who broke from the shifters. "How long for you guys?"

"Roughly ten hours, Gabriel replies. "I tried to come back for you, but the portal pushed me back out. We all tried it. We couldn't locate the never door, not even Cian." He tilts his head in the Leprechaun's direction. "The prince closed all access."

I glance over my shoulder. "Rhiannon has no way back."

"That false god is a planeswalker," Gabriel replies, face hard. "He can create a door to anywhere in the multiverse she wants to go, including your house.".

The warning is meant to scare me, but it doesn't. I trust Phyr. I don't know why, but something deep and intuitive as my very light trusts him. "He's going to contact my father for me."

Jada pulls away. "My grandfather is alive?"

"I think so, sweetie." I smile, it falters at the next thought. "I don't know if I want you to know him. He doesn't sound pleasant."

Gabriel's gaze dips to the mirror still clutched in my hand. A muscle in his cheek feathers, but he makes no comment.

Lucinda approaches. She asks the one question no one has. "You good?"

"It was just a couple minutes for me."

"Makes sense. Time passes differently on other worlds." She shakes her head. "That's not what I meant, though. What was it like to talk to your other parents' people for the first time?"

"It was a little overwhelming meeting someone who knew me, but I don't remember," I admit.

Her gaze takes all of me in. "Looks like they treated you like a fae princess, flower crown, snazzy dress, and all."

I touch the top of my head and flowers had been worn into a crown.

Jada's gaze passes between Gabriel, Lucinda, and me. "Can we go home?"

I nod and squeeze her. "I'd like that."

"Go on to the car. I'll be right there," Gabriel says, then leaves us to speak to all of the shifters.

"Glad you're okay!" Leilani says with a wave. Cian stares, mouth gaping, and then lowers his head as if in deference. Leilani rolls her eyes and steers him toward their truck.

"I'll be there in a sec," Lucinda calls over her shoulder to the couple. She takes my arm while Jada and Roxy head for the SUV.

Roxy touches my hair as she passes by. "You look like one of those fae core e-girls. All you need is the pointy ears."

"What I need is a sweater," I reply, shivering.

Lucinda takes off her jacket. "Shit. I'm surprised Gabriel didn't offer his."

Frankly, I am too. I thank her and slip the fleece on. I'm not completely warm, but my teeth stop chattering.

She draws close and speaks in a low voice, "*He* wanted to go in claws and fangs bared to get *his* potential mate. The council had to veto an all-out assault on a faerie."

I sigh. "I'm glad you vetoed. An assault would only keep me from ever getting this geas removed." My unbound light is my only hope to fighting back if Velja tries to whisk me away.

Lucinda hums her agreement. "That's what I said. I figured if you stayed behind, you did so for a reason. This territory doesn't need a war with the fae when we got Hell's attention."

I shiver at that. Both would be my fault.

"When we tried the never door and Gabriel realized it was sealed, he lost it." She ran her hand over my hair. "Now I see why. Ancient enemy of Gabriel's trying to seduce his new girlfriend. Looks like that fae prince wanted to make you their concubine or bride or something."

"There was no seduction involved," I say, remembering the booted toe waking me. "He's apparently an old friend and promised to tell my father I'm looking for him."

Lucinda's eyes drift over my half-covered dress. "After putting you in a see-through gown. Uh huh." She glances at her car. "I better go. The lovebirds want to leave. It's been hard on Cian."

GABRIEL SAYS nothing when he gets in the SUV except to ask if I'd like some heat. I accept. The girls doze off after a few moments. Their sleep noises the only sound.

"The fae gave you that mirror?"

"Um, yeah. I'm not dumb enough to steal from one of them."

He flicks the bar for the turn signal, changing lanes. Traffic is heavier than when we came, the light is fading. "I need you to tell me everything exactly as you remember it."

I recount how I woke up and the conversation with Phyr. I see no harm in it. "What gets me is that I never ever thought about the fact I can't remember my childhood. If I try to remember, to reach to my earlier years, I feel pain like when I tried to use more light than the geas allows."

"If your father went to such lengths, he doesn't want you to remember." Gabriel sighs.

I agree, but I want to know why. Does he know about the grimoires and the spell His Creepiness wanted me to power? Why would an Earth-banished fae care about what happened to this world? What is his stake? Why did my mother want me to hate fae? So many questions and nobody to answer them.

"I want to hate Phyr. He kept you to show me that he can take you and do whatever he pleases, and there's nothing I can do about it." Gabriel grips the steering wheel, knuckles whitening. "He's risking his life to help you get your light back. For that, I'm grateful."

"You immediately assumed he was with me for nefarious reasons. I'm obviously unharmed. Why?"

He swipes a hand over his face and flicks the windshield wipers on. The rain has started to pour and the light of day is fading into darkness. "You were in that dress and beautiful...and he was...you got to admit that Phyr is absolutely gorgeous."

He thought Phyr was attractive. "You were jealous?"

"I was concerned." He blows out his breath. "I thought he'd kidnapped you, played mind games with you and then was going to use you as a tool against me. The Miriam I know wouldn't hold with someone dressing them up like a fae bonding ceremony doll."

I blink. "A what?"

"He made every effort to make it look like you'd bonded, you know—fae have an equivalent to shifter mate-bonding, but your scent isn't different. You barely smell like him at all."

"Fae can't lie so they speak in double talk, but he was very clear that he thought I'd come to him."

"Fae can lie, Miriam. It's simply painful for them. You know that."

"Well, he isn't interested in mating with me because he didn't take the bait. When I was out cold, he didn't kiss me awake like in a fairy tale. He nudged sleeping beauty with a boot and told me to get up."

Gabriel laughs. "Really? Like he was afraid to touch you lest he be besmirched?"

"Yeah." I laugh too. It *was* funny. "It must have been strange to have a childhood friend disappear and then just show up like that ready to get it on. No wonder he was suspicious of why I was there."

"Are you sure he truly knew you as a child. He could have gleaned it from your head. Fae are telepaths."

"I don't associate with the name he called me," I reply, looking out the window. "She died in Hell a long time ago so I could be free."

Gabriel reaches over and clasps my hand.

"I never want to be second to someone's ambition again, Gabriel. I was second to you-know-who." Softer, I add, "Second to Rafael's godhood."

He takes his eyes off the road long enough to give me an empathetic look. "My only goal is to make this territory a haven for all supes, that includes witches."

"I'm half fae." I hold up the mirror, the words and the incident new and strange. "I need them."

His jaw tightens and so does his grip on my hand. "I know and they need you, don't let them make you think otherwise." He gives me a pointed look before returning his eyes to the road. "You don't know what they're like, but I do. He isn't helping you out of the goodness of his heart. His actions demonstrated he considers you as his potential mate."

Funny. He said the same about you.

As if reading my thoughts, Gabriel says, "The difference between shifters and fae is that fae don't mate for love. He wants children with you."

I wrinkle my nose. "I'm forty-three. A little late for that."

"Um," Gabriel clears his throat. "You're half-fae, not just a little. The possibility isn't off the table. If you take after your fae side, you have centuries before you'll go through menopause."

I have a distinct feeling he wants me to know for a reason, but I'm too chicken to ask. "How long do shifters live?"

"Not much longer than a human lifespan."

"You've already lived longer than a human life-span?"

He swallows hard. "Yes. I don't know how old I am, so please, don't ask." A pained expression passes over his face and his lip quivers as he says, "I will outlive my pack. I will outlive most of the supes in my territory. I think about it a lot. I wish I had when I was younger..."

Kirsten, who was a full shifter, would grow old and die like a human. I now understood why Gabriel hadn't executed her. She'd eventually die, her lifespan a blip in long-lived eyes.

"Do you know how long fae halflings live?"

A faint smile touches his lips. "Some halflings are as immortal as the fae and just as powerful when they come into their power. Does that scare you?" He glances in my direction.

"No."

"It makes the thought of us even more appealing to me. I want something that will last, someone who could help me make real change, the kind that takes time."

Phyr's warning echoes in my head. "You've thought about all of this?"

"Ever since I learned you were a halfling," he admits, pulling off the highway and onto the street that leads into my neighborhood.

"Oh."

I haven't had time to consider a future with Gabriel, I'd been too busy thinking about protecting myself and Jada from Velja, and more importantly, His Creepiness. If I thought about Gabriel, it usually involved the spicier moments between us.

"I told the pack I want to court you, but we can take that courtship as slow as we want. Just know, you might face a few challenges."

"I don't have time for challenges. I have to figure out how to break my geas."

"Should I tell them we're just friends?"

I blow out my breath. "I don't know. I haven't had to announce intentions before. It seems odd to me."

I'd committed to Rafael as a front, but at heart, I'm still a witch, who was raised to believe love was freely given and no one's business but the couple. This mate for life business bothers me.

Gabriel pulls into the end of the driveway. I wake up Jada. She wipes the drool from her chin and disentangles herself from the still sleeping Roxy.

I get out at the same time she does. Gabriel follows.

The pixies flit from plant by plant, taking care of the garden after dark. They welcome Jada as she trudges ahead to the house. She gives them a tired wave, entering through the garage after using the keypad to open the door.

I hover next to the SUV. "Want to come in?"

Gabriel rests a hand on the SUV, propping himself. His gaze lingers on the diaphanous dress the faeries set me up in before settling on my eyes. "Yes." Then his gaze moves to the car. His sigh is heavy with reluctance. "I need to take Roxy home. You look like you could use some sleep."

I nod, feeling the weight of all the events draining me. "I could."

Suddenly I'm enveloped in Gabriel's arms in a bear hug. He buries his face in my hair, inhaling. "After all you've been through to escape Lucifer, I was terrified that you were imprisoned against your will. Again. I lost it. No one deserves to be someone's object."

Hearing that it wasn't territorial claims, and that he'd been truly afraid I'd lost my freedom, takes some of my misgivings away.

The scruff of his five o'clock shadow scrapes against my cheek as he slowly slides his face against mine. His mouth covers my lips. His kiss is a simple press and release but makes me weak in the knees all the same.

Gaze latched onto mine, he says, "You know I don't want to go, right?"

"I'm getting the distinct impression." I cup his cheek, seeing the exhaustion in his eyes for the first time. "You should get some rest yourself."

30

Jada taps her pencil on her notepad, looking out the window instead of translating the spell. The cool thing about demigods is that they learn at an accelerated rate. Wisdom and gaining knowledge quickly are virtues my daughter possesses.

"Why don't witches like to be part of the supe community?" she asks.

"Outside of the Pacific Northwest, there's really not much of a community. They all stick to themselves. Mr. Crowfoot is fostering something different here."

"Imagine that kind of change everywhere. We wouldn't have to care about angels or demons."

"That requires the rest of the archangels to be as lenient as Mr. Crowfoot or to take their hands out of supe business."

"Roxy thinks shifters should stop listening to angels. She says there are other shifters who feel that way."

"Her mom one of them?" I ask casually, but I suspect I'm on the money with the guess.

"I should get back to this," Jada hedges, suddenly interested in her work.

I go back to my grimoire on curse breaking. I'd found nothing so far that could break a fae geas. Since I stole very specific grimoires for the big combo spell, I found very little on fae, other than they were good to breed with for more power. This contradicted everything my mother had taught me. Her betrayal stung.

The same question keeps coming up in my mind. *Was she protecting me from my father? Or did she want to create a bias in me because she had her own intentions for me?* Now that I have a daughter of my own, I question so much about the way she raised me. The way she and the coven all thought it was a good idea to leave me, a teenager, by myself in the woods, telling me I could not leave until I summoned a demon. She'd pretended to be surprised but pleased when I told her I'd summoned the devil himself. Her eyes shone with pride when I showed my apple.

Everyone treated me like any other witch up until that point. After that, I got deferential treatment. They must have known he was looking for a witch with fae blood. They must have known the whole time what kind of a witch he was seeking. Was I created for the coven's sake? Did my father glean it from my mother's head and protect me with no memory of him, this geas?

Hurt and anger boil inside me. I wipe the tears with the back of my hand.

Jada's big brown eyes fill with concern. "Mami, I know that the devil wants these books. Roxy told me all about the demon that wants you to leave or they'll kill you. I'll go, if you're staying for me."

I want to choke Gabriel for sharing this with his daughter, but I should have told Jada myself. I'd grown so used to keeping the truth about me secret from her, I'd forgotten she is both old enough to handle it and deserves to know everything. "I'm staying for me and you. This is our home. These grimoires are our coven's legacy. Why should we run because some damned angel wants them?"

"I was thinking. Maybe if papi ascended to godhood, he could hear me the way his mami could hear him. I could try praying to him to protect us."

My gut churns. I am careful to keep my tone conversational and face neutral. "Have you tried praying to him?"

She plays with a corner of her notebook. "This is different. I think he'll want to know about this."

"He knew who I was hiding from and the danger I was in. If he was in a state of understanding our situation, I have no doubt that your father would come to our aid." The pain of the lie shudders through me. I bear it, gripping my grimoire. Raf left me, knowing damned well without his protection, I was open to attack.

"You can handle it, Miriam. You're stronger than you think. Find the strength inside you."

Had Raf somehow known I had the geas? He'd never talked to me about it and I never talked to him about it because it was such a source of pain with my last relationship.

"I know what you're thinking," Jada says, brows furrowed. "Do you think papi is energy now, not a sentient person with his human feelings...like when you were sick?"

I cringe inwardly at her casual reference to my mental breakdown after Raf's ascension. "That's how he explained it to me. It's a transitionary period."

"Huh. You never said that before."

"I wasn't articulate when I was grieving."

She chews on her bottom lip. "Can I still try to pray to him?"

Forcing a smile, I say, "Of course. You shouldn't deny yourself communication with your father. Perhaps he can just listen, even if he's not at a state where he can help."

A timer goes off on my phone. "Ah, the quiche is done. You want to keep working on that spell or help me prep for the brunch?"

She closes her notebook. "I'll help. I can't wait to see Tomi. Roxy is the best, all the supes are. I just want some normal kid talk for a change."

I understand exactly what she means. I didn't simply settle on this life. I enjoyed my friends and my role on the PTSA. After all the excitement of the past few weeks, I'm looking forward to the normalcy of this brunch.

We go downstairs and I set up the food in the dining room while Jada sets the table for eight. Shawn and Micah have a teenager named Tomi, an elementary school kid named Jennifer, and twin babies named Rashad and Keisha.

The doorbell rings. I welcome them and take Rashad, who's reaching for me, from Micah. We all gather in the dining room. At first, it's all about getting the kids settled and serving everyone food.

"You've outdone yourself," Micah exclaims before shoveling another forkful of quiche into his mouth. Keisha tries to grab at the fork with one hand even though she's holding a muffin in her other hand.

We all laugh.

"I think you should open a bakery," Shawn agrees.

A thought I'd had myself but never went through with, because I didn't want to be scared of who might pop into the shop. "I'd have to be in control of my finances to do that." I take a sip of my mimosa, eyes on Shawn.

Micha shifts uncomfortably, face reddening.

"Oh!" Shawn says, smiling as he takes a card out of his jacket pocket. "I've signed everything over back to you. This is the person you'll need to speak to about your trust. You can do whatever you like with it. Keep everything as is. Sell all the stocks and invest in a bakery if you want." His smile is broad, too broad.

I shake my head. I'm imagining his smile is fake and the eagerness in his eyes hold something else.

"Easy as that," I say, a queasy sensation disturbing what should be a happy moment. "It's all mine now."

Shawn sighs. "It was always yours. I simply managed it for you, so you didn't have to think about it. So, now that you are thinking about what to do with that money, I've seen some nice properties downtown. Let me know if you want to tour them, and I'll hook you up with a commercial real estate agent who owes me one."

The idea is appealing. "I'll have to mull it over, maybe talk to Lucinda about what it would take to open something up."

"You're just trying to get these muffins every day," Micah teases.

"Short of divorcing you and marrying Miriam, it's the only way I see gaining a dad bod you think is so sexy." He winks.

Micah's freckled cheeks blush a deep crimson.

Sometimes they acted like a young couple in the early stages of a relationship, but they bought the house behind us only a few years after Raf and I bought ours.

"How long have you guys been together again?" I ask, realizing I never had before. I'd hoped if I didn't ask too many questions about their past, they wouldn't ask too many about mine. It had worked, but left holes in my knowledge of my friends.

"I was barely eighteen when Shawn saved me. I'd been in a bad accident, lost my memory, and ended up on the streets. Shawn helped me get clean, get into community college, then I transferred to UW where I got my teaching degree. We were friends all that time, Shawn mentoring me." He makes goo-goo eyes at his husband that is just too cute. "We *got together* when I graduated and started teaching."

Micah tells the whole story while feeding grabby Keisha some of his fruit. Shawn smiles at his husband with so much reciprocated love in his eyes, I can't help but be a bit envious. I miss having that kind of intimacy.

Jada and Tomi go upstairs to hang out. Little Jennifer asks if she can be excused to ride her bike. Apparently, she's brought it with her and left it out front.

"Make sure you buckle your helmet," Shawn lectures. "No short-cuts on safety."

She gives him a smile missing front teeth, crinkling her freckled nose. "Yes, daddy."

"I'll clean up the kids while you two talk baskets," Micah says, rising and taking little Rashad from me.

Shawn and I watch him leave. "I think this silent auction is a golden opportunity to make connections in the business community. Your baskets will show off your skills and get you out of the house and out there again in the real world."

I rear my head. "What world do you think I live in, Shawn?"

He leans forward, licking his lips. "Look, you're just coming out of your shell. I'm saying that volunteering for something like this is the perfect opportunity to meet more people than other moms and dads."

I'd expect Chad to talk to me this way, but not Shawn. "Your husband is a stay-at-home dad."

"He's in a stable relationship and plans to get re-certified as a teacher when the twins hit preschool age. Raf told me that you only had a homeschool education, but you're obviously a wiz at baking and running the PTSA."

"Isn't the trust set up in a way that I'm comfortable for life?" I really want to know why he's pushing this bakery thing.

Shawn shakes his head. "That's not my point. Jada's going to be leaving for college next fall. She's already set up. Why, oh why, would you want to sit in your house all day or putter around the garden like a retiree? You're young and beautiful. You could have a life again. I bet you were something else when you were younger. Now's the perfect opportunity to move on. Take some risks. A new business would be the way to open up a whole new world."

Given the last twenty-four hours, I want to laugh in his face. I'd been to not only a different planet but a different universe. I have a fae prince delivering a message for me at his peril. I'm on the supernatural council of the Pacific Northwest. A friggin' archangel wants to court me. I have the devil himself trying to get me to bring on Armageddon. This man wants me to bake muffins for locals and calls it taking risks because he knows nothing of my life, yet feels he knows everything.

"I'll consider your proposal," I reply.

31

I didn't have a typical teenage experience of someone my age, waiting by a phone for a romantic partner to call me. His Creepiness was super indulgent because he was grooming teenaged me. Raf and I were friends, inseparable from the moment we met until he ascended. So, I didn't know what it felt like to be given the run-around. I only knew the unease of a middle-aged wife waiting for this or that oncologist to deliver test results, carrying my cell with me everywhere.

Waiting for Phyr to contact me feels more like the teenaged thing than the oncologist thing, and that has me questioning why. I keep the mirror handy everywhere I go, waiting for it to do—I don't know what. He hadn't given me instructions on how to use it.

I get out the hedge shears from the tool storage behind my house. The wisteria growing on the arbor needs trimming before it takes over the fence between my garden and the Johnson's yard, or makes its way to choke out the rest of the garden surrounding the arbor. Wisteria looks beautiful and gives off a divine scent, but the vines can do a lot of damage unchecked. I've heard cases of wisteria ruining the exterior of houses, finding cracks and crevices to creep into and deteriorate further, and even destroying the foundation with its roots. Gardening is filled with good lessons in staying diligent about your boundaries. Even the innocuous can become insidious if you lower your defenses and let things slip between the cracks.

Besides backyard real and philosophical battles, I also need to take my mind off everything. Delving into physical activity outdoors with plants does the trick.

As I cut the wayward vines, I let thoughts enter my mind. The first thing that pops in there, oddly, are Chad and Shawn's remarks. Chad always had to say "some of us have jobs to get to" at PTSA meetings —*snip, snip, snip*—as if paid labor has some sort of understood value that is greater than the unpaid labor stay-at-home parents do.

Snip, snip, snip—I get into a rhythm of the work.

According to Chad and Shawn's world view, making a company profits is the only way you can contribute to a society.

Snip, snip, snip.

That mindset devalues everyone who isn't able to do that. What if I were so mentally ill or disabled that I couldn't work? Do I lose value as a person? That sort of thinking led ancient humans to abandon babies on hillsides.

Snip, snip, snip.

Why does Shawn want me to open a bakery so badly? He knows that Raf set me up for life. Does he want me to meet and impress people like Chad and him? Does he think owning a business will make me more appealing in their eyes than a comfortable widow?

I rake all the trimmed vines into a pile and then load them into a yard waste bin.

Shawn never once asked if *I* wanted to meet people who felt like that. What could I possibly have in common with them? I would never get romantically involved with anyone outside the supe community. I could always start a business and fit into their world, but they would never fit into *my* world.

I pull the bin through the garden path, opening the gate to the front yard. After closing the gate behind me, I drag the bin to the curb. Brushing off my hands, I scan the neighborhood.

How many people live here, and not a single one of them saw the fight with the vampires because they were too wrapped up in their world: their phones, their computers, and whatnot inside. None of them looked outside. None of them saw me save Gabriel's life, all of their lives.

I shake my head, feeling sorry for them. I may not subscribe to their views but at least I recognize that they have one. Just because someone lives differently than the way others see fit, doesn't mean they don't have a valid life. It doesn't diminish their existence. When did self-worth start coming from employment?

Chad and Shawn can stick their opinion about how I live where the sun doesn't shine. I saved their lives, all of humanity really, simply by escaping my evil ex...my abuser.

A car pulls into the cul de sac, parking at the foot of my lawn, not in my driveway. Kirsten steps out of the vehicle. She's wearing classically chic pantsuit, sunglasses, and heels—I can't fathom why, since her husband Dave is old Seattle money wealthy. Her blond hair looks like she stepped out of a salon. She pushes up her sunglasses. "Can we talk?"

"I think we've said all we need to say to each other," I reply.

She shakes her head and rounds her car, still not quite on my property. "Look. I don't blame you for not wanting to speak to me. I messed up pretty bad."

Kirsten would mess up worse if she tried to walk past my wards with ill intent. She must not, because she steps onto the lawn before continuing, "I only ask for five minutes of your time."

"Okay." I say, hoping she's here to apologize. We've never been friends, but she's been to my house many times over the years. She's always been aloof, but so have I. Each had our own secrets to keep, I suppose. We are not friends, but we've always been polite to each other.

"I showed a shameless lack of self-control and let my wolf take over. I'm not a bad person, but the mate bond makes you crazy jealous. You have to know, it wasn't me doing that." Kirsten releases a shaky breath. "After Gabriel severed our bond, I realized how awful I was. I hadn't meant to hurt you."

"Could've fooled me."

She swallows hard. "Okay. I deserve that. I wanted to scare you. I thought if I showed you what we are, then you wouldn't want to be with him, but that was it. I wouldn't hurt you, not after you've been so good to Roxy."

"I don't think what you planned is any better than physically harming someone. If I hadn't been a witch, I could have been traumatized."

"I know. I know. I was just so jealous of you. No matter how well Gabby treated me, no matter how much I loved our family, being the alpha's mate, being the archangel's wife…it wasn't for me. I think I've always been a lone wolf, not a pack wolf. But, you're perfect for it with all your baking and mothering stuff. The pack will love you." Tears streak her cheeks. "I'm sorry about everything I said. The crush he always had on you wasn't because he lusted after someone else's wife or wanted to cheat on me. Gabby saw who he needed by his side in you. I love him enough to let him have that. If you two want to be together, I won't stand in your way…I hope you can eventually forgive me, and we can move forward."

"It must have taken a lot to come here and say this. Would you like to come in for some tea?" I half hope she says no.

Kirsten shakes her head. "I'd love to, but I have to meet Dave at the country club for lunch. I just wanted to clear the air here."

I can forgive her, but I would not be close to her. Not after the way she behaved. "I think we can be civil to each other, but I don't think we can be friends, Kirsten."

"I understand. We're not exactly the same type to be friends," she tosses over her shoulder, getting into her car.

As she pulls away, the light sprites swarm from the back, frantically buzzing around me.

"What's going on?" I ask.

They form an arrow, pointing toward the back yard. Fearing it's Velja, I don't move right away. One bites me.

"Ow!" I rub my arm. "Okay. I get it. It's urgent."

I sprint to the gate, throwing it open, not knowing what danger faces me on the other side. Spells run through my mind. Ones I'd learned by rote for self-defense. A stasis spell might lock the demon in place until I could banish her.

Some sprites close and lock the gate behind me. Others follow me into the garden, urging me to run faster. Some fly ahead, forming an arrow which points to table and chairs under the arbor.

I sigh with relief. The relief is short-lived, replaced by anxiousness about what news Phyr has to deliver. I dash to the table where I'd set the magic mirror. It emits an eerie glow.

I grasp the handle with a trembling hand. The reflective side is face down. I turn the handle slowly to reveal the looking glass. At first, all I see is my reflection. I hastily pick a few leaves out of my French braids. The glass ripples before Phyr's face appears.

"Your father wishes to meet you." His tone is neutral. His features could be carved out of stone for all the emotion they reveal. Now the wry grin and flirtatious tone is gone, the difference is severe.

My gut flips. "When?"

The corner of his mouth quirks. "Given our realms don't function the same, when is a complicated question. How works better."

I roll my eyes. "Fine. How?"

"He said to open a door between your world and his faerie. He'll be waiting on the other side."

I shake my head. "I don't know how to do that…How do *you* open doors between realities?"

"I'm a planeswalker, Tati. I see the fabric of the multiverse and all the ways to step between the weave." His brow furrows as if he's concentrating. "My siblings learned how to make never doors, by making caches. Can you make one?"

"I can."

"Good. You could when we were young. At least you haven't lost all memory." He smiles in the familiar way that you do with an old friend.

I find myself smiling back, though I don't know why. "What does making a cache have to do with making a bridge between realms?"

"Instead of placing objects in the interstitial space, they put themselves inside and puncture through another reality's membrane—given you're half fae, therefore possibly mortal, I don't know if you'll survive without a path made by a planeswalker. There would be no air."

I might not survive if I fight a demon to stay where I am, let alone if His Creepiness finds out that I've deceived him and stole the grimoires with the spell he wants. Jada and I will have to live the rest of our lives on the run.

A thought occurs and I could smack myself for not asking before. "Could you make a path for me?"

His mouth twists into a grimace. "No."

"No?"

"I've been explicitly instructed not to bring you through. Your father wants you to do it." He sighs. "Call it a test of worthiness."

"Oh." So much disappointment fills that one word.

Something akin to empathy fills his amber eyes. "I must go now." He yawns. "The mirror itself is a connection from your world to where I am. It is taking a lot of my light to make this communication through the null, and I grow tired."

"I appreciate the help you've given and the risk you took for me," I say, because I have nothing else.

"You don't remember, but you were kind to me when you didn't have to be kind to anyone. Fae do not forget a kindness. I have every confidence you'll find your way, Tati. I'll await your arrival in your father's realm."

"Before you hang up—er—I mean go. Can I ask you a question?"

"You may." He grins, eyes dancing. "Whether I answer or not, is at my discretion."

There. The Phyr I met in his faerie is back. "Can I reach you through this mirror or is it one way?"

"I'm not sure if the little bit of your defensive power your father left you is enough to power magic like this from your world."

"Oh." I sigh. "Thank you."

"Don't despair, Tati." His eyebrows furrow, grin disappearing as if he's truly concerned about my predicament. "I will always help you."

He cuts off the connection and the mirror simply reflects my puzzled face.

Besides Lucinda herself, I'm the first to arrive at Lucinda's Café for the council meeting. When I walk into the café, Jada and Roxy are cleaning the machines. Lucinda is wiping down tables. Closing duties.

Jada smiles in my direction. "Hey, mami!"

Roxy too. She has started to warm up to me since Kirsten's visit and when everyone thought I went missing in a faerie. Gabriel had been tight-lipped with her about what happened. So the girls enjoyed my story about waking up.

I place my purse behind the bar where the girls' stash theirs. "Need a bit of help?"

Lucinda shakes her head. "Nope. Can the girls get you something?"

I smile. "I'm good. Just ate."

She nods and goes back to cleaning the tabletops. "So, you'll need the kitchen next week, right? Shawn said something about Sunday."

"Yeah. I hope."

"Take care of these, will you?" she asks the girls as she sets the towel and disinfectant spray on the bar.

Jada grabs it and heads to the back.

Lucinda takes a seat in an overstuffed chair, propping her feet on the coffee table. She indicates for me to take the opposite.

"What do you mean, I hope?"

"I should wait until the council gets here. I have news to share with everyone."

Her gaze shifts to the door briefly before she says, "I don't think we'll have much time for the news. Tonight's going to be pretty intense. Aurora and the cryptids' families are calling for their release with the claim that they didn't actually kidnap, nor had the intention to kidnap, the witch." She rolls her eyes. "The families are calling the cryptids the real victims here, and Aurora agrees. Technically, there is no proof the witch didn't spell the apples herself and fabricate the story."

Gabriel and I spoke very little since my return. He'd been too busy. I found it odd Lucinda knew more about this than I did since it was directly related to my grimoire library.

"Did Aurora share this?"

"I learned a little from her and a little from my sources," Lucinda admits.

I chuckle and lift an eyebrow. "Your sources?"

"I am an ambassador here, Miriam, but I still have a role in Persephone's siren army. I have a network of informants in the territory that keep a lookout for Zeus and the other Olympian horndogs. It's my job as ambassador to make sure they behave when they make forays into this world."

"I met Persephone and Hades once," I say. "They're much kinder than most of the Olympians I'd met."

Lucinda barks a laugh. "No way! You met the queen? I had to serve for—a very long time before I met her." She picks a piece of lint off her sweater. "I don't envy your time with the handsy Olympians."

My face heats at the memory of Ares, and my gut gets a little queasy thinking about things past me did for His Creepiness. Things I'd rather forget. "They're not all like that but some..."

"It was Apollo wasn't it? He's just like Zeus."

I look at my hands, regretting I mentioned anything. "No. I've never met either." Zeus didn't like the Angelic Anocracy, but the Olympians had a treaty with the angels, as most deities did, not wanting what happened to the Tuatha dé Danann happening to them. "Zeus wouldn't even deal with the devil directly, but Hera would."

"I like Hera. You know, it's strange," Lucinda muses. "We've known each other for so long yet know so little about our lives before we met."

"Isn't it like that for most people who move from one place to another?"

A wry smile curves her lips. "I don't think we're most people. Even among supes, I'm sure your experience is rare."

"I hear that he often grooms witches."

"I've heard so too, but the difference is that you got away," she replies.

We both grow quiet. How many witches had he gone through since I left?

I glance at the storefront. Through the glass I see Gabriel's SUV and Princess's motorcycle pull in the lot. Cian's truck follows.

Soon, the council is seated and we begin. Gabriel starts with the formality of giving Princess temporary alpha status. The air grows thick with the tension between Princess and Aurora, and Gabriel.

The three begin to debate whether it is fair to keep the cryptids under custody when we have no proof that they knew what the apples would do.

"I'm keeping them under protective custody until we have the demon."

"You're making my case," Aurora rebuts. "A demon isn't going to show up at a compound full of shifters and an archangel. Let the cryptids return to their families and put shifters on guard duty."

"It's not like some of them live in houses," Gabriel argues. "I refuse to put shifters on duty in the Pacific Northwest wilderness, exposed to the elements and to attacks, when they can more effectively protect the cryptids at my place. Your cousin and the others knew very well that dealing with a demon breaks Angelic Code, and they also knew that nothing good could come of a gift from Hell."

"My cousin said she didn't know anything. Are you calling her a liar?"

Cian scoffs. "I know you want to protect your kin, Aurora, but will you listen to yourself? When you say the cryptids didn't know that demons are cunning and dangerous, you expect us to believe that's anything but pure gobshite."

A low growl emits from Aurora's throat. Her glamour flickers.

Cian shifts in his chair.

"Easy now. Friends can disagree without violence," Leilani says to Aurora, but the Bigfoot has her eyes on Cian

Gabriel gives Aurora a hard stare in response. There's weight to that stare that has nothing to do with attitude and all to do with he's a powerful being controlling his temper. He hadn't even wanted to bring the cryptids back, likely expecting this on top of pressure from the other side. I'd pushed him.

"Aurora, are you forgetting that this council risked our lives to find your cousin and the others?" I ask. "Gabriel put a target on his back walking into his enemy's territory for them Don't you think that it's only fair we continue the investigation as this council sees fit?"

Aurora stops growling. "At least let the families visit the cryptids you have in holding."

After a long pause, Gabriel cedes, "Fine. However, they will have to make appointments with my chief of security." He nods to Princess.

This seems to placate Aurora. She'll be dealing with her girlfriend instead of Gabriel.

"The question is," Leilani pauses, gaze scanning the room, "How are we going to trap this demon?"

I raise my hand. "I have a solution. I can trap it but there's something I must do first."

"I want to go with you," Gabriel says after I finish relating my conversation with Phyr.

I shake my head. "I want to convince my father to remove the geas. How receptive do you think he'll be if I bring a nephil with me?"

A muscle feathers in his cheek, but he doesn't argue.

"I could go with you," Lucinda offers. "The fae and the Underworld have no quarrel, and I'm trained to navigate the interstitial space you'll have to cross."

"Thank you."

"I'm down to go," Leilani says, cheerfully as if we're planning a weekend getaway, not traversing the inter-workings of the multiverse. "My mother has nothing to do with the fae or Heaven or Hell. I can monitor your vitals and I'm great at negotiating. Are you coming to give us a bit of luck, boo bear?" She turns to Cian.

"I want to, love, but I fear the fae who created that geas wouldn't welcome a solitary Leprechaun. The Tuatha dé Danann don't appreciate my kind treating with the Angelic Anocracy to take a lesser role than full gods. I might hinder her case as much as Gabriel here, no offense, friend."

Gabriel holds up a hand. "None taken."

Aurora does not offer to come. I don't blame her reticence and don't take it personally. If I found my cousin caged like an animal and no one saw fit to question the decision, I wouldn't want to be among fae either.

33

Jada crosses her arms, refusing to get out of the car.

A horn blasts behind us and a volunteer traffic guard is urging me to pull forward.

We've had the conversation. She goes to school, and I go to meet my father. Gabriel will pick her up if Phyr doesn't bring me back at the same time I leave.

"Lucinda and Leilani are waiting for me."

"I'm supposed to take an algebra test today. How am I supposed to concentrate knowing you're on a dangerous quest?"

"What should I write in the excuse email? 'Please excuse Jada, I have to travel the multiverse to meet a powerful being, possibly a god, and this is causing her to lack focus. Don't worry. I have her hanging out with a pack of shapeshifters and an archangel so she'll have adult supervision.'"

The traffic monitor volunteer knocks on Jada's window. My sweetheart of a daughter shows how well I raised her and flips her off.

I roll down the window. "Give us a moment." Rolling it back up before the rightfully offended volunteer could respond. Cars start to circumvent mine.

"You could die." Jada's voice quavers on the word 'die.'

"That is not certain. What is certain is that I will be woefully under-armed to fight a demon if I don't have this geas taken off my light."

"Gabriel could smite any demon that comes around."

"And level every house in a three-block radius. Why do you think he didn't just blast the vamps? Smiting is a power meant to destroy cities or wipe out entire armies, not take out one demon at a time."

A tear slides down Jada's cheek. "I want to come, mami. I'm not a baby and I'm powerful. I want to protect you."

"I know you could, but that's not your job." I catch the shimmering tear with my finger, wiping it away. "I promise, I'll be back. I doubt my father would want to meet me only to kill me."

Jada puffs her cheeks, blowing out her breath. "If you're not home when school is out, I'm coming after you."

Before I can reply, she wrenches open the door and slams it behind her, joining the throng of students entering the building.

The traffic monitor motions for me to pull forward urgently.

I refrain from flipping the volunteer off, but oh, do I want to. Instead, I pull out, driving home.

Lucinda and Leilani are waiting on my porch when I park in my driveway.

"Jada wanted to come. Try telling a demigoddess she's just a kid and you've got my morning."

Lucinda and Leilani both laugh.

"I'm so glad Arianna takes after Rob," Lucinda says. "I couldn't take another siren in the house. Let alone a teenage siren."

I welcome them inside. "Wait in the kitchen. Feel free to make yourself at home. There's something I need upstairs."

I retrieve the gilded mirror from the grimoire library upstairs, rushing downstairs so I don't make them wait too long. I feel guilty that they had to stand around my porch waiting for me. Even more so because Lucinda hadn't sent a text saying they were waiting. Knowing

Jada since she was a toddler, my friend likely knew my daughter would put up a fight. Jada always liked to play my protector, even when she was little.

"What's that for?" Leilani asks, nodding to the mirror.

"My phone-a-friend option in case we get stuck," I reply with a wink.

Both women raise their eyebrows in response.

"Phone-a-friend?" Leilani asks.

I wave my hand over the mirror. "Ever hear of magic mirrors in fairytales?"

Leilani attempts to suppress a smirk. "Are you an evil queen?"

"Perhaps." I waggle my eyebrows, stuffing the mirror in my backpack filled with supplies. I've packed protein bars and water, salt, and an iron dagger Gabriel gave me. I almost didn't pack the dagger. The weapon measures almost as long as my forearm, ancient, and definitely has a vibe of having spilled fae blood.

"Oh, stop it, Miriam." Lucinda chuckles. "I think she means it's like the one the beast gave beauty so she could see her father."

"Bingo." I point at Lucinda and then hike a thumb at the backpack. "Except this one is a two-way means of communicating."

"You know. I'm a demigod and I gotta say that's some weird shit," Leilani says, still smirking.

"I am half witch and half fae, and I have to agree. Wait until you see the fae who made it. He looks straight out of a fantasy movie."

Leilani's eyes light up. "I bet he's hot." She grins dreamily. "A Thrunduil kind of hot, isn't he?"

"Phyr is...incomparable." Is all I'll admit.

"High praise from you," Lucinda remarks. "Raf was gorgeous."

Leilani nods in agreement.

"Ready to find out for yourselves?" I ask. I'm nervous and afraid, but the question and answer session brightened my mood.

After I get the go-ahead from both of them, I let my second sight settle in. Magenta light surrounds Leilani and a silvery light with magenta threads emanates from Lucinda—likely because Sirens' gifts were given by Persephone.

I focus on the tapestry that binds this world together, separating this universe from others. I focus my green light into my hand, snipping at the threads. Then I make a hole big enough to enter. Once inside, I make a bubble in the Null large enough to fit myself and my friends.

Sweat beads on my brow from the effort. "Go in. It should be safe."

Leilani cocks a dubious eyebrow. "*Should*?"

"Come on. You're immortal." Lucinda says dragging the larger woman through.

"Doesn't mean I can't question!"

I follow them immediately after. I've made caches my entire life, but I've never ever been inside one, let alone the Null. My own light is the only barrier between us and the Null. The Null itself is like a bargain bin of yarn, the color of magic the strings.

"Whoa. This is so dope. It's like dark but filled with color," Leilani remarks, spinning in a circle.

We're all standing upright, at least from our perspective, not floating around. My cache either obeys the laws of the world I come from, or is obeying how I perceive reality should be. I make a mental note to ask Phyr why.

"This is so cool. I can breathe," Leilani says, surprise coloring her tone. "It's like you made a pocket universe for us."

"I can't keep the door open to our world and look for the breadcrumbs Phyr might have left for me," I say.

Lucinda glances at the open portal to our world. "Is that a problem?"

"We'll only have the air that exists in this space at the time I close it."

"I can hold my breath for long periods while I monitor how you're doing and give you two a little boost when you need it," Leilani offers with a wink.

"I can get us back home if you can't find your way before we run out," Lucinda assures me, holding up a coin. "It'll be via the Underworld, but I'll get us there."

I smile at them both, grateful for friends. Next, I seal the cache I've created, so we can move forward. I examine the threads of magic in the tapestry of the Null, picking out the brightest of the green threads.

"What are you doing?" Lucinda asks.

"Can you see the threads?" My gaze bounces between them.

Leilani scrunches her face. "I don't see anything but swirling rainbows. What do you mean threads?"

Lucinda steps closer. "I can. Looks like a bunch of strings. If I travel from my realm to the Underworld, I go to a ley line and use a coin. I think these threads are ley lines—or at least how our brains perceive ley lines in the Null."

I point out the thread I've chosen. "I believe Phyr made this thread brighter than the other greens to show me the way."

"So which direction should you follow it?"

I chewed my lip, unsure. Now that I'd built it, I no longer had to maintain the cache, but—"I don't know how to use the thread."

"Grab it and see what happens." Leilani suggests. "Oh! We should hold hands, first."

I rear my head.

She holds up manicured nails in mock surrender. "Hey, I'm only making suggestions. You don't have to take my advice."

Lucinda rubs her chin, squinting at the threads. "You know what? I think Leilani is onto something. Instead of grabbing with your hand, try to connect with your light or a conduit of your light. The coin I have catches a ride on a ley line to the Underworld."

I think about how the spell to cast a demon out works. "To open a portal between Earth and Hell, you use salt as a conduit for your magic. Perhaps the salt, drawn a specific way, and words and light poured into the pattern, pierces the membrane of our world and catches onto a ley line in the Null leading to Hell." I couldn't control where the hellhound went because the spell wasn't meant to go to a specific place, simply to catch on any ley line once the hole was opened.

"The apples must have been a conduit too," Leilani suggests.

She's right. "Biting into them must trigger some sort of chain reaction of magic that catches onto a ley line that leads directly to Gehenna." Which is likely why His Creepiness never taught me the spell behind the apples. The asshole didn't trust me not to tell anyone.

"Do you have something fae that could act as a conduit?"

I recall what Phyr had said about how the mirror worked. I shrug off the backpack, theorizing the mirror is likely spelled to use the same ley line system to communicate between our world and the faerie where Phyr awaits with my father. I extract the mirror.

Lucinda, Leilani, and I link arms. "I hope this works, I'm feeling lightheaded," Lucinda says.

I am too. The amount of breathable air depleted while we puzzled out how to follow these ley lines.

I thought of Phyr's words. I didn't have enough light to power the mirror, not in my world, but there was more than enough in the thread. I simply had to connect the mirror to the ley line. Phyr provided the means but not the how.

"How would you use the coin here?"

"I'd hold it out to any of the magenta threads, from the Underworld, then I'd take the ley line back to my post."

"Here goes nothing." Extending the hand holding the mirror, I reach for the brightest green thread.

When Jada was in elementary school, Raf and I used to take her to a waterpark. There was this fully enclosed waterslide that twisted and turned, jettisoning your body into the air where you'd stay airborne for at least five seconds before plummeting into a pool. I used to scream down the entire slide, fearing that moment where I had zero control over which way my body would eventually fall.

I hated that ride.

I would rather buy a lifetime pass to that park and ride that damned slide every day for the rest of my life than ever take a ley line by this method with only the exterior of the cache as a barrier again.

"That was wild," Leilani exclaims, excitedly looking about as we rise to our feet.

Dusting ourselves off, the three of us took in our surroundings—a rose garden surrounding a reflection pool. A silvery castle that seems made of glass or crystal peers down at us, the enormity of it too much to take in at once.

I stuff the mirror in the backpack.

The faerie feels old in the way the weight of history presses upon you when you visit an ancient ruin. There's more than that. The light within me is in tune with this place and everything about it feels right, familiar. Home.

Leilani rubs her arms. "This place is sweet. Are you from here?"

"I don't know. Maybe?" I bite my lip and look around. "The light within me comes from this place." I feel it more than know it.

The water ripples. A fae with white iridescent scales covering their body emerges from the dark depths of the pond. The fae stares at us unblinkingly from pitch black eyes with no sclera and white pinprick pupils as they step out of the pond. Nothing except a sword strapped to their back clothes the fae.

We stand in shadow as a winged lizard the size of a large cat swoops down landing next to the newcomer.

"Holy shit, that's a dragon," Lucinda says, backing toward me.

The fae opens a slit for a mouth, speaking to us in the same language as Phyr had when I first met him.

"We don't understand," I say in English, hoping, like Phyr, the fae understands me.

The fae draws their sword in response. The lizard hisses, creeping toward us slowly, like a predator about to attack.

"Two can play at that game," Leilani says. Her clothes tear as she transforms into a lizard three or four times the size of the one coming at us.

This gives the other lizard pause, but only for a moment.

"Crap," Lucinda says, shifting to her siren form in a flash of light.

"You brought allies, powerful ones," a resonant tenor says in accented English behind me. "I wonder who will win."

I glance only briefly, not wanting to let the lizard and the sword-wielding fae out of my sight.

The fae behind me has shimmery silvery white scales as well.

Their face is beautiful, all angles and the sort of arrogance that comes with having the power of a full god. Their hair is the same pink as the rose garden. White antlers protrude from the wavy rose locks. They're dressed in clothes that scream more Purple Rain costume-y fashion than an actual 18th century fop, except for the crown. A circlet sits upon their head, pulsing with a bright green glow. The pulse of the faerie itself. I know this as if I were taught it, yet I have no memory of it.

"You'd gamble with a life of a fae when there are so few left?" I ask, narrowing my eyes on the newcomer.

The fae takes me in, no expression on their features. "I simply said that I wonder."

"Tell them to put the weapon down and send the dragon away," Lucinda says in her siren-compelling voice.

The magic pounds at my flesh. *I* have a hard time resisting obeying her.

"I will, but not because you attempted to force me," the fae replies, seeming completely unaffected by Lucinda's voice. Their green eyes narrow on Lucinda. "No one tells a dragon what to do." The fae then turns to the other and says something in their lilting language.

The fae says something to them before returning to the pond. The dragon circles Leilani once, grinning with an uncanny intelligence in its eyes before taking off.

"That was your cousin, Niamh, Tati." The fae says, nodding toward the reflection pool.

I glance in the direction, perplexed that I'm related to the scaled being, let alone this antlered and shimmering skin one at all.

"Why were they so hostile?"

"They thought you were back to kill me and claim my crown, and power over this faerie for Lucifer."

I shiver. "I'm here for my father's help."

A smile touches the handsome fae's lips. "You may call me Oberon and your father, since I did not carry you."

34

The interior of the castle doesn't bustle with servants. The quietness of the place bothers me. I feel as if I know every turn, yet I have no memory of this place.

"Have I been here before?" I ask outright as we mount a spiraling stairwell.

"You were born here." Emotion flickers in Oberon's features there and gone. By my side, he leads us through an opening to another floor.

The great hall is cool, but not chilly. Tapestries decorate the walls like a medieval castle, but there are also touches I don't expect. The lighting isn't torches or candles. The bulbs seem electric, but they are not. I can see the green magic that is infused into everything in the castle, judging by the green sheen.

"Oh shit. Gabriel is going to trip," Leilari whispers behind me. She's resumed her human form and smells overwhelmingly floral. She adds, "Halflings born in faeries are considered fae under the Angelic Code."

Before we'd entered the palace, Oberon spun her a dress of rose petals replete with a rose petal crown. His idea of a consolation gift for the rude welcome, I suppose.

I shoot her a warning look. She should know better than to mention Gabriel. The animosity between the fae and angels rivals that of Heaven and Hell, perhaps more so. They never allied with His Creepiness because, at the end of the day, he was an angel and wanted the fae to submit to him.

"Don't be cross with your companion. I know about the archangel and his politics. It's the only reason you're allowed here."

I stop dead in my tracks. "What?"

Leilani bumps into me, almost knocking me over. Fortunately, she's quick as she is tall, setting us both straight.

"Allow me to explain. In here," Oberon gestures to an entrance to a grand dining hall. All the tables are ornately carved, but empty, except the one at the head.

Phyr sits at the grand table next to a large, empty chair, I assume is meant for Oberon. On the other side of the empty seat, a pink-haired fae who resembles Oberon down to the antlers takes a loud bite of a fruit that resembles a Golden Delicious apple. The fae chews slowly, appearing bored.

Another fae, with silver skin and hair as black and long as Phyr's sits to the right of Oberon's doppelgänger. They sip dark liquid from a crystal goblet, ignoring our presence. Their eyes are fully black like Niamh's.

Oberon turns to me. "Given Phyr's description of how much the archangel is smitten with you, I'd assumed he'd follow you here."

"I didn't want to bring him," I reply, gaze on Phyr. His face is completely devoid of expression. He only glances at us as he cuts his food, almost as if he's disinterested in our presence at all.

"Pity," says the Oberon look-alike in a soft soprano voice. "I would so enjoy disemboweling the nephil."

The black-haired fae snickers. "Why kill him right away, Maeve, when we could show him a good time for centuries?"

"Little sister wouldn't like it. Would you, Tati?" The pink-haired fae taunts. "You always ruin our games, telling on us to father."

"I still say Phyr's horns would look better on me," the black haired one drawls, eyes on me for my reaction, no doubt.

Phyr grows absolutely still.

I feel my hands ball into fists. "Whoever you are, you'd better learn I won't tolerate bullies."

"Nix, do you hear that?" The pink-haired fae leans toward the silver-faced one. "She called us, her dear siblings, bullies."

"I heard. Doesn't bother me. I never liked her." The fae directs their gaze to Phyr, giving him a look of mock sympathy. "You, on the other hand, must be heartbroken she doesn't remember how well you licked her boots."

Phyr digs a fork into his food, looking like he couldn't care less about anything but what was in front of him. "I assure you, I have no more sentiment regarding her amnesia than you do, Nix."

"There's a hex on her memory," Oberon says.

I rear my head. I'd assumed the memory loss was tied to the geas.

"Could be pretending to forget," Maeve says, before taking another bite of the fruit. "You did order us to leave her alone until she could fight back."

"After all the trouble she caused, all the promises she broke, I can believe Gracia capable of any manipulation.' Nix leans forward. "You truly don't remember any of us or this palace, Tati?"

"I don't." Given this reception, I didn't know if I wanted to remember this place. My gaze lands on Phyr, who doesn't meet it.

"There's much to discuss. Have a seat, my dear," Oberon says, pulling out a chair at one of the smaller tables and smiling at Leilani.

Leilani sits, smiling back. She gasps as a platter of food and a goblet appear before her.

Maeve rolls their eyes at our father. Nix stares at me as if they can see the geas or hex, or perhaps my liver. Phyr continues to eat, disinterested.

Oberon offers a chair to Lucinda, platter and goblet appearing before her. Lucinda sits but doesn't touch the meal before her. I hope that Leilani knows enough about the fae to not eat the food either. My father then offers me the large chair next to Phyr at the great table.

I almost refuse, but Maeve's face hardens, if that is possible. Nix looks down, curtaining with their hair whatever emotion their face would reveal. I've been given some honor.

Oberon produces a chair between Maeve and me. The table extends. No one but us newcomers is impressed.

"You figured out how to get here, so that makes you a planeswalker," Oberon announces.

Nix snickers. "Or, an enamored planeswalker opened a back door for her."

"Did you?" My father leans forward, raising a sculpted, pink eyebrow at Phyr.

"I had to give her a means to communicate. Tati figured out all on her own that the mirror I'd given her would act as a beacon to my location."

"That's true," Leilani says, putting down her empty crystal goblet. "Miriam puzzled it all out and Lucinda helped." She pats Lucinda's hand.

Lucinda stops Leilani from putting the food in her mouth.

"Miriam," Oberon says quietly. "You do not go by Tatiana?"

Raf had chosen Miriam. "Someone renamed me."

"Good. It mocked our mother calling the halfling Tatiana," Nix hisses.

Oberon shrugged. "I honored my favorite child with my favorite partner's name."

I'm growing impatient with the bickering. "Will you remove the geas?"

"Yes. On one condition: the archangel agrees to allow you a fae guardian of my choosing."

A hungry look fills Maeve's eyes. "I would be happy to guard my sibling."

Not wanting Maeve anywhere near me, let alone Jada, I say, "I don't know if the archangel will allow that."

"You doubt your charms. Phyr has looked into his mind. The archangel will allow you anything you wish."

I cast a cutting glare in Phyr's direction, disliking he'd shared what he saw.

"Our sister must be just like her mother," Nix says over their goblet's rim. The goblet refills by unseen means. "Seduction, lies, and false friendship. No move too low to get what she wants."

In my periphery, Lucinda and Leilani exchange glances. I don't know what they think of all of this, but I don't think they like it.

"There's no plot," I say. "I want to protect myself and your granddaughter from Lucifer."

"Daughter?" Oberon asks softly. "Did you know I have a granddaughter, Phyr?"

"No." The answer is soft.

I can sense his muscles tensing, bracing for the pain the lie would bring. Why hadn't he told Oberon about Jada? Now I wish I hadn't. Phyr must have had good reason because not telling Oberon seems to be costing him.

"Why would he hide it from you?" I ask, redirecting Oberon's gaze and attention to me.

"Tati forgets her pet *loves* her," Maeve says, eyes lighting with delight. "So much so he'd let her betray him without retribution."

Phyr sets his cutlery aside with a decisive clink. "There are so few Unseelie left. The child is a blessing, not a betrayal."

I'm thoroughly confused why Jada would be a blessing or betrayal.

"I agree," Oberon says. "Also, my terms have changed. I want visitation rights to my granddaughter. Work it out with the angel, Tati dear. I did not get to see you grow up, but I will get to see this infant."

I don't correct him about Jada's age. There's enough tension in the room. Besides, part of my mind is racing. What had I promised Phyr?

Nix chuckles. "With all of her other children infertile or dead, do you think your mother feels the same, Phyr?"

I see his hand tremble as he reaches for the goblet. "I'll claim Miriam's daughter as my heir and consider our agreement met. I only ask to be the guardian of the two."

"No. Family should be her guard." Maeve sticks out their lips in a pout. "Your commitment is fulfilled. We are blood."

"What say you, Tati?" Oberon says, "Who would you like to protect you? Your siblings or someone from another house?"

I don't answer right away. I'm certain I don't want Maeve or Nix anywhere near Jada. I also don't want to offend Oberon by *not* choosing one of my siblings. I consider naming Niamh, since Oberon said they were my cousin, but I don't know if I could accommodate a water fae and make them comfortable. Plus, I don't know Niamh.

Phyr and my siblings watch me deliberate, but not directly. All seem to be consumed with consuming the feast. Lucinda and Leilani only look nervous.

"Phyr has a rapport with the archangel. It's best if he comes." I'd watched enough fantasy shows with Raf to believe I got the court intrigue right.

Oberon smiles as if I'd made him proud. "Clever."

"I think she and Phyr planned this outcome all along," Nix says. "Or at least he did."

"Remember when they ran away together?" Maeve adds. "Are you sure we can trust them? They're always *plotting*."

"I trust Phyr doesn't want war between our houses." Oberon waves his hand in dismissal. "Go on. Tell your archangel my terms. Once I see my granddaughter, I'll lift my geas."

35

Even at a table of supes, Phyr sticks out like a sore thumb. The princeling leans back in the chair as if he's a king conducting court, lazily observing the Pacific Northwest Supernatural Council. I sit to his right. My nerves are wound tight. Gabriel sits on the opposite end of my dining room table. Lucinda sits directly to my right and to her right sits Leilani. Opposite me Aurora sits, Princess next to her, and Cian to her left.

Except for informal greetings at the front door for the newcomers, no one has spoken yet.

"Now that we're all settled. Would you mind telling me what a full fae is doing in my territory?"

"Because my bloodline is royal," I struggle to say the word 'royal' because I don't like all that is implied. "My father has agreed to release me of the geas on the condition I have fae guard."

Gabriel rubs his brow. "For how long?"

Phyr grins. He seems to enjoy how uncomfortable he makes the others, especially Gabriel. "For life, of course. She's heir to the Unseelie throne."

Cian visibly flinches.

Gabriel's eyebrows sink and his eyes narrow to slits. "Heir? Fae are immortal."

Phyr's responding grin is more a flash of teeth. "We can die, as you well know."

To his credit, Gabriel doesn't push that point further. However, he rallies into a new line of questioning. "Where, exactly, do you plan to sleep? Do you plan on hovering over her bed guarding her?"

"The guest room," I reply, annoyed Gabriel is concerned about the wrong things. "We're getting off track here. There's another term my father demanded. He wants the right to visit Jada."

Cian clears his throat and gives a slight shake of his head. "I don't trust Oberon wants only that."

"A fae guard and visits with his grandchild are the only way he will release the geas?" Gabriel clarifies.

I nod.

Princess scoffs. "This is bullshit. How do you know she hasn't planned this with the fae all along?"

"Because a geas is no easy commitment," Cian says. "It's her very soul binding her magic. A promise. Not even Oberon would take such a spell lightly."

"So says the fae," she replies.

Cian's fair skin reddens. "I'm no liar."

Gabriel clears his throat. "I interrogated Miriam under the influence of my angel dust to make sure she wasn't an agent of the devil or anyone else."

Only Leilani and Phyr, who likely puts nothing past his enemies, don't seem to be shocked by this.

"Why didn't you share that before, alpha?" Princess looks hurt. She's his beta, second in command, and chief of security.

Gabriel shifts uncomfortably. "The situation was an angelic matter, not pack."

My chest tightens. I don't remember the interrogation, but the guilt on his face is plain.

"Doesn't angel dust have aphrodisiacal effects?" Phyr asks, his tone and expression casual.

"Yes. I didn't molest her, if that's what you're thinking."

Phyr smiles wide enough to show fang. "No, but you do want her for a mate, don't you?"

Leilani interjects before Gabriel can reply, "I was there to make sure nothing happened between them. It was a standard interrogation, nothing harmful."

"Standard," I whisper. He'd drugged me and she watched. My eyes sting and my throat tightens. I thought of Leilani as a friend.

"Please don't be hurt. It wasn't personal," Leilani pleads. "I didn't know you, and the devil has planted supes in our midst before."

Lucinda shoots Gabriel a nasty look. "We've known her and Raf for years, Gabe."

"She's masqueraded as a latent for all that time. I had to be sure." Gabriel turns to me, his eyes wet. "Miriam, I swear I was only thinking of the territory. You know how close he's gotten to me."

I did. "Kirsten's betrayal has nothing to do with me."

"I'm confused," Phyr says, looking anything but. "Why didn't you simply ask her outright without influence of your angel dust? Fae cannot lie."

Gabriel responds with the alpha glare I've seen him give Princess and others. "As I've said before, I didn't know Miriam was half fae."

Phyr chuckles softly. "Her light is bound but her scent is not. Or, is it a rumor our scent is irresistible to angels?"

"I was attracted to Miriam long before I smelled her," Gabriel admits, frustration evident in the way his fists curl and uncurl.

Phyr leans forward. "Did you smell her faeness before you gave her the angel dust?"

"Yes." Gabriel says through clenched teeth. "Why?"

"I'm here to protect her. You knowingly gave Miriam, a halfling, something that is multiple times more addictive to us than any other species."

The knife in my chest twists when Gabriel doesn't deny he knew what he was doing.

"I was looking at Satan's former Harbinger of the Apocalypse, the Destroyer of Man and Heaven. I had to make sure you no longer had his ambitions in your mind. You know I wouldn't harm you."

I do, but I bite my lip to keep from crying. What would he have done if I *had* been a spy? Turn me to his side by the same sort of addiction, use me as a pawn to pass between himself and his enemy? I would like to think he wouldn't do that, but I'd trusted Gabriel, Raf had trusted Gabriel, and he gave me angel dust. Twice.

"Council, let's put it to a vote. Will we allow Phyr, a full faerie-born fae, in this territory to guard Miriam, and her father to visit his granddaughter? A show of hands for all in favor?" Gabriel lifts his hand.

I raise my hand. Lucinda, Leilani, and Aurora raise theirs. Cian blows out his breath and then grimaces at Phyr as he slowly raises his hand. Princess keeps her hand down.

"Your reason for opposing the bargain, Princess?" Gabriel asks, not hiding his annoyance.

"It's against Angelic Code to let a faerie-born fae on Earth."

My heart lurches. It takes me a moment to realize she's talking about Phyr, not me.

"As Archangel, *I* interpret the Angelic Code for this territory," Gabriel argues. "I am the law."

"You asked my reason. I gave it." Princess folds her arms across her chest. She shoots a cutting look at Aurora, who suddenly finds her hands interesting. "I cede that I'm outvoted."

"Alright." Gabriel says, turning to me. "Here are my terms you will pass onto your father, Miriam. He will get one hour a week with you and Jada in this house. You will contact me before the visitation will take place. I will arrive before your father. I will give you privacy by being in another room but will remain on the premises and must watch him leave with my own eyes."

Gabriel's gaze passes from me to Phyr. Taking on that 'I am the archangel' tone, he declares, "If you want to stay in this territory, here are my terms: You are here to defend Miriam and Jada. You will not *trick* anyone into having sex with you to impregnate them. If you have sex with a resident of my territory, they will be someone who knows *what* you are, your true appearance and capabilities, therefore can fully consent. No pretending to be human or impersonating someone else. You will not *eat* residents of my territory, whole or in part. You will not harm or murder residents of my territory. No making residents of my territory your thrall for kicks. No mind manipulation at all."

I shudder because Gabriel has reason to believe a fae would do this.

"I like your priorities. Listing whom I can fuck before whom I can eat, kill, or enslave. Shows me what you're afraid of most." Phyr's smile would be dazzling if there wasn't so much malice in his amber eyes. "Anything else, archangel?"

"Yes. You may not start any religion or seek out those who still worship the fae or demand individuals with fae blood of lesser rank to pay you homage." Gabriel briefly glances at Cian. "You must glamour your appearance whenever you leave this house and you may not tell humans about the existence of the supernatural. Do not attempt to play with my rules or twist my words, or I'll consider the deal broken, and you *will* face my wrath. Understood?"

Phyr examines his nails, expression bored. "Oh, I understand. I understand that you know nothing of my kind other than the propaganda angels feed you, but I'll agree to your terms."

"Good. Meeting adjourned."

Cian and Leilani leave, the latter giving me an apologetic glance on their way out. I don't feel forgiving, so I look away.

Princess remains seated, gaze on the table. Aurora pushes back her chair, asking Lucinda, "Can I get a ride with you?"

They leave and Princess follows.

Gabriel turns to me. "Can I speak with you privately?"

"Not so far I can't hear her shout for help," Phyr says, face grim.

"In your eyes, I deserve that," Gabriel admits.

"We can go to the garden," I offer, not wanting to be in an enclosed space with him.

We say nothing until Gabriel slides the door behind him.

"You know he's purposefully driving a wedge between us, right?"

I have no doubt, but I simply cross my arms and look away. "You drugged me."

"I didn't know about your addiction when I did it. I'd almost died. You used strange magic. There were vamps." He stabs his fingers into his dark curls. "I fucked up."

"You drugged me."

"I'll never do it again."

I pick a flower more out of frustration than the need to pick a flower. "I don't know if any of this is real between us."

"It is for me. That's why I had to be sure. I needed to protect my territory and my heart from falling for someone who could destroy both." He stepped closer but didn't crowd me.

I wouldn't look at him, but his need to touch me is palpable. Mother help me, I want him to as well. That's what scares me the most. I want to turn to him and let him comfort me the way he did in my car after Velja scared me. I want him to kiss me and caress me, and more. Much, much more.

Instead of turning to him, I shake and cry.

"I'm sorry. I'm so, so sorry I've caused you pain." His own voice is shaky. A tentative hand rests on my shoulder.

"I have to go pick up Roxy and Jada. Do you want me to come back inside when I drop Jada off?"

I shake my head. "I can't think when you're near and I need to think this through," I whisper. "I'll call you after I contact my father."

"I'm sorry," he says once more. The hand slips away and he's gone.

36

I'm all alone. The rain starts to come down in the usual mist, but then it thickens to fat drops. I'll be soaked if I remain outdoors much longer, but I can't bring myself to turn around. I let the rain wash away the hurt and the longing I still feel.

I go inside to find Phyr grimacing at the television and entertainment center. He squats in front of the blank screen scrutinizing the receivers and wiring behind. He could have witnessed everything that transpired between me and Gabriel through the window, my tears afterward, but he makes no comment on the scene in the garden or my appearance. When his amber eyes turn to me, he gestures to the entertainment unit.

"I sense currents of energy around this. Copper and other metals, surrounded by substances that do not exist in faeries." He cocks his head to the side. "Tell me, is this of human or witch design?"

"Human. These are machines that power this portal for information and entertainment."

He cocks his head, eyebrows raised. "Information. What sort?"

"Anything you want to know about the modern human world. Actually, everything and anything about this world." I gesture to the universal remote, Raf's old wireless keyboard, and a mouse. "These are tools to input and query information from the machines."

Phyr scowls. "The angels allow this?"

"Angels aren't around in force anymore," I reply, figuring it wouldn't hurt to tell just one fae. "Just the Archangels."

"An occupation but not a full colonization. I'd thought this world would be fully ruled by the angels at this point. I'm quite surprised they leave it alone."

"Between you and me, I think the angels don't want this world, but they also don't want anyone else to have it either."

"Interesting." Phyr rubs his chin. "Can you show me how to access the portal of knowledge?"

"Sure. Why not?" I figure that teaching him how to use the internet and watch television would distract us both from everything.

We get comfy on the couch as I instruct him how to use the devices as best as I know how. Phyr picks up pretty quickly and soon is expertly surfing the web, using the TV as a screen. He's interested in history of what happened since fae were kicked out by the angels, particularly the Celtic peoples but not limited to. I sit with him while he watches videos and reads blogs on the internet.

"Mami! I'm home!" Jada cries barreling down the hall and into the living space, stopping dead in her tracks. "Who are you?"

Phyr drops the remote and his jaw goes slack, eyes widening as if he's never seen a teenager before. He murmurs something in the beautiful fae language.

"This is Phyr, the fae who helped me find your grandfather. He'll be staying with us for a while. He's new to this world, so be nice."

"I'm always nice." Jada rolls her eyes at me, dropping her backpack on the floor and kicking her boots off. She tosses her jacket over one of the stools at the breakfast bar.

Phyr watches her as if she's performing a complicated spell, not a typical teen freeing herself of anything she deems unnecessary to wear indoors and leaving it wherever.

She thrusts a hand at him, grinning ear to ear. "Hi, I'm Jada. I've never met a real fae before."

Phyr swallows hard, somehow gathers his composure, and rises to his feet. He bows with a flourish, gracefully taking her hand and kissing the air above it. "It is my sincere pleasure and honor to meet you, daughter of Ta—Miriam."

Her tan cheeks flush with color. "Wow. So old school! Like a fairy-tale prince."

His mouth quirks, until it spreads into a full smile. "Not like. I *am* a faerie prince, young one."

"Dope!" She turns to me, lifting her eyebrows and grinning. "Since we have company, did you bake?"

I'm pleased and perplexed at how well Jada is taking we have a horned fae in our midst. I also realize I hadn't offered Phyr anything to drink or eat since we've arrived. I'd been too busy showing him the guest room and getting his belongings set up, while coordinating with Leilani and Lucinda to call the council to gather here.

"I can fix you both an early dinner." I rise from the couch. My time as a fae princess in castle feasting halls is over. As I circle the sofa and breakfast bar, I toss over my shoulder. "Jada, show Phyr anything he needs to know about using the internet."

"If you prepare your own meals in this realm, I would like to be more useful than a fixture in your home," Phyr says, joining me in the kitchen space. He eyes the kitchen dubiously. "Is this your hearth?"

"Yup."

I have a lot more going on in my kitchen with all my drying herbs and tools than most kitchens. The appliances would also be unfamiliar to him.

"It is not a fae hearth but give me a task. I am a quick study," he assures with a grin. There's something different about him than our other two encounters, an easiness.

I feel easier too. "I believe you."

"I'll help too, mami," Jada offers, grinning ear to ear.

I decide to make empanadas, Jada's favorite.

While I collect the ingredients and tools for making the simple dough, I assign them to gathering the ingredients for the sofrito: cilantro, onion, green pepper, garlic, vinegar and oil.

I chuckle along with Jada's giggles while we watch Phyr sniff and react to the ingredients as she teaches him how to peel and chop.

"Well hello, little creature," Phyr says as the cat makes his way into the kitchen.

"PC is a cat," Jada informs, loading the coarsely chopped ingredients into the food processor.

"Ah." Phyr smiles in a way that he says he knows but doesn't want to tell her. He watches PC weave around his legs, my cat deciding the fae is worth rubbing his scent upon. "We don't have cats in faeries."

We all laugh as both the cat and Phyr startle when Jada turns the food processor on.

She turns to Phyr. "If you don't have cats, what do you have for pets?"

Phyr lifts an eyebrow, a grin touching his lips. "Why humans, of course."

A shudder passes through me. My gaze swings to Jada's airy laughter.

"You sound like my *abuelita*."

Phyr cocks his head. "Your what? I'm unfamiliar with that term."

"It's Spanish for grandmother," I say.

"Yeah, abuelita is a goddess. They're super weird."

"The fae are gods." His amber eyes darken. "Even if this world forgets. The Angelic Anocracy allows other gods?"

I waffle my hand. "Treaties to accommodate demigods. Most gods have left their fleshly forms. No one wanted something like the Fae Wars." I switch subjects. "Jada knows about her grandmother through her father's stories."

My daughter unhooks a frying pan from the rack hanging above the gas-range stovetop, setting the pan on the burner. "Papi had lots of them."

"Had?" Phyr's gaze darts to the family photos on the wall and then to me and Jada, I think comprehending for the first time that her father had lived here longer than it took to make Jada. I didn't know what he assumed about Raf since I had not said much.

"My husband Rafael is no longer with us," I explain, so used to the words instead of saying he shed his cancer-riddled physical body to become a god.

He rears his head, face scrunching as if he'd tasted something sour. "You married, vowing yourself to one and only one person?"

I roll the empanada dough out on a cutting board, maybe using a little more force than necessary. "Yes."

Something flickers across his face. "Did you owe him some sort of debt or were you seeking an alliance where he needed a vow?"

Jada chuckles, seemingly amused by our exchange and Phyr's genuine abhorrence of marriage. She pours oil into the pan and turns the burner to a low setting.

"No." I blow out my breath, getting a glass out of the cupboard to cut the pastry dough into circles for the shells. "It's what people do who are in love and live the life we lived."

Jada retrieves the ground beef and a jar of olives from the fridge.

He follows her, tone softening. "I'm truly sorry about the loss of your father. I know that sort of grief. I lost mine at a young age, too."

"It sucks not having papi to talk to but at least I know I'll see him again one day." She pours the sofrito in the pan first. Sizzling and sputtering oil precedes aromas that make my mouth water.

Responding to Phyr's curious tilt of his head and furrowing of his brows, she explains, "Papi ascended to godhood."

"We fae who can construct faeries consider ourselves gods, but when my father left his corporeal form, his light went to a place we call The Summerlands—an eternal paradise, I hear. It sounds incredibly boring, feasting all day and lying about. I'd rather live and experience new things."

"Me too." Jada tilts her head. "Where do witches go when they die, mami?"

"Our light becomes part of the fabric of the multiverse." I collect the scraps of dough that didn't make it to the first round of shells so that I can roll the ball out to make more. "Some sects believe we are reincarnated."

Phyr stops and turns to me. "Witch beliefs have mingled with human religions?"

"No, it's the other way around."

"Since we're not full witches, what will happen to us?"

"I don't know."

"May I try?" Phyr asks, pointing with pursed lips toward the rolling pin.

I stand aside, allowing him enough space to roll the dough, but supervise.

"Papi was certain I'd ascend, but I don't know." She adds ground beef and seasonings to the softened veggies. "I'm barely an Orisha."

"Perhaps you'll have a choice," Phyr offers. "Nothing is certain in life, why should it be in death?" Phyr grimaces uneven thickness of the dough he's rolled out. "What have I done?"

"Here," I sidle closer, resting my hands over his. "Apply even pressure."

His breathing changes as we roll out the dough together. I back away as soon as the dough is flat and even, pretending Jada's perfect picadillo needs more olives.

The truth of the matter is my heart quickened the moment my hands touched his and an electric tingling shivered through me—wholly unexpected and completely unwelcome. I have enough man problems with Gabriel to add another into the mix—even though neither is technically a man.

Forty-three is too old for a love triangle of any sort.

I keep my physical distance for the rest of the preparation and don't sit next to him at dinner as the three of us discuss life, death, and beliefs of the fae, witches, and otherwise. Phyr fully charms Jada, but he makes no mention of the adoption. I don't either. I didn't quite know what it meant.

Long after we've all said goodnight and I've settled into bed, I lie awake, wondering if my father is actually going to release me from my geas or make more demands. What will happen once my light is released? Will I be the same? Will it be enough to banish Velja? If I do, will she tell His Creepiness and will my power be enough?

My chest tightens painfully as I think about Gabriel's betrayal and Leilani's part in it. Do I have burgeoning feelings for him or is it the effect of the angel dust? Did he care about me or what my unleashed light could do for his territory? Suddenly, doubt that I *should* be free of the geas creeps in. What if I make things worse? Will it change me?

A light rap on my door takes me out of my anxious thoughts and into the moment. I get out of bed, expecting Jada to say she can't sleep and to have lots of questions about Phyr. To my surprise, I find the fae at my door.

His torso is bare, revealing tattoos. My gaze roams over the beautiful, intricate patterns covering his bronze skin, ending where black cotton pants hang low on his hips.

"Do you need something?"

"Yes," his voice is smokier than before, deeper. His amber gaze runs over me. I'm in a spaghetti strap tank and sleep shorts, suddenly aware I'm bra and panty-less.

I am forty-three, too damned old for this.

Phyr taps my forehead. "Your thoughts are loud. Could you please shut me out?"

My cheeks flush. "I don't know how."

A grin creeps up the corner of his shapely mouth. "Obviously. I didn't think you wanted to share all that."

He slants his head. Those otherworldly amber eyes focused on my mouth. Suddenly, I'm seeing myself from his perspective. I'm much more beautiful in his eyes than I see myself. Vision-me radiates like a medieval painting of a saint. He's got it bad.

I'm-he's snaking his arm around vision-me's waist and pulling my body to his. Conflicting emotions, fear one of them, superimpose over my own feelings. My-his hand roams over every curve, slipping our hand under vision-me's tank top. I-he leans down and presses his lips to mine. Arousal coils in the center of my actual body.

"Hey!" I push the thought out and build a wall of green light around my mind shielding myself from any more intrusive thoughts. "I thought fae couldn't do that to other fae,"

I get my bearings, realizing Phyr hasn't laid a hand on me. We're still standing at arm's length.

His brows furrow with concern. "Do what?"

"You didn't send me thought porn?"

He blinks, confusion playing one his features. "What is porn?"

I clear my throat. "In this case, a sexual fantasy."

His eyebrows raise, surprised. "Do you have a food fetish? I was thinking about going downstairs for the leftover empanadas and drinking all your cream."

I gauge his body language for a lie. Shit. I see none.

He shakes his head. "Tsk. Tsk. Miriam. You need to learn to read fae who have learned to lie better."

My mouth drops.

He makes space and then genuflects. "Now that you know how to shield from being read and reading me, I bid you goodnight."

I roll my eyes, understanding what he did there. I almost thank him for teaching me how to shield but think better of it. "Goodnight, Phyr."

He turns and I see the tattoos covering his chest and arms also cover his lean, muscular back. I can't help but wonder if tattoos go all the way down to his feet and if they're for aesthetic or magical purposes.

I want to ask. Instead, I say, "If my thoughts were loud, why didn't you simply shut me out?"

He twists his torso but doesn't completely turn. In profile, his face is a stunning study of planes and angles. His horns, regal. "I—I thought it best you knew how to protect yourself from those who could read your thoughts."

"Well," I smile. "Now I do."

"Indeed."

"I'm going to contact my father after Jada heads to school tomorrow."

"Removing your geas would be wise, even if it causes a few problems in the beginning."

I scoff. "A few problems."

Phyr turns fully. His fae light burns in those amber eyes turning them deep emerald green like my light. The tattoos light up, also green.

"Beautiful," I murmur. I can't help myself.

"Beautiful?" He sneers at the word, at his tattoos as if they're offensive. "This is nothing compared to what I could be if we had not muted ourselves for the angels."

I furrow my brow, confused about the point he's trying to make.

"We fae were once *gods*, carrying within us a supernova's worth of faelight. I'm reminded every time I use my magic that I am not a god but could be."

"I don't think I'm that powerful."

Phyr's hand gently cups my cheek. His eyes are so serious, no trace of the mischief I've witnessed before. He dips his head so that our faces are close. We've been this close before. My body knows his touch. Memories beat at an invisible barrier. My heart gallops in my chest as if it can pound away the geas.

"My dear friend, I fear it is more than your fae light that you have let dim. What did the devil do to you?"

A lump forms in my throat. I attempt to swallow back the tears, knowing he has a reason for this tenderness and deep inside without memory, I know it too. "That story is too long when we both need sleep."

He nods slowly, understanding limning his handsome features. "It's as I feared. Be warned: Gabriel thinks he is unlike Lucifer. He is not. All angels, fallen or otherwise want to control everyone and everything."

"There's good in him. I've seen it."

"Good. Bad. It doesn't matter. None of the politics matter. There will always be someone thirsty for the throne. At the end of the day, you must think of those who matter to you most and what you must do to protect them."

I place a hand over his. "Why are you here? Are you protecting your family?"

"Yes," he replies, without hesitation. "Goodnight."

His hand falls away, and Phyr is in his room, door closed behind him.

37

I set a tray carrying a tea service and pastries on the coffee table in the sitting area of the great room. Gabriel watches me in an overstuffed chair, hands gripping the armrest. He'd asked to help. Phyr told him in no uncertain terms that he could not handle the king's food.

"Are you ready?" Phyr asks. He's in full armor, sword sheathed on his back.

I'm not. Not at all. I clear my throat and put on my PTSA smile. "You can get him now."

"Only her father, and one guard, no other fae," Gabriel says, his tone even, but his eyes carry a threat.

Phyr genuflects, disappearing as he straightens.

Gabriel stands. "I want to apologize. I was up all night, thinking about how you would see this. I should have trusted you all along, the way you've trusted me all along."

"Will the amount of power I wield once the geas is lifted make me a threat?"

"Your father is a king, I get it. There's a lot of kings and queens, and princesses and princes among the fae. It's not like he's *the* king."

"Who is *the* king?"

"You're not Oberon's kid. Someone would know."

A frisson skitters across my shoulders. I hadn't told Gabriel my father's name and I doubted there is more than one Oberon. "Would that matter if I was?"

"Yes." He draws out the single word. "Oh shit. Is he?"

I open my mouth to reply, but our attention is distracted by Phyr's return.

He kneels and bows his head, announcing my father, "His Majesty, Oberon King of the Unseelie."

My father appears looking like a mix of a period drama style dress and fantasy novel cover, where he plays the morally gray lead. His green-eyed gaze locks with Gabriel's. The latter doesn't seem to breathe for a moment.

"Your father made you an archangel. Congratulations," Oberon says smoothly, smiling as if they're old friends. "A large step up from the Anocracy's sword."

Gabriel nods. "Archangel is a different sort of position now. I'm a protector of my territory, not—"

"An infant murderer?" Phyr suggests. "An innocent fae child exterminator?"

Gabriel's gaze snaps to the other fae, eyeing his sword. "At the moment, the only reason you are here is because I care for Miriam's well-being."

"Then we agree on one thing, baby killer."

Phyr hadn't been this aggressive before and I can't help but wonder if it's an act for my father.

Oberon sets a hand on Phyr's shoulder. "We are in the archangel's territory. Let's let the past be in the past and fetch my granddaughter."

"She's in school—a building where young receive an education," I explain, unsure if they have formal schools in faeries. I gesture to the tea service. "Would you like some tea and pastries?"

Oberon's gaze flicks from the sweets and tea to Gabriel and finally to Phyr.

"Made by her hand," the fae explains to his high king. "I watched."

My father takes a seat on the sofa, and I sit next to him. Gabriel resumes his seat in the armchair. Phyr positions himself standing next to where I sit, like a formal guard.

I serve my father his tea first. Gabriel serves himself a pastry while I pour. Oberon lifts an eyebrow at Gabriel, his gaze sliding to Phyr. The fae exhales loudly through his nostrils, kneels, and gets himself a pastry as well. I serve Oberon a pastry and then pour the remaining three cups at the same time, telling Phyr and Gabriel to fix theirs how they like it and prepare my own cup. I'm not playing whatever silent game is going on here.

Oberon watches my every move as if I'm the most fascinating creature he's ever seen, smiling the entire time. His smile has fangs.

I take a seat.

Gabriel leans forward. "Has Miriam explained to you the terms of your visitations?"

Oberon dips his head. "I'm amenable."

"So, you'll lift my geas?"

"I cannot." He raises a pastry to his mouth, taking a bite.

I blink, Phyr makes a choking sound, and Gabriel appears ready to pounce on my father. I struggle for words. Instead of making an intelligent and rational argument like an adult, I say, "But, you said—"

My father cuts me a look that silences whatever protest formed in my mouth. "I know what I said. I cannot lift the geas because *you* must lift it."

I furrow my brow. "How do I do that?"

"First you must remove the hex on your memory that your mother wove into the geas so that you can remember your goddess given name."

"Can't you just tell me?"

Oberon shook his head, offense clear on his face. "The goddess Danu whispered it in your ear. Only you and she know it."

"No one can remember what was said to them they day they were born."

"Fae can," Phyr says. "The goddess sears that single memory into your mind for as long as you live. However, Gracia is a powerful witch within her own right and clever. She tied her hex to the geas to circumvent that memory, I'm sure."

"Why did you put a geas on my power?

"The geas itself was your idea, not mine." He smiled, revealing fangs again. "Even as a small child, you were clever too."

I could hardly process the compliment. My mind was spinning.

We finish our tea with my father. He asks me to give him a tour of my home. I show him everything, since he's curious about every room. Everything except my grimoire library.

Gabriel and Phyr remain with Oberon while I pick Jada up from school. When we return she nearly bursts out of the car, excited to meet her grandfather.

My heart flutters at the way her face lights up and the way the High King's face softens when I introduce them. There's something familiar about the way that he regards her that touches my memory.

"I've never met one of my relatives before," Jada says, dropping her backpack on the floor.

Oberon's green eyes glisten. He holds out his arms. "I have never met a grandchild of mine. Likely because you are the first."

I cast a glance in Phyr's direction. He nods, grief fills his eyes. Grief because his people are almost extinct.

Gabriel chooses that moment to excuse himself to take a call in the dining room.

The tension that existed in all the fae present eases a bit.

Jada and Oberon sit together. She grabs one of the pastries. "Mami is such a good baker."

Oberon agrees.

"She might make a business of it."

My father lifts an eyebrow. "Do you not have enough wealth, you must lower yourself to a trade? Do gold and gems still hold value? Phyr, why didn't you tell me my daughter's coffers were empty?"

"She is quite wealthy for the modern Earth. Trade is the new form of power in this world."

"Yes. The world has changed," I agree, not wanting anything to do with fae gold or gems. "Besides, a bakery is a legitimate means to occupy my time and expand my wealth. The siren Lucinda has a shop that sells coffee." I don't know why I'm pushing a business I'm not sure I want.

Oberon lifts an eyebrow to Phyr.

"A commodity of great value, perhaps more than tea," Phyr provides.

"I work there after school," Jada provides, grinning. I don't think she knows. "It's super fun. I get to meet so many people."

Phyr responds to Oberon's mortified look, "Through the knowledge portal, I have learned that bakers and cooks have more renown and more influence in the modern world than ancient human kings of old had within their kingdoms. Taxation is no longer the way of the monarchy to gain wealth, but a means to support programs that benefit the people. The governments are selected by the people and can lose their position in as little as two to four rotations of this world," Phyr replies. "If your daughter becomes part of the baker elite, she would have influence over billions."

He smiles at me. "Very clever."

Phyr and I have very different ideas of what I want to accomplish as a baker. Also, I'd found him this morning sleeping sprawled out on the sofa with the television on and remote in his hand. I made a mental note to check his browser search history.

"Knowledge portal?" Jada cocks her head and then understanding blooms on her face. "Oh, the TV has web browsing."

"I'm intrigued, granddaughter. Phyr told me all he knew about this information portal. I would like to see this clockwork wizardry myself."

I worry my lip, unsure if showing my father how much the world has changed is a good idea, given Phyr's reaction to modern appliances, my car, and things as simple as showers and water heaters. The fae seem to know nothing of the modern world.

Jada giggles. "I can show you."

"Not today." Gabriel, done with his phone call in the dining room, returns. "I'm sorry but the visit must end."

We all turn.

"Why?" Jada asks, big brown eyes luminous. "We've only begun talking."

"It's political, my dear," Oberon says. "Think of me as a visiting dignitary from a formerly hostile country. We must keep peace."

She nods.

Oberon and Jada say their goodbyes. I say nothing about a ring he passes to her. I don't want to piss Gabriel off and have him change his mind, now that he knows Oberon can't directly take my geas off me.

My father touches my face. "I cannot wait to see your true form, Tati."

I blink, wondering exactly what that'll be.

After Phyr escorts Oberon back to faerie, Gabriel says, "Walk me to my car."

"ARE YOU ALRIGHT?" Gabriel asks, outside.

I shake my head. "I don't know how to feel. I don't know how to remove the hex. I've never even heard of a spell that would weave into a fae geas."

He maneuvers around me until he's standing directly in front of me. I almost run into him. His hands shoot out, preventing the collision. He keeps his hands on my shoulders, steadying me, halfway between my front door and his SUV parked in my driveway.

"Your mother would." Gabriel nudges his head over his shoulder toward the house. "And you have a planeswalker who will do anything for you."

I didn't know about all that, but I think Phyr would do anything to help me with the geas.

"The problem with that is my mother thinks I'm dead and that can't change. Besides, she's the one who put the hex on me, kept it on me, even after His Creepiness wanted the geas off. I think she had her own reasons."

A muscle in Gabriel's cheek tics. "Maybe she would take it off if she knew its purpose is null. You know who your father is now."

I hold a flicker of hope my mother had tied the hex to the geas to protect me, not just from remembering my father and my childhood in faerie, but also from being what His Creepiness wanted me to be. That flicker dies as a tiny voice says that theory makes no sense.

My past clicks in place. The World Destroyer spell required a powerful witch, the kind who existed before our world was destroyed. My mother had seduced my father into giving me that kind of power. He tried to prevent the end of humans by placing a geas on my light. He knew why she'd seduced him and fae were so desperate for children he'd let her do it.

A wave of vertigo hits me—realizing my existence might have been part of a plot for His Creepiness's purpose is too much to handle.

Gabriel squeezes my shoulders, bringing me out of my thoughts and back into the moment. "You alright?"

How long had he allowed me to stand there puzzling out my past?

"My mother won't help. She didn't want my power bound. She wanted me to forget my life in faerie. I had to believe the coven was my whole life and Lucifer's purpose my only purpose. I have to be willing to serve him and power the spell, or she'll do nothing."

I shiver and it has nothing to do with the chilly autumn afternoon.

Gabriel rubs his brow and his face lights up. "She'd need a grimoire for the hex, right?"

"Yes," I agree. "Even if she came up with the hex, my coven is meticulous about record keeping. She'd write it in her grimoire. If only I'd known there was a hex, I could have stolen that grimoire when I had the coven's trust." I sigh loudly, frustrated.

"You have a planeswalker. You could be in and out of your old coven's library without anyone knowing."

"It's not that easy."

"What do you mean?"

"The grimoire library isn't a room or two. We're talking a real library, thousands of grimoires. I wouldn't have the faintest idea of where to find the grimoire with the hex."

"How did you find the ones you stole?"

"I convinced an archivist that you-know-who wanted them." My stomach knots with the memory. I'd used some of his angel dust I'd collected on her. I am not proud of what I did, but I was saving the world. In that light, being angry with Gabriel for drugging me seems hypocritical. "I can't do that now."

He bites his lip and looks away.

I know what he's thinking. His angel dust could influence a witch. I don't want to go down that route again. I'd been young and desperate. It was a matter of survival and protecting others.

"We're going to convince someone to show us the grimoire she used."

Gabriel cocked his head. "How?"

I point to the front window where Phyr watches our exchange. I point at him. "Fae trickery."

38

Gabriel, Phyr and I sit around my dining room table. On a large sheet of construction paper, I draw a rough draft of what I remember of the coven's compound setup: The farmhouse, the library, the stockyard and gardens. "This square is the entrance to the library. From the ground, it looks like any other entrance to a storm shelter. The entire building is underground." I point to the farmhouse. "My mother's room is located on the fourth floor. That's where I need you to open a door."

"While I talk with my mother, you will take Gabriel to the library where you will convince an archivist to find the grimoire with memory suppression spells."

A grin ticks at the corner of Phyr's mouth. "Convince?"

"You know what I mean."

Gabriel chimes in, "I will allow this one concession to the rules I've set in place for you."

Phyr's grin spreads to a full smile. "Oh, I don't mind enthralling a witch into giving me what Miriam needs, but I am curious. If I'm doing all the work, why do you need to come along?"

A muscle in Gabriel's cheek feathers, but he keeps his tone casual. "If Miriam runs into trouble, I want to be in close proximity."

Phyr folds his hands on the table. "Oh, that makes sense. I thought maybe you didn't trust a fae with an entire library of grimoires and a whole coven of witches at his disposal."

Gabriel's eyebrows lower as he narrows his eyes. "You stay here, don't you? If I trust you with Miriam, I trust you with some musty old grimoires that likely mean not nearly as much to the fae as she does."

"Fair point." Phyr shifts his attention to me. "Since I've never traveled to this place, I will need a few things. Do you have anything of your mother's?"

"A drop of blood, nail clippings, and some hair."

Both of them gape.

"What? Aren't those things all families keep?" I ask, knowing damned well those things are necessary for counter spells and protection against the person who might hex you. If I had the right counter spell to the current hex, I wouldn't need my mother—I kept a part of her exactly for that. I don't want Gabriel to know the ways a witch could protect themself, which bothers me.

Gabriel's mouth opens and raises his finger as if he's going to ask a question. With a shake of his head, as if dismissing whatever thought came to mind, he clamps his mouth shut again.

"No, Miriam. Most people, even fae, do not keep parts of their families' person." Phyr says with a droll grin. "I had meant a personal affect, but any of those would do too. Also, I'm going to need a grimoire, previously stored in that underground library."

I stiffen. "I'd rather give my mother's blood."

Phyr chuckles. "Fresh from her body, no doubt, but I will need something that has been in that library a long, long time, long enough to have left a temporal marker on that space."

Something occurs to me. Planeswalkers can open portals to the past. That's why there were so few fae, especially planeswalkers. The fae kept going back to fight in the war with the angels, thinking there'd be a different outcome. Phyr could manipulate when a door opened. He'd opened the door ten hours after everyone else portaled on purpose. Cocking my head, I ask, "Could you take me to the past?"

"What do you mean?" Phyr asks, leaning forward, intrigue limning his fine features.

Gabriel's brows lift as it must dawn on him what I want to do. "Are you thinking of going back in time when you were still trusted?"

I nod. "Exactly, so."

Phyr is silent for a moment, his face serious, as if he's contemplating. His voice possesses a cautious tone, unusual for him since we left the faerie a few days ago. "I can, but I'm wary of doing so. You would have to avoid past you."

"This won't work," Gabriel holds up his hands. "No offense, but I'm sure you've aged."

It would only be offensive if he equated aging with losing value somehow. I wave him off. "I can simply use a youthenizing spell."

Phyr jacks an eyebrow up. "A euthanizing spell? Are we planning to kill?"

"Haha." I roll my eyes. "A glamour to appear younger. Happy?"

"No. Not at all." Phyr answers without a trace of humor. "But, I will be when you gain your memory back."

Sometime later, I have a grimoire in my hands and a youthful glamour on my face that freaked me out when I first saw it in the mirror upstairs.

"So, this is why you keep body parts, to masquerade as others?" Phyr asks, but it's Gabriel who watches me closely, as if he's wondering the same thing.

I grin. "Yes. I frequently masquerade as my mother so I can get the senior citizen discount."

Gabriel chuckles. "Frugal."

The joke falls flat on Phyr. His brow furrows as he cocks his head. "Is this seniority in citizenship one that requires advanced age and what does this seniority allow them to discount?"

I bite my inner lip to keep from laughing.

"Senior citizen simply means elderly," Gabriel explains. "The discount she's referring to is a reduction in price for certain goods."

"Oh, I see. This society is based off commerce. It would make sense people would be categorized by where they rank in consumership."

With a halfcocked grin dimpling his cheek, Gabriel asks me, "Ready?"

"As I'll ever be." To Phyr, I ask, "You?"

In answer, he places one hand on the grimoire and slips the fingers of the other hand around my chain—a necklace I've owned since I was sixteen. I hold my breath as his amber eyes unfocus, appearing as if he's in a trance.

After what seems like an eternity, a triumphant smile touches Phyr's lips. "Found it. Take an arm, Archangel."

Gabriel loops an arm through Phyr's. The latter leads me by the necklace into the library.

We're completely in the dark. I curse under my breath. I'd forgotten the library had no electric lighting. The odor of old books, oil and a musty scent I associated with being in the underground library hit me, bringing a wave of nostalgia.

A green flame flickers in Phyr's hand, illuminating hundreds of grimoire-lined shelves on either side of us all the way to the high ceiling, invisible in the faint light. Power thrums in this aisle of ancient books—which should be no surprise since the grimoires are filled with spells written in witches' blood. However, this much magic in one spot is dizzying after not being exposed to it for decades.

"You can't keep that on," I whisper, nodding to Phyr's hand.

He grimaces. "How will we see?"

"He has a point," Gabriel chimes in.

"Trust me. I can find my way."

After the flame is doused, I grab Phyr's hand. He follows me as I make my way down the aisle. I know they're directly behind me, I'm physically connected to Phyr, but not being able to see either of them freaks me out a bit.

I turn a corner. My chest lightens as I spy light ahead. An archivist carries a lantern. Her face lost in the play of shadow and golden light.

I backtrack to the aisle where I started out. I turn to Phyr and Gabriel and whisper, "I'm going to approach her. Stay here."

Phyr letting go of my hand is the only response I receive from them. I veer around the corner again.

"Oh, thank the Mother!" I exclaim.

The witch turns, a sharp inhale the only sign I startled her. "Who's there?"

"It's me—Mir—Tatiana."

Her dark brows furrow and she tilts her curly head. "Why are you in the dark, Tatiana?"

I recognize her now. The witch is neither young nor old—at least her dark skin doesn't have wrinkles of advanced age. She's someone I hadn't been close to, and I can't remember her name.

"My flashlight died while I was figuring out where to return this grimoire. I've been wandering forever. Do you know where the memory hexes are?"

She arches a dubious brow. "*You* had shelving duty?"

My stomach dips and I feel the sting of her words. After I'd summoned the devil himself, I no longer had any other duty than whatever he commanded me to do.

I lift my chin and behave as I would when I was His Creepiness's thrall. "No, silly witch. I'm doing research for—" My throat catches on his preferred name. How easily I had tossed it around before! I laugh, a cackle. "Why am I even bothering to explain to you? You know exactly who."

"Sorry, you just took me by surprise. Please don't tell *Him* I was rude." The way her voice quakes and she lowers her eyes in deference makes my stomach sour.

There'd been a time I'd expect no less, now it only makes me sorry for the bratty way I treated everyone in the coven. If I'd been nicer, I could have had friends to rely on instead of a demon who took pity on poor, addicted me.

"Show me where I can find the grimoires containing hexes on binding memories, and it's a deal."

I hold my breath as she eyes me for several moments. By her facial expressions, she's burning to ask questions. Fortunately, I've found a witch with more sense than curiosity.

Allowing her to lead me through the maze of grimoire shelves, I walk a few steps behind so Gabriel and Phyr can keep up. I'm glad I wasn't a talkative teenager.

My pulse thrums in my ears when she presses the button to call the old cage-style elevator at the end of an aisle. It takes everything in me to not turn around and check with the guys about what I should do, or rather, what are they going to do when I follow her onto the elevator.

I bite my lip so I don't scream at the sudden sensation of fingers touching the nape of my neck. One of them, likely Phyr by the lightness of his touch, unclasps my necklace. The archivist turns sharply. She squints into the darkness behind me.

I glance over my shoulder, spotting no trace of either of my companions. *Shit. He's fast.*

"Did you see that?" The archivist asks as I turn around.

"See what?"

She shivers and takes an unconscious step back. Her mouth spreads in a smile that doesn't reach her eyes. "Nothing. Must have been my imagination."

The elevator mechanisms screech and groan until the carriage comes to a halt. After flipping a handle, the witch pushes the metallic, accordion gate to the side, leaving room for me to get on.

Focusing on the carved rock wall behind the elevator so I won't look back, I step onto the carriage. Turning slowly to face the front, there's nothing but shadows and the buzz of magic behind the archivist as she joins me. She pulls the gate shut. She pulls a lever to the number two slot. I place my hand on my chest, sticking out two fingers from my partial fist and hoping Phyr and Gabriel catch on.

My stomach bottoms out as the elevator jerks and then descends at a rapid pace.

The archivist takes me in. Her gaze scrutinizing. Suddenly she lunges forward, hitting the stop button. "*Who* are you and *what* have you brought into this library?"

I cock my head. "I don't know what you mean?"

"I know you're a witch but what are your companions?"

I swallow hard. "Are you alright?"

She holds out a hand. "You are looking at a master caster. Your spell work is superb, but you are not Tatiana. She took her life." Grief colors the witches last sentence.

"I'm Tati but not the one you know."

Confusion contorts her features. "Come again?"

"I'm going to show you something. It might be frightening and difficult to believe, but it's the truth, sister."

She crosses her arms. "Alright."

I remove the illusion.

Her eyes flare. "Tatiana, you're—" She shakes her head, disbelief and confusion warring on her face.

"I was Tatiana over twenty years ago. After I faked my death, I went by a different name. I have come from the future because you're all in grave danger."

Tears fill her eyes. "We grieved you."

I hold up my hand. "They cannot know I'm alive. I'm working on something. Something that will free all witches from the rule of men."

Angels weren't technically men, not even fallen ones, but she understood what I meant.

"Is that why you stole the grimoires, including that one?"

Her eyes widen in shock as I open a cache and stuff the grimoire inside. "Yes. They're all safe."

"Where?" she murmurs.

"Will you help me find the one I need?"

"You want to remove your mother's hex, don't you?"

I nod slowly, unsure why she would know about this hex and Lucifer didn't.

"Your father found you, didn't he? That's who helped you pull it off."

Rage, white hot, burns inside me. They *knew* all this time. "I escaped on my own. Will you help me or not?"

The archivist is silent for a long time. "I will let you see the spell and commit it to memory, but I will not let you steal another grimoire. Not only that, I want the grimoires you stole returned."

"I cannot. They contain—"

She laughs, a bitter cackle. "I know. I'm not going to give anyone that kind of power and the means to use it any way they wish. I don't know who you sided with, but you couldn't have gotten away with what you did to age as much as you have and not sided with anyone."

Just then Phyr appears and Gabriel directly after him. Phyr takes one look at my face sans illusion and then spins on the witch.

The witch screams, backing against the grate of the elevator. Her hip bumps the lever and suddenly we're plummeting.

Unfazed, Phyr tsks. "Make it stop."

The witch's eyes shift from wide with fright to glassy dullness. As if moved by marionette strings, she obeys his command.

"Now, find us the grimoire she needs to lift the hex."

The witch nods slowly, again obeying without question. She's totally utterly under his thrall.

I shudder, glad Phyr is on my side. Now I see why angels fear fae and my mother wanted me to have nothing to do with them. With that kind of power, you could do terrible things.

"You brought me here too late. They know."

Phyr puts a finger to his lips. "She looks like a puppet, acts a like a puppet, but she's in there."

Understanding his meaning, I nod, but we would have this conversation later.

"This is better than me using angel dust on you?" Gabriel whispers in my ear as we follow Phyr and the archivist.

"Compulsion is temporary," Phyr answers over his shoulder. "So, yes."

Gabriel gives me a sidelong glance.

I shrug, pushing forward.

After some time and another jaunt through a maze of aisles, the archivist stops. I don't like the feel of this section of the library. It prickles my skin.

"Give me the grimoire Gracia used for the spell on Tatiana."

The witch doesn't obey at first.

"Oh, we have a fighter. Several millennia ago, a witch would have been successful in breaking my thrall. Dear heart, your blood is much too watered down by human to be my match." His amber eyes glow green, and his tone changes from light and teasing to stern and vibrating with power. "Give. Me. The. Grimoire."

Even with the compulsion so strong *I* feel it, the witch is reluctant. Her movements slow as if she's resisting. Hatred fills her features in turns with a glassy-eyed expression, but the witch selects a grimoire and hands it to Phyr.

"There, there. Good girl. What's your name?"

Her nostrils flare, but she answers, "Evelyn."

He smiles in a way that reveals his fangs and taps his head right below his horns. "Your lovely face and pretty name will stay here longer than your entire bloodline will exist. In case you feel the need to tell anyone about this, about who you saw, remember, I am a planeswalker. There is nowhere and nowhen you can ever go where you or anyone you love, or ever will love, that is safe from *me*."

The witch's dark skin blanches an ashen gray.

An involuntary shudder tumbles down my spine at the warning.

39

Several days pass. I only sleep when my body ceases to allow me to stay awake. I eat when Jada or Phyr bring me food. Interpreting and understanding the witchcraft behind hexes impeding memory or free will requires all my focus. I always thought of myself as a master spell caster but *several days* have passed, and I've barely made a dent in the grimoire; not to mention the archivist saw through my illusion. Self-doubt and insecurities set in. Have I spent so long living as a mundane that I am no longer the witch I thought I was?

I rub my bleary eyes. No use spiraling into this line of thought. I simply need to focus harder, push myself more.

Phyr enters the room with a plate and glass on a tray. He's dressed in loose cotton pants and a sleeveless tunic, both black. Apparently, black is his signature color. Except for when Gabriel comes around, my fae "guard" has stopped wearing his armor. A sign he trusts me, too. Given how dangerous his life must have been, I appreciate that he trusts me not to cast a harmful spell on him.

I look up and smile, holding back my thanks. He's been in my house nearly a week and his behavior has been nothing but trustworthy thus far, but my mother's warnings still echo in my mind. To show my gratitude I say, "Smells good."

"It should. You made it. I simply warmed it for you. I prefer heating food in the air fryer." He places a plate of *arroz con pollo* and leafy salad on a side table.

The amalgam of garlic, onion, cilantro, peppers, and cumin aromas wafts from the plate, a comfort. The chicken, rice, and bean dish was the very first meal Raf ever cooked for me. I associate the smells with love and safety.

Phyr picks up some of the dirty dishes lying about. "Why don't you eat and then take a nap in your room? It's been days since you rested properly. You need sleep."

"I'm fine. What I *need* is another witch." I set the grimoire aside. "A master spell caster, who understands complex hexes." Unfortunately, I'd burned the bridge with my former coven. My stomach knots. There's no way to know if that witch gave me up back then to the rest of the coven and therefore His Creepiness. I'd hoped to have the hex removed and geas lifted by the time the past caught up with the present.

He tilts his head. "If you need a witch, Rhiannon is good at spell casting."

I recall the repulsion ward she'd cast in Wallace Falls. She may have learned orally, as most witches outside my coven do, but I could translate the written language of witches for her.

"Can you take me to her?"

The corners of his mouth curve in a grin reeking of smugness. He gestures to the plate. "After you eat and get some sleep, I most certainly can."

"You are not my father!"

He arcs an eyebrow.

I blush, realizing how childishly cranky I sound.

"Definitely not." A grin curves his handsome mouth. "If you'd refuse to take proper care of yourself, Oberon would have no qualms simply lulling you into slumber."

I have the distinct feeling he had already done this when I was a child. Phyr takes the dirties away leaving me to my meal. I devour the food in a short amount of time, finishing the meal off with a glass of red wine from one of the local wineries. Phyr returns, sits and pours his own glass.

"Nap time, dear."

I glower at him as I rise from my chair. "Want to tuck me in? Make sure I fall asleep like a good girl?"

"I would love to join you in your bedchamber, but we both know you're not a good girl. Never have been." His amber eyes sparkle, as he grins behind his wine glass before taking a sip.

Was he flirting?

"What is that supposed to mean?"

Shit. Was I flirting?

His eyes dance with amusement. He enjoys my curiosity about the past the way all fae love to lord secrets over others, but I'm too damned curious to avoid his bait.

"Well?"

After another sip of his wine, he replies, "You led me into quite a lot of mischief when we were children."

I look down at my glass. "How old was I when we left?"

"Our acquaintance was not brief." He pauses to sip his wine. "You are of the long lived and those who are long lived have long childhoods."

"That is why your siblings had such strong reactions to your reappearance. There is history between the four of us."

"I thought I've lived forty-three Earth years." I sit back down in my chair. Witches don't celebrate birthdays. I had to believe what my mother told me. "I don't know how old I really am."

An odd look passes over his face, there and gone. "You're still young for fae."

"How many Earth years would you surmise I lived in faerie?"

"Time passes differently there. I don't know? A hundred, perhaps two hundred years?"

I blink. I'm not middle-aged. I'm *old*.

"We were close?"

He gazes at his wine. "Absolutely. Close enough for me to recognize you despite you no longer having the form or face of a young woman."

"My mother is a witch, not a fae. If she spent that much time in faerie, how could she be still alive and barely have aged?"

"Oberon controls all things in his faerie."

"How so?"

"The ruler of the fae *is* the laws of nature, or rather, the rules bend to their will. He wants a star. A star forms. He wants his wife to not age, a wrinkle wouldn't dare etch into her face."

"Holy shit."

"That is what it is to wear the crown, to be a fae god. That is why the ancient Celts worshiped us."

How much was kept from me hurts. It proves my theory I was planned to be an instrument in my mother's machinations. She kept me in faerie until I was about to reach maturity, trained me as a witch when we returned to the coven so that it *felt* like I'd lived a whole childhood there, and then sat me in a forest where there was no doubt who I would summon to anyone but me.

It hurt. It hurt so much to be nothing but a pawn, that my mother not only knew what He did to me but had made me for that life. She hurt others along the way. I had held a grudge against her before, but I'd thought of her as a victim too, not an accomplice.

I rise from my chair on unsteady legs.

"You're right. I need a nap."

"No tuck in?" he teases.

I don't answer. I'm too distraught.

When I slip under the covers, my racing thoughts feel like they'll keep me awake. Every time I try to grasp onto a memory, the past slithers through my fingers. I fall asleep rather quickly. Tears might have ushered me there.

According to the digital clock on my nightstand, I rise four hours later. Dusk. It wasn't a full-night's sleep so to speak, but enough that I feel more refreshed and alert than I have in days.

In the shower, I try to console myself that at least the revelation about my true age means I wasn't actually sixteen when I'd met His Creepiness. I promptly decide my age at the time doesn't matter. I was a pawn *made* for his purpose and that galls me to my core.

After I dress in fresh clothes and put together my travel backpack, I find Phyr and Jada lounging around in the family room. They're watching a cooking show with celebrity chefs.

They both lift their heads.

"Want to go to Phyr's faerie?" I ask Jada, figuring this is the safest way she'll ever see one. I only plan on staying long enough to talk to Rhiannon.

"Can I?" she directs the question to the fae prince.

He doesn't reply right away, then finally nods with a terse smile. "Of course."

"Yay! I'll get my boots," Jada says rising.

Phyr opens his mouth as if to say more, but he closes it again. His gaze tracks Jada running upstairs before landing on me.

"I don't know how to tell her that as my heir, the faerie is also hers," he says, his amber eyes landing on me. "What do you advise?"

"We could tell her together, but I'm not sure I fully understand how it works."

"Understand what?" Boots in hand, Jada reenters the room.

"A long time ago, your mother's house promised my house a child."

Jada wrinkles her nose but doesn't interrupt.

"Your mother's siblings are temperamental, and quite frankly, cruel. When I was told I had to choose between them by the king himself, I nearly died of fright. Your mother skipped into the court and sat on her father's knee, unaware of the situation and giving me a reprieve at once."

"If mami was a part of her father's house, why wasn't mommy part of the choosing?"

"Her mother had tried to lock her in her room because multiple fae courts were present and she hates us, but your mother escaped, wanting to see the courts for herself. She asked her father what was happening and when he replied I was choosing a consort, she asked if she could be in the pickings."

I listen, fascinated as Jada.

"Her siblings protested because the tying of the two houses with an heir would give them great power in the fae courts. However, your grandfather loved to indulge your mother, so he said yes. Your mother was breathtaking in her strange humanish beauty, and Oberon's obvious favorite, so I made the best decision of my life. Both fae royal houses were happy until your mother disappeared. After the news of your mother's death, there had been talk of me having to choose again." His amber eyes land on me. The gratitude in them overwhelming. "Danu blessed me with the appearance of your mother."

"So, are you here to—uh hook up and have a kid?"

Phyr cocks his head and arches an eyebrow. Then comprehension settles on his features. He lets out a raucous laugh. "Not quite. I have no desire to have a child with an unwilling person, so I named you the child between us. This faerie we travel to is yours, or will be yours one day, if I do not prove truly immortal."

Jada lowers onto the sofa. "Whoa. So, like you're my new dad?"

"I would not dare to think to replace your father. Think of me as a benefactor—or what would be a modern word for someone who is not blood relation but responsible for the wellbeing and material comforts of a child if their parent perishes?"

Jada tugs on a combat boot and then the other. "Sounds like an adoptive dad to me."

"Godfather would be closer," I reply. "Without the whole church thing."

"K." Jada nods as she tightens the laces on her boots, apparently satisfied with that explanation. "Fairy godfather it is."

"*God*father," Phyr purrs, an amused grin touching his lips. "I like the sound of that."

I roll my eyes. "Ready?"

Phyr pushes to his feet in a swift, graceful motion. "As I'll ever be."

Through the portal he creates, the three of us step into a forest.

Rhiannon's cottage ahead looks the same. The tree cages are gone, thank goodness.

Jada looks around, brown eyes wide while she takes it all in. "Whoa. You live here?"

"This is the home of a friend of mine and an acquaintance of your mother's," Phyr explains. "I live in a castle in another part. Next time, we'll visit there.'

She grins. "Cool. I've never been in a castle before."

He smiles back but it doesn't reach his eyes.

We walk together to the cottage. I knock. The wooden door swings open slowly.

Rhiannon's eyebrows creep up her forehead. "You're back?"

"I have a favor to ask of you."

The witch jabs a thumb at her chest. "A princess has a favor to ask of *me*?"

"Yes. I need your assistance with a spell."

She gestures to the interior. "Come in!"

We all go inside. I introduce her to my daughter. Jada, thankfully, has enough manners to not mention Rhiannon's stench or the state of her clothing. The rock witch offers us food, which we all respectfully decline.

I explain the situation as succinctly as possible, but Rhiannon has lots of questions.

"Most of what I understand of hexes is that the recipient must be asleep for the removal, like surgery. When I do figure out which hex is the right one, I won't be able to perform it alone."

"I can remember any spell you tell me. Steel trap mind." She taps her temple with her fist. "I'm good with figuring out counter spells on the fly, too."

I must not be holding back the shock from my face, as she laughs. "You grimoire-trained witches don't know how to MacGyver anything. The problem with grimoires is that you treat spell work like a scientific recipe and not what it is."

"And what's that?" I ask despite fearing her answer.

Rhiannon waggles her fingers in the air like a talent show magician. "Magic!"

Jada chuckles and Phyr snorts. I hold my tongue. The geas is tied to my light, my soul, and the hex is tied to the geas. I don't want duct tape and paperclips holding my soul together.

Rhiannon claps her hands together. "Let me gather a few things, I take it I'll be staying more than one night."

"Yes. Likely," I reply, hoping I don't have to resort to Rhiannon's improvising spell work. There has to be a counter spell in the grimoire.

I just have to find it.

40

To my great surprise, the first thing Rhiannon asks is to use my bathtub. I wince internally. There's more than a little grime caked on her. The mess would be awful to clean, and I wasn't sure sitting in her filth would get her truly clean.

"Would you mind using the shower?"

"I've never used one," she admits. "Our coven only had a tub we all shared."

I take her to my bathroom and get the shower started for her, pointing out what all the shampoos and soaps are for. I hand her a wide-toothed comb, several washcloths because I believe one won't do the trick, and a big fluffy bath towel.

"Would you like to borrow some clothes of mine—to blend in?"

"You're the first person to be kind to me since I left the coven." A tear slides down Rhiannon's grimy cheek. "Well, the princeling has been kind but in an aloof fae kind of way, and he's always so bossy. 'You can live here but if you're eaten by a fae because you didn't hide your scent, I'm not going to feel sorry for you.'" She mocks his accent. "'Stay away from the castle. If anyone asks, I said you could live here, but you're not to say we're friends. Killing and eating the forest creatures even if they're not hominids is wrong. They're sentient. Fine, I'll build you a Nowhere door to Earth so you can get human food, but you better not bring back trouble. If you're going to collect cryptids, you have to remember to feed and water them and give them exercise.' Blah blah blah."

"He built the Nowhere door for you specifically here?"

"Yeah. He said the pixies say this territory was a safe place."

"How would the pixies know that?"

"They flitter between this world and the faerie."

Anger wells up inside me like boiling water in a lidded pot. I leave Rhiannon with a steaming shower and access to any of my clothes, storming downstairs to Phyr.

"Do the light sprites in my garden spy for you?"

He spins on his heel and face me. "They were your dear friends. However, I did send them to find and guard you when you left."

"So, you know *everything*?"

He nods slowly. "Everything that happened in their presence, yes."

"Who did you share the information with?"

"No one."

"Not even my father?"

He shook his head.

"Why?"

"Because he would have started a war that we could not win to get you back. Too many fae have died over angelic and demonic machinations. I'm sorry for what you went through, but you must believe that I knew you well enough to know you'd defy even Lucifer himself. Eventually."

The doorbell rings.

I waver between this argument and answering. A light knock and Shawn's voice makes the decision. *Shit.*

"Either make yourself scarce or glamour yourself to appear human." I shoot over my shoulder.

I swing the door open and plaster on my PTSA smile. "Well, this is a surprise."

There are bags under Shawn's eyes, he hasn't shaved in at least a few days, and he's slouching. He's wearing a suit, but it's disheveled. The twins are in a double stroller behind him on the sidewalk. Tomi, the eldest, stands next to the stroller, arms folded across his chest. His eyes are red. The middle child is riding her bike on the cul de sac's sidewalk, ringing her bell.

"Yeah. Um. Sorry for the intrusion." He rubs the crown of his head. "Have you seen Micah?"

I shake my head, worry knotting my gut. "No."

He glances over his shoulder. "Watch the twins. I need to talk to Miriam in private."

Behind him, Tomi rolls his eyes and groans.

"You want to keep that phone, you'll do it, mister," Shawn snaps.

"I—uh." Didn't have time for whatever this is.

"Darling? Who's this?"

An arm slips around my waist. Phyr's in black jeans and a button down, his skin is the dark olive of the Mediterranean, not bronze. The horns are gone and his jet hair is slicked back in a ponytail at the nape.

"This is my neighbor, Shawn. Shawn, this is an old friend I grew up with."

Phyr shoves a hand forward, the sameway Jada had when she introduced herself. "Bréanainn."

Shawn straightens, suddenly alert. "What did you say?"

Phyr's responding smile has no fangs. "Never mind. My Irish name is too hard for an American tongue. Call me Brendan."

Shawn takes his hand. "Can I speak with you alone a sec, Miriam? No offense Brendan, but it's about something personal."

Phyr grins. "No problem." He presses his lips right next to my ear, whispering, "I will not be far."

A shiver of pleasure dances down my neck from where his lips brush against my skin. He releases his arm from my waist and is gone.

I lead Shawn into the dining room.

"I thought you were dating Gabriel Crowfoot."

"I am," I close the doors to both the entrances. "Sorry, I have nothing to offer in the way of food. I wasn't expecting more company than I already have."

I send a prayer to whatever gods will listen that Rhiannon keeps her strange self in the shower for the duration of this visit.

Shawn studies me a moment and then shakes his head as if dismissing whatever love life I have going on as not his business. He grips the back of a dining room chair and blows out his breath.

"Right. Better get straight to it. Micah and I had a fight two nights ago. He said he needed space. I haven't heard from him since." He smooths a hand over his head. "I was wondering if the kids could stay with you while I look for him."

I had a demon coming, the witches are aware I'm not dead, and I have a hex to remove. The last thing I need is to babysit four children. "Have you reported his disappearance to the police?"

He shakes his head. "No. I don't want the police involved. Micah —had a temper when he was younger. He would take off. I usually could wait it out, but we have kids now, and it's scaring them."

"Do you have any reason to believe he's in danger?"

Shawn cuts a scathing glare. "He's a gay man in the United States, so yeah he's in danger."

"I'm sorry. I didn't—"

Shawn holds up his hands. "No. I'm sorry. That was unnecessarily rude." He scrubs his face. "I'm worried he'll lose his temper and get into trouble. He's come so far, Miriam."

Given how Shawn treats me, I can see how he might say something to set Micah off.

"Look. He loves his family more than anything in the world. He'll be back. You just have to be patient or involve the police."

"So, is this your way of saying no to watching the kids?"

"I have a lot going on, Shawn."

"What? An old boyfriend is in town and now you suddenly have a life? Micah and I were there for you, and we had things going on too."

I close my eyes and take a deep breath. "I get that you're having a hard time with your marriage and Micah's disappearance is frightening, but flinging my mental breakdown in my face and making disparaging remarks about how I choose to live is not going to guilt me into doing what you want."

"I wish," Shawn begins. "I wish for one moment you'd open your eyes and see how much you don't see. There is a world out there you're a part of and know nothing about. You and Micah both get to pretend it's not there because Raf and I protect you from the ugly truth."

Before I can respond, before I can even digest what he said, Shawn is out the door.

Phyr enters the dining room, looking like a fae again. "So, you have an angel who's fallen from *grace* and living as a human for a neighbor? Interesting community."

"What?" I spin to Phyr.

"I never forget a face. He was an angelic soldier once, a powerful one."

I rub my temples. Shawn, an angel fallen out of grace with the Angelic Anocracy—meaning stripped of his power—was one revelation too many. He knew what I was, or at least, what Raf told him I was? Raf knew there was an angel next door and didn't tell me? Did Gabriel know my neighbor was a fallen angel, and if he didn't, what new problems would that cause?

For now, I decide that it's not my issue to figure out.

"I wonder what it's like to start over and live a whole new life in this bizarre version of the Earth I once knew," Phyr murmurs. He turns to me. "Was it terrible to give up magic and be no one?"

"You want a firsthand account?" I plant my hands on my hips. "Weren't the pixies' reports enough?"

His shoulders slump. "You're not angry with me because I had the pixies watch over you. You're angry that I knew about Lucifer and didn't intervene."

The pixies didn't abandon me when I spent time in Hell. They'd seen everything I went through. He'd seen everything. *How could someone who suggests that we were close do nothing*, I want to shout. Instead I look away, blinking back tears. I don't know why I feel so raw about this, but I do.

"Tell me, Miriam. Would you have preferred if I'd been your savior, caused a war, shed blood for you?"

"No." I sob. "Yes."

He breeches the space between us, the sudden movement forcing me to look at him, to see the anger blaze in his amber eyes, but his tone remains oh so fae neutral. He smiles, but there's no humor in it. "Would you like me to go back in time and rescue the younger you? I could. You know it's within my power."

My first instinct is to say yes. I'm glad I don't. If he did go back, I would have never met Raf, fallen in love and had my precious Jada sleeping upstairs. I wouldn't have the conundrum I face now, but I would have caused war between Hell and the Fae, decimating the dwindling population of the latter. Lucifer would've destroyed the faeries and all who dwelled in them to get me back. I was his key to one-upping his estranged brethren. Phyr would die defending me, Oberon too, perhaps, for nothing. I would have likely run back into Lucifer's arms, if I hadn't had to go through the crucible of saving myself.

"No."

"I could challenge Lucifer now. Duel him to the death. I would lose, but maybe the thought of me acting like a possessive, lovesick fool excites you?"

I roll my eyes.

He reaches for me, stroking my cheek. The barest of touches. "I did not save you, but I never abandoned you, Tati."

I recall all the times the pixies found me strung out, gave me water and herbs. How the pixies found Raf and led him to my half-dead body in the Everglades. How the pixies kept Jada from going near that hellhound. How they warned me of the vampires attacking Gabriel.

My throat tightens and tears sting the back of my eyes. I hadn't been alone. I'd always had my childhood friend. "You saved my life."

"You saved your life. I only provided what assistance I could from afar." His finger traces the edge of my jaw, causing electric sparks to travel over my skin. "Do you know why I had the pixies watch over you, long, long after I lost all hope of you ever coming back?"

I lick my lips. "No."

Dark lashes sweep downward over Phyr's amber eyes as his gaze dips to my mouth.

My heart thuds as his head lowers to mine. His grip on my waist tightens. A kiss between us would not be simply a kiss. We would complicate an ever-increasingly complicated situation.

"As long as I'm alive, you don't have to sleep with my siblings?"

He barks a laugh, dropping the hand and taking a step back. "Exactly so."

"Why'd you make a joke and ruin the romantic scene?"

We both turn and my jaw falls to the floor. Rhiannon—all washed up, long brown hair untangled and free of branches and gods knew what, face free of grime but displaying freckles and delicate features, dressed in a pair of my leggings, and *of course*, my most expensive cashmere sweater—is drop dead gorgeous. She's also devouring a bag of popcorn like she's watching a movie. How did neither of us hear her enter the dining room?

"Plot-wise, it's good to develop some sexual tension before Miriam remembers all that you were to each other and your enduring love for her is requited," she adds around a mouthful of popcorn. "Oh. I want to see *that* kiss."

Phyr arches a jet eyebrow. "Are you comparing our life to a fiction?"

She furrows her brow. "Yes. This is totally a romantic subplot, but you know, with the archangel, there's a love V."

"A lovey?" I immediately regret asking. I want no part of her less lucid moment.

"A love triangle implies that all three parties are potential love interests for each other." She draws a triangle in the air. "What you have here is a V. Gabriel and Phyr have the hots for Miriam, but you don't have the hots for each other." She draws a "V" in air.

"The hots?" Phyr tilts his head.

Rhiannon laughs. "Sexual desire!"

Phyr rubs his chin, his eyes distant as if lost in thought. "I would not mind this triangle. I think I'd prefer it to a V. Gabriel would feel less threatened by me and my presence welcome rather than tolerated. The question is, would I be able to stomach a nephil who has killed so many fae?"

"Oh, that's enemies to lovers! He's a curmudgeon, but he's a pretty curmudgeon," Rhiannon says dreamily. "Imagine rubbing up on all those muscles."

My cheeks heat. I don't have to imagine. I wipe my brow, unable to believe this conversation is actually taking place. Gathering my composure, I clear my throat. "We should get to work."

Rhiannon salutes. "Okey dokey, smokey."

I lead her upstairs into the grimoire room, leaving Phyr to ponder an enemies-to-lovers narrative. Inside the library, she spins in a circle, awed.

"I can feel the magic pulsing in here. Shi—" Her face has a rare-for-Rhiannon moment of shrewd lucidity. "This is 'the treasure' the demon wanted, isn't it?"

"Yep."

"What's the devil want with a bunch of old witchy books?"

"Grimoires," I correct, taking a deep breath. "He wants the World Destroyer spell. To end humanity, the source of Angelic Anocracy's power."

"World Destroyer?"

I smile bitterly. "Did your coven teach you what happened to our old world?"

"The Council of Ofia destroyed the old world because the warlocks were well, terrible." She hugs herself. "It never sat right with me. All those innocent boys and there had to be grown warlocks, who weren't evil oppressors but just surviving, you know?"

"Witches died too," I confess. "Anyone who didn't agree with the Council of Ofia."

Her eyes widen. "Whoa. I did *not* know that."

"That knowledge is shared only by the few." A tear wets my cheek. "Lucifer always talked about how witches would form a great army and take over this world, rid it of the ones who persecuted us. He used our bias against us."

"Wait. If he wants witches to power the Council of Ofia's spell, then what about the ones who live here? What was the plan?"

A bitter laugh escapes my lips. "He promised me all the witches would have a place in Hell."

Rhiannon wrinkles her nose. "Yeah. No thanks. Wait. Just one witch can power something that big?"

"The original spell was designed so that a full witch from the old world could power it."

She scratches her head. "I mean. Those witches were like gods. Aren't we a bit watered down from what we once were?"

"That's where I come in his plan, under my geas is enough light to power the spell."

"So, after I help you remove your hex and you remove your geas, then you'll have the kind of light that can power a world eater?"

"In theory."

"You'll also have enough power to destroy these grimoires and that fucking awful spell?"

Although it pains me to destroy the other knowledge contained in these grimoires, I understand this is her price for her help. I hedge, "Maybe."

"I can read and write in Kairska," she admits, tugging at the hem of my sweater. "I will help you transcribe every bit that isn't a piece of that spell, but you must use the power you unleash to destroy them."

Could two witches, three if we include Jada, transcribe all the knowledge in these books? It would have to work.

"Deal," I say, handing her the grimoire of hexes. "Since you can read, we can get this going."

41

It takes two more days, and all of my patience, for us to find the spell my mother used. It takes another day for Rhiannon and I to devise a counter spell since the grimoire had none. When I phone Gabriel to tell him the good news, he insists Leilani be there to monitor me while Rhiannon removes the hex.

When Leilani shows up the next day, so does Cian, Gabriel, and Lance—I recognize the handsome shifter from the witch search party. Lance waves but remains outside as the other two come inside.

"You can come in," I say, wondering if it's a shifter thing to be invited in.

His dreads sway as Lance shakes his head. "Thanks, but I have orders."

"He's on guard duty. I have more shifters posted throughout the neighborhood," Gabriel explains. "Close the door, please. I'll explain."

I close the door and look at him expectantly.

"Hellhounds were spotted along the Sammamish River. They didn't engage with the shifters that came into contact with them, disappearing before they could apprehend the monsters, but the hounds were hunting something."

An icy shiver slithers down my spine. The Sammamish River, also known as the Sammamish Slough, runs through Seattle's Eastside. Humans walk, jog, and bike the paved trails running along the river. Parents push their infants in strollers. It is not an isolated area. His Creepiness wants something there bad enough to not care if he exposes himself to Gabriel's scrutiny. It could be taken as an act of aggression, leading to war.

"Understood."

I lead them all into the great room. Phyr sits at the breakfast bar eating while Rhiannon sets up for the counter spell. I offer seats to Leilani and Cian at the breakfast bar. All the other furniture is shoved out of the room except one overstuffed chair.

"There were more sightings of strange wolves up in Wallace Falls," Cian adds to Gabriel's report. "Those are state lands, so we don't have to worry about idjit hunters, but the gossip in Gold Bar is fierce. Lots of speculation."

"Hellhounds in Wallace Falls make sense," Gabriel says, taking a seat in the overstuffed chair in the living area. "They are likely looking for the missing cryptids. What doesn't make sense is the bold move of sending packs into the suburbs. One? There's precedence of a few coming into archangels' territories and nothing coming to fruition, but entire packs? He's pushing the limits of the treaty." His face is grim. As it should be. The situation is a threat. "I have every pack in my territory hunting for hellhounds and/or demons with the order to kill the former on site and to report demons."

"I worked magic in Wallace Falls," I say, covering my mouth. Magic Lucifer himself had taught me, I don't add.

"You will have the aid of my army if you need to defend your territory against Lucifer *if* you don't involve the rest of the Angelic Anocracy," Phyr says, abandoning his meal to join the conversation.

Gabriel cocks an eyebrow and folds his arms across his chest, dubious. "You have Oberon's permission to make such a claim?"

Phyr's gaze flicks to me briefly. "I have over twenty thousand fae warriors at my disposal under the High King's approval."

"Didn't know the fae even had that much left." Gabriel seems more than a little more than impressed.

"It's the entirety of our army." Judging by the coolness of Phyr's expression, saying so costs him to admit. "Our high king's bloodline is at stake."

"As is the opportunity to enter my territory," Gabriel replies grimly. "Let's hope it doesn't come to the fae having to pay such a high price."

"Let's," Phyr agrees.

Both their gazes swing to Rhiannon.

"Is that my cue to say the counter spell is ready?" She makes a sweeping gesture to her layout. "'Cause it's not. Have some snacks or something. Miriam baked."

I assist Rhiannon with the setup while Leilani, Cian, Gabriel and Phyr eat the croissants I baked this morning. It feels odd to have a snacking audience.

Phyr and Gabriel continue their conversation in low tones. I'd love to eavesdrop, but Rhiannon has me running to the garden for herbs I grow but haven't had time to have dried and stored in the past few weeks. My life is completely different from the one I had when the hellhound showed up on my morning run. Normal routines like cutting and drying herbs have gone to the wayside.

It takes at least an hour before I'm lying supine on the floor, surrounded by candles. Rhiannon sits cross-legged behind my head, fingers hovering over my temples. She rubs the herb concoction she's mashed in a mortar with a pistle over my forehead, murmuring under her breath.

The tingle of magic brushes my skin, spreading until my body hums with the sensation scalp to toes. When I was pregnant with Jada, long before I felt her kick, there was a fluttering sensation the doctor called quickening. I felt something akin to quickening in my chest directly under my sternum. Instead of ticklish fluttering it was as if something slithered there.

My gaze drifts between Leilani, Gabriel, Cian and Phyr. They all watch in grim silence. I finally settle on Phyr, who observes with narrowed eyes as if he *sees* what the spell is doing. He's so focused that he doesn't even notice I'm staring at him.

The quickening in my chest shifts from slithering to tugging.

I lift my gaze, tilting my head so that I can see Rhiannon above me. Sweat beads on her forehead. All of her visible skin possesses a dewy sheen. Her dark hair is damp around her face.

A scream tears from my throat as my chest surely renders in two.

One moment I'm in my living room, and the next I'm in a strange meadow.

I'm holding hands with a bronze boy with small horns sprouting from his head. He is running with me. We pass a dryad and a flock of pretty sprites. The boy and I are giggling but I'm also a little afraid. We've stolen something. Something important, but it's oh so funny we've gotten away with it.

We reach a grove of twisted gray trees with scarlet leaves and golden fruit. I exchange a broad smile with him. We're safe. He takes the velvet box from the cache where he stored it and opens the box.

A crown of thorns and gold and jewels sparkles inside, even in the shade. I take the crown with shaky hands.

"Echtas Nnomen allat," I command the boy in High Fae. The words are strange sounds for a moment then I understand what I've said: *Tell me your name.*

"I cannot," he replies in the same language. "Only one can ever know your true name. The one you mate-bond with. They're the only fae you should ever trust with it."

"I'll tell you mine," I offer, setting the crown upon my head. It belonged to the dead queen Tatiana, the one I'd been named after officially. I hate the name, the empty space next to father where mother should sit. Father still loves Maeve and Nix's mother and she's been dead longer than my mother has been alive and that is a very, very long time. My mother had to be at least thirty when she came to faerie and has lived here for at least a hundred years. I hardly have a concept of years. It was a mom's world thing. Earth. The place all fae dream of seeking again.

My whole life in faerie flashes in my mind every single moment, many of them filled with Phyr, but then I'm back in the grove with the boy again.

Fear limns the boy's features. "Please don't."

"You'll be my consort. Besides, I'm going to mate-bond with you when we're old enough, why not tell it now?' I scowl. "Have you seen the future? Do you bond with someone else?'

"Never," he swears, and I think he's about to say more but his mouth clamps shut as if he's keeping secrets. I hate when he keeps secrets from me. I tell him everything. Phyr is my only friend.

I take a step toward him then another. Phyr is frightened of me, of my power, but not as fearful as he is of my siblings.

Maeve and Nix could be very cruel—a thousand memories of cruelties flood my head. Their "little jokes" stopped only by Niamh's watchful eye and Phyr's many sacrifices, taking my place turning their attention to him. I've done the same for him when they go too far with him. He's not an only child, they could kill him and be forgiven —my father's favor, the only thing that keeps my siblings from killing me. They've come close, too often.

My mother, father, cousin Niamh, and Phyr are the only ones who show me any affection. The rest of the high fae fear or hate me.

Phyr shows me affection, but affections and loyalties change in this place, and I am not as beautiful or clever as the fae. I have witch blood. I am a halfling. I need his name as guarantee Phyr will never turn on me and side with my siblings.

My heart flutters in my chest. I must gain his trust.

The most beautiful face I've ever seen fills my vision, iridescent and shining like a polished mirror. Hair like rays of sunlight. Eyes the color of the darkest moss, but glowing with power greater than father could ever hope to have. Shapely lips as glossy as dew spread in a smile.

Danu leans down, whispering, "Morrígan."

I'm no longer in the bassinet but in the shady grove with the boy. He's utterly still as I take his hand in mine. My heart flutters wildly as I take in his scent. When we grow old enough, I will do with him what mother does with father. She's told me all about what transpires. How fae are different, that they choose what they want to have in the private spaces or nothing at all like Niamh.

I gently tuck his long hair behind his ear. He shivers but doesn't seem afraid anymore. Phyr had been "they," androgynous as Niamh, until I told him I'll need a boy someday because I couldn't change down there.

"Do you really not want to know mine?" I whisper.

His breath is ragged. "Of course, I want to know, but I daren't ask."

I whisper my most sacred secret in his ear and then pull back, smiling. "Now tell me yours."

His eyes sparkle amber surrounded by a sea of white, so wide and terrified. He shakes his head slowly. "You don't know what it will do to us. We have a long time until we're ready for the sharing of names."

"I shared and you *let* me." I take a step back, covering my mouth and blinking back the tears. My throat hurts. "You're going to use it against me. Aren't you?"

"I'll never tell," he vows. "I'll never say your name out loud until you say I can." I see him cringe as the pain settles in, not the pain of a lie, the pain that comes when you make a vow that Danu binds you to uphold.

I hear horns in the distance. Both of us start.

He holds out a hand. "Let me take the crown back to the display room. I can be in and out and no one will ever know you wore it."

I shake my head, creating a cache and stuffing the crown inside. "I don't want Maeve or Nix to have it." *Ever.*

His head whips in the direction of the castle. "You said you wanted to wear it for a while, *not* keep it."

"You said you'd be my bond-mate someday but won't tell me your name," I shoot back. "Guess both of us are liars."

"You will leave me, and I will be so inconsolable, I will volunteer to go back to the war against the angels in hopes that I'll die. I won't. Not in a thousand, thousand different scenarios will I die. You will grow old and so will I. I will be lifetimes older than you when we meet again and you will look upon my face and not know me, not trust me. I will be a stranger to you, and it will eviscerate me. I've seen in all the possible futures where I do nothing but suffer and long for you. Let me keep my damned name, Tati!"

"Why did you seek our futures?"

He looks away. "Your father asked me to. He was worried your mother has plans for you. She does. They're not good."

"No. They're not."

We both turn to the resonant sound of my father's voice. He enters the grove, regal and handsome as ever. A rueful smile touches his lips.

"Phyr, say goodbye and go home," my father commands.

The boy's amber eyes turn to me, taking me in as if he'll never see me again. "I'll see you again."

I throw myself at him, hugging him with all my might. He stiffens at my embrace at first and then tentatively hugs me back. It's unseemly of fae, but I'm overwrought. Phyr is a boy, but a powerful planeswalker and never, never wrong about the future. He steps out of the embrace and into the ether, gone from this faerie to his realm.

"Tati, come here," my father commands, gently.

I obey.

He wipes my tears with his thumbs. "Do you know what a geas is?"

I shake my head.

"It is a way one fae is beholden to another. Phyr is now bound by geas to never say your name unless you tell him to, but you also will always be connected to him. Which means you'll be able to find your way back to him. I want you to always be able to find your way back to me."

Though I'm embarrassed that he saw the whole dumb moment transpire and knows I took his dead wife's crown, I know he's not angry with me for it. Father loves Maeve and Nix but not as much as he loves me. He's said so in front of everyone. Oberon's genuine love for me is part of the reason they hate me.

I nod. "I want that too, papa."

He smiles, the adoration in his eyes warming me. I always feel his love and Phyr's affection, but not mama's. She's nice but doesn't look at me the way they do.

"There are those who would use you for your light, Tati. I want you to promise me to not use more than you need of your light than necessary to sustain your life."

"Okay."

"I want you to say, 'I, your name, promise to not use my light other than necessary to sustain my life and small magics. I will not release myself from this vow until I tell Phyr my true name for the second time."

I make the promise, whispering my name. The pain of the geas binding my soul is too much. All goes black.

I awake again in my living room, surrounded by everyone. My gaze locks with Phyr's. "Come here. I need you."

He does as I bid, eyes wide likely because I said it in High Fae. I hadn't done so intentionally. My mind was still thinking in the language.

"I need you to give us space," I say in English to Rhiannon. I don't want to risk her overhearing what I am about to whisper. My true name frightens me, there is power in the name itself, more than what knowing it could wield over me. My true name means something to the fae and might to others.

I sit up. Grabbing his arm, I pull him close. In the fae tongue, I say, "I remember everything, my friend, and it was you who was naughty."

A smile touches his lips.

"Your promise still stands?"

His face and tone grow solemn. "Always."

The memory of how he refused me his name when I'd given mine freely still fresh—I whisper my true name in his ear, knowing I can trust the geas between us even if I didn't know if I could trust him.

"Shield yourselves," I hear Phyr shout.

There's movement around me, a flash of golden white light. Green light, blinding and fierce, thrusts from every pore of my body until I'm consumed by it. Phyr is still there with me, unbothered by the energy I'm emitting. I *see* him for the first time. He's made of it, the fae light is woven into his flesh, but I'm not the same. I'm of two forms, one pure energy, a fae god, and the other flesh and blood— like Rafael.

"Draw it in," Phyr shouts in my face. "Angels are drawn to our light."

"I don't know how," I answer, my voice strange and resonant, akin to my father's.

As soon as the words leave my lips, Phyr presses a hand to my face —a jolt passes between us. The contact is more than skin on skin, he's breaching the barriers I've built. "You do. Remember."

I'm not sure if he says the words out loud or thinks it at me. A memory, an early and fuzzy around the edges, of my father teaching me to contain my light within my half-witch body. My physical form seems impossibly small compared to the supernova within me and I'm even more frustrated and confused than I am now.

In the memory, I build a cache within me—a secret store to make it seem like I have less light than I do, but accessible if necessary.

"I remember," I whisper.

Phyr's hand leaves my face. He stays close, hovering over me. Worry limns his usually stoic face. I see my constant childhood companion in the fae prince before me. The memories are fresh now as if I've just experienced them, and the emotions are as raw and big as in my youth. I tuck them away to examine later when I didn't glow like a freaking green star.

I withdraw the light, pouring it through a door within my body into the interstitial space of a cache I create. I leave as much light as geas had allowed. No wonder my mother hadn't realized there was a geas until we'd left the faerie. Discovering it after she made me forget the father and friend I'd wailed for, no doubt.

I look in Rhiannon's direction. I can't thank her. Not because she's one-sixteenth brownie. Now I understand why fae don't thank, how Danu binds them to words of debt and gratitude through their light. I simply nod and say, "Time to keep my end of the bargain."

42

Turns out Gabriel's gift from his father to speak any language means he speaks both the High Fae Phyr drops into, that I remember now, and the tongue of witches, Kairska. Not only can he speak it, he can write in it. So can Roxy—who was just as shocked as I was when Gabriel said that she could read the grimoires.

Rhiannon, Jada, and I are the only ones with witch's blood to transcribe the grimoires, but the rock-witch figured out a spell-hack that made it so Roxy and Gabriel can use our blood and their magic to do transcribing.

The five of us set to the work of transcribing over thirty grimoires. Phyr, Lucinda, Cian and Leilani, as well as Lance and few other members of the pack rotate feeding us. Phyr also spends time doing the forbidden—surfing the web. Gabriel allows it when I say that Phyr is bound to me through many, many childhood debts. I don't tell him the debts are mutual. I don't tell him we have shared trauma thanks to my siblings, and clung to each other out of necessity.

I take a break from transcribing, stand and stretch. "I'm going to go out to the garden for a bit."

Rhiannon glances up, nods, and then goes back to work. Her hair is in a messy knot, emphasis on the messy, and she's in my sweats.

Whatever clothes she'd packed are staying in her bag. Thank the Mother.

Gabriel gives me a thumbs up but doesn't look up from his work. Roxy ignores me, also engrossed.

Jada yawns and stretches. "I think I'm going to take a shower and wake up."

Something occurs to me that hasn't occurred to anyone. It's silly I hadn't thought of it before.

"We don't have to rush to get these copied. We could go back in time to steal the grimoires at any time."

Gabriel's quill stops moving. He looks up slowly. "Could we go back before Lucifer knew of the spell's existence?"

I shrug.

"No," Phyr says from the doorway. He's carrying a tray of food.

Everyone, including me, make quick work of stacking the grimoires, stoppering blood inkwells, and transferring them onto a buffet.

"Why?" Gabriel and I ask at the same time.

"Because there are fixed points in the skein of the universe. Lucifer knowing about this spell is one of them."

"What if we went back to get the grimoires before I was even born?"

"No." He sets the tray on the cleared table roughly, spinning on his heel and leaving.

I follow him into the kitchen. "Why?"

He turns to me. "If we go back to steal the grimoires before you are born, then you will cease to exist and so will Jada. Your whole reason to be is to power that spell, remember?"

"Okay, so that's not an option," Gabriel says behind me.

"I suggest using machinery to copy the grimoires and destroying them. This transcribing will take months and you do not know when this demon will return. It's better if you summon them and get it over with."

"You could beat Lucifer at his game and use the spell on Hell," Gabriel says.

"That is an excellent idea," Phyr agrees, surprising me.

Somehow, they're on the same side?

I step back so that both of them are in view. Gabriel leans against the door frame and Phyr stands next to the cupboard with the plates. "No," I meet each of their gazes. "Billions of innocent demons would die."

The dubious look on Gabriel's face says he's too indoctrinated to believe there are innocent demons. Phyr holds a neutral expression, he couldn't care less but doesn't want me to judge him.

"And, so would *I*," I add, appealing to their selfishness. "I would burn out my light powering the spell."

"Then that's out," Gabriel says. "Phyr has a good idea about the copying and summoning. We'd be at an advantage."

"Copy the spells? Go to the high school and use the copier to print out the remaining spells?"

"Destroy the pages with the keystone spell, of course, and then destroy the grimoires."

It would mean having all the spells without the protection of witchcraft or possible errors, but it was a better solution than hurrying to copy all the spells before Velja showed. Plus, it was a Sunday. No one would be in the office.

An hour later I open the grimoire and set it on the giant school copier. There's no security on the weekends and the office is dark and empty. Four hours later, all the spells are copied.

An hour after that, I am inside a cache with the grimoires. I release my light, the energy unbound lights up the cache. I imagine from afar I'd look like a star and smile at the notion. Focusing my power, I say a simple fire incantation and pour my light into it.

A tidal wave of protective backlash, I shield against hits. With my faelight protecting me, it's uncomfortable but not harmful. Wards broken, the grimoires set ablaze like dry kindling. All those witches' blood and sacrifice to pass on their work, gone in a matter of seconds. Tears streak my cheeks. No matter how much they put in it, how much knowledge they passed, the spells would destroy a world. No one should have that power.

I don't return to my home right away. Allowing myself to see with my other sight, I examine the threads of the multiverse. My light unleashed allows me to see mysteries and wonders at the micro and macro level my witch eyes could not.

As I observe, I unlock the secret to rendering a pocket universe, a faerie of my own. I have the light, the elements necessary. Instead of destroying, I could, I *would* become a *god* with the sort of power that would make me a formidable enough enemy to keep His Creepiness away, but what would become of *me*?

"You would lose your purpose in coming here and leave those who need your aid behind. You are not ready for your own faerie. Creating one is the last step in becoming what you are meant to be, but there are many steps before it," a soft voice, answers my thoughts.

I don't have to turn. The interstitial space isn't like standing in a room. I'm suddenly aware of Danu. She's stunning as in my memories, and my heart does a little flutter at the sight of her.

"I'm meant to be *the* Morrígan, bringer of death, a war god?"

Danu's shapely mouth spreads in a smile. She's heart-achingly beautiful. It's not just her appearance, but her presence is old and wise and farseeing at the same time. "No, you are not a Morrígan of the past. You will reap peace, not sow seeds of war, lovely one."

My cheeks flush and suddenly I don't know what to do with my hands. I'm in the presence of an ancient god, creator of all fae, and I'm crushing like a young fan girl.

"Until recently, you found ways to isolate yourself, never allowing closeness. You hid instead of seeking allies. You're not meant to become your truest form alone. Now that you've gathered witches, halflings, cryptids, demigods, fae, nephilim, fallen angels, sirens, and shifters to your side, face those who would use you for their purposes and say no."

Danu fades, leaving me to realize I've been away much too long.

43

I pull into the parking lot in a space facing Lucinda's Café. I glance to the passenger seat. Phyr's horns and bronze skin are glamoured away. He's still striking in his leather jacket, gray shirt and black jeans, passing for human. He could walk away, disappear into a crowd, and simply blend. Someone who looks like him with his fae mind manipulation abilities could live really well in this world without ever landing on the Angelic Anocracy's radar.

Phyr grins. "What?"

"You don't have to do any of this. You could simply leave and never have to worry about...anything, really."

His grin widens into a smile and for the first time, I notice he has dimples. "I'm a planeswalker. I've always been able to do as I please."

"I no longer require a guard, not really. Why haven't you gone back?"

"He has the hots for you," Rhiannon suggests from the back.

Jada chuckles as she swings open the rear door. "So gross."

"But true!" Rhiannon retorts.

Phyr glances over his shoulder. "True, but I am not motivated by desire."

"Sure, sure," Rhiannon says, slamming the door behind her.

She and Jada head for the café.

Phyr's gaze slides back to me. "I am here now for the same reason I befriended you when we were children. You make a formidable ally."

I raise an eyebrow. "We don't have to have each other's back against my siblings anymore."

He licks his lips, pressing a hand against the dashboard. I forget how big Phyr is because he's more slender than Gabriel. "You are incorrect in that assumption. They want us dead more than ever. However, we have more than our former playmates to worry about now."

My heart thuds in my chest. "It's my battle, not yours. Your presence will involve the fae."

Phyr shakes his head slowly, mouth spreading to a grin that doesn't reach his eyes. "The fae were involved the moment he used a witch to seduce our High King, treating *Oberon* like a stud and you, a blessed of Danu, like a pawn." His bitterness about the insult creeps into his tone. "I will not stand aside while someone manipulates your sensibilities with substances again." His amber gaze swings to the windshield, where Gabriel is exiting his SUV in the space diagonal to my passenger side.

I swallow hard, reaching for my purse. "He's apologized."

"Words are nothing. He is not bound by them as we are," Phyr retorts, popping the door open.

He's right. Gabriel's actions are all I can rely upon, and today, I'm going to ask him to vote on something he's not going to like.

Gabriel joins us on the way into the café, nodding to us by way of greeting. As we reach the door, he asks, "Can I borrow you for a sec?"

"You cannot borrow a person, nephil," Phyr digs but his tone is playful.

"Can I borrow a moment of your time, alone, Miriam" Gabriel amends with a smirk in Phyr's direction.

I gesture to the door. "Go on in, Phyr. Let everyone know that we'll join shortly."

As soon as the door closes behind the fae princeling, Gabriel asks, "Did you *really* destroy the grimoires?"

"Yes."

He studies me for a few moments then he blows out a breath, relieved. "My father contacted me. I had to answer about the presence of hellhounds. He usually doesn't check up, but I think Princess might have gone over my head on this one." He grimaces at the café. "I let him know the hellhounds were searching for a spell but I found it first and destroyed it. I'm glad you went through with it." He runs a hand through his hair, pausing at his nape and holding it there. "If the grimoires turn up, I'll be punished."

"They're gone." I touch his arm. "Your own father would punish you?"

Emotions war on Gabriel's face. Finally, he says, "He's only trying to protect humans."

"Because human belief gives angels power."

"Exactly so."

I rear my head. I'd expected an argument. His agreement surprises me.

He squints as his gaze scans our surroundings. "I used to believe the Angelic Anocracy really were guardians. He wanted the grimoires." His nostrils flare. "He even had the audacity to be angry that I'd destroyed the spell instead of giving it to him. He has no respect for this world, only his authority over it."

I gape. An archangel openly speaking against the Angelic Anocracy?

He sighs heavily. "I think we could manage this whole supernatural community better if we didn't have to worry about interference from other worlds. Wouldn't it be nice to find a way to seal off Heaven and Hell from this universe?"

I think about how Danu told me that I could face anyone as long as I did it with friends. "Or, claim this world as belonging to the humans and the supernaturals who live here, and make angels ask permission to come here like the fae have to."

Gabriel considers this for a moment. "If only all the archangels were nephilim, it might be something I could broach with them."

"How many are nephilim?"

"At least two thirds." He holds up a finger. "One, *one* angel has considerably more power than several nephilim. The Anocracy made sure there would never be another rebellion."

"Angels don't trust their own children." I shake my head. "Doesn't that seem wrong to you?"

"An angel betrayed them, why not the ones with one foot in this world? Besides, many nephilim sided with Lucifer before. That's why the angels destroyed Sodom and Gomorra."

"My whole purpose was to bring on the apocalypse, destroy this world and take away the Angelic Anocracy's power source." I gesture to a Chinese restaurant storefront with a laughing Buddha. "Abrahamic religions aren't the only religions among humans. Beliefs are already divided. What if everyone learned the supernatural community was real, that gods were real, *all* of them?"

"It would upset the current order."

I step closer to Gabriel, forcing him to look into my eyes. "How is their order our problem? No one deity. No one belief would reign. You wouldn't have to wear the mantle of being the guardian of the entire Pacific Northwest supernatural community upon your shoulders. You could make this council real and share the yoke."

"How about we wait until after this meeting to give this some real consideration?" He grins, cheeks dimpling. "Maybe you and I could discuss what that would look like over dinner at my place?"

"Sure." I nod, realizing this might have been something he has considered all along. Why he's helped me all along. It would take a powerful ally to pull off going public and face the backlash.

He opens the door to the café and gestures for me to go in first.

As I enter, part of me wants to peek inside his head. I could. Thanks to the lifting of the hex and geas, I now remember how and have the ability. Something inside me, call it my conscience or moral compass, doesn't allow me. Maybe it's fear and not morality.

Inside, Phyr sits next to Jada at a side table away from the main group, observing her talk animatedly with Roxy. The rest of the council is present and seated. A few non-council members, too, that I don't recognize.

Gabriel had mentioned he was going to invite the supernatural leaders from the local Native American tribes since my plan would affect them, too. Apparently, he's tied through his mother to one of the tribes. According to Gabriel, unlike the shifter community at large, who have aligned with the Angelic Anocracy, most indigenous shifters don't recognize the Anocracy as their superiors and definitely don't ascribe to the Guardian role. His mom was viewed by her family as sort of a traitor for leaving and falling for an angel for a bit, and then aligning with the alpha of the PNW.

I take a seat, waiting for Gabriel to begin. Gazes shift from me to him.

"Thank you for coming." Gabriel nods to the strangers.

We all rise and say who we represent. Gabriel does not defer alpha role to Princess, which surprises me, but she comes as a beta of the Guardian shifter community and her vote counts.

After she's betrayed him to the Anocracy, I'm surprised he's allowed her to come to this meeting at all. Unless this is some sort of test of her loyalty.

"The war between Heaven and Hell has not touched these lands for the entirety of time. Lucifer moves in now because we had something he wanted. We destroyed it, but he does not know this. I will defer to Miriam what she plans to do about that."

I clear my throat. "My plan is simple. I will summon the devil and tell him I've destroyed what he's sought."

Gasps all around.

"Why would he believe you?" one of the strangers asks, an elderly woman with jet hair streaked with silver at the temples. She's in a hoodie and jacket, PNW casual. Her aura shines blue and magenta. She's both shifter and demigod.

"I'm half high fae and he knows fae cannot lie." *Without pain*, I don't add.

"Does the Angelic Anocracy know you're going to summon their enemy?" the same woman asks.

"No. It isn't their business," Gabriel says. "This is about protecting the Pacific Northwest, our people, not the war between Heaven and Hell."

"Why does that demon wear a mask?" She points with her lips at Phyr.

"I'm an Unseelie prince, not a demon," he replies for himself. "I wear a mask because I am too beautiful to behold."

Everyone who doesn't know that Phyr is a full high fae exchange nervous glances. The fae had a bad rap among supes, apparently.

The elderly woman simply lifts a dubious eyebrow. "I heard fae weren't much better than demons."

"We're much worse." Phyr grins and nods at Gabriel. "According to this one, we'll seduce you and make you our thralls. Perhaps I'll start with you, pretty one."

"Try it and see how badly you fail." She chuckles. "Pretty one? Ha! I could be your grandmother."

Phyr shakes his head. "No, my dear. I'm the elder here."

Both her eyebrows lift at that remark.

Gabriel clears his throat. My cue to take control of this meeting back.

"I'm going to summon the devil, but I'm going to need your help," I begin and then tell them my plan.

WITCHES NEVER WASTE. I draw a circle with a mixture of Jada's old sidewalk chalk that I've ground up and mixed with my own blood, chanting a spell. Jada places candles on the north, south, east, and west, murmuring to the four winds the spell she's learned. Rhiannon whispers over the herbs she grinds in the stone mortar and pestle. I find our chants soothing.

Not far from us, Phyr is casting an illusion that will keep all the supes present from Lucifer's sight. I really wish I could watch. His illusion is amazingly accurate.

In case my plan does not work, and the spell isn't enough to contain a former archangel of the highest friggin' order, we've set up the summoning circle deep in the Cascade Mountains so far removed from civilization we don't have cell service—much to the dismay of *everyone*. My reasoning is that if a fight ensues between all of us and him, it won't affect mundanes.

All my new and old friends, cryptids, shifters, demigods, witches, and fae have never worked together before. I enjoy the sweet taste of pride and gratitude that I could bring them together. Tart shame, that I'd hidden for years instead of reaching out, mingles with the more palatable sentiments.

Setup complete, I kiss Jada's forehead and squeeze Rhiannon's hand before they disappear behind Phyr's illusion.

I lift my head to the flap of wings. Gabriel lands just outside my summoning trap. He's beautiful in the moonlight in his angelic form. Imperfect creature that I am, I am caught up in that beauty and his dazzling wings. There is an inexplicable attraction between fae and angels which makes me wonder why they fought at all. That attraction is the entire reason why I'd fallen for Lucifer in the first place, I'm sure. That and his angel dust, which is why Gabriel approaches.

He leans in and whispers, "Take what you need."

I can smell the angel dust on his wings. The scent is intoxicating. I pull him to me and lay a kiss on his lips. He's shocked at first and then reciprocates. I slide my hand down a silky wing, eliciting a shudder.

He breaks off the kiss. "That should be enough." He cradles my face with his hand. "I'll be close." He steps back and launches himself in the air.

I have to fight every instinct to not lick my fingers. Gabriel let me in on a little secret among angels. Lucifer cannot manipulate me with his dust if I have another angel's dust in my system. If Lucifer drags me to Hell, what is on my fingers will protect me until Gabriel and Phyr showed up.

I stand at the center of the circle, lifting the dagger and slicing the inside of my arm. Blood wells and drips into a chalice set up to catch it.

When I was sixteen, I nearly filled the damned cup before he showed up.

Three drops and the ground trembles. The air shimmers. The stench of smoke and sulfur fill my nostrils. Thick smoke snakes from the chalice filling the circle until I'm surrounded by it.

"So dramatic," I whisper under my breath.

"Tatiana." The resonant voice purrs from somewhere within the near suffocating cloud.

"Yeah. It's me."

The smoke clears to reveal an angel. His hair is a curtain of black silk just as dark as his wings. The angles of his face are sharp and pretty. His eyes are pitch, without iris or sclera, but shimmer like two moonlit pools. His skin is golden and almost human, but not quite. Human skin doesn't radiate. He doesn't hesitate in his approach. Arms snake around my waist possessive as they'd been twenty years ago, pulling me against him. Joy and wonder limn his features. A smile touches his beatific face.

Gag.

"You broke the geas. I'm so proud of you."

I find it strange I can look at him and his enthusiasm and feel— nothing. What he'd wanted and his happiness had meant so much to me. I wing an eyebrow, utterly confused. "Why?"

"You've done what no one has ever done. Allied an archangel and a fae prince, witches and shifters. Demigods and cryptids, too?" His face lights up with such...joy?

My mind races to comprehend why he's so happy about this. More importantly why I'm letting him hold me. Wriggling out of his grasp, I take a step back.

"I have. Only to tell you that I won't be used as your weapon. I've destroyed the grimoires, so back off."

"I will," he replies touching his heart. "However, what will stop the Anocracy from throwing you out after they learn you're the heir to the Unseelie throne born in a faerie?"

"Me." Gabriel lands outside the circle. Flapping his wings, he clears out the smoke.

Phyr approaches from the shadows, hand on the hilt of his sword, but he doesn't draw too near. This is part of the plan.

Gabriel on the other hand, positions himself at my side. "I say who comes in and out of my territory."

Lucifer turns to him, smiling. "Until your father makes you get rid of her like he told you to get rid of your wife."

Gabriel's eyes flare, but he keeps his mouth clamped shut.

"What will you do then, *nephew*, toss aside another mate, possibly the love of your life—I know she was the love of mine—simply to appease your papa?"

A muscle feathers in Gabriel's cheek. "That's my business and none of yours."

I expected him to say he wouldn't set me aside. I expected him to say she's my ally, not my mate. Not this. This isn't part of his plan.

"It *is* my business. I love Tatiana and want her happiness." He touches his chest. "Why else would I allow my consort to live after betraying me?"

There. There it is. That hint of anger he's been hiding.

"Lucifer," I say, drawing the King of Hell's dark gaze to me. "He's not my mate. I'm part of Gabriel's Pacific Northwest supernatural council because this is my home, and I'm not going anywhere. So please stop trying to challenge my leader like a jealous ex-lover. It's embarrassing."

One of his eyebrows quirks and his mouth twitches. I know that look. Lucifer likes to give the impression he's all knowing, like a god. One of his spies must have told him Gabriel and I were in love, mated. It must burn to learn we're not. Lucifer's ego is so big and so easily bruised. He probably lied to himself that, that was the reason I didn't return to him, I was simply addicted to another angel. Which means he doesn't know about Raf, or more importantly, Jada.

Lucifer being Lucifer, he rallies. "My point stands. The Angelic Anocracy will not tolerate your presence here and my fear is that he'll betray you to keep his position."

Gabriel lowers his voice but the lethality in his tone conveys his rage as he says, "My council, my pack, and my territory are where my loyalties lie. So stop trying to sow seeds of doubt in my people."

He turns to Gabriel, one eyebrow raised. "Careful. That sounds an awful lot like rebellion."

My heart lurches in my chest when Gabriel shrugs and Lucifer's eyes light up.

The devil licks his lips—a tell that he's about to make a deal. "In that case, I will offer you my assistance. My army in exchange for—"

"We got this," I say before he offers Gabriel something none of us can walk away from. He is called the ultimate tempter for a reason.

"You don't and he knows it." Lucifer nods to Gabriel. Turning back to me, he says, "I don't ask for much. Use of my army in exchange for twenty-four hours alone with you, dearest Tati."

Young me would have found the gesture incredibly romantic, proof of how much he loves me. *Gag.* Twenty-four hours is all Lucifer would need to spin an inescapable web of lies—if I didn't know him. I know too much now for him to be able to con me.

"No," Gabriel says before *I* can answer.

Lucifer's lips curve in a *got you* grin.

I burn with frustration. Gabriel shouldn't have given away how much that would bother him.

Before Lucifer can attack with another angle, I say, "We don't want your army, but I'll agree to your terms if you agree to mine."

Gabriel gasps. "You're not seriously considering this?"

I hold up a hand, signaling I got this. I know Lucifer way better than he ever would. I turn to the devil. "First, you'll withdraw any presence within this territory. Second, you'll give up the silly notion *we* were ever in love."

His nostrils flare. A hand seizes my throat. At the same time the ground rumbles, impenetrable darkness surrounds us.

I'm suddenly cold and hot at once. I've pissed off an ancient creature that is a god unto himself, so powerful the entire Angelic Anocracy could not destroy him. Maybe I should have went about this better.

44

I can't breathe and, just as importantly, I can't cast any spells without my voice. I have a child's knowledge of how to use my fae light, certainly not enough to battle the King of Hell. Clawing at his arm is like clawing at titanium armor and my kicks might be as futile as a tantrum-throwing toddler.

"You owe me your very existence," he hisses in a quiet voice.

All I can see is his face, beautiful features twisted in anger.

"Your loyal mother endured an abomination to create you. Risked her life to free you of their murderous realm. I treated you like my equal, my consort. All because I was in love with a selfish little halfling brat. You made me look a fool to my army, my people who have stood by me longer than your baby mind could fathom, and still I love you."

He eases up enough on his grip enough for me to swallow some air and then tightens it again before I can speak the words that would save me from him. He wants to keep me alive long enough to tell me how pissed he is with me, apparently.

I fight to think. The rationed oxygen and his hypnotic voice makes it hard to do anything but concentrate on him, on my impending death.

Something dawns on me. I summoned him. Angels, demons, witches and others had to travel between worlds by spells and rituals, but fae don't. I'm not a planeswalker like Phyr, but I could open a cache. I reach out my hand, pouring my light into a cut in the fabric of the universe, extending it. Then I threw my weight into him, pushing us both into the cache and sealing the door behind us.

Lucifer lets go of my neck.

Air rushes into my lungs, which makes no sense because we're in a space outside of air and atmospheres. I don't fall. I'm right side up despite no ground beneath my feat, or at least it feels that way. Curious.

It's pitch black. I wanted the space to have air and it simply came into existence. My *will* is doing this.

"What did you do?" he roars from somewhere in the darkness. "Where are we?"

"In a world of my making," I explain in a raspy voice. I light the space with a ball of my fae light in my palm. The ball floats, illuminating Lucifer.

He waves his hands and makes odd gestures, muttering words in a demonic or angelic tongue. I'm not sure which. The whole thing looks absurd enough that a strangled laugh escapes my lips.

He spins on me, eyes narrow.

"You hold no power here." My voice sounds a little rough, but I feel my fae light healing me, repairing the damage a grip only a fallen angel could do. If I'd been only a witch, the damage would have killed me.

His black eyes narrow to slits. "Are you certain of that?" He lunges in attack but doesn't grow closer.

This is my faerie, and I won't let him.

I smile. "Oh, yes."

He folds his arms. "You figured out how faeries work. Good for you." His head swivels as if he's looking for a way out. "Do you plan on keeping me here forever?"

"You wanted twenty-four hours alone with me."

He clucks his tongue, shaking his beautiful head slowly in mock admonition. "Tati, you should know I was lying to bring you home without a fuss."

Feeling stupid, I close my eyes and sigh. I really should've known. Why would I think Lucifer would appear for any other reason than to make me his minion again? Why did I think my power and how I've changed would change him?

"We cannot remain here forever, Tati."

"Then we need to come to an agreement."

He crosses his arms, eyeing me dubiously. "The only thing I'll agree to is not starting a war with your new friends."

That was too easy. I motion with my hand to hurry on with the rest. "Go ahead with the 'but.'"

"You must return with me." He draws near, fanning his wings. "I think you'd enjoy being at my side again. You're more mature. Less prone to fits of passion. You'll be more appreciative of what I have to offer."

I don't take the bait to ask him how he knows these things.

Lucifer continues all on his own, "The youthful Tati would have used this opportunity to murder me to take over Hell. You still have that ambition, or you wouldn't have aligned yourself in a position of leadership. We could unite the fae and my people against the Angelic Anocracy."

He isn't entirely wrong about who I was. Some people dream of being famous or a powerful leader of one form or another. I'd wanted to rule at his side, running everything in the way that we saw fit. However, the way that he wanted to go about it was all wrong.

"True leaders are servants of the people. The ends don't justify the means when eight billion lives are at stake."

"So, you don't mind living under the Anocracy's thumb, knowing how the fae and the demons, and the Fallen suffer?" He arches a dark eyebrow, grinning maliciously, oddly still appearing so heart-achingly angelically beautiful. Lucifer is proof looks have nothing to do with goodness.

I worry my bottom lip, thinking. I don't want to cower in fear at the thought of the Anocracy banishing me from my home just because I was born in a faerie. It sucks that they get to make that decision based on bias.

An idea occurs to me. "I could usurp the Anocracy's authority without shedding a single drop of blood."

Lucifer cocks his head, eyebrows lifting with interest. "I'm intrigued."

"Supernaturals come out of the closet."

His brow furrows. "Come again?"

"We use mundane media to demonstrate that supernaturals exist."

"That would be breaking their greatest law. No other gods before theirs, and there are plenty of gods." His burgeoning grin broadens to a full smile. A smile so beautiful he's almost difficult to behold. "I like it.

"To say there is no one true religion and that all we're correct in one way or another?" He shrugs. "It will upset the balance for a while, I suppose. Are you willing to see what might happen when you force their hand? Sodom and Gomorra aren't just fairy stories."

"Neither are fairy stories just stories," I retort. "The fae are gods."

He pulls a face, giving away he doesn't like the fae referred to as gods any more than Gabriel does. Interesting. He hasn't seen his creator in eons, yet he still believes. Talk about daddy issues. Lucifer lifts and drops his shoulder. "More like distant cousins of angels, but we digress. I must admit, I like this plan. Mind if I take credit for it in Hell?"

I wave a dismissive hand. "As long as you keep your minions out of the Pacific Northwest."

"You keep saying that. It's very American centric and unlike you. There isn't simply one Pacific Northwest in that world."

Knowing he's baiting me, not truly caring about a world he once would have gladly destroyed, I reply, "Stay out of my territory."

"What about everywhere else?" he asks, all innocence in tone.

I blow out my breath and throw up my hands. "I have no ambition beyond protecting where I live."

He sits on what I say for a while before saying, "I have one more condition."

Folding my arms across my chest, I eye him warily. "What's that?"

"You will turn to me as an ally, if you find yourself at the mercy of Gabriel—I mean my brother, not my ambitious nephew." A real grin, one that reaches his eyes, plays on his lips. "You can't stuff the entire Angelic Anocracy into a faerie."

"Agreed," I stick my hand out, forgetting Lucifer has no idea how humans do business.

He eyes my hand with a touch of sadness shaping the angles of his features. "I'd much rather seal our deal with a kiss."

Ew. I'd rather eat moldy bread.

I nod to my offered hand. "Take the deal or leave it, Lucifer."

A smile touches the same pretty mouth that used to tell me all the honeyed words I wanted to hear. "No you wouldn't. You would rather shove the moldy bread in my mouth and tell me to enjoy it, or I wouldn't get any more."

I bark a laugh. The pain in my throat reminding me he'd tried to squeeze the life out me.

As Lucifer predicted, Phyr enters my cache as if he were stepping into a room. Worry limns his bronze features, but his amber gaze simply observes the handshake with an amused grin.

"Not the scene I expected."

I do not miss Phyr's hand gripping the hilt of his sword ready to strike, nor that he does not ease his grip.

Lucifer wings an eyebrow. "What did you expect to see, princeling?"

"A mutilated corpse."

"I would not harm her," Lucifer lies, touching his chest.

"Could you escort Lucifer to Gehenna?" I ask, letting go of the King of Hell's hand—hopefully for the last time. "We're done here, and I don't think he's wanted back on Earth."

Phyr nods. As he slices through the fabric of time and space with a hand, he says, "It wasn't her I thought I'd find dead."

Lucifer chuckles. "I like you."

Phyr angles his head, taking in Lucifer's measure. "Most do." More darkly, he adds, "Until they don't."

The two disappear.

Within a space of the breath, Phyr returns.

"I faced his and won," I whispered, disbelief painting every word. Tears come unbidden and my body trembles.

"Did you dip into his mind?" Phyr asks, his eyes roam over my body as if assessing for injuries.

I shake my head.

"Good. The place is a twisted labyrinth and none too pleasant." Phyr's broad shoulders shudder. He lays a gentle hand on my arm. "My friend, I don't think he ever cared about the spell. He believes you will bring about the kind of war which, quite frankly, terrifies me to behold. In his mind, you're doing exactly as he wants."

I shudder. I am stronger for making this space. Lucifer would never make a move that wasn't calculated. He wouldn't have choked me out of anger. He was pushing me to become the goddess of war.

"We need to get back," I say, part of me sad to leave before I made my own true faerie.

"Not the way you came. That darkness has impenetrable spell-work." He offers me his hand. "Don't say anything when we come through until I tell you to."

"Why?"

"It will—" he seems to grasp for words, "—weird people out."

I smile at his use of modern expression and take his hand much more eagerly than I took Lucifer's. I follow Phyr through a portal to a time I'd already lived unfolding.

We're at a distance, nestled between trees. I now see the way Lucifer was baiting me, getting me to say something that will *seem* to anger him. From this angle, I see that Lucifer had started the shadow and smoke barrier spell, which would envelop us, long before his hand shot to my throat.

"I had to observe this a few times to figure out that you'd made a cache and threw the two of you in it," Phyr whispers behind me, his breath tickling my ear.

Everyone gathers around the circle filled with impenetrable darkness, waiting.

"We didn't dare enter that thing."

We watch Phyr—or rather, a past version of him—argue with Gabriel and then simply disappear.

"That's our cue," Phyr whispers.

"Wait."

I turn and face him. His blue eyes are luminous in the dark.

"I'm glad you came for me, and I'm even more glad you didn't intervene."

He studies me for a moment, his haughty features indecipherable. "I serve you, not my wishes."

"You're the best friend ever." I throw my arms around him and squeeze.

Phyr reciprocates, resting his chin on the top of my head. "I forgot you that you do this."

"Hug?" I ask into against his leathery armor.

"Yes. Your mother hugged too. I wasn't aware adults that weren't lovers embraced this way."

I step back and smile. "Good friends do." I glance over my shoulder and sigh. "Let's go."

We head toward the supernaturals gathering around the darkness spell. Phyr whistles. They all turn.

I dip into my light, using my other sight to see the spell work of the shadow and smoke. "Everyone, step back." I pour my light into the darkness, breaking Lucifer's spell like a fan dispersing smoke, zapping away the runaway tendrils of darkness, trying to lurk.

Gabriel and Jada approach when I'm done, Roxy not too far behind. Jada clamps onto me in bear hug.

I squeeze back. "I'm okay," I reassure her, but my gaze is on Gabriel. "We won't be seeing any more of Lucifer."

For now, I add silently.

45

The chilly winter rain comes down at a steady drizzle. I load the last of the gift baskets filled with baked goods into the back of my Subaru, glancing over my shoulder. Behind me, Phyr locks the back of the bakery. Rhiannon and Jada wait in the backseat, chatting.

I shut the trunk and turn fully. Phyr's armor is glamoured to appear as a black tux. His sword, a fashionable bag. I'm a little jealous of how much control he has over his fae light, yet I'm learning, and memories are still coming back. I will eventually have as much control.

His gaze sweeps over me appreciatively. "Did I say that you look ravishing?"

I'm in a silver evening gown that hugs my full-figured frame. It's all me. I don't know how to glamour myself or my clothes to appear differently.

"I'm trying to get over the fact that not too long ago, I was a widow, a witch with a secret past that almost destroyed my future. Now I'm a member of a supernatural council, a fae princess, and... still a witch."

"You forgot a prominent business owner," he replies with a smile.

"We opened last week. Let's hold off on calling ourselves prominent."

I glance at the back of our bakery. I liquidated a trust and poured some of the money into a bakery downtown near Shawn's law office. I supplied half of the costs.

My childhood friend had gifted me a bag of gold to go in on the mortgage and the business with me. Pantsuit's eyes bulging when he plopped it on her desk was priceless.

Gabriel allowed Phyr to stay and even pulled a bunch of strings to get Phyr documents. He was an Irish immigrant, apparently.

The two formed some sort of agreement between them to lay off trying to get me to bear children or be a mate while I got my new life settled. Both still flirted incessantly despite that agreement.

"I have no more secrets; I am who I am—at least to the people who matter. After tonight, I won't have anything to hide from the community at large," I say, returning my gaze to Phyr.

He takes a step closer. "Would you call yourself settled?"

His gaze is on my lips.

"I don't want children."

"Neither do I." He grins and cups my chin. "I have an heir. I want to know if you are content."

"I am. But tonight is *big*. Nothing will ever be the same, you know?"

"I will be there for you." His hand rests on his bag, which I know is really the hilt of his sword.

I swallow hard, fighting back tears. I don't want to ruin my makeup. "I know."

He always has.

We lean closer.

My phone chimes in my clutch. Likely a text from Gabriel about tonight. He and Shawn took turns working my nerves about the auction.

"We better get going," I say, and dart to my car door. I don't know what I'm doing. Kissing Phyr would only complicate my life after I've made it simple.

"Ready?" I ask everyone after Phyr and I slide into the car.

"Yup," Rhiannon calls in the back.

Jada has her earbuds in and doesn't look up from her phone.

Phyr leans toward me, face serious and gives my hand a squeeze. "There is nothing to be nervous about. If this is an 'epic fail,' as Jada would say, we'll leave to my faerie."

"If you do, I got dibs on living in the castle," Rhiannon chimes from the back.

Jada, who is also in the back, takes out one of her earbuds. "Castle? What castle?"

"Plan B," Phyr replies.

"K. Pops." My daughter smiles, reinserting her earbud.

Phyr wings a dark eyebrow at her response, but a smile tugs at the corner of his mouth. I don't know when Jada started calling him Pops, it's just one of those things that's became part our life, like Phyr, Oberon, and Rhiannon themselves, the last of the three Jada calls Auntie Rhi. I've just went with it. She had none of my past in her life and now she's surrounded by witches and fae. So am I.

Witches, who have defected from covens, have been showing up in Gabriel's territory. Halflings and more lesser fae have come out of the woodwork, too. Other supes that have heard Gabriel is about his people, not the Anocracy, and have shown up. These supes aren't loners. Whole families have moved into the area. Gabriel's pack has grown and we've had an influx of new supernatural children in our school district. Lucinda and I have had a secondary unofficial PTSA to help those families adjust.

I check my phone just before I pull out. It's not from Gabriel. It's from Shawn.

"You've come so far. Can't wait for you to shine tonight, Shawn," I read out loud.

"Ten bucks Micah put him up to it," Rhiannon says from the back.

Shawn has been a lot nicer since his husband returned. Poor Micah had gotten lost hiking. I'm glad he isn't hellhound kibble. I hadn't had the chance to hear the story from Micah himself. I've been too busy with the store. At least I'd see him tonight.

As I pull out of the parking lot, Jada says, "I wonder what the other kids at school are going to say. Do you think I can still do cheer next year?"

My chest tightens. I want to assure her everything will be okay, but I don't know. "I'm not sure, kiddo. Let's hope so after the mundanes see their friends and neighbors as the people they've always known."

"They're going to lose their shit," Rhiannon adds, oh so helpfully. "Then they'll eventually get used to the concept and in fifty or sixty years no one will remember what it was like before the supes came out."

"Thanks for the encouragement," I say, dryly.

Phyr grins in my peripheral.

I take the 520 exit to get on the highway heading from the east side to Seattle proper. It's a Saturday night so the traffic isn't too heavy. When we reach the city, Phyr takes in the size of the buildings. We pull up to the back of a hotel to unload my vehicle.

We all get out. I spot Lance among other shifters, working security for the evening. He looks handsome in his tux.

"Need some help?" Lance says in way of greeting.

"Sure," I say.

"Be careful," Phyr warns. "I don't want any of my marzipan butterflies to chip." I'm an excellent baker, but Phyr had gone all out with decorating.

Lance helps us unload, complimenting my dress, Jada's rainbow bantu knots, and then shyly tells Rhiannon she looks lovely.

Micah appears with a trolley for the baskets. I haven't had the time to get the tea, as Jada calls it, on what happened between him and Shawn. Micah would never hike alone without telling anyone.

We go through staff corridors with people bustling back and forth. By the way their eyes flash gold, all of them seem to be shifters. We reach a staging area behind a curtain where all the items to be auctioned off are on long tables set up for the purpose. Phyr, Rhiannon, Jada, and I get to work setting up the baskets of baked goods. I make sure my business card is on each one. The cards are pink with silver lettering featuring a hearth as the logo, the name of my business Eastside Hearth. I'm named as proprietor and the shop's number is listed, an email, and a website an old friend of Raf's set up for me.

Lance escorts Jada, Phyr, Rhiannon, and I through another corridor to the entrance of a ballroom. He whispers something to another shifter posted at the door. It takes me a minute, but I recognize Nate from the excursion to find the cryptids. The reason it took me a minute is that his hair and eyebrows are no longer blue and green. It's a brown that looks dyed. He wears it slicked back in a ponytail and he's clean-shaven. All of the shifters working are in tuxes, no hair in vibrant colors and trending styles, their usual look. I spot Princess in a black cocktail dress with pearls. Her blonde hair, usually in a messy modern mullet, is all pinned and smoothed into a chignon at the base of her skull. Her makeup is subtle. Gabriel must have made them conform to some sort of conservative ideal of what he thought would make them look nonthreatening.

I grimace. That isn't the point. I don't have to like Princess to admit she has great biker gal vibes and fits in fine in Seattle's alt vibe. Nate's blue and green hair isn't out of the norm for Seattle either. On the contrary, they appear less Seattle and more east coast old money. It bothers me Gabriel has made them change to fit some sort of stereotype of normalcy when they were perfectly normal before.

Gabriel himself appears.

I would have to lose my vision to not be impressed. His curls are cropped closer, but the fit of the suit on his muscular frame makes the nephil look like a god slipped into modern clothes.

Shawn is at his heels, doing his best Idris Elba impression. Micah is nowhere to be seen. My heart sinks. I really want to talk to him. I have only heard second hand through Shawn that his husband is back. I know Micah didn't stay home with the kids. Their brood is staying with some aunt of Micah's while the two work out their problems that lead to Micah's disappearance.

Gabriel takes my hand and kisses my cheek by way of greeting. He whispers, "You look ravishing in that dress."

My pulse quickens. He smells...so good.

"Mind if I borrow Miriam to introduce her to some people before the auction starts?" Gabriel asks Phyr, slipping an arm around my waist as if it's only a formality and he doesn't give a shit about my company's reply.

I glance over my shoulder as Gabriel ushers me away between him and Shawn.

Phyr wings an eyebrow and glances at Jada. "Was he talking to me or you? Because I'm not sure which of us he just snubbed."

Jada giggles.

For what seems like an eternity, I'm shaking hands and hearing a myriad of names as Gabriel, a prominent businessman, and Shawn, a prominent lawyer, introduce their small business owner friend Miriam. Gabriel is always touching me in some way as he introduces me to Seattle's elite. I see Chad and Lucinda in passing—they're part of running this show, but they don't seem to have the same kind of time as I do. Micah is nowhere and I'm starting to get worried.

"Where's Micah?" I manage to whisper to Shawn between introductions.

"He couldn't make it," he says waving a hand.

Micah couldn't make it to any of the meetings that lead up to this either. I have that uneasy feeling in my gut I get when I'm being lied to. I open up the boundaries Phyr taught me to create and open myself to Shawn's mind.

"Where did you say Micah was?"

Shawn barely glances in my direction before Gabriel introduces us to some Seattle tech billionaire or another. The names and companies all started to meld a while ago.

Shawn's head has nothing but images of searching. Flying over the neighborhoods, finding something of Micah's in a park.

Suddenly I'm shut out like a massive wall is erected between Shawn and I. He glares at me.

"Stay out of my head, Miriam," he warns in a low hiss.

"Sorry. Didn't mean to. Still getting used to—what I am." I smile awkwardly.

He smiles but it doesn't reach his eyes. "I suppose getting used to previously unknown abilities are hard. It was for Micah."

I open my mouth to ask what Micah is, but the ambient music pauses. Chimes follow. That's our cue. My stomach drops. Micah forgotten for now.

"Time to get this show started," Gabriel says, guiding me with a hand at the small of my back.

Shifters, working as ushers, guide attendees to tables. I'm ushered to a table with the entirety of the Pacific Northwest supernatural council. I'm seated at a round table on Gabriel's right. Princess takes a chair at his left. To her left, Aurora is already seated. To my right Lucinda sits and to her right, Leilani and Cian complete the circle of council members. The PTSA table is nearby. Shawn sits with them.

I scan the crowd to see Phyr sitting with Jada, Rhiannon, and Roxy. My stomach does a flip when I see Kirsten sitting with them. I see the native elders who are also supes have a table.

Shawn and Lucinda rise and take a place on a small, raised dais, standing side by side. A curtain is drawn, revealing the table of auction items we'd unloaded earlier. They go ahead with the auction.

Crews from several local news stations are present. They line the sides of the ballroom, cameras pointed at the dais. I spot a table with a sign that says press in bold letters. I don't know how Shawn or Gabriel convinced the media to go to a PTSA fundraiser, but they're here.

The auction seems to go in minutes, though my guess is that it took at least an hour or two. Lucinda and Shawn call for the PTSA to come to the stage. I join them on stage.

Chad leans over and whispers, "Where's Micah?"

I shrug, stepping a pace away from him.

The guests wait for the closing statement. Instead Shawn whispers something to each of the mundane members of the PTSA board. They step off stage. Chad glances over his shoulder at me with a quizzical look like he can't figure out why he has to go, and I'm staying.

. . .

"Before we end tonight's auction, I would like to thank a different set of people who made this evening possible, unseen pillars of the Seattle and the Eastside's communities," Shawn says into a mic.

Sweat pearls on my forehead and I'm not quite sure what to do with my hands. This is it.

I meet Phyr's gaze. His hand is on his bag-sword.

"We have been your friends, neighbors, and allies in many things over the years," Shawn begins. "We've served you coffee and baked goods." He nods to Lucinda and I.

Phyr, Jada, and Rhiannon rise, as planned. So do others in the audience.

Shawn continues, "We own construction companies and security companies making sure your homes are built well and the place you live safe."

Gabriel stands, as does Cian and others.

"We're your doctors and lawyers." Leilani, who is a family doctor stands, and so do several other members of the audience.

"We're your shopkeepers, firefighters, and bankers."

I notice Pantsuit from my bank in the audience for the first time as she rises. More people stand along with her. I notice the shifters all moving to set stations among the tables.

"We live among you, protect you, serve you, but we haven't trusted you with something we've been holding back for a long time. We are not human. We are supernatural. Shifters, who can take on the form of animal."

Wet popping sounds and the rustle of clothes precede shifters morphing to their animal forms.

Someone shrieks.

Some rise, rushing toward the exits.

Others freeze in a wide-eyed panic.

A bear and the wolves stand in the way of the exits. Princess, in her giant honey badger form, guards Gabriel.

Shawn continues, "Cryptids, ancient dwellers of the forests, are among us."

Aurora drops her glamour, revealing her Bigfoot form, as does a Moth-person.

Cries of disbelief ring out through the audience. The last head count for attendees was around five-hundred and sixty, and that didn't include the news crews.

I lock eyes with Jada, who is in panther form next to Roxy's wolf form. Phyr and Rhiannon stand close by.

"Witches are among us."

Rhiannon spreads her arms, working a simple spell to make the candles on the tables float. She'd believed shaking the building would be great fun. Thankfully, Gabriel convinced her none of us would show our entire hand.

Shawn's voice again fills the panicked room. "Fairy stories are not stories."

Cian stands on the table and shrinks down to two feet tall. Phyr drops his glamour. I let my light shine through my eyes and let my hands glow.

"Sirens are not myth!"

Lucinda shifts to her siren form, careful not to speak. Still, much of the audience turns their attention to her, calmer.

"Do not fear. Angels rule us all."

Shawn takes off his tux's jacket and lets four giant multicolor wings sprout and unfurl. Gabriel transforms into his angelic form, flying from his table to land between me and Shawn. The rest of the council joins us on stage. Leilani stays in her human form, carrying pint-sized Cian.

"I am the Archangel of the Pacific Northwest and this is the supernatural council," Gabriel announces and then nods to me.

"I represent the High Fae of the Unseelie courts and witches unaffiliated with covens. I own a bakery and I'm the secretary for this PTSA. I've lived on the Eastside for almost twenty years. You have nothing to fear. We are all part of your community," I say, hearing my voice quaver over the mic.

Each of the council say who they represent. I attribute the audience's calm to Lucinda's influence. I speak for her, too, since she cannot without enthralling everyone. "She represents the Olympian Mythics and is a retired soldier from Persephone's army."

After everyone has introduced themselves, Shawn announces, "We'll be taking questions for the next forty-five minutes. Afterward, you'll have to make an appointment with the archangel."

BONUS MATERIAL: Keep reading for sneak peak of Eastside Witch Hunt (Midlife Supernaturals #2)

EASTSIDE WITCH HUNT (MIDLIFE SUPERNATURALS #2)

BY T.J. DESCHAMPS

1

A man in an ill-fitted suit, standing on a literal soapbox, shouts from the street corner, "End times are nigh. Accept the Lord in your heart and you will be saved in the last battle."

At one time, no one would have listened to him, believing him mad. This man isn't alone. Another man in a suit, and two women in winter jackets and modest floral dresses with rain boots sticking out from the ankle length hems, hold up signs with Bible verses about Armageddon. What were once madmen's words ring true, a balm even, if they echo familiar teachings in times of upheaval. Facing the truth, facing the unknown, and accepting we don't know everything, seems like the mad choice.

News that all supernaturals exist and live among humans hasn't gone as well as I'd hoped it would. Obviously. Some have accepted it. Some have become fans, writing the members of the Supernatural Council of the Pacific Northwest letters, and printing our faces on t-shirts. We didn't want fame. We'd meant to take power away from the Angelic Anocracy, the shadow government of the entire world.

One of Soapbox Evangelist's companions, a woman in a long,

shapeless dress, holds a Bible up in one hand, a brochure in the other. "Thou shalt not suffer a witch to live," she hisses at our approach. Another cries, "Repent and be saved."

Her proclamation reminds me of the comedian Eddie Izzard's skit called "Cake or Death," where the character gives everyone the choice, "Church or England, cake or death," and makes as much sense. I look straight ahead, pretending to ignore her. I'm not foolish enough to actually ignore someone shouting at me, but I won't feed into her b.s.

The evangelists are not alone, but neither am I.

Phyr and Jada are with me. Phyr wears a glamour, an illusion to make him appear human. The fae sneers in their direction. He won't do anything. The local archangel Gabriel, my sort-of boyfriend, has my friend on a tight leash. If Phyr breaks any of Gabriel's conditions the fae had agreed to, he's bound not by the archangel, but by the Goddess Danu, to keep his word.

That's the downside of being a high fae. Danu makes us, even halfling fae witches like me, keep our word. We suffer pain if we lie— Danu's sense of justice. She meant to temper our power with these limits. It only made fae craftier.

The man and his companions' eye Phyr with, well, fear. Even in his human guise, Phyr is uncommonly handsome: black hair, sharp, imposing features, amber eyes that take everything in and discard it at once, and the lean-muscled build of a fae warrior. Instead of black leather armor, he still wears an Enchanting Treats t-shirt from our shop under a leather jacket, paired with jeans and black combat boots. Even with the frilly logo for our bakery, he looks like a badass. His sneer reveals straight white teeth, his fangs obscured by a glamour.

Jada snakes an arm through mine. Her voice is the barest of whispers. "They're everywhere."

We've had protestors and religious zealots in front of the bakery for the past few months. Most people ignored them, but some stopped and listened. Some people stop now.

I squeeze my daughter's hand and say in Kairska, the language of witches, "Do not be afraid, my sweet. They're only human."

The man shouts as we pass, "The angels and saints will weep! The beast and the harlot will terrorize the righteous! But, lo! Do not lose faith! Our savior comes!"

I'm not too keen on the way he emphasizes the word "harlot" with his eyes on me—especially since I'd once been Lucifer's consort. Could he see it? I push the thought from my head. Of course, a mundane person couldn't see past what's before him.

Phyr's hand goes to his hip, gripping the air. Invisible, Angel's Bane, his sword, rests there.

I give him a slight shake of my head. No. I will not lose my dear friend again over these idiots.

"Wouldn't you like to be saved?" the woman pleads with me. "It's not too late. Come to the Paradise Center! If you accept Jesus's sacrifice, his blood will cleanse you of all sin so that you may live in paradise."

"I prefer bath bombs to blood, thanks," I mutter under my breath.

Mundane humans have it all wrong. Well, mostly wrong. Lucifer had told me the true story, or at least his version of it. Their god abandoned the angels and humans to do who knows what. He promised to return before he left. That was eons ago.

When Lucifer was still part of Heaven's leadership, he'd wanted to let humans be and keep angels' things among angels. He thought his creator would come back if things got bad on Earth. What would later become the Angelic Anocracy believed it was their job to guide humans to believe in their god, and with enough of that belief, he would return.

Factions formed.

They fought.

Thousands of angels died, more than in any other war.

Lucifer, tired of seeing his brethren die over humans, allowed them to strip him of his Grace. He and his followers escaped to a realm called Hell.

The Angelic Anocracy ran a smear campaign to make sure he

wouldn't attempt to garner human worship for himself. Turns out, the widespread rumor of Lucifer as this anti-god, anti-human villain called Satan gave him more power than he'd ever had as an angel.

Sometimes I wonder if Lucifer knew all along that becoming the villain would work out better for him. Sometimes I wonder if he'll ever get over the heartbreak of his father abandoning him and his angelic brethren, making him an outcast, a bad guy. He may have accepted the role to survive, but Lucifer wasn't happy about it.

Family squabbles. Am I right?

WE ENTER Lucinda's Café despite the sign reading "closed." Magic of the protective wards I've set in place brushes my skin, recognizing me. A few months ago, the owner didn't need the wards.

Times have changed since.

Lucinda, the proprietor, and my best friend, greets us. She stands about five-foot two to my five-foot six. Her curly deep brown hair sits in a topknot. She's dressed in leggings and a hoodie. Lucinda is a triathlete and has the build of one. She's also a siren.

"Roxy is in the back. Why don't you join her?" Lucinda gestures to a set of double doors.

Roxy is Jada's bestie. She's eighteen, and used to be the biggest pain in my butt. I'd thought that the girl was a delinquent, with her cagey attitude and rough manners. Turns out, the alpha abjured her mom from the pack and the pack hazed the poor girl.

Gabriel, her father, is not only an archangel. He's in the unique position of being an alpha to the Greater Seattle shapeshifter pack.

Weird combo? You bet. However, I don't have room to talk. I'm not a full fae or witch, and my daughter is a witch, demigod, and fae. American melting pot, supe edition, I suppose.

Jada waves to the Supernatural Council of the Pacific Northwest, who all sit in overstuffed, colorful chairs and sofas that give the cafe a nineteen-nineties sitcom feel.

Princess, the honey badger shifter, sits on a couch. She's in her badass biker chick jeans and a leather jacket. Her dark hair is slicked back. A helmet rests between her black boots. Gabriel's beta, she's here to represent shifters.

Next to her on the sofa, Aurora, a tall willowy blonde, sips tea. She represents the cryptids' interests.

Opposite Princess and Aurora sits Cian, the auburn-headed construction worker-slash-Leprechaun. He represents the low fae unaffiliated with the high fae courts.

Next to Cian, a demigoddess of a Hawaiian pantheon and medical doctor, Leilani turns to smile at me. She possesses a lovely smile and the most gorgeous hip-length ringlets I've ever seen. She's also the bubbly, sweet type when she's not in giant lizard form.

Last, but certainly not least, is Gabriel, the Archangel of the Pacific Northwest lounging. Noticing my arrival, he pushes to his feet. My eyes go up and up to meet his gaze. He's six-foot four wall of lean muscle. How would I describe him? Angelic perfection with the raw animal magnetism of a shifter.

Rawr.

He also has wavy brown hair that he's let grow into loose curls. His eyes are green, and his lips are shapely and full. They feel really nice too. Right now, those pretty lips are set in a grim line.

Uh, oh. Disapproving face.

I'm the last to arrive at the council meeting. Shit. Gabriel hates tardiness.

Before I can apologize for our lateness, Phyr asks in a mild tone, "Did you see your fan club outside, Archangel?"

Gabriel's grimace deepens. "Yes. I was starting to worry they'd detained you." He answers Phyr, but his eyes are on me.

"If they threaten Miriam's person," Phyr warns, "I have sworn vows—"

I cut him off, "I can handle myself."

The pissing contests between these two have become the constant bane of my existence. I wish they would kiss and make nice.

Now, there's a thought.

"Did they threaten you?" Gabriel's voice lowers into a deep grumble, definitely not in a human range. His wolf has become more protective of me over the last few months, and we haven't even yet done the deed. I don't want to know what he'll be like once we do. I'm not into alpha-holes. Been there. Done that. Got the scars to prove it.

"Thou shalt not allow a witch to live" rings in my head. "They offered to make me clean with a blood of Christ bubble bath."

He snorts and some of the tension eases in his shoulders. Gabriel gestures for me to have a seat to his right. I settle there. Lucinda fixes herself in an overstuffed chair opposite the archangel.

Phyr remains next to the door. He appears at council meetings to stand watch, not as a representative with a say. A couple of months ago, we didn't need a guard, but not all mundanes are pleased about supes living among them. Obviously.

"I'm sorry about those creeps. They said some of the same crap to me and Aurora." Princess nudges her head to her girlfriend seated next to her.

"It's scary," Aurora confides. An almost seven-feet-tall blonde with long, willowy limbs. Her outfit befits the owner of a scented oil and candle shop: colorful broom skirt and loose peasant blouse. She's a gentle giant with hippie tendencies. Aurora wears a glamour to hide a Wookie-looking Bigfoot in those hippie clothes.

I spare her a rueful smile.

Laughter bubbles up from the back. At least Jada and Roxy are having fun.

"Shall we begin?" Gabriel asks, standing.

We all nod. The sooner we stop talking about the assholes outside and get something done, the better.

"I am here today as the Archangel of the Pacific Northwest. I cede my power of alpha to represent the Greater Seattle shapeshifter pack to Princess."

The magical transfer of power scrapes like wool on my skin.

Princess stands. "I represent all the shapeshifter packs of the Pacific Northwest."

Each of the council members stands and names who they repre-sent. There's an air of solemnity because we all take our positions seriously.

Gabriel clears his throat. "I would like to update you on Heaven's stance."

A hush falls across the council. We regard the archangel with expectant gazes and clasped hands.

"The Angelic Anocracy is still not speaking to me directly, at least not officially. I've heard through back channels there is deliberation on whether they will remove me as archangel and replace me with a full seraph. If you choose to ally with the new archangel, then I would leave immediately. I promise I will take no action against you."

My heart aches for him. Gabriel loves his father. I can't help but feel personal responsibility for the rift between them. He broke the angelic code for me. I had Lucifer powerless. I could have ended the conflict between Heaven and Hell by murdering the King of Hell with my faelight. Instead, we made a bargain.

Also, Gabriel has had to make the same speech with all the shifter packs in the PNW. He's been an exemplary leader. No alpha broke allegiance to him. Still, some members of other packs have broken with their alphas and moved out of Gabriel's territory. None have challenged him. At least we have that. All of the shifters know he's not stripped of his angelic powers, his Grace, and his claim to alpha status is still legendary.

It's no surprise that no one leaves. We decided to defy the Angelic Anocracy and come out of the supernatural closet together.

"I cede the floor to Cian, representative of the low fae."

"I saw on the news," Cian says, his Irish accent slight but there, "that Congress is trying to decide whether or not supes are citizens. There's also talk of immigration doing deeper investigations of all resident aliens and marking the files of those suspected to be super-natural."

Phyr and I exchange a glance. He's here on paperwork Gabriel had pulled strings to get. I'm not as American as I'd thought either. I recently learned that I was born in my father's faerie. My mother is an American citizen, but I no longer go by the name that she gave me. Tatiana died, confirmed by my death certificate online. That's what I get for faking my death so thoroughly that my mother filed one.

"There are supes in the House, Senate, and the Supreme Court, as well as in the ACLU and other legal organizations that would battle any bill claiming us as anything but tax-paying Americans," Gabriel replies, unconcerned. "They know I can expose them all. We're fine."

Mutually assured destruction. Great.

"Enough supes to not be worried?" Lucinda asks, echoing the concern etched on everyone's face.

Gabriel clears his throat, looking as if he doesn't want to share what he knows. "The president is a shifter. We've spoken."

Princess chuckles at my startled expression. "Shifters run this country, Miriam."

I blink. So that's how the Angelic Anocracy ruled without being present except for regional archangels. This was new information. Also, being half shifter and an alpha would put Gabriel in a pretty position.

"Most shapeshifters don't want to be commanded by an off-world agency anymore," Gabriel adds. "Which works in our favor. This council might set precedence for an official type of office."

Had he planned on coming out longer than he'd let on? I exchange another glance with Phyr.

"A shift in the power dynamic is coming," Leilani sighs. "We all wanted it. We all knew coming out would be a catalyst to that shift, but it seems to be happening faster than we anticipated."

We discuss possibilities awhile, until the discussion takes its natural course and dies down.

I bring up a topic in my official capacity. "As representative of the high fae, I must ask, when are you going to grant fae permission to enter your territory?"

"I'll speak to Oberon on the matter. Arrange a meeting."

Bristling that he doesn't make it a request, I stare. Just call me Miriam, supernatural secretary.

"I have sad news. A cryptid has gone missing," Aurora says, breaking the silence.

Gabriel rubs his brow. "Who?"

"Robby." When we all stare blankly at her, the bigfoot shakes her head and throws up her hands. "Robert? You've all met him." With an exasperated sigh, she grumbles, "The moth man."

Gabriel pulls a face.

"Oh, him." I'd forgotten his existence until now.

Princess rolls her eyes. "Ugh, him? He was so whiny. We were protecting him from a crossroads demon, and he demanded raw, vegan organic dishes served on ethically sourced plates and cutlery."

I bite my lip to keep from laughing. Robby is a cryptid, and a suburban Pacific Northwesterner through and through.

Aurora holds up her hands defensively. "Yeah, yeah, I know he's a bit of a pill, but he's missing, and his people are asking questions." Her gaze shifts briefly to Phyr, distrust in her eyes.

"Are you accusing me of kidnapping him?" the fae prince asks in a mild tone.

Aurora brushes her tie-dyed skirt. "We found him in your faerie."

"Between my duties at the bakery, learning about this world, and spending time with my family, I assure you I don't have the time to kidnap an irritating mothman."

Gabriel sighs. "We all know Rhiannon trapped him before he could trap her." To the Princess, he says, "Beta, put someone on it."

She nods.

Cian pipes up again. "A halfling living in a trailer near Sultan runs a small cleaning business. She stopped showing up to work and won't answer her door, but her car is in the driveway."

That grabs Phyr's attention, and mine.

"Do you know her?"

Cian waffles a freckled hand in the air. "I know of her. She's a brownie. Her cousin says she started going to church, talking a lot about end times, and walking the righteous path. Then she was gone."

Princess leans forward. "Pack alphas as far west as Forks and east as Wenatchee, and one down near Eugene have reported members who started acting strange, withdrawing, and not participating in gatherings. The alphas did check-ins, but none of them were home. I would suspect they left their pack, like some do, but all their belongings are still there. Family photos, mementos. That's not seceding from a pack. What bothers me is the alphas aren't concerned. They think they'll just show up."

Gabriel adds, "Normally I wouldn't think anything of it either. Some shifters like to take a hiatus from the pack occasionally, go out to the woods, and just be their animal. Given there's also a cryptid and a brownie missing, maybe we should alert the alphas to put some hunters on it to investigate."

His gaze travels to the members of the council. "Anyone else have someone missing to investigate?"

I say, "I'm going to check in with the local witches, make sure they're doing well."

"I'll check on the nymphs and oracles," Lucinda says. "I'm due for a visit with them."

The meeting comes to a close. Gabriel resumes his position as alpha.

He touches my shoulder as we both rise. "Can we talk in private?"

THE ONLY PRIVATE place in Lucinda's Café is the back office where the girls are doing homework and gabbing.

Gabriel smiles at the scene and then looks over his shoulder at me.

I don't know what he wants me to see. Yes. Our girls get along. They've always gotten along. Then I see it from his perspective. They would make good stepsisters. Did Raf see it that way when he asked Gabriel to look after us before he ascended?

I shudder inwardly and don't like my future pre-planned, even if my former husband meant well. I've gotten over Raf leading a double life, one foot in the supe world and one in the mundane, but I would be damned if I partnered with someone because we made a good insta-family.

Gabriel clears his throat. The girls look up in unison.

He smiles. "Can we have a moment of privacy?"

"But I'm hungry," Roxy whines.

"I'll take you for sushi on the way home."

The girls collect their things.

Jada eyes us for a second, then closes the office door behind her.

Gabriel and I started dating a few months ago, but neither of us had ever actually dated before. We decided to take things slow. We had to. More and more, witches have been showing up in the territory, after having left their covens. I also have a bakery and two new members of my household. Well, Phyr has been my friend my whole life, but we've spent many years apart. Rhiannon, a witch I took in, is a lot.

It's also Jada's senior year and we're looking at colleges. She'd wanted to go to Howard University, but after supes came out, she decided to stay closer to home.

I lay none of this on him because he knows. He's busy too. He's been the public face of all supes. Handsome, gregarious, good at oration, Gabriel handled most of the press. Apparently, he's been talking to *the* president as well.

"Is there something wrong?" I ask, worried he'll want to delay his arrangement with my father. Again.

"Yes." Suddenly he's in my space, hands cupping my cheeks. "I miss you."

"Oh, yeah?" I hedge, grinning.

He angles his head so his face hovers just above mine. "Should I show you how much?"

He's so close that heat radiates from his body and his breath fans my face. He smells so good, evergreen forests and fresh mountain air in combination with an indescribable scent I attribute to angels.

My hand trembles a little as I reach for his beautiful face. The stubble of a beard rough under my fingers makes him feel real, instead of a perfect angel. I like real. Normal. I want what Raf and I had, something mundane but precious in its normalcy. With Gabriel, there are so many complicating factors: our positions in the supe community, our kids, our friends, and the conflicting interests we have from time to time.

I focus on his shapely mouth, wanting to bite his plump lower lip, or trace my tongue over the shapely peaks of his upper one.

"Show me," I command in a breathy voice.

He breaches the small distance, the contact between us electrifying. Power pulses from him. I'm more sensitive to it, in the same way I can feel the energy of a crystal, or the threads of magic that weave the universe.

He takes his time, a leisurely kiss appropriate for two people reacquainting.

Conversely, need coils within me, winding so tight I think I will burst. I deepen the kiss.

He makes a sound that's almost a growl. His hands find their way to my waist and then his calloused palms are smoothing all over my body, heat flaring in their wake.

My inner light pulses. So much of his wild lupine magic mixed with angelic might. I want to consume it. Consume *him*.

Something's not right. Still I kiss him harder, nipping at that juicy bottom lip. I rake my hands down his muscular back. The material shreds under my nails. Wet warmth soaks my fingers.

Gabriel breaks off the kiss wide-eyed. Blood trickles from his mouth.

My mouth tastes like pennies. I bring my hands to my face, noticing there's blood on my razor-sharp claws. Claws? I have claws. Sick realization that I'd *bit* Gabriel and tore up his back sinks in. The room spins. I shut my eyes to stop the vertigo.

A steel grip clutches my shoulder. "Miriam?"

I can't answer. If I open my mouth, I'll vomit.

"Miriam?"

I shake my head. The motion nauseates me.

"I'm going to get Phyr. He'll know what to do."

I open my eyes. The blood keeps running from Gabriel's injuries. My heart sinks.

"I should heal you." I reach to touch him, pausing at the sight of the bloody claws extended toward him. The blood smells good to me. Too good.

"I had ways of healing from injuries before I met you." Gabriel takes a step back, holding up his hands cautiously. "Just stay here."

I will not say it doesn't sting that Gabriel doesn't want me to heal him. Given that I like the smell of his blood, I don't blame him at the same time.

When he leaves, I close my eyes and take a deep breath, relieved. With his scent not as strong in my nostrils, I don't feel as out of control.

I take a seat at Lucinda's desk, careful not to touch anything with my bloody hands. All I want to do is go home, wash this off me, and forget. That's a lie. That's not all I want. Part of me hungers for Gabriel to come back, and begs me to follow him. It takes all my will to keep my butt planted in the seat.

Phyr enters the office, his face grim. He's lacking the leather jacket he'd sported earlier. Likely, he gave it to Gabriel to cover the shredded shirt.

Embarrassed by my behavior, heat floods my cheeks.

No illusion masks his bronze skin covered in tattoos—protective spell work. He offers a cup with the cafe's logo. "Drink this. It'll dampen the effects."

I take the cup and sniff. Not coffee. The liquid smells slightly sweet. A feral part of me, the same part that grew claws and sprouted fangs, wants to down it. Another part, a logical, witchy part, suspects the contents are something I don't care to drink. I narrow my eyes at the dark contents with crimson edges, then lift my gaze to Phyr, noticing a bandage around his wrist.

He frowns. "Yes. It's my blood."

I rear my head. "Why are you giving me your blood?"

He rubs his brow. "I really wish someone else would have explained this to you."

"Explained what?"

Phyr's face and body language emote he'd rather be anywhere than here. "There are bodily changes when a fae child transitions into adulthood. Drinking my blood, a fae who has gone through the passage, will make you less...scratchy and bitey when you're feeling amorous."

"Sounds like a cure for puberty." I sigh. As I eye the liquid dubiously, I recall a mate-bonding being a big deal between adult fae when I was a child. "I saw a bonding ceremony once. They drank each other's blood." And had sex right on the altar. The other fae watched regardless of age, but my mother dragged me away. "Will drinking this bind us?"

Phyr rolls his eyes. "I've shared the blood of many fae, and I am not bound to any of them."

"If drinking someone else's blood relieves the physical need to bond but doesn't actually bind you, what does?"

His gaze fixes on the cup as if he *could* will me to drink and get it over with—making me wonder why he's so eager to avoid the conversation.

I gesture at him and the cup with my bloody hand. "I want to know before I drink."

"There is a specific ceremony for mate-bonding. Remember when I found you on an altar dedicated to the ritual?"

I remember waking on a stone slab in a sheer gown covered in flowers. The memory triggers another of a bondmate ceremony. One of the fae was wearing a similar dress.

Oh, wow. The fae of that faerie assumed I'd come there to bond with their prince. Phyr, knowing how I'd lived my life through the pixies who followed me, must have had his doubts. No wonder he wasn't happy to see me.

"How could I forget?" I grin. "You kicked me awake."

He grins back. A bit of mischief sparkles in his amber eyes and some of the tension in his body eases. "I nudged you gently with my boot, well aware you didn't understand what you were being set up to do."

"Some reunion that."

"Indeed."

I take one last look at the contents of the cup before I drink. The taste isn't unpleasant. My fangs and claws retract, and my hands, albeit bloody, are my hands.

"Your change has finally come. Talk to your father," Phyr advises, unease in his features. "It is his duty to explain."

ACKNOWLEDGMENTS

I'd like to thank Emily Paper for swooping in and finishing the editing job after Rhiannon Rhys-Jones lost her dear husband Dustin Gross. Gibbit, may you and Sharie find the healing you need and may his memory be a blessing to you both. We'll do the next one and many more as soon as you're ready.

Thank you Paul Carpentier for stepping up as a final proofreader at the last moment.

I would not be the author I am today without Cascade Writers, GrottoGarden, Speculative Twist, and NaNoWriMo groups. Thank you for all the invaluable feedback!

I'd like to thank my "Coven", the friends who inspired me to write the strong, capable women in this book.

I'd like to thank my co-parent and ex- husband, Felix Deschamps. You've never read a word I've written, but you always enthusiastically believed all my projects would be a movie.

Last, but not least, I'd like to thank my kids. You were all the inspiration for Jada.

ABOUT THE AUTHOR

T.J. Deschamps writes fantastical stories with diverse characters and subversive themes. She lives in Seattle's Eastside with her three children, three cats, and a singular adorable tortoise. In her spare time, T.J. likes to read, lift weights, collect oddities, and dream of becoming a feral bog witch. Sometimes she dances.

facebook.com/TJDeschampsauthor
twitter.com/MmeDeschamps
instagram.com/writer.reads

ALSO BY T.J. DESCHAMPS

Midlife Supernaturals

Eastside Witch Hunt (Midlife Supernaturals #2)

Eastside Mórrígan: (Midlife Supernaturals #3)

Eastside Rock Witch (A Midlife Supernaturals Novella)

Midlife Olympians

Westside Oracle (Midlife Olympians #1)

Westside Harpy (Midlife Olympians #2)

Westside Titan (Midlife Olympians #3)

Faerie Tales

The Ballad of Brave Janet

Tam Lin

Warrior Tithe

Vow Unbroken

Coming 2024:

International Supernatural Enforcement Agency (I.S.E.A.) Files